The

TIGER
CATCHER

By Paullina Simons

FICTION

Tully
Red Leaves
Eleven Hours
The Bronze Horseman
Tatiana and Alexander
The Girl in Times Square
Road to Paradise
The Summer Garden
A Song in the Daylight
Children of Liberty
Bellagrand
Lone Star

NONFICTION

Six Days in Leningrad

COOKBOOK

Tatiana's Table

CHILDREN'S BOOKS

I Love My Baby Because . . .
Poppet Gets Two Big Brothers

The
TIGER
CATCHER

The End of Forever saga

PAULLINA SIMONS

wm

WILLIAM MORROW
An Imprint of HarperCollinsPublishers

HarperCollins books may be purchased for educational, business, or sales promotional use. For information, please email the Special Markets Department at SPsales@harpercollins.com.

Originally published as *The Tiger Catcher* in Australia in 2019 by HarperCollins Publishers Australia Pty Limited

FIRST EDITION

Library of Congress Cataloging-in-Publication Data has been applied for.

ISBN 978-0-06-239476-7

19 20 21 22 23 LSC 10 9 8 7 6 5 4 3 2 1

For Tania, my last child, the joy of my life

A safe fairytale is not true to either world.
J.R.R. Tolkien

The Transit Circle

I SHOULD HAVE KISSED YOU. JULIAN LAY NAKED ON HIS BED, clutching the red beret, staring at the ceiling. *I should have kissed you the last time I saw you.*

After half a night passed like this, he gave up on sleep, jumped up and began to get ready. He had a lot to do to be in Greenwich by noon. Don't dawdle, the cook told him. You have very little time. You have a picosecond inside of a minute. And don't get stuck. Where you're going, the opening is wide enough for one man, but not for all men.

And what was Julian's wise response to this?

"How long is a picosecond?"

"One-trillionth of a second," the exasperated cook replied.

Julian dressed in black layers. He shaved. He slicked back his unruly brown hair and tied it up so it didn't look like what it was—a bushy mane on a man who long ago stopped giving a damn. Julian was square-faced, square-jawed, straight-browed, granite-chinned, *once*. His hazel eyes looked gray today, huge, sunken into his gaunt cheeks, the dark bags under his eyes like somebody clocked him, the full mouth pale. He had lost so much weight, he had to punch a new notch in his belt; his jacket could've fit two Julians inside.

It took him a while to get out; he kept forgetting this, that. At the last minute, he remembered to text his mother and Ashton. Nothing too alarming—like *I'm sorry*—but still, he wanted to leave them with something. Jokes to make them think the old Julian wasn't too far away. To his mom: *"I used to feel like a guy trapped in a woman's body. Then I was born."* To Ashton: *"You can't lose a homing pigeon, Ash. If your homing pigeon doesn't come back, what you've lost is a pigeon."* But he did leave a separate note for Ashton on his dresser.

As instructed, Julian left his cell phone at the flat, his wallet, his pens, his notebooks. He left his life behind, including the words he had written just yesterday called "Tiger Claws."

What do you ask of life
At night the world you can't change
desire drunkenness rage
Flies by
While you lie flat on your back
Under claws and lizards
In the purple fields.

He brought four things: a fifty-pound note, an Oyster fare card for the tube, the crystal on a rope around his neck, and the red beret in his pocket.

At Boots at Liverpool Street, he bought a flashlight. The cook said he would need one. And then the trains were slow like he was slow. Julian waited forever for a change at Bank. At Island Gardens, he looked down into his hands. They had been clenched since Shadwell. Lately he'd been staggering, foundering, drowning. Without time, his wandering life had filled up with nothing but watery impressions, his days were without architecture, without frame or matter, a muddle, a madness, a dream.

But not anymore. Now he had purpose. Lunatic, foolish purpose, but hey, he was grateful something was being offered to him instead of nothing.

In Greenwich, the flat landscaped park below the Royal Observatory is lined with crisscrossing paths called Lovers' Walks. Deep inside the park, on top of a steep hill with a wild garden, for centuries the British astronomers have studied the skies. Today, on a blustery day in March the garden was nothing but bare branches whipping about, blocking the view of what Julian was climbing to the top of the mountain to find.

He felt idiotic. Did he buy a ticket? Did he loiter until the appointed hour? The cook told him to find a telescope called the Transit Circle, but the Observatory was home to so many. Where was this enchanted spot where all impossible things became possible? Julian caught himself scoffing and felt ashamed. His mother taught him better than that, told him never to mock the thing you were about to fall on your knees in front of.

"Which way to the Transit Circle?" Julian asked the cashier behind the table.

The pretty girl smoothed out her hair. "George Airy's Transit Circle? Right through there. I can take you, if you like. Will it be just one ticket for you?" She smiled.

"Yes," he said. "And no, that's fine, I'll find it. Do you sell pocket watches?"

"Yes, in our gift shop. Do you need a compass, too? Maybe a tour guide?" She tilted her head.

"No, thank you." He wouldn't look up, wouldn't meet her gaze.

With the girl hovering nearby, Julian bought a watch in an unopened box. She wanted to test it to make sure it worked, but he said no. He didn't want her touching it, imprinting his brand-new timekeeper with her own spirit.

"You won't be able to return it if something's wrong with it," she said.

"That's all right," he said. "I'm not coming back this way." Whatever happened, he wouldn't be coming back.

"That's a shame." She smiled. "Where are you going?" When he didn't answer, she shrugged, a friendly girl marking time. "Look around," she said. "Take your time."

Julian had almost nothing left from his fifty. He hid the remaining pound coins in a souvenir vase along with his Oyster card. Was that wrong, to hedge his bets? No, he decided. Even people who sought out miracles were allowed to be cautious. That was him—a cautious man seeking out a miracle. He had some time to kill so he wandered around killing it. It was only eleven o'clock. He tried to remember all the things the cook told him, but there had been so many. "At noon, the sun will pass through a pinhole in the glass crosshairs overhead," the cook said. "A beam of light will strike the quartz in your hands. The blue chasm will open. You must hurry. The rest of your life awaits."

It sounds difficult and complicated, Julian said. The cook stepped back from the grill and judged him up and down, a cleaver in his hands. "You think *this* part is complicated? Do you have any idea what you're about to do?"

No. Julian had no idea. He knew what he had been doing. Lately, nothing. But way back when, he did things, like mark time with his baby down the road from his Hollywood dreams. Sun beating down on palm trees and lovers, Volvos parked in secluded corners. Windows open. Joy flying in, like wind. Julian wasn't a skeptic then. Well, like he always said, there was a time for everything.

"Where's the Prime Meridian?" Julian asked a gruff older guard inside one of the rooms in the pavilion.

"You're on it, mate," the guard replied. His name tag said Sweeney. He pointed to an enormous black telescope. "You're in the Transit Room. And that's the Transit Circle, right on the meridian line." Over nine feet long, Airy's telescope looked like a field gun aimed at the stars. It was flanked by a set of glossy black stairs, their base set into a square well slightly below the main floor.

Through the open door, pale sunlight. The brass line marking 0.0 longitude was riveted into the cobblestones in the courtyard. Julian watched the tourists hamming it up on the line, one foot in the east, one foot in the west, standing on each other's shoulders, taking pictures, posing, laughing. He checked his new watch.

11:45.

His hands trembled. To steady himself, he grabbed the low iron railing that separated him from the telescope, the retractable roof open, the patchy sky above him.

He was so utterly alone.

A strange, vast, rainy, foreign city. London like another country unto itself. Julian glanced back at the guard. The portly man sat on a stool, an elbow on the wood table, indifferent to Julian, as was the whole universe. There was a window behind Sweeney, a glimpse of taupe leafless trees blowing about in the sharp wind. It had been so gusty in London the last few days, like an eyewall of a hurricane passing through.

11:56.

Reaching into his shirt, Julian pulled out the stone that hung on a leather rope around his neck. Leaving it in its silver webbing, he laid it into his shaking hand. In the gray light, the crystal didn't sparkle or shimmer. Silent and cool, it lay in his open palm. Once the stone had been in her hands. There was sun then, a sparkling mist of dreamlike bliss, the beginning, not the end—or so he thought.

Was this the end?

Or was it the beginning?

"The crystal oscillates a million times a second," the cook told him—a cook, a magician, a warlock, a wizard. "And you oscillate with it. *You* are the oscillator. *You* are the chain reaction, the chemical ignition, the voltage soaring through your own life. Go, Julian. The time has come for you to act."

There is no other time.

Until the end of time.

Running out of time.

11:59.

Julian gripped the crystal. His vision blurred. The memory of pain is what causes the fear of death. The heart grows numb. There's a sense of suffocation. As the lungs become paralyzed, the heart cannot breathe.

So it is with the memory of love.

O my soul and all that's within me, the beggar cried, raising his palm to the sky.

Ladies and gentlemen, it's *show*time!

In the picosecond before the clock struck noon, in the blink he still had between what was and what was yet to be, Julian asked himself what he was most afraid of.

That the inexpressible thing being offered to him was possible?

Or that it wasn't?

There'll be another time for you and me.

There'll never be another time for you and me.

As the sun moved into the crosshairs at noon, he knew. He would do anything, sacrifice everything to see her again.

Help me.

Please.

I should've kissed you.

Part One

The Ghost of God and Dreams

*"Like a ghost she glimmers on to me.
And all thy heart lies open unto me."*
Alfred, Lord Tennyson

"I love acting. It is so much more real than life."
Oscar Wilde

HOW TO PREPARE FOR A DISASTER

Every day we fake it.

We fake at everything.
At friendship, adulthood, love.

The goal is to wing it like you mean it. And hope that eventually form will follow function.

You can't overprepare. You can underprepare. And you can not prepare at all. Those are your choices.

Accept that, and do what you can.

AMONG THE THINGS YOU CAN DO

- Carry a multi-tool.

- Protect your head. You can't do without it, not well anyway.

- Clocks are useless. Flashlights are not. Neither is vinegar.

- Learn how to live without things you can't live without, especially the magic beans. Examples: Electricity. iPhone. Klonopin. Your dreams.

- If you can, leave them with a joke.

  "What's the difference between Port Authority and an attractive lobster?
  One is a crusty bus station, the other a busty crustacean."

That's how you prepare for a disaster.

Exit Quote:
"I hated every minute of training, but I said, 'Don't quit. Suffer now and live the rest of your life as a champion'."
— Muhammad Ali

CRUZ/BENNETT PRODUCTIONS
thanks you for 11 years of loyal support

1

The Invention of Love

"I'M DEAD, THEN. GOOD." THOSE WERE THE FIRST WORDS SHE said to him.

Julian and Ashton flew to New York from L.A. with their girlfriends Gwen and Riley to see the star-studded adaptation of Tom Stoppard's *The Invention of Love* off Broadway. The play—with Nicole Kidman in the starring role!—about the life and death of British poet A.E. Housman, originally written for men, had been reimagined and restaged with all women, except for the part of Moses Jackson, Housman's *objet d'amour*, which was played by some male newcomer, who was "ominous like a powder keg," the *New York Times* had reverentially written.

At first, when Gwen had suggested going, Julian balked. He knew something about *The Invention of Love*. His unfinished masters, a papercut inside him, included Stoppard's play as part of the assignment.

"Oh, you think you know something about everything, Jules," Gwen said. She was always dragging him to cultural things. "But you don't know about this. Trust me. It's going to be fantastic."

"Gwen, if we're going all the way to New York, why don't we see *La Traviata* at Lincoln Center instead?" Julian said. He wasn't particularly a friend of the opera, but Placido Domingo was Armand. That was worth a cross-country trip.

"Did you not hear when I said *Nicole Kidman* is A.E. Housman? And Kyra Sedgwick is her sidekick!"

"I heard, I heard," Julian said. "Is Ashton going to agree to this?"

"He will if you will. And what, you think *Ashton* would rather see Placido? Ha. We have to expand his horizons. And clearly not just his. Come on, Jules, don't sulk, it'll be fun. I promise." Gwen smiled toothily as if her promises were stone-carved.

They made a weekend out of it. Ashton hung up his favorite sign on the door of his store: GONE FISHING (though he didn't fish). The four of them like the musketeers often traveled together, spent weekends down in Cabo or up in Napa. They flew into JFK on Friday, had dinner at La Bernardin, where Ashton knew the owner (of course he did), and they got to eat for free. Afterward, they met up with a few friends from UCLA, went drinking in Soho and dancing in Harlem.

Hungover and slow, they spent Saturday afternoon at MOMA, did some window shopping on Fifth Avenue. When Saturday night rolled around, Julian was almost too tired to go out again. He had bought a fascinating little book at the MOMA gift store, *The Oracle Book: Answers to Life's Questions*, and would have liked to order room service and leaf through it—looking for answers as the book suggested. He had opened it randomly to two provocative replies, answers to questions he wasn't asking.

One: *You've drawn the seven of cups. Is this what you really want?*

What was *this* referring to in that sentence?

And two: *A solar eclipse hints of an unexpected ending.*

What ending was he expecting?

Dressed for a Saturday night on the town—the men in dark jeans, fitted shirts, and structured blazers; the girls made up and blown out, in high heels and open necklines—they had pre-theatre sushi at Nobu in TriBeCa, all but Riley because it was B day and Riley didn't eat on B days, and cabbed it to the Cherry Lane Theatre in Greenwich Village.

And wouldn't you know it, Nicole Kidman had an understudy!

The sign on the board read: "Tonight, the part of A.E. Housman will be played by Ms. Kidman's understudy, Josephine Collins."

A loud unhappy hullaballoo rippled through the ticketholders. It was a Saturday night! Why would the star of the show be out without a word? "Did she fall down the stairs? Did she catch a contagious disease?" Gwen asked. No one knew. The box office was mum. The social media was quiet. Since the only name above the title of the play on the marquee was Tom Stoppard's, refunds were out of the question.

Julian thought his girlfriend was going to have a polar icecap meltdown right on the pavement. Gwen was upset at the poor woman at the ticket window, as if Nicole's absence was the woman's fault. "But *why* is she out?" Gwen kept repeating. "Can't you tell me? *Why?*"

Julian tried to make it better. Giving Gwen a small commiserating pat as they took their seats, he said, "Josephine Collins is a good stage name, don't you think?"

Gwen glared at him. "You never say anything to actually make me feel better when I'm upset," she said. "Like you don't even care."

Julian glanced at Ashton on his right. His friend was chatting with Riley, chuckling over some private joke, their blond heads together.

He tried again. "You did amazing, Gwen, really. These seats are incredible." And they were. Third row center.

"Oh yes, they're excellent," Gwen said. "All the better to see the understudy from."

Ashton elbowed him. "I keep telling you, Jules, in some situations, it's best to shut the hell up. This most definitely is one of them."

Julian stared straight ahead. After an interminable minute, the red curtain rose.

The understudy stood center stage in the footlights.

"I'm dead, then. Good," she said to him, and swiveled her hips.

A slouching, heavy-lidded Julian sat up in his seat.

The play may have been fine. It may have been terrible. Gwen spent the moments during applause and the intermission in a ceaseless harangue against the understudy, so it was hard for Julian to form a coherent opinion about the play.

But he formed an opinion about the understudy.

The accidental girl was in front of Julian for over two unsuppressed hours.

She was remarkable. Though she was young and played an old man looking back on his life and finding it wanting, she brought melancholy and elegance to the stage, she brought wit and pain and outrage. She brought it all. Everything she had was left on the stage in front of Julian.

She might not have been as tall as Nicole Kidman, but she was just as sinewy, all long limbs and whiteout skin and bleached-out features. Unlike Nicole, she had brown eyes and a whisper of a breathy voice. She sounded like a teenager but with an earthy grownup exhale at the end of each sentence. The juxtaposition of her feminine self, sauntering about, playing a gruff professor had a powerful effect on Julian. The sturdy Housman verse coming from her barely audible, husky throat seduced him. Her swiveling hips seduced him. *Love is but ice in the hands of children,* she murmured in her impeccable British accent, standing on the banks of the River Styx, stretching out her slender arms to him. He fought the urge to leap up in his seat. How many tomorrows would the gods give me? she kept asking. How much time do I have? she cried.

And then, stepping out of Housman and into Chekhov, she said this from *The Three Sisters*:

Oh, where is it, where has it all gone, my past, when I was young? When I dreamed and thought with grace, when my present and my future were lighted up with hope? Why is it that when we have barely begun to live, we grow dull, gray, uninteresting, lazy, indifferent, useless, unhappy. The adults relieve the monotony of their days with gossip and vodka. Where is the artist, the scholar, the saint, where is the one who is not like all the others, who inspires envy, or passionate desire? What do you want, Julian? WHAT DO YOU WANT?

His mouth dropped open. Did he mishear? *The Oracle Book* was speaking to him out loud. Bewildered, he leaned forward. Ashton nudged him to sit back. Did the girl just call out to him by name?

∞

"It was ghastly, wasn't it?" Gwen said when it was over. "How pretentious was she? Oh, she thought she was all that. How in the world did she land such a complex role? Banging the producer, most likely, don't you think?"

"How would I know?" Julian said. "Why are you asking *me*? I know nothing about her." Was she really British? Surely you couldn't fake an accent like that.

"Why are you getting defensive?" Gwen sighed, taking his limp hand. "I'm sorry, okay? You were right. We should've seen *La Traviata*. But honestly, what did you think? Ghastly, wasn't it?"

That wasn't quite what Julian thought.

Gwen wanted to stage door for Kyra Sedgwick's autograph. "So the evening is not a *total* waste." They squeezed in by the blue guardrail. "After this, we're walking straight to Art Bar," Gwen said. "First round's on me. We will drink to forget."

"There isn't enough alcohol in all of New York," Riley chimed in. "I also didn't care for her, Gwennie. She rubbed me the wrong way, though I can't quite put my finger on why."

"What do you think, Jules?" Ashton said. "Is there enough alcohol in all of New York for you to forget her?"

"I shouldn't think so."

Ashton was teasing but not smiling. Julian turned his gaze to the backlit pink posterboard by the stage door.

"She grated on me," Gwen continued to say to Riley. "It's fine to bring something new to a role. But it can't be a total departure."

"She was a woman playing a man, how much more of a departure can there be?" Julian asked.

"She wasn't manly enough. Did you hear her voice?"

"I heard her," said Julian.

"I could barely. Plus she wasn't tall enough. It was *so* distracting."

"Were you distracted by her height, bro?" Ashton said, nudging Julian.

"Nope."

"Well, pardon me for expressing my opinion," Gwen said.

Julian pointed out that he, too, was expressing his opinion.

"Yes, but *I'm* making an intellectual argument against her lack of quality," Gwen said. "What are *you* doing?"

Julian let it go. He didn't know what he was doing.

It was a June summer night in New York, warm, overcast, windy, a crackle in the air of three million people alive in the street. People were pushy, the way people in New York sometimes are when they've spent a lot of scratch on tickets and feel it's their due to get a signature on a playbill. They stand with demanding arms out, as if they're doing the actors a favor and not the other way around.

The petty things Gwen continued to say about the understudy irritated Julian. He stepped away, letting other men and their dates wedge between him and his date. An echo of the girl's words continued to ring in his ears and thump in his chest. *I'm dead then, good; love like ice in the hands of children...*

Kyra Sedgwick came out on the arm of Kevin Bacon, her skinny, youthful actor husband. A guy in the crowd loudly made a six degrees of Kevin Bacon joke. Kevin Bacon smiled as if he wanted to deck him. A few minutes later, the only man in the cast—the beefed-up, "explosive powder keg" who played Moses Jackson—strutted out. Julian didn't catch his actual name and didn't care to. A few steps behind Mr. Universe, the understudy followed. Julian's breath caught in his throat.

The barricades grunted under the heaving mob; there was shouting, Kyra, Kyra. Kevin, Kevin. Julian liked that Kevin Bacon wasn't even in the play, yet was signing. A measure of true celebrity, Julian thought with amusement. This was some superstar shit.

Even Mr. Universe signed a few playbills. Not Julian's understudy. She stood to the side like the last unbought maiden at an Old West wench auction. No one recognized her with the blonde wig off and her wet hair pulled into a tight bun.

It started to drizzle.

Extending his hand with the playbill in it, Julian waved it around to get her attention. How do you act like a gentleman and not an asshole when you're waving around a thing to be signed? But when she saw him making a fool of himself, she stepped forward, all breath and grateful smile. He held out the playbill for her in the palm of his slightly shaking hand, watching the top of her wet dark head as she signed her name, large, ornate, nearly illegible, *Josephine Collins* with a bold flourish.

Before Julian could tell her how good she was, how astonishing, the steroid with a mouth summoned her from afar. The only thing missing was a finger snap. She fled.

And that was that.

∞

Back in L.A., Julian almost forgot her.

Ashton's store was as busy as ever, three of Julian's brothers were having birthdays, Father's Day was coming up, a baptism, his mother was hosting an end-of-school party and needed Julian's help finding a florist and a caterer, and Gwen was hinting at a romantic getaway to Mexico for the Fourth of July, hoping perhaps for an engagement ring in Cabo.

Every once in a while, Julian remembered the girl's first line.

Not even remembered it. He dreamed it.

In visions of blazes and icy glades, her pale face would appear lit up against the black, and from the center stage in his chest her voice would sound, asking what he was waiting for, telling him that the soul had no borders.

2

Book Soup

A FEW WEEKS LATER JULIAN RAN INTO HER AT BOOK SOUP ON Sunset. Ran into her was probably a misnomer. He was in the poetry stacks, killing time before meeting up with Ashton, and she waltzed in.

Skipping up the short stairs, she headed for the black shelves by the windows, to the film and theatre section. From his hidden vantage point, his head cocked, Julian watched her scanning the spines of the books. It was definitely the same girl, right? What a coincidence to find her here.

She had on a blonde wig in New York and cocoa hair now, swept up in a messy, falling-out bun. She was wearing denim shorts, black army boots, and a sheer plaid shirt that swung over a bright red tank top. Her legs were slender, long, untanned. No doubt. It was her.

Julian didn't usually approach women he didn't know in bookstores. Plus he was out of time. He glanced at his watch, as if he were actually contemplating accosting her, or perhaps looking for a reason not to. Ashton in thirty.

His insane buddy wanted to go canyoneering in Utah! Julian's job as a friend was to talk him out of it. So Julian had gone to Book Soup to buy the memoir of the unfortunate hiker who had also gone canyoneering in Utah. The poor bastard got trapped under a boulder for five days in Blue John Canyon and had to cut off his own arm with a dull pocket knife to survive.

Over lunch of spicy soft-shell crab tacos, cilantro slaw and cold beer, Julian intended to read the salient passages to Ashton about how to save a life.

But before he could get to the life-saving travel section, Julian got sidetracked by the L.A. poems of Leonard Cohen and then by the hypnotic synth-beat chorus of Cuco's "Drown" playing on the overhead speakers.

And there she was, bouncing in.

It was almost noon. Julian had just enough time to hightail it to Melrose to meet Ashton at Gracias Madre. At lunchtime, the streets of West Hollywood pulsed with *hangry* drivers. The girl hadn't even seen him. He didn't need to be sneaky. He didn't need to be anything. Put Leonard Cohen down, walk out the open door onto Sunset. Stroll right on out. Throw a dollar into Jenny's jar. Jenny the blind waif loitered outside the store at lunchtime by the rack of newspapers. The homeless needed to eat, too. Walk to your car, get in, drive away.

Without traffic, it would take him seven minutes. Julian prided himself on being a punctual guy, his Tag Heuer watch set to atomic time, Hollywood's legendary lateness insulting to him.

Julian did not walk out.

Instead, casual as all that, he ambled across the store to the sunny corner by the window until he stood behind her, Leonard Cohen's love songs to Los Angeles clutched in his paws.

He took a breath. "Josephine?"

He figured if it wasn't her, she wouldn't turn around.

She turned around. Though not exactly *immediately*. There was a delay in her turning around. She was makeup free, clear-skinned, brown eyed, neutrally polite. Everything on her smooth healthy face was open. Eyes far apart, unhindered by overhanging brow lines or furrows in the lids, forehead large, cheekbones wide, mouth pink.

At first there was nothing. Then she blinked at him and smiled politely. Not an invitation to a wedding, just a tiny acknowledgment that she was looking at a man whom she didn't find at first glance to be overly repellent, and to whom she would deign, grace, give one minute of her life. You got sixty seconds, cowboy, her small smile said. Go.

But Julian couldn't go. He had forgotten his words. *Going up*, it was called in the theatre. When everything you were supposed to say flew out of your head.

She spoke first. "Where do I know you from?" she asked, squinting. There was no trace of a British accent in her voice. "You look so familiar. Wait. Didn't you come to my play in New York? *The Invention of Love*?"

"Yes." He cleared his throat. "You remember?"

She shrugged. "Yours was the only playbill I signed." Her voice—not just her stage voice but also her normal sing-song speaking voice—was gentle and breathy, a girl's voice but with a naked woman's lilt to it. Quite an art to pull that off. Quite a spectacle. "What are you doing in L.A.?"

"I live around the corner," he said, ready to give her his street address and apartment number. "You?"

"I'm just visiting. Auditioning."

"From London?"

She chuckled. "Nah, that was fake. I'm Brooklyn born and raised—like Neil Diamond."

"Don't you have a show to do?"

She shook her head. "Nicole came back."

"Why was she out that night?" Gwen was *still* carrying on about it.

"You're upset about that, too? The theatre got so many complaints."

Julian stammered. "No, not me."

"Would you believe it—Nicole's driver took a wrong turn into the Lincoln Tunnel." Josephine chortled. "He had a brain freeze. He drove to Jersey! I mean, Jersey is always the wrong turn, but then they got stuck behind an accident coming back, and—well, you know the rest."

"Wow."

"Yeah. My contract ended a few days later," she said. "They didn't renew."

"I'm not surprised," Julian said. "Nicole must've been afraid for her job. You were fantastic."

"Really?" She beamed.

"Oh yeah," he said. "You stole the show. They don't forgive that in the theatre."

The girl thawed. She said some things, a thank you, and a you really think so? Julian barely heard her. His sight grew dim.

That night was the only night she took the stage.

In front of him.

Blinking, he came out of it. "Plus," he said, "you couldn't make up a better stage name than Josephine Collins."

"How do you know I *didn't* make it up?" She twinkled. "And what's *your* name?"

"Julian."

She shielded her eyes—as if from the sun, even though they were inside—and assessed him. "Hmm. You don't look like a Julian."

"No? What does a Julian look like?" He resisted the impulse to check his attire, as if he forgot what he'd put on that morning. "I'm no Ralph Dibny," he muttered, not meaning to say it. It just slipped out. In the comic book universe, Ralph Dibny was an ordinary man in ordinary clothes who drank a super-potion that changed him into an extraordinary contortionist.

Josephine nodded. "Agreed, you're no Dibny—unless you're made of rubber. Julian what?"

"Julian Cruz. Did you say *rubber*? You know who Ralph Dibny is?"

"The Elongated Man? Doesn't everybody?" she replied in her dulcet soprano.

Julian didn't know what to say.

"Are you *sure* you're not a Dibny?" Josephine stood clutching a book to her chest as if they were in high school. "Why else would you look like a geeky middle-school teacher?"

"I don't look like a middle-school teacher," Julian said, and the girl laughed at his on the fly editing, as he hoped she would.

"No?" she said, studying him.

Why did Julian suddenly feel so self-conscious? She reviewed his well-groomed, square-jawed face, she assessed his hair—kept carefully trimmed—the crisp khaki slacks, the sensible shoes, the button-down, blue-checked shirt, the tailored blazer, the impeccably clean nails digging into the cover of Leonard Cohen. He hoped she didn't notice his large, tense hands with their gnarly knuckles or his broken nose, or his light hazelnut eyes that were forcing themselves into slits to hide his interest in her.

"Okay, okay," the girl said, her face lighting up in a smile. "I'm just saying, like Dibny, you look like you might have some hidden talents." Teasing him suggestively, inviting him to tease back.

What happened then wasn't much.

Except the skies opened up and the stars rained down.

"You don't need to be Dibny," Josephine added. "You can live up to your own rock star name, Julian Cruz."

Julian Cruz the rock star forgot how to talk to a girl. Awkwardly he stood, saying nothing. Why did his earth-tone fastidiousness irk him so much today? He was normally so proud of it. He hid his face from her in a dazzle of tumbling stars.

"Listen," Josephine said, "I'd love to stand and gab with you all day about our favorite superheroes, but I've got an audition at one."

"Is that what the book is for?" He pointed to her hands. *Monologues for Actors from Divine Comedy.*

"No, the book's for my 4:30." She zeroed in on him, blinking, thinking.

Not knowing what to say, Julian took a step back and lifted his Leonard Cohen in a *so long, Josephine.*

"Here's the thing," she said, taking a step toward him. "I was gonna catch a cab, but they're so hard to find around lunchtime, so I was wondering…is there any way you could help a girl out and drive me to the audition? It's at Paramount, not too far."

On the radio, Big Star were in love with a girl, the most beautiful of all the girls in the world. "Not a problem," Julian said, flinging away Leonard Cohen.

"I don't mean to impose," she said. "New York's so much easier, I just hop on the subway, but here without a car…"

"It's no big deal." Ashton who? Friend for how long? "So you live in New York?" he asked at the counter as they waited to pay.

"I do. Is that good or bad?" Cheerfully her dark eyes blinked at him. She was fresh faced, eager, sincere. She had a few freckles, a dimple in her small chin. There was something wonderfully animated and inviting about her open face, about her pink vivid mouth.

His car was parked by the Viper Room, a block up Sunset. "The audition is for Mountain Dew," Josephine said as they hurried past the blind homeless Jenny, smiling as if she could see them. "But the 4:30 is for something called *Paradise in the Park* at the Greek Theatre. Have you heard of it? Apparently, they need a narrator for Dante and also a Beatrice."

"Have I heard of what? Mountain Dew? Beatrice? The Greek?" Julian opened the car door for her. He'd been leasing a Volvo sedan the last couple of years. It was spotless inside.

She didn't notice the car or the cleanliness, or if she had, didn't care. She was starved, she said, she hadn't eaten since the night before. He offered her a bite-sized Milky Way from the glove box, behind his seatbelt cutter, flashlight, and multi-tool—items she also ignored on the way to the chocolate. "I really need to start making some money," she said, theatrically chewing the hard caramel. "This Milky Way tastes like it's been there since Christmas. I'm not complaining, mind you. Mine is a beggar's kingdom." Flipping down the visor mirror, she took out a small bag from her hobo purse and started doing her makeup. "I didn't know Ralph Dibny drove a Volvo." So she did notice. She threw blue shadow over her eyes and some more shade at him. "What are you, fifty?"

"What? No—"

"Only married fifty-year-old men with kids drive Volvos."

"That's not true," Julian said, "because I'm none of those things, and yet I drive one."

"Hmm," she said with a purr, casting him a sideways gaze. "You're not a *man*?"

Julian turned off his phone. Switched it off cold. Last thing he needed was Ashton's scolding voice coming through the car speakers, intruding on his Technicolor daydream. He just hoped Ash wouldn't think Julian had been in an accident. Ashton wasn't going to take it lightly, Julian blowing off lunch and a set walkthrough at Warner.

Well, *hadn't* Julian been in a kind of accident? On an unremarkable day, a nothing day, a Tuesday, he was suddenly doing remarkable, out-of-character things. Standing up his friend. Approaching strange women. Giving them rides. The open-ended nature of life was such that on any day, at any moment, this was possible. But just because the world for others was free to these possibilities didn't mean it was thus free to Julian. He lived his comfortable life mostly without impulse and therefore without miracles. He barely even believed in miracles, as Ashton never failed to remind him.

With the traffic on Santa Monica at a standstill, Josephine got antsy, while Julian became a praying man, don't change, red light, don't change, please. "So what do you do, shuttle back and forth between L.A. and New York?" he asked her. "Why not move out here?" Oh, just listen to him! He gripped the wheel.

"I tried that," Josephine said. "I couldn't make it. I don't mean, I couldn't get work. I mean I couldn't live here. Hey, can you give me a heads-up before the light changes and you start driving? I'm putting liner on the inside of my eye." She told him that to her, L.A. always carried a vague ominous quality. At first Julian thought she was joking. L.A. ominous? Maybe some parts. Parts he didn't visit. "I don't feel *real* when I'm here," she said. "It feels like I'm in a dream that's about to end. Hey, Julian, remember you were supposed to give me a heads-up? I could've poked my eye out."

"Sorry." He slowed down, like *now* that helped. "In a dream like a dream come true?" Smooth, Jules. Real smooth.

"No," she said. "Like a walk-on part in someone else's acid trip."

He wanted to make a joke but couldn't, he was too busy praying.

A few minutes to one, he pulled up to a Paramount side gate off Gower. The guard there knew him. "Hey, C.J.," he called out to the smiling security man.

Josephine was impressed. "You're on a first name basis with the guard at Paramount?"

"How you doin', Jules," C.J. said, peering inside the Volvo. "And where's our boy Ashton today?"

"Who's Ashton?" Julian said with a wink.

A smirking C.J. was about to lift the gate, but Josephine leaned over Julian to flick her audition pass into the open window. Julian smelled her meadowsweet musky perfume, verbena mint soap, and the chocolate Milky Way on her breath. Pressed against the back of the driver's seat, he inhaled her and tried not to get lightheaded—or worse.

"You're fine, young lady," the guard said, waving her on. "You're with him, go on through. Do you know where you're going?"

"Do any of us really know where we're going, C.J.?" Josephine said cheerfully. They drove past. "Who's Ashton?"

"My get-into-Paramount card," Julian replied, looking for her soundstage. "Also, Warner's, ABC, CBS, Universal, Fox. Really my get-into-life card. Run, it's right here. Or you'll be late."

At the gray door to Soundstage 8 marked "Auditions," Josephine said sheepishly, "Um, do you think you could wait? I won't be but a minute. Five tops. I'll buy you lunch after. As a thank you."

"You don't have to do that," he said.

"I want to. But also"—she coughed with a beseeching smile—"maybe after I buy you lunch you could drop me off at Griffith Park? The stupid Greek Theatre is so far. And then that's it, I promise."

After she disappeared inside, Julian texted a rushed half-sentence apology to Ashton, switching the phone off again before he could get an outraged reply.

3

Lonely Hearts

JOSEPHINE CAME OUT WELL OVER AN HOUR LATER, FELL INTO his Volvo, and said, "God, that took for*ever*."

"Did you get the part?"

"Who knows?" She was unenthusiastic. "One of the other girls said she knew Matthew McConaughey, Mr. Mountain Dew himself. I hate her." Said without malice. "She's got connections. What time is it? I'm starved, but the Greek is on the other side of town. Where can we grab something quick?"

He took her across Melrose to a place called Coffee Plus Food. It was almost closing time, so they were nearly out of coffee plus food. The joint was also blissfully empty of people. It was just the two of them and the cashier, a bored, unsmiling Australian chick. They sat at a round steel table by the tall windows. Josephine tried to pay, but Julian wouldn't let her. She ordered three sausage rolls ("I told you I was famished"), an avocado salad, a coffee, and the last morning bun on the tray after he assured her that the morning buns were not to be missed, like an attraction at Disneyland.

"I'd like to go to Disneyland someday," she said, devouring the pastry. Even Ashton's Riley, who ate primarily kale, allowed herself the morning bun. It was crispy and caramelly, a cinnabun mated with a croissant and glazed with crunchy sugar. "It's like love in a bun," Josephine said, her happy mouth sticky. She said she'd have to come back for another one before flying back home, and Julian restrained himself from asking when such a hideous flight might take place.

"What do you do, Julian?" she asked as she started on the sausage rolls. "What do you teach?"

"Nothing, why do you keep saying that?"

She twinkled. "You left your house this morning dressed for school."

Julian was going to tell her that he did indeed teach a story writing night class at the community college, but now wouldn't give her the satisfaction. They were off for the summer anyway, so technically he wasn't a teacher.

"Teaching is a noble profession," she went on, the smile playing on her face.

"I know," he said. "I come from a family of educators. I'm just not one of them."

"So what *do* you do?"

"A bunch of things. I run a blog, I write a daily newsletter..."

"Ooh, a blog about what?" she said. "Teaching?"

Now Julian really didn't want to tell her.

"Come on, what's your blog called?" With buttery fingers, she took out her phone. "I'll look it up."

He wished he had named his blog, "Deep Thoughts from a Viking Lord." Instead he was stuck with the truth. "From the Desk of Mr. Know-it-All."

"I knew it! You tell other people how to live!" She laughed. "You have that look about you."

"What look is that?"

"The fake-quiet-but-really-I-know-everything look." She was delighted. "Is it like an *advice* column?" Grinning, she leaned forward. "Do people drown you in their suffering?"

Sometimes yes. "Mostly they write to ask how to get rid of birds that fly into their houses."

"Not for advice on *love*, are you sure?"

He tried to keep a poker face. "It's not *that* kind of blog. I'm not Mr. Lonely Hearts."

"No?"

How *could* one maintain a poker face against such onslaught?

A few years ago, he started distilling his website into a daily newsletter. He picked a handful of questions, tied them up with a theme, and offered a few life hacks and pithy sayings to go along with them. *The soul is a bird inside your house*, Nathaniel West wrote. *Better one live bird in a jungle than two stuffed birds in a library.*

The young woman clapped. "I can't *wait* to bookmark you," she said. In her voice, even a word like bookmark sounded erotic. "Do you have advice for frustrated actresses?"

He wanted to impress her with his own inappropriateness by telling her to never go topless unless it was essential to the story. "Dress to the camera," is what he said.

Flicking up the collar of her see-through blouse, she crossed and uncrossed her bare legs. "Done. Bring me my pasties and a fedora. What else?"

Did she just say pasties? Mon *Dieu*.

"Once," Josephine said, "a casting director told me not to try so hard to be someone else. Just be yourself, she told me, and I'm like, you idiot. I'm auditioning for Young Nabby Adams on *John Adams*, isn't the whole *point* to be someone else?"

Julian laughed.

"I get a *ton* of advice," she went on, "especially *after* I don't get the part. Don't be so desperate, Josephine. Relax, Josephine. Have fun! Drop your shoulder! I'm like, where were you before my audition? If that's all I had to do, I'd be winning a Tony by now."

"How long have you been at it?"

"How old am I? Oh yeah—*that* long. I prefer stage to film," she announced, like it was a badge of honor. "It's more real. And I'm all about making it real."

"So why do you come to L.A. then?" Not that Julian was complaining. But L.A. was a make-believe town.

"Why? For the same reason Bonnie and Clyde robbed banks."

He laughed. "Because that's where the money is?"

"Yes! It's not acting I love, *per se*. I just love the stage. I like the instant feedback. I like it when they laugh. I like it when they cry." She twirled a loose strand of her hair. "Do *you* like plays?" She batted her lashes. "Besides *The Invention of Love*."

"Yes, that's one of my favorites. Oscar Wilde is pretty good, too. I once played Ernest in high school."

"I was Cecily *and* Gwendolen!" Josephine exclaimed with a thrill, as if she and Julian had played opposite each other. Grabbing his hands from across the table, she affected a stellar British accent. *"Ernest, we may never be married. I fear we never shall. But though I may marry someone else, and marry often, nothing can alter my eternal devotion to you."*

The name *Gwendolen* made Julian stop smiling. Casting aside his enchantment, he politely drew his hands from her and palmed his coffee.

Josephine, puzzled at his sudden wane, pivoted and refocused. "Sorry, you were in the middle of telling me what you did for a living, and I interrupted you with myself. Typical actress, right? Me, me, me. You run a blog, you said? Sounds like a hobby, like it's even less lucrative than acting. And trust me, there's *nothing* less lucrative than acting."

"I thought actors cared nothing for money, they just wanted to be believed?" At the Cherry Lane, she had made a believer out of him.

"That's first." She smiled grandly. "But being booked and blessed wouldn't be the *worst* thing that happened to me."

"Well, there's money in blogging," Julian said. "I get paid from Google ads, plus I run a pledge drive twice a year. Whoever sends me a few bucks gets my daily newsletter."

"How many people pledge?"

"Maybe thirty thousand. And two million unique visitors to the website. That helps raise our ad rates."

She became less casual. "Two *million* visitors? I may be in the wrong business. Who is *our* in that sentence? You and the famous Ashton?"

"Yes, the famous Ashton." Who was probably calling in an APB on Julian at that very moment.

"Is he the other Mr. Lonely Hearts?"

Why did everything out of her mouth sound like she was playing with him? Playing with him like seducing him, not toying with him, though she may have also been toying with him. "He can't be the *other* Lonely Heart," Julian said, "because I myself am not one. But yes, we're partners in everything. Enough about me." No red-blooded male talked about himself while across from him sat no less than Helen of Troy. "What have *you* been in? Anything I can watch tonight?"

"I was in a national Colgate commercial a year ago. You could watch that." She flashed her teeth at him. "Recognize me now?"

She did look incongruously familiar. Maintaining a calm exterior took *tremendous* effort.

She told him she was also Mary in *The Testament of Mary.* "You didn't see that? Yeah, nobody did. It was well reviewed and was even nominated for a Tony but ran only *three weeks.* Go figure, right? Only on Broadway can you have both great success and abject failure in the same show." She chuckled. "To increase *Mary*'s ticket sales, the producer told the director to shoot a commercial with a shot of the audience hooting it up, having a great time, and the director said, 'You gotta be careful, Harry, you don't want your *actual* audience jumping up in the middle of your show yelling, what the fuck were *they* laughing at?'" Josephine laughed herself, her face flushed and carefree.

Her flushed, carefree face was quickly becoming Julian's favorite thing in the universe.

They'd been in the café for over an hour. Julian was still clutching his cold cup of coffee. Suddenly she sprung from her seat. "Oh, no, it's almost four! How do you swallow time like that? Let's go, quick!"

"*I* swallow time?" Slowly he rose from the table.

The traffic on Gower was of course at a standstill. "Can we make it?"

"No, Josephine, we can't."

"Oh, come now, Mr. *No-at-All*. I told you, I go on at 4:30."

"Will never happen. We're four miles away in heavy traffic."

"Mr. Pessimist," she said. "What did Bette Davis reply to Johnny Carson when he asked her how to get to Hollywood?"

"She said 'Take Fountain,'" said Julian.

"Very good! So you *do* know some stuff. Follow Bette's advice, Julian. Take Fountain." She flapped open the book she had bought. "Look what you did, you kept me yapping so long, I forgot to prepare a monologue. I don't know a single line for Beatrice."

"Start with, *In the midway of this, our mortal life, I found me in a gloomy wood...*"

"And then?"

"That's all I know," Mr. Know-it-All said.

"What am I supposed to do with that?"

"Perhaps you can go off book on another line or two from your years in the theatre?"

"From Beatrice? From *Divine Comedy*?"

"So audition for the narrator," Julian said. "You'd make a great Dante. You were a very good Housman."

"Please don't stare at me, drive," she said. "Is this jalopy a car or a horse buggy?"

"The Volvo is one of the best, safest cars on the road," Julian said, offended for his oft-maligned automobile.

"I'm thrilled you're safe," she said. "Can you be safe and step on it?"

"We're at a red light."

"I've never seen so many red lights in my life," Josephine said. "I think you're *willing* them to be red. Like you *want* me to be late."

"Why would I want that?" Face straight. Voice even.

"That's what *I'm* trying to figure out." Almost as an aside, she added, "You know, if I get this gig, I'll have to stay in L.A. for the summer."

Julian's jalopy grew wings and in it he flew to Griffith Park, screeching into a parking spot seventeen minutes later. "Ashton is right, miracles really do abound," he said. "I've never made it here in less than a half-hour."

"Really, hmm," she said. "How often do you do this, Speedy Gonzalez, take strange stranded women to the Greek?" Flinging open the door, she motioned for him. "Come in with me. You can be my good luck charm."

The theatre was nearly empty except for a few dozen people sitting in the front rows. Built into the cliffs of the untamed Santa Monica Mountains, the open amphitheatre was a little disquieting with its spooky silence and vacant red seats, the shrubby eucalyptus rising all around.

At the side gate, a girl with a clipboard stood in Phone Pose—head down like a horse at the water—texting. Josephine gave her name—and then Julian's! He pulled at her sleeve. The girl didn't see his name on the call sheet. "Must be an oversight," Josephine said. They began to argue. "Clearly *someone* has made a mistake," Josephine said. "Go get your supervisor immediately."

Thirty seconds later, they were taking their seats in side orchestra, him with a number and a sticker. "That's a great hack I learned from the theatre life, Julian," Josephine said. "Today, I give it to you for free. Never yell down to get what you want. Always yell *up*. You're welcome."

"Why did you do that?" he whispered.

"Shh. She wouldn't have let you in otherwise. You saw how she wallowed in her petty power. You want to perform, don't you?"

"I most certainly do not."

Josephine gave his forearm a good-natured pinch. "You said you were Ernest in high school. You must know something from Wilde by heart. I did."

"Am I you?"

"What you are is number 50. You have ten minutes. I suggest you start practicing."

"Josephine, I'm not reading."

She stopped listening. They sat next to each other, their arms touching, her bare leg pressed against his khaki trousers. She was mouthing something, while his mind stayed a stubborn blank. Anxiously he stared at the stage. He was nervous for her, not for himself. He knew that despite her shenanigans he wasn't going up there, but he really wanted her to get the part. A large sweaty man with messy hair recited Dante from the first canto. After four lines he was stopped. A bird of a woman followed. A pair of identical sisters got seven lines in before they were shooed off.

"If you can get through your monologue," Julian said quietly, after watching the others, "you'll be all right. Here's a hack for you. You're rehearsing, not auditioning. Act like you already have the part."

"But I *don't* have the part. How the heck do I do that?"

"You *act*," he said.

Her number was called. "Number 49. Josephine Collins."

"Wish me luck," she whispered, throwing Julian her bag and jumping up.

"You don't need it. You have the part." Julian watched her let down her long hair and become someone else on the stage, someone who projected without a microphone into the 6000-seat amphitheatre, someone who didn't speak in a breathy femme fatale voice, someone with a British accent. She stood tall, eyes up, chin up, her body in dramatic pose, and shouted up into the empty seats.

What power is it, which mounts my love so high,
That makes me see, and cannot feed mine eye?
The mightiest space in fortune nature brings
To join like likes and kiss like native things—

The casting crank in the front row stopped her. "Miss Collins, what is *that* you are reading for us?"

"Shakespeare, sir, from *All's Well that Ends*—"

"This is an audition for *Paradise in the Park*. You're supposed to be reading for either Beatrice or Dante."

"Of course. I was showcasing my abilities. How about this"—she lowered her voice to a deep bass, looked up, beat her breast—"*through me you pass through the city of woe, through me you pass into eternal pain*—"

"Thank you—next. Number 50. Julian Cruz. Mr. Cruz, have *you* prepared some Dante for us?"

4

Gift of the Magi

BACK AT HIS CAR, THEY LINGERED. SHE CALLED HIM chicken for telling the director he had nothing prepared, and he agreed, not wanting to take her home. She tied up her hair and put away her fake glasses. She looked like herself again, simple and perfect. The ends of her sheer blouse swayed in the breeze.

"I wish it wasn't so late in the day," she said, glancing at the hills around the theatre. "We could take a walk up there. I could show you something."

"Show me anyway," he said. "Wait—up where?"

"What, you agreed too fast? No, no backsies. I'll have to show you another day."

"Okay—when?"

She laughed. They leaned against his gray Volvo, drinking from the same water bottle. Julian's thoughts were racing. "What's your favorite movie?"

"Dunno. Why?"

"Come on. What is it? *Titanic*?"

"Ugh, no, I don't care for all that dying in icy water, don't care for it one bit," she said, peering at him through slitted eyes. "*Apocalypse Now.*"

Julian did a double take. "*Apocalypse Now* is your favorite movie?"

She stayed poker-faced. "Sure. Why is *that* surprising?"

"No reason." He fake-coughed. "I've never seen it."

Now it was her turn to do a double take. "You've never seen *Apocalypse Now*?"

"No. Why is *that* surprising?"

"Because it's such a guy movie. We should watch it sometime."

"Okay—when?"

She laughed. They lingered a bit longer.

"Listen—I gotta head back," she said.

"I thought you were hungry," Julian blurted. "What do you feel like eating? We can go anywhere. My treat. I may not know about Vietnam movies, but I know my L.A. food. Are you in the mood for a taco? Factor's on Pico? A pizza? Marie Callender's coconut pie?"

Her mouth twisted as she struggled with some internal thing. "Don't think I'm nuts," Josephine finally said. "But I feel like breakfast for dinner. Hash browns?"

"I know just the place. Best hash browns in L.A."

"Am I dressed for it?"

"For IHOP? Absolutely." Julian opened the passenger door.

"You know what they say," she said, getting in. "When the guy opens the door for you, either the girl is new, or the car is new."

"Ha," Julian said. The girl was new.

∞

"So who do you stay with when you're in L.A.?" he asked. They were sitting across from each other, their second plate of hash browns half eaten between them on the blue table.

"My friend Z."

Did Julian dare ask if Z was a Zoe or a Zachary? He dared. "Who's Z?"

"My best friend Zakiyyah."

"Ah." An exhale. "Is she in the business, too?"

"She used to be." Josephine drummed her fork against the table. IHOP on Sunset was empty, because what kind of fool came to IHOP at night.

"What's her actual name?"

"Zakiyyah Job. Job as in Bible, not employment. And Zakiyyah like pariah."

"You two have incredible stage names. You're lucky."

"You should talk, *Julian Cruz*," she said. "Anyway, Z is lucky. Jury's still out on me. Seven years ago, we moved out west, paradise is here, the whole thing. We set up house, started going to auditions. I thought we'd be all right—me being white and her being black and all—but with colorblind casting, the agents were bending over themselves to hire her, not me. Sometimes she was better. Sometimes I was better. It was hard to tell, because she always got the part, and it got between us." She sighed. "One of us had to choose a different life if we were to stay friends. So we flipped for it."

"I should think," Julian said, "that first you'd want to flip on whether or not you wanted to stay friends."

"Nah. We're from the same hood. Z is like my sister."

Julian knew something about flipping for it. When they first met Gwen and Riley, he and Ashton flipped for Gwen. Because tall, gorgeous, California girl-next-door Riley with glossy blonde hair and glowing skin looked too high-end for mortal man, even Ashton, who was no slouch himself in the looks department. Ashton said that no one who was that put-together on a Wednesday night happy hour at a local dive in Santa Monica would ever be easy on a man's life. She looked and moved like a movie star. And Gwen looked like the movie star's best friend. So they flipped for Gwen. Ashton lost. That was shocking. Because Ashton never lost anything.

"I was pretty confident," Josephine continued, "because I never lose a coin toss or even a game of rock, paper, scissors. But Z won. I said, let's play best of five. She won again. I said, best of seven. She won that, too."

"Was this major life decision fueled by tequila by any chance?"

"A whole bottle full."

"Thought so."

"She won every time. Finally I said, okay, one last time, winner take all, sudden death. We fortified ourselves with the rest of the tequila. And guess what happened?"

"You won?"

"Why," she said with a half-smile full of whimsy, "because you believe in the Willy Wonka philosophy on lotteries and life in general?"

Julian laughed. "I do, actually. You stand a better chance if you want it more."

Josephine nodded in deep agreement. "And no one wanted it more than me. Yet I still lost. Sometimes, no matter how much you want it, you still lose." She didn't look upset, just philosophical. "After I threw up and calmed down, Z told me I could have it. She would become something else."

Julian was impressed. After he won, he did not give dibs on Gwen to Ashton. "Why would she do that?"

"She said because ever since I was old enough to recite 'Three Blind Mice,' I stood on every table," Josephine said. "I invented a stage everywhere I went." She fell silent, poking the remains of the cold potatoes. "Of course, now Z is doing fantastic, and I'm still waiting for my big break." Zakiyyah was an art therapist for the California public school system. She traveled to districts around the state and trained elementary-school art teachers how to apply their craft to the Special Ed curriculum to help troubled kids who could not be reached by conventional therapy methods. Julian thought Zakiyyah's newfound career was an ocean away from the stage. One job: me, me, me. The other: you, you, you. How did one make a quantum leap like that?

"Why do I plow on, you ask?"

"I didn't ask. I know why," Julian said. "Because the theatre is all there is." His throat tightened.

"Yes!" Josephine exclaimed, her bright eyes gleaming. "It's not so much a career as a sickness. You gotta love it, otherwise there's no good reason for being obsessed with something that offers rewards to so few."

Julian agreed. "That's good advice for many things, not just the theatre," he said. "But you'll get there." He wanted to tell her that he had never in his life felt what he felt when she stood in front of him on the darkened stage at the Cherry Lane. *Oh where is it, where has it all gone, my past, when I was young.* "Besides, if it's what you do, and you can do it, then you do it." Julian set his jaw. "Because sometimes, you *can't* do it. And then, there's nothing worse."

Josephine mined his face. "You know something about that?"

"Little bit. The irony is," Julian said with a thin smile, "that after all that drinking and coin tossing, you didn't stay in L.A. and your friend did."

"That's true. We came here together, and she, who said she couldn't stand the constant sun and the fake life chose to stay, and I, who loved both, returned home instead."

"Why didn't you stay?"

"I told you, I couldn't live here," Josephine said. "Though of course, I didn't know that when we flipped for it."

"That's the time shift paradox." Julian was trying to find something to say to make her feel better. She looked as if she needed it. "The hindsight paradox. You can't act on what you do not know and cannot know."

"No, I'm fibbing, I knew it," the young beauty said, her doleful voice echoing in the empty restaurant. "I felt it in my soul. I thought the heaviness inside me was because of tension between me and Z. It was only after she went back to school and I kept going to auditions and yet the pervasive sense of doom wouldn't lift that I realized it wasn't me and Z that was wrong. It was me and L.A. that was wrong." Breezily she waved her hand around, la-di-da. "So six years ago I returned to the absurd delights of the New York stage life." She smiled. "Every few months I fly out here, try out for a few things so I can keep my SAG membership. I visit my friend and get away from the theatre to see if I can live without it. And I can't. I fly out to L.A.," Josephine said, "so I can know who I am."

5

Normandie Avenue

NORMANDIE AVENUE WHERE ZAKIYYAH LIVED WAS POORLY lit. The residential through street lined with tall scraggly palms and working-class homes was wide but sketchy.

"It's all she can afford," Josephine said.

"I said nothing." A moment later: "Is it safe?"

"Well, it's not as safe as your Volvo, but what is?"

In a minute she was going to leave his Volvo.

"Z and I haven't had much trouble," she went on. "If you don't count that drive-by shooting last time I was here."

"And who'd want to count that?"

"It happened in front of Z's house. Cops blocked the road for hours. Z was at work, but I had a callback and couldn't leave until they cleared the scene. Story of my life."

"Why doesn't she move?"

"Because I'm back in New York. When we were both paying rent, it was easier."

"Why doesn't she get another roommate?"

"Who'd want to live here, have you seen the neighborhood?" Josephine shrugged. "On the plus side, it's cheap. It's next to the freeway. Rosie the landlady is nice. She makes us enchiladas because Z works late and is often too tired to cook. Though she's a really good cook."

"What about you? Do you cook?"

"Oh, sure. I cook," she said. "I make shame toast."

"I like it already," said Julian.

"Wait until you taste it. You'll love it."

"Okay—when?"

She laughed like he was the headliner at the Comedy Cellar.

Zakiyyah lived in a yellow house under a yellow streetlight. He pulled up to the curb and put the car into park. He debated turning it off. Julian wanted to come in. He wanted he didn't know what.

"You'd like Zakiyyah," Josephine said. "She's in education, like you."

"I'm not in education, Josephine. I'm in entertainment."

"You literally teach people how to use vinegar. You call that entertainment? *I'm* in entertainment."

"Anyone can make Oscar Wilde entertaining," Julian said. "He did all the work for you. To make vinegar entertaining, now *that* takes talent."

"Okay, so you're an entertaining academic," she said.

"See, where I come from, that would be considered a compliment."

"Where I come from, too." She stretched, her arms hitting the roof of the car. "Z and I are on the second floor. We have a balcony." She pointed to the side of the two-story house. "We have flowers on it. Can you see them? Red azaleas. Yellow petunias."

"You're lucky someone doesn't come up and steal them." He glanced up and down the street.

She wasn't offended. "I mentioned this about the balcony," she said, "in case you wanted to stand under it and recite a life hack or a poem or something."

Swaying from her, he had nothing in reply, nothing clever.

Slowly she picked up her bag from the footwell. "I'm just messing with you. Thanks for today. I had fun."

"Me, too."

She opened the door and turned to him. Julian was about to cry nonsense into the confused air, literally to open his mouth and pour forth on her his plans before getting lost, how much he had once wanted a different life, how it hurt to let it go, and how hard it was to make peace with it, but the upside-down longing for her that felt like plunging into orchards of roses, thorns and all, made it impossible for him to breathe and therefore to speak.

Her hand was still on the open door, her right foot already out.

Leaning across, she kissed him softly on the cheek, close to his mouth. She smelled of chocolate cherries, of palm trees, of fire. A sense of something helpless rose up inside him.

After he watched her wave and vanish, he sat in front of her house, staring at the crumbling yellow balcony with the wilting azaleas, his fists pressed into his chest. He opened the window so he could hear the Hollywood Freeway on the next block, lights of cars flying past, whooshing like a turbulent ocean. A mile north, at the end of the long, straight Normandie, rose the giant inky forms of the Santa Monica Mountains, and etched into them the HOLLYWOOD sign whitely lit against the high darkness. Normandie was a through street, and cars often sped by before climbing up the hill behind Julian and disappearing. Directly across from Z's place stood a low apartment building behind a locked gate, like a halfway house, a cheap duplex, gated off. All the lights were on. It was loud. Barbed wire hung over the barred windows and the stucco balconies, draped down, dangled like icicle lights at Christmas.

Julian peered closer. No, it wasn't barbed wire. How retro. How WWII of him. It was razor wire. That was the modern way, the L.A. way. When regular barbs weren't deterrent enough, the straight-edge blades sliced your Romeo throat as you climbed up to sing a sonnet to your lover. Josephine, Josephine.

Why would a house need razor wire on its windows and balconies?

Julian didn't want to think about his day. He wanted only to feel. When he was thirteen he had a mad crush on a girl in the schoolyard. The crush was so bad it had rendered him speechless. Every time he was within fifty feet of her, he would start to sweat and pant. In the middle of the school year she had open heart surgery and died on the operating table, and that was that. It was the last time Julian had felt this way. Since then, he kept in control of himself. None of the later women he was with, and some of them had been awe-inspiring, made him feel like that tongue-tied kid at recess. He tried to avoid it at all costs, the feeling of being out of control. It was so debilitating. He wanted a sane love life. He wanted a sane life.

And until today, that was exactly what he got.

6

Gwen

WHEN GWEN OPENED THE DOOR, AT TEN AT NIGHT, SHE stared at him like he was about to tell her someone had died.

Gwen was right to be worried. They had a weekly schedule from which they rarely deviated. They went out on Thursday nights, and she stayed over at his place. They went out on Saturday nights, usually with Ashton and Riley. The four of them had Sunday brunch together. On Wednesdays he and Gwen tried to grab lunch if Julian didn't have meetings and she wasn't swamped. She was a legal secretary for an entertainment law firm.

She lived in a ground floor apartment with two other girls. All three had been watching *Desperate Housewives*. The other two waved to Julian, annoyed by the interruption. "What's wrong?" Gwen said. "Were we supposed to go out today?"

"No, no."

"I didn't think so. Tuesday is not our day." She smiled.

"Can we talk?"

Gwen glanced at the couch where her roommates were waiting. "Can it wait till tomorrow, Jules? Because we have fifteen minutes left of our show and then I gotta hit the sack. I have to be in at eight. Contract crisis. Can it wait?"

"No."

Gwen grimaced.

He didn't want to talk in the kitchen, and Gwen was already in pajamas. There was no way he was getting her into his car for a distressing heart to heart. "Let's go to your room."

Smiling and misunderstanding, she took hold of his wrist. "Girls, finish without me."

In her room, she fell on the bed, while he took a chair across from her, his hands tensely threaded.

"Why are you all the way over there?"

"Gwen…"

Sitting up, she cut him off. "No. Don't start any conversation with *Gwen*. Jules, I'm so stressed at work, I never work fast enough or long enough. Tonight I was there till eight-thirty. If I've been off, it's because I'm overworked."

"You haven't been off."

"I'm so tired all the time. I can't deal with any bullshit right now, Julian," she said. "Can't this wait until I have more energy?"

"It can't. I'm sorry, Gwen. I don't know how to say it. There's never a good time for this." He stiffened his spine, took a breath.

She squeezed her eyes shut, her hands together. "Julian…are you…breaking up with me?"

"Yes, I'm sorry. Please don't be upset. Don't cry." He came to sit by her on the bed, tried to touch her. "You're a great girl. You won't be alone for a minute. And I hope we can stay friends—"

"You're not serious!" she cried, slapping away his arm. "We can't break up! We have brunch reservations at N/Naka this Sunday! We've been waiting three months for them!"

"About that—"

"And we're going away to *Cabo* next month. You already booked the hotel."

"About that…"

"Why are you doing this?"

What could he say? What could he say that would hurt the least?

"I did something wrong," Gwen said. "Look, I'm sorry. I'm

always having mood swings. It's not you, Julian, it's me. I have to take something. My therapist says I need something."

He took her hand, held it despite her protest. "You're not having mood swings. You don't need to take anything. It's not you. Honest. It's me." He took a breath. "I met someone," Julian said. "And I don't want to sneak around on you, or on her. I don't want to end anything or begin anything like that. I'm sorry. I didn't expect it, it's not something I looked for, it's not something I wanted."

Wasn't it, though? Wasn't it something he looked for? As he meandered through the streets of Los Angeles, the city of angels, trying new bars, new cafés, new restaurants, new movie theatres, new stores, as he grazed the beaches and the boardwalks, sat outside eating and drinking al fresco, wandered the malls, the cemeteries, hotel lobbies, what was he looking for, what was he searching for? Yes, he was grabbing ideas for his newsletter, photographs, flowers, phantoms of life. But was that it, really? For ten years he'd been scouring L.A., in a roam not just of the body but of the soul. Was he searching for someone? Staring into the face of every woman he met, the question behind his eyes ever present. Was she *the one?*

One thing Julian knew for sure—and had known from the beginning. Gwen was not the one.

"We've been together so long!" Gwen said. "Don't I deserve better than this?"

"You do," Julian said. "Better than me."

"But why waste three years of *my* life?"

"Sometimes," Julian said, "when you're on the wrong road, you have to get off, go back, start again."

"You're calling me the wrong road? Fuck you!"

"No. *I'm* the wrong road."

"I thought your mother raised you better than this," Gwen said.

"What am I doing?" Julian said. "I'm trying to do the decent thing, the honest thing."

"The decent thing would be not to break up with me."

"Not the honest thing."

"The decent thing would be not to hook up with someone else!"

"I haven't hooked up with anyone else. It's brand new."

"But you want to!"

"Yes," Julian said. "I want to."

HODGEPODGE

- Synonyms for **HODGEPODGE**: medley, farrago, mishmash, grab bag, gallimaufry

- You can tell many, if not most things about a person by the kinds of shoes they wear.

- Muhammad Ali says when you work out, don't do sets of repetitions. Do it until it hurts. And then, do it a few more times until it really hurts. Until it's agony, you ain't working it.

- Want to watch a movie with a girl? Ask her what her favorite movie is. When she tells you, say you haven't seen it, even if you have. If she likes you, she'll say, we should watch it together.

- When you go out into the world, always dress as though you're about to meet the love of your life.

Exit Quote:
*"You must yourself into the
destructive element submit."*

— Joseph Conrad

7

Ashton and Riley

Having fallen overboard, Julian swam the rest of the night in a sea of Josephine. His morning newsletter reflected this. It was a hodgepodge framed by an odd Joseph Conrad quote (was there any other kind?).

It was his turn to open the store, and Julian got to Magnolia Avenue before nine. To his surprise, Ashton was already up and inside. Usually on the mornings Julian opened, Ashton slept in. And granted, his friend looked barely awake and barely dressed, but still. Ashton kept a buzz cut so he wouldn't have to fuss with his hair, but had not yet shaved, his dirty-blond stubble darkening his face.

Riley stood next to him. That was a bigger surprise. Riley tolerated the store like everything about Ashton—with fond resignation. But she didn't show her face on weekdays when she had to be at work. Riley was the organic-produce regional supervisor for Whole Foods. Early morning was her busiest time.

Ashton and Riley both stood at the glass counter by the register, glaring at Julian, their arms crossed. Of course Ashton, who took nothing seriously, was glaring at Julian mock critically, and his arms were mock crossed. He was mimicking Riley to present a supposed united front and hiding from her his persistent yawning.

"What's up." Julian rattled his keys.

"Why don't you tell us," Riley said, her skirt suit without a wrinkle, her honey blonde hair blow-dried glass-straight, her makeup impeccable, her posture like a ballerina's. She stood in fine contrast to her slumped, torn-tank-ripped-jeans-and-half-awake boyfriend. "Did you end it with Gwen last night?"

"Ah." Julian should've known Gwen would call Riley immediately.

"Why did you do it?"

"Do I have to explain everything to you?" He was being glib. Gwen and Riley were best friends. He knew he'd have to explain himself. He just didn't want to.

"Gwen's very upset, Jules," Riley said. "She says you wasted her time, made her believe things that weren't true. She doesn't understand what happened. She told me you were planning to propose in Cabo next month!"

Julian shook his head. That was Gwen wishcasting.

"Breaking up is bad enough," Riley went on, "but why did you lie to her?"

"I didn't lie—"

"Yes, you did. You told her you met someone."

Ashton was shaking his head, too.

"What are *you* shaking your head for?" Julian said.

"Who could you possibly meet? I saw you Monday night, and you hadn't met anyone," Ashton said. "But suddenly yesterday you met someone?"

"That's how it works," Julian said. "That's why it's called *meeting* someone."

"Yeah, 'kay," Ashton said. "Look, if you want to lie, fine, but why be so bad at it?"

Riley twisted to Ashton, her shoulder-length bob swinging. "Do you mean it would be okay for him to lie if he was better at it?"

"That's not what I meant."

"What did you mean, then?"

"Hey! This isn't about me. He's the one who's lying and breaking up and shit. What are you getting on *my* case for?" Ashton threw Julian a wait-until-I-get-ahold-of-you glare.

Julian rubbed his chin with his middle finger in reply.

"Look, Jules," Riley said. "I don't have time for this. I was on the phone with Gwen until two in the morning and had to be at work today at seven. We have a shipment of uninspected cherry tomatoes coming in from Arkansas, and yet here I am with you instead of my tomatoes because of the mess *you've* made. Bottom line is, Gwen and I talked it over, and she said she'd be willing to make some changes—if that's what you need."

Julian shook his head. "It's not what I need."

"You know, Julian"—and here Riley used her slow, wise high-handed tone—"if you thought your relationship needed work, why didn't you just talk to her? You two have been together a long time. You don't think she deserved a conversation?"

"We had a conversation," Julian said.

"But you didn't have to make things up if all you wanted was to shake things up."

"That's not what I want, and it's not what I did."

"Really?" Riley stuck her hand on her hip in a kettle pose. "You didn't lie when you told Gwen that you and Ashton flipped a coin—for *her*!—and you won? Why would you say a thing like that?"

"Yes, Julian," Ashton said, now scowling for real. "Why the *hell* would you say a thing like that?"

"It's not obvious why?" Julian said. "To make Gwen feel better."

Riley swirled to Ashton. "Is it true, Ashton Bennett? That you and I only hooked up because you *lost* a coin toss? That I was your consolation prize? Because you know, sometimes that's *exactly* how you treat me."

"No, sunshine, of *course* it's not true," Ashton said, putting his broad arm around Riley's shoulder and drawing her to him. Riley was tall, but Ashton was taller. "You heard him, he only said it to make Gwen feel better." Icy blue glare from Ashton's ice blue eyes. "Right, Jules?"

Julian swore under his breath. "Ash is right," he said. "I only said it to make Gwen feel better." He closed his fist around his sharp keys.

"Julian, you've always had trouble talking through things." Riley was using her calm, psychoanalytical voice. "You're a little broody, you keep your emotions bottled up. That's not good. You keep acting like nothing's bothering you…"

"Nothing *is* bothering me."

"And then, instead of working things out, you tell Gwen you met somebody."

"But I did," Julian said, "meet somebody."

"Shut up," Ashton said. "Stop making everything worse with your talking."

"I already told you, Gwen's agreed to make changes," Riley said. "While she doesn't condone your passive-aggressiveness, she's willing to do what needs to be done to re-commit to you."

"Let me get this straight," Julian said. "My breaking up with Gwen to her face is passive-aggressive, but her sending a proxy to discuss our relationship, that's facing the matter head on?"

The unflappable Riley continued; she had a list to get through on her way to the cherry tomatoes. "Gwen says she's willing to go to a boxing match with you in Vegas if that's what you want."

"That's not what I want."

"She will also," Riley went on, "stop hassling you to get a real job."

"That might be good advice not just for Gwen," Ashton said.

Riley flipped up her exquisitely manicured hand to stop Ashton from speaking. "Excuse me," she said. "I can't deal with *you* right now. I'm trying to salvage *their* relationship." She took an exasperated breath. "Gwen also said," Riley continued, resuming her professional, no-nonsense manner, "that she'd be willing to do that other thing you want to do with her that she's been saying no to."

"That might be good advice not just for Gwen," said Ashton.

"Ashton Bennett, this is not the time for your jokes! Jules, my opinion?" Riley airbrushed over her body. "It would help you spiritually if you had a mud bath. In the ocean flats at low tide, followed by apitherapy. Both will do wonders for your anxiety problem."

Julian tried not to exchange so much as a blink with Ashton. "Apitherapy, Riles? Is that where I'm attacked by bees or where I'm stabbed by needles?"

"Not attacked," she said defensively. "You are judiciously stung by bees to rid yourself of impurities, spiritual as well as physical."

"I don't need to be stung by bees," Julian said. "I spend my days looking for hacks to prevent *other* people from being stung by bees. And also—I don't have an anxiety problem..."

Julian's cell phone rang. It was 9:07 a.m.

"Hello?" Josephine's voice breathed into his phone. She could seduce the monks in all the missions in California with that liquored-up voice.

"Yes?" Julian kept it cool. He lifted his one-minute finger to Riley and Ashton—frozen in scolding poses by the counter—and turned his back on them.

"Who is this?" Josephine said.

"Who is *this*?" Julian said. "You're calling me."

"Well, I know I'm calling *you*," she said, "but someone called *your* number from my cell phone at 4:49 p.m. yesterday and I know it couldn't have been me because I was on stage. Yet there it is. Your number in my phone."

What was Julian supposed to say?

"Good morning, Josephine," he said quietly.

"Hi, Julian." She giggled. "You could've just asked for my number. I would've given it to you. Listen, what are you doing right now?"

"Like today?" he said. "Or this minute?"

"Sooner. I have a situation. Can you come by? Hey, why

are you talking so low?" She lowered her voice, too. "Who's listening?"

Ashton appeared next to his shoulder. "What the hell? We're not done."

"Be right there." Julian hung up and turned to his friend. The two men were alone in the store. "Where's Riley?"

"She left," Ashton said. "She couldn't wait around for you to be done with your call. She said we weren't finished with our conversation."

"Oh," said Julian, "of course not." He jingled his keys. "Can you hold the fort for a bit? I gotta run out. Be back in a jiff."

"How long is a jiff in Julian-speak, two days? It's your day to open the store, remember? I'm supposed to be in bed. Slumbering. And why did you tell Gwen about the coin toss? What the hell, man. And who was that on the phone?"

"Tell you later. Move." Julian tried to get around Ashton.

"Where are you going?"

"To see a man about a horse."

Ashton didn't budge. "Who was that on the phone?"

"Nobody. Move."

"Make me." Ashton bumped Julian.

Julian pushed him back, not hard. "Do you *want* me to make you?"

Ashton's light blue eyes blinked merrily. He kept trying to grab the phone out of Julian's hands. "You blew me off for lunch yesterday," he said. "Was that when you met this *somebody*, who's now calling you at all hours of the morning? Are you ever coming back, or do I have to call Bryce?"

Bryce was one of their college friends who thought he was Ashton's *other* best friend. "Don't threaten me with fucking Bryce," Julian said. "I'll be back."

"By the intense horny look on your face, I don't think you will, no."

"Drama queen," Julian said. "We have a wardrobe appointment at Warner."

"Yes. At eleven."

"Probably won't be back by then," Julian said. "Can you push it to this afternoon? Ashton—can you please—" They continued to bump and deflect, a well-rehearsed pantomime of friendly combat.

"Jules, please don't tell me you met some chick yesterday and after one afternoon with her broke up with your long-time girlfriend and are now racing off like you've been summoned for a breakfast booty call."

"So stop cockblocking me if you're such a genius."

"Wait!" Ashton said. "I have one very important question—" Impatiently Julian waited.

"What does she look like?" Grinning, Ashton finally let Julian pass. "You know she's only using you for your body."

"I should be so lucky." Julian didn't glance Ashton's way, not wanting his friend to see even a reflection of the wet impression the girl had left on the dry sponge that was his heart.

8

The Red Beret, Take One

AT NORMANDIE, JULIAN TOOK THE STAIRS TWO AT A TIME, though he still managed to glance at the maximum-security house across the street. It didn't look right, even in daylight.

"Good morning, Julian," Josephine said, opening the door. She'd just stepped out of the shower and was flimsily dressed in a tank and sleeping shorts. "Isn't that what they say in Hollywood, no matter what time of day it is—good morning?"

"Yes," he said, "but it's actually morning." They hid their smiles.

Zakiyyah's apartment was small and clean—an open plan kitchen/living room with three half-open interior doors, one bathroom, two bedrooms. A small Formica round table, an old light beige sofa, a couple of bookshelves. A TV. A treadmill. A guitar in the corner. Magnets on the fridge, a stack of bills and magazines on the counter. The apartment of a working girl who was never home. It was sunny and quiet, except for the constant hum of the freeway.

"Who plays guitar?"

"Zakiyyah. I have a favor to ask you." Josephine tilted her head.

Julian would've done it without the head tilt.

"So the good news is," she said, "I got a callback for Dante. Shocking, I know, given yesterday's Shakespearean debacle." But the bad news was, the callback was for the part of the narrator, an old man in a historical wig and glasses.

"You're an expert at the old man part," Julian said. "Just channel your inner Housman."

"It's the wig that's the problem. Callback's at eleven. How do I become a gray-haired old dude in an hour?"

Looking over her pink scrubbed face, Julian agreed it was not the easiest of tasks.

She held out a can of aerosol. "Can you spray paint my hair?"

Shaking his head, he stepped back. He didn't like to do things he'd never done.

"Come on, I need your help. You can do things other than sit in front of a computer, can't you?"

"I do plenty of those." He wished that hadn't sounded as suggestive as it did.

"Is one of them color a girl's hair?" She flung around her damp dark mane for him to see. It smelled of foamy coconut. "Do it, do it," she said. "And afterward, I'll take you to the top of the mountain to amaze the crap out of you." Her body smelled freshly washed of foamy coconut, her arms and throat glistening with lotion. The muscles in Julian's legs felt liquid.

He had another idea. "Why don't we just get you a wig? Seems a lot simpler."

"Audition's in an hour."

"I know a place."

"I'm broke."

"It's free. Can you get dressed in five minutes?"

"What do you mean? I *am* dressed."

No makeup, tiny shorts, ripped gray crop top, no bra (do *not* think about that) bare feet, hair all over the place. She looked dressed for after-sex waffles, not a callback. He said nothing.

"Okay, fine." Two minutes later she emerged from door number two in denim shorts, boots, and a see-through white shirt over her crop top. Her bare stomach showed. "Better?"

He said nothing.

In the car as she did her makeup she told Julian Dante's play paid real money! Rehearsals began in a few days. It ran a month.

"Though I'll have to memorize ninety-nine cantos. Doesn't seem possible."

"You can do it," he said. "They're such romantic cantos."

She grunted. "Realms of the dead are romantic?"

"Sure," Julian said. "Clad in weights, Dante searches for Beatrice in heaven and hell because he cannot find her here on earth. That's not romantic?" He smiled.

"I dunno," she said. "Does he find her? See, even Mr. Know-it-All is not sure. And the endlessly mutilated sowers of discord are definitely not dreamy. There's a lot of damnation before Dante gets to Beatrice, is what I'm saying. Inferno, purgatorio. Why is it even called a comedy? How far's the wig?"

"Almost there." Magnolia Boulevard was just on the other side of Hollywood Hills.

"Magnolia…isn't that where the vintage shops are?"

Julian pulled into a spot at the curb. "Yep. And here we are."

They were parked in front of a large storefront whose cinnamon-colored awning read "THE TREASURE BOX."

"The Treasure Box?" she said. "What kind of store is that?"

"The kind where you might find what you're looking for. It's Ashton's. Well, mine and Ashton's. But he does most of the work. I just count the money."

"He's got a wig?"

"He's got a lot of things." Julian switched off the engine.

"Really? Like what?"

"Anything. Everything." He watched her apply red gloss to her lips. "About Ashton…"

"I need to be *prepped* before meeting him? Why, is he super cute?" She grinned.

"That's not it." How to explain Ashton to this innocent? "He likes to tease. A bit like you. Remember that and ignore him."

"Like you ignore me?"

"Just like that."

Ashton was on the phone behind the register. He had showered and shaved and was wearing pressed black jeans and a white shirt open at the collar. His leather shoes were buffed. The doorbell trilled as they walked in, and Ashton raised his head. He couldn't drop his call when he saw Julian with Josephine but, by the expression on his face, really wanted to.

Josephine's mouth dropped open, too. Even a grizzled cynic would have a hard time not fawning over the cornucopia of baubles and beads that was housed under Ashton's expansive roof.

Real and fake furs, old lamps, figurines, designer bags, red carpet dresses, tuxedoes, movie memorabilia of all kinds were on sale and display. From *Casablanca* (the bar glasses) to *Back to the Future* (Marty's Hoverboard), incredible real artifacts from imaginary places abounded. Ashtrays from *Chinatown*, a replica (not actual-size) of the Starship Enterprise, an actual-size Han Solo frozen in carbonite, Halloween costumes, shoes and hats, and all the bling in between, including signed framed photographs of the stars, including Ashton's treasured possession, a poster of a joyous Bob Marley from 1981, signed by the man himself a few months before he died. There were albums, playbills, scarves, a wall of arcade games from PacMan to Donkey Kong, a wall of original art by local artists, and next to it a table with brushes, paints, and blank canvases for sale. There was a display of vital herbs and vitamins, a nod to the health-obsessed Riley. There was a red door bathed in black light and a neon sign above it that read, "*Haunted House* ⬏ *this way.*" Yes, there was even a Haunted House, which ran year-round, and all the zombies and ghouls inside it were for sale. Ashton replaced them with new ghouls and zombies as needed. The Treasure Box was a store that no one but the treasure-hunting, adventure-seeking Ashton could've devised or imagined. Everything he was and everything he loved was in that store.

"This is the most *amazing* place I've ever seen!" Josephine said in a thrilled whisper. "Can we come back?"

"Maybe. Follow me." Julian popped into one of the narrow side rooms and was relieved when he quickly found what he was looking for: a long-haired 18th-century wig made with real gray hair.

"Perfect," she said. "This is fantastic, oh!—but expensive."

Julian put a finger to his lips and sighed, hoping he could sneak her out before Ashton got off the phone. Alas.

Ashton barricaded the door to the small room, blocking the daylight with his tall frame. "Hey, Jules. Whatcha up to?"

"Not much," Julian said. "We're in a hurry."

"Hurry? But you just got here. And who's we?"

"Oh, sorry. Ashton, Josephine; Josephine, Ashton."

"Nice to meet you, Ashton," Josephine said, smiling over Julian's shoulder.

"Yeah, you, too."

"You have an incredible place here."

"Thanks." He stared at her and then blinklessly at Julian, who rolled his eyes, mouthing *stop it*. The three of them stepped out into the main area, where there was sunlight and windows and space to put between one another.

"Where do you get this stuff from?" Josephine asked, walking around, touching the dresses and the silk scarves.

"Here, there," Ashton said. "Hot sets mostly. Before they shut production on a show, Julian and I walk the soundstages, mark what we want, and after they wrap, we return with my truck."

"You take the furniture, too?"

"Why, do you need some furniture? A couch? A *bed*?"

"No, just curious." She didn't blink.

Ashton, stop it.

"We get the larger items for free," Ashton said, "because that's first to be hauled to the dumpster. Basically we sell other people's trash."

Julian wanted to knock his friend on the head. "Josephine, we have to go."

"A teacher, a writer, *and* a small business owner?" Josephine said to Julian. "You sure wear a lot of hats, Jules."

"Oh, you have no idea," Ashton said, mouthing *Jules?* to Julian.

"I'm not a teacher," Julian muttered. "Not really."

"And people pay you guys money even for the big stuff?" she asked.

"Yes, in our business, trash is a collector's item," Ashton replied. "We have an entire room next to the Haunted House of sofas and tables from the sets of *I Dream of Jeannie, Bewitched, Mork and Mindy,* that sort of thing."

"How fantastic! Can I see? After the Haunted House, of course. That's first."

"Another time," Julian said, trying to shepherd her out. "Or you'll be late." It was like shepherding out water. Josephine was studying the props as if she couldn't care less about the callback.

"Excuse me," Ashton said to her, "but have we met before?"

"I don't think so."

"I could swear I've seen you somewhere. I never forget a face…" He tapped the counter. "New York! A few weeks ago. *The Invention of Love.* Weren't you the understudy?" He peered at her.

"Yes! Oh wow! You were there, too?"

"Yes," Ashton replied. "I was there, *too.*" Even his small smile vanished.

"Did you enjoy it?"

"Yes. Not as much as Julian—obviously—but I enjoyed it. It was out of the ordinary."

"But not extraordinary?" Josephine grinned amiably as if she couldn't care less whether Ashton liked the play or not.

Mutely Ashton stared at Julian, who was signing out the wig and wouldn't return his friend's pointed gaze.

"Ready to go, Josephine?" Julian said.

She didn't reply, her eye spying something hanging on the wall behind Julian. "What's that?" she exclaimed. It was a lambskin dark red beret. She pried it off the hook, turned it over once or twice, and put it on her head, stepping into the center of the store and smiling at both men. "What do you think, guys?"

One man suppressed a smile, the other had no hint of it on his somber face. Julian didn't understand why Ashton was being so unfriendly. He elbowed Ashton, who did not elbow back.

"This thing's fresh to *death*," Josephine said, gazing in the mirror with approval at her own reflection. "Is it expensive?"

"No, it's not expensive," Ashton said. "It's priceless. It's vintage Gucci. From the forties. But it's not for sale. It's Julian's. It's his lucky hat."

"It is?" Josephine stared in the beveled mirror. "Jules, where did you get this marvelous thing?"

"Yes, *Jules*," Ashton said, "where'd you get it? Tell the girl."

"I don't remember," Julian said.

"There you go," Ashton said. "He doesn't remember. So what do you say? Can she have the red beret you found somewhere and haven't parted with in a decade?"

Like it was even a question.

Josephine nearly skipped in place. With a grateful smile, her adorned head tilted, her fingers splayed, she did a two-step, a shim-sham, twirled around, swiveled her hips, and sang a few lines of the chorus of "Who's Got the Pain" from *Damn Yankees.*

Ashton, his light blue eyes dipped in indigo, gave Julian a long anxious stare soaked with question, unease, and, for some reason, despair.

"Let's go," Julian said, grabbing his keys.

Josephine looked Julian over as they got ready to walk out, at his starched gray-check shirt, gray khakis, black suede Mephistos, tailored greige sports jacket. "Julian, we're going into the mountains after my callback."

"Yes, so?"

"Well, you've put on your teacher uniform again, not your mountain climbing gear."

"Oh, you're adorable, Josephine, to think that's a uniform," Ashton said, stepping between her and Julian. Forcefully he shook his head to underscore his words. "That's not a uniform, dear girl. It's a costume."

9

Phantasmagoria in Two

"ARE YOUR SHOES AT LEAST COMFORTABLE?" JOSEPHINE asked him in the Greek parking lot after the callback. Her outcries of woe killed it, she said—because of the lucky beret.

Julian didn't know how to answer her. All his shoes were comfortable. Comfort was his MO. "Why, is it a long way where you're taking me?"

"It's up a mountain." She poked him. "You want to back out?"

"Who said? No, I'm in. Maybe you should've asked Ashton. He loves to do that stuff."

Josephine fell quiet as the sun played footsies with the sparkles on the rattlesnake weed. "I don't think he would've said yes. He didn't seem too friendly. I don't think he likes me."

"Of course he does." Julian deflected since he wasn't sure *what* had been up with Ashton. "He was off his game. He's not a morning person."

They began their uphill climb through the loamy sand in which juniper and spruce grew and eucalyptus was profuse. Josephine was in front of him. Flame trees turned everything to fire. The jacaranda and the pink silk trees looked and smelled like cotton candy and made Julian feel he was in a sweet blooming garden full of redbuds and desert willows and lemon-scented gums. He wanted to point out to her their bright and gaudy surroundings, but what if her response was, yes, sure a *garden*, but what kind of garden is it, Julian, Eden or Gethsemane?

What was wrong with him? *Gethsemane!*

As he was thinking of something less idiotic to say (frankly, *anything* would be less idiotic to say), there was a rock in his way, and he tripped over it. She was too fast for him. He could barely keep up, while she was practically sprinting through the peppergrass. It was hard to flirt walking up a steep hill on uneven terrain in a single file. He tried (not very hard) to keep his eyes off the smooth white backs of her slender thighs. His gaze kept traveling to her lower back, bared above the waist of her shorts. He wanted to dazzle her with his knowledge of blessed thistle and golden fleece, of Indian milkweed and fragrant everlasting, of the perennial live-forevers, but he couldn't breathe and dazzle at the same time.

She returned to him, fanning herself with the red beret. "Julian Cruz," Josephine said, one hand on her hip, "come on, a little more hell for leather. We have less than fifteen minutes."

Hell for leather? "I didn't know there was a deadline."

"There's always a deadline. You should know that, Professor Daily Newsletter. I know you're a novice at walking…"

"I'm not a novice at walking."

"We have until noon," she said. "And then it will be gone."

"What will? The sun? The mountains?"

"You think you're clever, but you'll see. If we miss it, that's it. Tomorrow you'll have a million things to do, and I have my Mountain Dew shoot. Yeah, they called while I was at the Greek. If I get this Dante gig, that'll be two for two. I don't know what's happening," she said. "I haven't gotten two jobs in a row in like never." The beret went back on her head.

"Maybe I'm your good luck charm," he said. "Lucky hat, lucky Julian."

"No time for chit-chat, Mr. Talisman—spit-spot." In her combat boots, she disappeared up ahead, around a cottonwood.

"If we miss it, we could definitely come back another day," he said after her. "I'm not saying we're going to miss it—"

"We're going to keep coming back day after day because you can't hurry up today?" she called back. "What makes you think you're going to be able to hurry up tomorrow?"

"I'm hurrying. I'm running uphill."

"What you're doing is called self-paced running," Josephine said. "That's another phrase for walking." Ahead of him, she continued to scoff and mutter. "I can tell you work from home. People who work from home have absolutely no sense of urgency. They never have to be anywhere. It's always dope-dee-doe."

"I'm not dope-dee-doeing." Julian huffed, wanting to tell her he didn't only work from home, he also worked out. And drove all around L.A., loading and unloading trucks full of heavy things, and taught a class. Suddenly he wanted to tell her everything.

Josephine was barely flushed when they made it to the crest. "How you doing, cowboy? Hanging in there?" She smiled. She was flushed enough.

All he could do was pant. "*Where* are you taking me?"

"To show you magic."

Pushing through the brush, they went off trail until they reached some scrubby silver dollar gums and a lonely laurel fig. She was happy, open-mouthed, panting, wiping her wavy hair away from her damp forehead. "It's going to be amazing today, I can feel it," she said. "Look how sunny it is."

He saw. It was blindingly sunny. They swirled around in a 360, taking in the view. Miles of Los Angeles valley simmered below. They were high in the hills, floating in the shivering air, soaring above the vast spaces where people lived. The ocean in the westerly distance was in a mist, downtown L.A. a haze of matchbox towers. All the roads with a million white houses and a million palm trees led to the sea. Up here, the air was thinner, the oxygen weaker. It was time for nosebleeds and birds of paradise and whispering bells. The summer flora was blooming, the mustang mint and golden currant vivid in the high noon sun. There was a smile on her lips and thunder in his heart. He knew there was magic in these hills. All he wanted to do was kiss her.

She sucked in her breath, a bird of paradise herself, a whispering bell. "We're standing above the fault in the earth called Benedict Canyon," she said, rummaging in her hold-all until she pulled out a clear stone on a thin rawhide rope. Silver wire was braided and wrapped around the stone like a basket. She placed it in the palm of her hand. It was a chunky rough teardrop with sharp multi-faceted edges, translucent in part, occluded in part.

"What's that?" He studied it with mild curiosity at first. But the stone tweaked something inside him, peaked his interest. Stirred some indefinable emotion. He felt an electric buzz through his body as he stared at it. The buzz wasn't entirely pleasant.

"A quartz crystal." Josephine lifted her arm to the sky. The crystal sparkled in the sunshine.

"Not a diamond?" Julian smiled.

"Ha. No. I've had it appraised, believe me." She brushed her hair away from her face. "My grandmother gave it to me. It belonged to her cousin in the old country."

"Old country where?"

"Not sure. Near Blackpool, maybe. Or Scotland." As if the two were interchangeable. They walked a little farther until they reached a clearing, a hidden mesa in the sun encircled by chest-level exposed rock, a stony enclosure. "Jules, you're standing in a cave of quartz!"

"Do I want to be standing in a cave of quartz?"

"Aha. Mr. Know-it-All doesn't know everything. Yes, at certain times of the day, the quartz glitters like diamond dust. If you're lucky, you might find yourself inside a rainbow."

What man wouldn't think himself lucky to stand next to beauty in girl form, rhapsodizing about magic diamond dust inside rainbows. He was motionless, catching his breath, interested, bedazzled, open to her, open to anything.

Their eyes flickered between the crystal in her hand and each other, the sandy desert hills falling away below them. In the valley, the outlines of Beverly Hills and Century City gleamed, farther west the yawning maw of the Pacific. Her flushed face was so near, all Julian had to do was move his head half a foot forward and kiss her open lips. His head slowly tilted sideways.

"How long till noon?" she asked.

He rocked back to check his Tag Heuer. "A minute."

"Excellent." Her palm faced up. "If you can think on your feet, you can make a wish. At noon, for a brief moment, the stars and the earth and the whole of creation will be so perfectly aligned that any wish asked for in faith can be granted."

Clearly Julian wasn't quick enough on his feet, or he'd be kissing her. "Why are you holding the crystal like that?"

"Trying to catch the sun with it."

"You're a sun catcher." He gazed at her.

"I'm a wish catcher," she murmured. "Around us are the oldest rocks in the Santa Monicas. Like forty million years old. You're standing inside stone as old as time itself. You can touch time with your hands." She took a breath. "Do you want to touch time with your hands, Julian?"

I want to touch you with my hands, he thought. His wish must have been apparent in his eyes. She blushed.

"What happens to the crystal when the sun hits it?" he asked. "Does it get hot?"

"Julian, I've led you up a mountain," she said. "This is no time to be a cynic. We're standing inside a volcano. The river beds below us have dried up, the land looks stern from here and is sometimes cruel, even ruthless, to weakness."

"I know that all too well," he said.

"Man, despite his fire and chaos, has made barely a ripple in these hills."

With slight shame Julian thought that you could tell a lot about how he had chosen to live by his languor in the land of palm trees and summer, by how he had breezed through a decade of his chill life in which he made barely a ripple, and which had made barely a ripple on him.

"Is that what you're going to do, Julian Cruz?" Josephine asked. "Be carried unfulfilled to the grave?"

Not anymore.

"All the colors of your world are about to disappear," the ephemeral girl whispered.

A bright flash stopped Julian from speaking. The sun reached zenith. The rays hit the lucid gem in her hands. The light flared and dispersed through the prism, sparks of fire bounced off the glittering quartz of the cave. A moment earlier Julian and Josephine had stood amid green and sepia. Now they were dancing inside a kaleidoscope of purples and yellows, a phantasmagoria of color, an electrical unstoppable aurora. The hills vanished, so did the trees, and the valley below, and the sky. Everything was drowned out. Everything *else* was drowned out. Julian could barely see even her, and she stood right next to him. It almost looked as if she herself had dispersed, had broken into a million moving shards of the deepest scarlet. For half an inhale, the blinding red blanched his pupils, and she was gone.

He blinked, and she was gone.

In the reflection of the vanished world, with flames exploding in his eyes, Julian couldn't say what he *saw*, but he *felt* so intensely that it took the breath away from him. He felt love, and pain that doubled him over, he felt crushing fear, and desperate longing, and deepest regret. He felt terror. He felt profound suffering. It hurt so much he groaned.

With a gasp, he blinked again, and there she was, restored to him, the crystal in her hands, dancing sunbeams around her. When he could breathe, the weight inside him shifted. Not lifted. Shifted.

The sun moved a quarter of a degree. The colors faded. The world returned to what it was.

Almost.

The pressure in his chest remained, the saturated heat of a punch in the heart.

He couldn't speak. The lens through which he saw the world had become distorted, had lost focus in its very center.

Josephine took his hand. "Told you," she said, squeezing and releasing him.

"What *was* that?" It was like waking up from a nightmare. For a minute you didn't know where you were. Julian still didn't know where he was.

"What did you wish for?" she asked.

"It's not what I wished for. It's what I saw."

"What did you see?"

Julian didn't know. He wasn't sure. Something he didn't want to see. He stared at her enthralled, yet unsettled.

Josephine dropped the stone back in her bag. "Sometimes," she said with a melancholy tinge, "when I come here, I don't know what to ask for because I don't know what I want. I want so much to believe it's all in front of me, and I wish for a break, or a role of a lifetime, for accolades, for applause. But sometimes it feels as if everything is already behind me."

"It's not," Julian said, for some reason certain. "It's all still up ahead."

"I hope you're right," she said. "My biggest wish still hasn't happened. I want to be in London, on the West End stage."

"Why London?" he said. "It rains all the time. New York has great theatre, too."

Longingly she smiled, imagining her perfect future. "We wish for what we don't have," she said. "I want to sell out the legendary Savoy." She swiped her hand through the air. "Have my name above the marquee—Josephine Collins tonight at the Savoy!"

"I've never been to London," he said. "Have you?"

"Only in my dreams." She put her hand on her chest.

His heart still hurt.

"You know the same man who built the Savoy also built the most beautiful theatre in the world," she said. "The Palace on Cambridge Circus."

"I did not know this."

She nodded. "He loved his wife so much he built her a theatre so she could attend the opera any time she wanted. Imagine that. The Palace Theatre is the man's love for his wife made real." She smiled.

"How do you know all this?"

"Because I adore the story of how much that man loved his woman," Josephine said. "How do you *not* know this?"

Reluctantly, they started back downhill. "What did you wish for?" he asked.

"Today I asked to be in *Paradise in the Park* so I could stay in L.A.," she said. "How about you?"

"Me, too," said Julian.

10

Griddle Cafe

"WHAT DO YOU WANT TO DO NOW?"

"What do *you* want to do now?"

"I'm starved."

"I know just the place."

Hours later they were still sitting across from each other at the Griddle Cafe on Sunset at a square table on the sidewalk, hot out, cars whizzing by. Julian perked up once he got some food in him. There had been something foggy and surreal about the minute with her at the top of the mountain, the floating evanescence mixing and churning with unfathomable emotion.

Dante's people called. The part of the narrator was hers if she wanted it. Could they send the contracts over to her agent? Could she start rehearsals the day after tomorrow? Things were looking up. She was never taking off the red beret. "But do you know what the producer said to me even as he was giving me the job?" Josephine said. "What took you so long to come out here, Miss Collins?" She stirred her coffee.

"I heard you tell him you were twenty-eight."

"And he said *exactly* and hung up."

Julian laughed. "Last month Ashton was on the phone, angling for a walk-through at CBS and the producer asked how old he was. Ashton said thirty-two, and the producer said, 'Do you *look* thirty-two?' Ashton was like, do I need to look younger than thirty-two for a set walkthrough on a cancelled sitcom?"

Josephine shook her head. "Everybody's looking for eternal youth. Especially in this town."

"Eternal something maybe."

"So, is your friend a good guy?" she asked. "The truth now. Even if he is ornery and thirty-two. Should we introduce him to my Zakiyyah, see what happens?"

"Okay, Dolly, pipe down," Julian said. "He's not ornery. He's taken."

"Taken, shmaken. How attractive is his girlfriend?"

Julian took out his phone and showed her Riley.

Josephine acted unimpressed. She took out her phone and showed him Zakiyyah.

Julian acted unimpressed.

"She was Miss Brooklyn!" Josephine said.

"Riley was voted most beautiful in high school."

"Did you not hear me say that Z was Miss Brooklyn?"

"Ashton doesn't date beauty queens."

"*Obviously*," Josephine said, and they both laughed. "Is Riley in the business?"

Julian shook his head. "Ashton also doesn't date actresses. He got burned a few times, and now says they can't be trusted."

"Really, he says that?" She eyed him with a twinkle. "What do *you* say?"

"I don't know." Julian eyed her with a twinkle. "I've never dated an actress."

She fell silent, continuing to stare at Riley's photo. "Do you like her?" she asked.

"I like her a lot, why? We're good friends," Julian said. "She's wonderful entertainment. And she hates being teased."

"And that makes you tease her all the more?"

"Naturally," said Julian. "Every outing with her is a wellness summit. Sometimes to help me cleanse my spirit and align my chakras, she tells me to eat paper." He couldn't hide his genuine affection for Riley. "To rid herself of impurities, she eats on alternate days. On B days she drinks only lemon water flavored with maple syrup. She tells me to write in my newsletter that maple syrup is the perfect food and I tell her, yes, especially over waffles."

Josephine snorted the strawberry shake through her nose.

They finished their red velvet pancakes with cream cheese frosting. Their elbows on the table, they slurped the last of the milkshakes through their straws. The tables around them were empty; only they were left.

They talked about the plays she'd been in (*Danny Shapiro and his Quest for a Mystery Princess* was Julian's favorite). They talked about their favorite books (*The Fight* for him, *Gone with the Wind* for her), subjects they liked in school, comfort food, swimming pools, and then engaged in a crossfire over the Dodgers and the Yankees. ("You live here," she said, "so maybe you have to pay lip service to this, but you do know in your heart of hearts that the Dodgers suck, right?") After half an hour, the argument subsided unresolved. ("What, you're offended?" she said. "That's not a surprise, I'd be mad too if I rooted for the Dodgers.")

They told each other their official stories. She was born and raised in Brooklyn, near the Verrazano Bridge, not quite Coney Island, not quite Bay Ridge, a small congested working-class community so removed from the rest of the world that she was ten before she set foot in New York City. She thought Luna Park on Coney Island was what all beaches looked like, and her concept of New Jersey was map-related, as in, it was a mythical place beyond Staten Island. "*New Jersey* is mythical?" Julian said.

Her father ran a vaudeville joint called Sideshows by the Seashore, and she worked with him until he died, and the place changed hands. Her younger sister died of leukemia a few years later. To make her sister feel better, Josephine sang and played the piano, and her sister danced in time to her singing. She said that since then, that was how she thought of all children—in the image of frail girls dancing. Dying but dancing.

Josephine had a close but contentious relationship with her mother, less close and more contentious in recent years. Her mother worked for a private academy near their house and kept her job two decades so her daughter could go to an elite prep school for free. She wanted Josephine to attend Columbia, to become a professor, a doctor of letters. Josephine had other ideas. She got into the School of Performing Arts instead and felt vindicated—for two seconds. Then she realized she was in a school with five hundred kids just as talented as her. Someone else always danced better, sang better, recited louder. Acting was a zero-sum game, especially on stage. In middle school she'd been the unsinkable Molly Brown, the star in every play, but at Performing Arts she was barely the sidekick. After graduation it got worse. She didn't get into Juilliard, but now competed for parts with everyone that had.

She found a steady job building stage sets at the Public Theatre while continuing to audition. Her not getting a college degree was the greatest disappointment of her mother's life, and Julian, who knew something about disappointing mothers (and fathers), wanted to ask, even more than one of her daughters dying, but didn't.

Julian revealed his own official story. He was raised in middle-class suburban Simi Valley, the fourth of six sons born to two teachers: Brandon Cruz, a third-generation Mexican, and Joanne Osment, a third-generation Norwegian.

The children: Brandon Jr. and Rowan, followed by Harlan, Julian, Tristan—Irish triplets, one born every ten months—and then Dalton, ten years later. His parents still lived in the same starter house they'd bought right out of college. His mother raised six kids in it while also running the guidance department at the high school, unstoppable "like a Viking." His father had been head of the school district and was now president of a local college. As a kid, Julian read and watched sports. He went to UCLA. Ashton was his freshman roommate. They'd been friends ever since.

"Is that it?" she said.

"Pretty much," he said.

"UCLA and that brings us to today? I know you're not twenty. What did you major in?"

When he didn't immediately reply, Josephine laughed. "I bet it was English."

"My parents were paying for my room and board, what was I going to do?"

"Major in English and become a teacher, obviously."

"Am I a teacher?"

"Yes—in your secret heart, Julian, I bet you are."

"Trust me, Josephine, in my secret heart, the last thing I am is a teacher." Julian squinted at her, the button-eyed waif, the vision with the long blowing hair, the teasing girl with the constant smile on her lips. It was hot, and as they chatted and she swirled the straw around the bottom of her shake, he debated if it was too soon to ask her to go with him to Zuma. It was a hefty drive to Malibu, but the sun would set as they swam. The beach was secluded, and at high tide the waves crashed hypnotically against the shore. Too soon?

Was it too soon to invite her to his apartment, a few blocks away, and watch Marlon Brando bring on the apocalypse in Vietnam? Was it too soon for a scenic drive on Mulholland? Comedy at the Cellar? Dinner at Scarpetta? Tea on his sofa? A walk to the jewelry store? Was it too soon to place his lips against her alabaster throat, God, what wasn't too soon.

"Even superheroes need steady and loyal sidekicks," he heard her say. The word *superheroes* rerouted him back to Sunset Boulevard and their small squat table. "In your formula, what am I?" Julian asked. "The superhero or the sidekick?"

"Maybe you're the superhero and *I'm* your sidekick."

"Or you're the superhero and I'm *your* sidekick."

Her grin was wide. "I bet Ashton's right about you. You're the superhero who pretends he's the sidekick so no one notices his powers."

"When did Ashton say this, and what powers might those be?"

"You tell *me*, Julian Osment Cruz."

He narrowed his eyes at her animated face, trying to hide from her not his powers but his weakness. She was so fresh and funny, so red-lipped and delightful. He loved how to hear her, how to hear every sound that sprang from her mouth, he had to lean almost across the table. He loved that her every breath drew him closer to her. He loved her clean unpainted nails, her long fingers unadorned by rings. He wanted to touch them. He wanted to kiss them.

She was a wonderful audience. She had a great laugh. Was it terrible of him to want to do other things to her that he knew might delight her, to impress her with some of his other skills besides joking and finding great food in L.A.? What a brute he was. Making a girl laugh while fantasizing about other kinds of love. Wishing to give her pleasure in all ways, physical and metaphysical. The desire was strong and would not be bargained with. Lust and tenderness rolled around the crucible inside him, their mercury rendering him mute. At the Griddle Cafe!

He stared too long at her slender fingers, and in the shadows cast by Sunset, he thought he saw a white circular mark around her fourth digit. He blinked. Nope, nothing there but a trick of the light.

"Who *are* you, Josephine?" he murmured. I want to know you. I need to know who you are. I'm here. Do you want to know who I am? He nearly reached out and took her hand across the table.

She drew a breath—he wanted to say she drew a sexy breath, but that was the only way she knew how to draw it—and misunderstood him. He wanted real, she gave him fantasy.

"Maybe Mystique?" she said.

Happily he assented. "Yes. You *are* Mystique."

"Yes," she said, but less happily. "I'm the blue girl, and my body is a green screen. I disappear when I need to and turn up as someone else in another city, not this one, and not my own."

Julian was about to pursue that analogy, but the annoyed hipster waiter informed them that the place was closing, "like forty minutes ago," and could they *please* close out their check, because he was off shift "like forty minutes ago." Julian checked his watch. It was after four! "What do you do to time," he muttered, taking out his wallet.

"What do *I* do to time?" she said. "But it's not too early to start thinking about dinner."

"Agreed. I'm quite hungry myself."

They were next to Rite Aid pharmacy. Rush hour traffic was heavy on Sunset. Across from them, up on a hill, stood the legendary Chateau Marmont. They both stared longingly at it.

"Where should we go?" she asked. "For dinner, I mean."

He looked over her shorts, her boots.

"What, my outfit's not good enough for dinner at the Marmont?" She did a hair flip. "Just kidding, I don't want to eat there. John Belushi ate there and look what happened to him."

"Um..."

"No such thing as coincidence," she said. "Lessee, where else can we go where I don't have to get dressed up?"

"The beach?" he said. "The restaurants there are pretty casual." Was it too late for a swim and a sunset at Malibu?

"Beach is good." Her eyes were half-hooded. "Anywhere else?"

He thought about it. "We could go to Santa Monica. Get some food truck grub, eat on the pier."

"We could," she said. "Or we could go to a Dodger game. Would you like that?" She winked.

He played it straight. "Dodgers are away this week."

"Probably getting their asses kicked in New York," she said. "Anywhere else?"

"You want to go to the movies?"

"Sure." She sighed with slight exasperation. "Or...we could go to your place, Julian. Didn't you say you live around here?"

"My place?" Julian repeated dumbly. "But there's nothing to eat."

She laughed. "Tell you what," she said, "let's go to Gelson's. Buy some steak. Do you have a balcony? A grill on it perhaps?"

He didn't know what to say.

He said okay. He did have a balcony. And a grill.

"I don't have to come over if you don't want me to," she said.

"No, no." We both know I want you—to.

"I can't believe I had to invite myself over," she said with a headshake as they waited for the light to change on Sunset and La Cienega. He had taken hold of her elbow to keep her from crossing against the light. "I just don't know about you, Jules. Are you always this polite?"

Their eyes locked.

"No," said Julian.

They stared into each other's open faces. He slipped his arm around her lower back, touching the sheer fabric of her white blouse, her bare skin hot under his fingers. He drew her against him. Her breasts were at his chest.

Before the light turned green, he kissed her. He didn't need Zuma Beach or the setting sun. Just a red light at an intersection, his palm on her back, his head tilted, her arms splayed.

"Are we moving too fast?" she breathed. "I'm afraid we might be."

"Absolutely. Like meteors."

Her arms swept around his neck. "Maybe we should go to dinner, go to a bar, get a drink, wait for night…"

"Josephine," Julian said, his hands running up and down her back, his insistent lips at her warm, peach-scented, pulsing neck, "if you want some magic, you've come to the right city. We can Hollywood up anything around here, even daylight. We Hollywood it up real good. Come with me and I'll show you. In L.A. it's called *day for night*."

They stumbled against the post and forgot to cross. The light changed, and changed again.

DUENDE

A word for which there is no equivalent in the English language.

It's a Romance word that means magical or enchanting.

A certain indefinable radical something that has a supernatural ability to evoke passion, a trembling of the spirit.

Something irrational and miraculous and nearly painful that sends a chill down your spine, a flamethrower's power to profoundly affect another human being.

Almost like religion.

ALL GREAT LOVE SONGS MUST HAVE DUENDE

"Something"
"We Found Love"
"When a Man Loves a Woman"
"All of Me"
"Everything I Do, I Do it for You"
"Lovin' You"
"Crazy Love"
"Dang"
"God Only Knows"
"For Crying Out Loud"
"I Will Always Love You"
"Lovesong"

All great love stories must have Duende

Exit Quote:
"I will always love you."
— Robert Smith, The Cure

11

Duende

Los Angeles, the city of angels, the city of dreams.

It's easy to fall in love in Southern California.

If it's so easy, the exquisite girl whispers, exquisitely naked on your bed, then have you fallen in love a thousand times before me?

Take two: It's easy to fall in love in Southern California with her.

She likes your apartment. You keep it clean. Did you clean it, she asks, because you thought I might be coming? And you want to tell her the truth, that you keep it clean because it's your nature, but instead you tell her the romantic truth. Yes, you say. I hoped you'd be coming. I cleaned it for you.

You have so many books, she says approvingly, standing by your wall of books and your black heavy bag hanging from a hook in the ceiling. Why do you have a punching bag, Julian? Is it for exercise?

Yes.

Well done. About the books, I mean. John Waters would be proud of you. Proud of me, rather.

Who?

John Waters. Her clothes thrown off, your clothes thrown off.

What does John Waters say? Like you even care. She is so beautiful. Your hand glides across her body.

He says, if you go home with somebody and they don't have books, don't fuck them.

Ah. *Now* you care.

Your heart reforms around the Aphrodite in your bed, the sun god's daughter, naked and pulsing, her arms open, everything open and she moans and beckons to you to come to her, closer, closer.

You fall inside the throat of a volcano, inside the one space that has no inside and no outside. You sink into the pink-tinted, over-saturated world where nothing exists except her and you.

You kiss her clavicles, her eager mouth, you press yourself upon the raw softness of her body. Her lips are vanilla. She is honey and easy all over like pink cotton candy. And yet it's you who feels like spun-out sugar, and when she places you on her tongue, you melt.

You draw the room-darkening shades and you pour her peach champagne. Now she has a real drink and there is no more day, just endless night.

Her body is beauty, in need of love, of care, of caress. She's an acrobat, she twists and curves like a tumbling immortal. You've been turned inside out yourself. She can see your heart, it's visible to her smile. And you can see her heart, it beats for you between her breasts.

After love she falls asleep and later says she wasn't sleeping only dreaming.

We're both inside the same dream, you whisper. You stole the show, Josephine. They don't forgive that in the theatre.

The next morning and the next you write rhymes about mist rising from the satin sheets, recite sonnets for her on the sidewalks of Sunset while pressing her warm palm against your love-struck face. At Griddle Cafe, you devour red velvet pancakes and drink chocolate shakes and tell her the poems write themselves. The sidewalks of Sunset near the homeless camped out by Rite Aid have become your Elysian Fields.

If the sonnets write themselves, she murmurs, then have you fallen in love a thousand times before on this red velvety sidewalk?

No, beautiful girl. You haven't fallen in love a thousand times before.

You've been on the prowl since your senior year in high school. You've been with quite a few women. You ask if that's a strike against you. Does it make you less appealing?

No, she purrs. *More.*

You have a new two-bedroom with a balcony. And a wall of books. You both beam. You've made John Waters proud.

But that's not a balcony, she says. It's too small.

It's still a balcony. It's called a Juliet balcony.

Why, she asks.

Literally because of Juliet, you reply.

You get some love for that, for the poetry of it.

Julian, she whispers, her arms over her head, holding on to your headboard, did I explode in your heart.

Yes, Josephine, you exploded in my heart.

After love, when she is barely able to move, you tell her you also have a roof deck with a Jacuzzi and a view. You're barely able to move yourself. Your bruised mouth can hardly form words. Funny how both love and a fight can wreck a body.

In the cool desert night, you slip naked upstairs and jump into the hot tub. She murmurs her approval of the spa, of the colored lights, of the champagne that goes with it, and of the man that comes with it, and in it and in her. But there's hardly any view, she says, gazing at you over the foaming bubbles.

There is. If you look left, you can see the schoolyard across San Vicente.

I bet you can hear it, too, she says, crawling to you in the roiling water. At recess, the screaming kids. And if you can see *them*, can they see *us*? She straddles you, lifting her wet breasts to your wet mouth.

You wish someone could see you. You desperately need a witness to your bliss.

You give her the spare toothbrush, a pair of your boxer briefs, you share with her your shampoo, your soap, your shirts. She shares with you stories about Brighton Beach and making out with gropy boys under the bridge and about Zakiyyah looking for Mr. Right her whole life and instead finding loathsome Trevor. She tells you about the bright city and sharp loneliness.

She asks what color the lights were when you first saw her.

Red, you reply.

You watch *Apocalypse Now*, a romantic comedy if ever there was one. It takes you days to finish as you pause for love, for Chinese, for dramatic readings from *Heart of Darkness*, and she mocks you for having that wretched Conrad tome handy on your John Waters bookshelf. You pull *The Importance of Being Earnest* and act it out in your living room, laughing, naked, loud. She knows it better than you, which fills you with shame. You used to know it by heart but forgot. You inhale two bottles of wine as you roll around the floor and reenact Cecily and Algernon, slurry on the comedy, sloppy on the love.

You've lost all sense of the days, lost track of the hour. You sit and wait for her in your Volvo, gripping the wheel in your lovesick hands. You make some calls. Everyone you know is unhappy with you. Everyone except her. She is delighted with you.

Why didn't you choose to live up in the Hollywood Hills? she asks. You could get a place anywhere. Why here, overlooking the back of some hotel?

You didn't choose the Hollywood Hills, you explain in the wet afterglow with the jets purring low, because up there, a box to live in costs five times as much and the drive down takes *forever*.

You didn't choose to live in the hills because of *money*?

And a long drive, you say, defending yourself, caressing her.

Where do *you* have to run to? she says. You work at home. You could sit all day in a tub on a roof deck on Mulholland that overlooks the ocean and wisecrack about vinegar.

Who's wisecracking now? Believe me, I did the *smart* thing.

She smiles. But not the *beautiful* thing.

You want to drive into the mountains, Josephine? You offer her the hills, the canyons, Zuma Beach, and all the music other men have made if she will love you.

All she wants is your body.

Sometimes you act as if that's all you've come for, you say in jest.

How do you know it's not all I've come for, she says.

In jest?

She whispers she's been starved for tenderness. There's no time to waste.

You recall to her Ben Johnson's lament over the brevity of human life. "O for an engine to keep back all clocks."

She disagrees. There is nothing brief about you, she says, as she stands before you naked, her bouncy breasts to seduce you, her lips to relieve you, her hips to receive you and maybe one day to give you children (her joke, not yours, and you're less terrified by it than you should be). She wants tenderness from you? You're as gentle as your brute nature will allow. She wants the beast in you? Her wish is your command.

Julian, I barely know you and yet I feel like I've known you forever. How can that be?

You have no answers. You were blinded from the start. A comet has crashed to earth.

You forget to go to Whole Foods, forget your friends, the newsletters, the bills, the store, the lock-ups to scour, the trucks to rent. You forget everything. It's like you left your past behind when you met her.

She is hungry? You feed her. She is thirsty? You give her wine. She wants music from you? You sing to her about Alfred's coffee and sweet corn ravioli at Georgio Baldi. You kiss her throat. You've wanted to kiss her for so long, you say. She laughs. Yes, Jules, it must've felt like the longest twenty-four hours of your life.

You offer to take her to Raven's Cry at Whisky a Go Go, but not before you buy her the best steak burrito on Vine, and she says how do you know so much about food and love and how to make a girl happy, and you reply, not a girl—you. You two stay in for love, you go out for food. So how about that Whisky a Go Go, Josephine? Ninth Plague and Kings of Jade are playing. Tino and the Tarantulas are going to rock the house. But she wants love from you, and she'd like it to the rhythm of the mad beat music. Are you going to make me feel it, she cries.

Yes. You're going to make her feel it.

Oh, Jules, she says, her arms wrapped around you, pressing you to her heart. Beware the magician, we say in the sideshows, he's here only as a diversion. Do not let him into your circle. Boy, you did some magic trick on me. You drew me in with your irresistible indifference, and now you're like flypaper.

Who is indifferent? he says. She must mean a different Jules.

When did you first want to kiss me? she asks. You tell her it was when she revealed herself to you in the crimson footlights at *The Invention of Love*. You have not let the first day, the first hour, the first moment of meeting her come and go. You knew. You knew it from the start. Your soul lay open to her as she now lies open to you.

You're inventing some crazy love yourself so she doesn't become bored of you.

Fat chance of that, the divine creature coos.

Rejoice, Josephine, you whisper, your head lowered, kneeling between her legs, *for your name is written in heaven*.

And for some reason, this makes her cry.

No, no, don't stop, she says, wiping her face. Nothing's wrong. But let's put on some Tom Waits while you love me. He's my favorite. Let's listen to him sing *time time time*, but you don't finish until he is finished, okay, Jules?

As long as it's not the fifteen-minute live version, you're fine with it, you say, always the joker, even then.

Afterward she sings to you about your endless numbered day for nights. Sometimes it sounds like she's saying *our endless day for nights are numbered*.

At Whisky a Go Go, a drunk fool crawls into your empty bar stool, and as you come back from the men's, you drop your shoulder and knock him to the ground and pretend it was an accident. Sorry, man, so crowded, didn't see you, do you mind, this one's mine. Julian! your girl croons, did you just knock that guy off the chair? I don't know what you mean, you say. He fell.

Later, after she rushed you home because she had urgent need of you, in her dizzying voice she purrs that you have surpassed her expectations. You demur, you do the humblebrag. You're pleased she's pleased, you say with a faux shrug. You have a knack for selling without selling. You have nothing to prove. First you sell, then you deliver.

She says she thought you might be the Nightcrawler who has the appearance of a demon and the heart of a preacher. But that isn't you. You have the appearance of a preacher and the heart of a demon.

And not just the *heart* of a demon, Julian.

Sometimes she stays with Z. And sometimes you haul your ass up and choke out a cheat sheet of advice even though you have no wisdom for anyone anymore, all your sayings swooshed into the trashcan icon on your laptop. Make a list of the things you thought you wanted and burn it—*that's* your advice. Because where you are, there's nothing but glory.

She makes you wish for a different car: a convertible, a dazzling two-seater with a chrome grille and suicide doors. You both love the beach at Zuma. You leave before sundown because the rings of hell are waiting for her at the Greek. But sometimes, if you are lucky, she makes love to you in the Zuma lot, her bikini thrown to the side. She straddles you in the backseat of your old man Volvo like you're sixteen years old and just learned to drive.

Like you just learned to do everything.

The taste of her is always in your mouth.

The rehearsals for *Paradise in the Park* are at night. At the Greek, you wait for her in the sea of ghostly seats that look soaked in blood and watch her glide across the stage as the sun sets and it grows dark. Julian, she breathes, I may speak Dante, but I dream of you.

Everywhere you go, you stroll hand in hand. The beaches of Venice and Hermosa are worn out with your lovers' walks. The flowers bloom. The nights are warm. The desert days are long.

This is the realest dream you've ever lived.

The Scurvy Kids and Slurry Kids play by the local hotel pool while the chairs are being cleaned for the guests to suntan in. There's a pounding soundtrack of hip hop and jazz, of indie rock and big bands, of grunge and electric blues, of Buffalo Springfield and Wasted Youth in Los Feliz and Hollywood. L.A. has never sparkled like it does these summer nights when Voodoo Kung Fu and the Destroyer Deceivers squeeze out every last beat of joy down by Luna Park, the city has never been a more shimmering blinding work of art.

At Scarpetta on Sunday nights, you sit outside in the verdant courtyard overlooking Canon Gardens lit up like Christmastime. You drink Fortuna cocktails—pear Absolut, St. Germain, and peach puree—and make wishes to the stars, you wish for this, you wish for that. You order steak tartare, and ravioli, and foie gras. Have you told each other everything? There doesn't seem to be much left to say, yet you talk and joke and argue, you never stop. You spend until three in the morning at the Laugh Factory on Sunset being singled out by some stand-up talent. "Look at you two, you got yourselves some white people love," the comic mocks you in his high-pitched falsetto. "Oh, baby, am I hurting your *arm*?" "What you talkin' 'bout, honeycakes, you *are* my arm!"

You sleep and eat and live and love and lie entwined. Your souls are without borders because your bodies are without borders.

Or is it the other way around?

Oh, Jules, she whispers. There is nothing better than you.

In the book that is my life, you say, in the chapter when I first met you are the words *and so begins my life anew*.

I want my own book, she says, not just a measly chapter.

From Zuma to Agoura it's easy to fall in love in Southern California.

You know what's not easy to do?

Find the ideal spot to ask her to marry you.

Sure, she's happy to be adored by you—for now—but does she understand that this thing between you isn't something that begins and ends.

Behold, I show you a mystery. We shall not all sleep, but we shall all be changed.

12

The Four of Them

JULIAN KEPT SUGGESTING THE FOUR OF THEM GO OUT. HE STILL
had not met Zakiyyah. And Josephine met Ashton only once, if you
didn't count that other time (and who wanted to count it) at two in
the morning when Ashton banged on his door like the KGB, and
when Julian opened it—with Josephine half-naked behind him—
he said, "Oh, so you *are* alive," and stormed back down the stairs.

Josephine said why should we all go out.

So our two sidekicks can meet.

Why?

So they can approve of our union.

Why do you care if they approve? What if they don't?

Why would they not approve?

People are strange, she said. Ashton doesn't like me.

He's just mad at me right now. Ashton will love you.

It's not Ashton I'm worried about.

Z? But I'm a nice guy, Julian said. I shave, I don't overpraise,
I'm polite, I reply to invites. I can make a joke, take a joke. Why
would Zakiyyah not like me?

I told you, Jules, people are strange.

∞

One problem was their work schedules. Weekends Zakiyyah
was off, but weekends were slammed at the Treasure Box,

and Josephine was about to premiere in *Paradise*, narrating the adventures of Dante and Beatrice six nights a week and a matinee on Wednesday.

At the end of June, Julian finally managed to arrange a Sunday brunch for the four of them. He couldn't get a reservation at the Montage in Beverly Hills, but they met nearby on an outdoor patio in cloistered Canon Gardens, at the cheap sandwich place across from the five-star luxury hotel.

Zakiyyah and Josephine arrived together. Josephine wore a loose lime-green beach cover-up and a bikini. She and Julian were off to Point Dume afterward. Under the red beret, her long hair was down. She wore minimal makeup and remnants of an arousing sunburn. She was a hipster goddess. She took his breath away. After she kissed him, she introduced him to Zakiyyah.

Josephine was right. Zakiyyah was attractive. But was she trying to turn herself down a notch? She had covered her well-developed body in a stiff blouse and a slightly frumpy too-long skirt. Her mass of corkscrew loopy black curls was poorly held back by a headband, leaving most of the emphasis on her glistening dark face, an unblemished face that needed no embellishment. And what a face it was, so symmetrically in balance, it looked fake. In her whole person, she was a sculpture of the idealized female form, carved out by an ardent lover of women: eyes big, brows arched, forehead high, cheekbones wide, lips full, body full, hair coiled and passionate. Upon introduction, Zakiyyah smiled the fake toothy smile of a beauty contest winner.

The smile faded rather quickly, though. Julian couldn't tell if it was his imagination, but he sensed a hint of...tension? Disapproval? Almost as if the smile had been forcibly turned on and then switched off a moment too soon. After it was gone, there was no denying the plain truth: an unsmiling face was a less beautiful face, even Zakiyyah's. Julian could put that life hack in tomorrow's newsletter.

They ordered soft drinks and waited for Ashton by tackling the weighty topic of sunny weather, tackling it with such enthusiasm, you'd think heat and sun were unique to Southern California. Josephine told a silly joke ("what happens when an egg makes a yoke? It cracks up"), Julian gazed at her besotted—and caught Zakiyyah's eye. You poor pathetic *fool*, the woman's expression read.

"Never mind her, Jules," Josephine said. "Z's all soured on love."

"Is that what I am?"

"Well, who wouldn't be—with horrible Trevor as a boyfriend." Josephine pinched Z's arm.

"Yes, shame Julian can't clone himself."

"If you think my Jules is nice," Josephine said, "wait till you meet his friend Ashton."

"Josephine!" That was Julian.

"Yeah, *Josephine*." That was Zakiyyah, unsmiling and unexclaiming.

"I'm kidding. I jest. Jeez, the both of you."

The more Julian observed Zakiyyah, the more he was convinced that she never wanted anything *less* than a career in film or theatre. She seemed to be the opposite of Josephine. Despite her obvious physical assets, Zakiyyah wasn't excitable, or whimsical, or seductive, she wasn't quick with a joke, and not in speech or dress or demeanor did she show herself to be someone who wanted *any* attention, much less someone who lived for lights and applause, like his girl. It was odd. Didn't Josephine tell him that the theatre had been their mutual dream?

Ashton finally arrived insultingly late and unforgivably underdressed. He wore ripped jeans and an unwashed navy T-shirt. He hadn't shaved. And worst of all: he was sullen.

The man was usually impeccably outfitted and a charmer, especially when meeting new people, *especially* when meeting women. And he didn't even apologize! He was cool toward Josephine, which wasn't a surprise, but even cooler toward Zakiyyah. She looked up, he looked down, she half waved, he half nodded. The only empty chair was next to her, so he had no choice but to take it, but his body language said he wanted out. He held the fanned-out menu between him and Z. After they ordered, Ashton turned to Julian, and when he saw Julian silently judging his attire, he pointed out they were having ham sandwiches. "What could you possibly wear that's too casual for a ham sandwich?" Ashton said. "A ham sandwich is something you have in bed with a chick while watching *Entourage* reruns." That was the least offensive thing he would say all afternoon.

Having been at the table less than five minutes, Ashton, instead of charming the girls, decided on a different approach. He became as obnoxious as possible. Without meeting anyone's gaze, staring either into his water glass or at the side of Zakiyyah's neck, he brusquely asked Z what she did for a living and cut her off halfway through her answer. Minutes later he returned to her with a "Sorry, you were saying?" Never mind, said Zakiyyah. When Josephine prodded Ashton to tell her about his extreme adventures in the American West, he dismissed her by saying he had always hated the outdoors, which was not only the opposite of true but a conversation killer.

"Really?" Josephine said. "But Jules told me you love hiking."

"*Jules* told you that, did he?" said Ashton. "It may be wishful thinking on his part. He's the one who digs the outdoors."

Fondly Josephine laughed. "Julian doesn't like the outdoors, what are you talking about," she said. "He *hates* the outdoors. Except for the beach. Otherwise, he is not one with nature."

Ashton took a long swig of Coke, wishing perhaps it were something stronger. "Is *that* what he told you?" After a strained moment, Ashton barreled on. "Paraphrasing Milton, I myself hate the outdoors with a steadfast hate. My main issue, you see, is that I don't enjoy any of the things that share the outdoors with *me*. If you saw my reaction to a tarantula or a snake, I can promise you, I would not be cool and I would not be manly. No, not since Julian's little mishap with the outdoors have I liked it. I'd just as soon stay inside Tequila's Cantina and drink all day. Drinking and being hungover is really the only exercise I get."

Before Julian could speed on to another subject, "What little mishap?" a dumbfounded Josephine said.

"You drink?" said Zakiyyah. "That's a surprise."

"I drink now, sure," Ashton said, "but not like before, in college. God, who could; right, Jules?"

She stared at Ashton with hostility and at Josephine with resentment. Why did you bring me here, she seemed to be saying and jumped up to use the ladies. Apologetically Josephine followed.

"Dude, what's *wrong* with you?" Julian hissed as soon as the girls were out of earshot.

"I don't know what you mean."

"You're supposed to charm them, not make them hate you— and by extension me!"

"I'm being myself, Julian," Ashton said.

"Really?" Julian said. "You feel this is how women usually react to you? Bolt and run? What if they don't come back?"

Ashton's gaze flicked to the sky as if to say please God. "They needed to powder their noses. How's that my fault?"

"What's wrong with you?"

"I can't be liked by everybody, bro," the blond man replied philosophically. "Not my fault they have a problem with me. I'm the same. *I'm* not the one who's changed." The two friends sat in silence for a moment. Just as Julian was about to speak, Ashton nodded in the direction of the returning women.

"What mishap did Julian have outdoors?" Josephine asked as soon as she took her seat.

"Never mind," Julian said, wanting to kick Ashton for opening his big mouth.

"Yeah, Josephine, never mind, Jules is right, it was *nothing*," Ashton said. "We were hiking, and he got lost, that's all. We couldn't find him for a long time. We were sure he was dead. But then," Ashton exclaimed, "we found him! Ah, yes, all's well that ends well, don't you agree? No use flailing about it now, when he's right next to you. It's great, by the way, how you two have hit it off. Sometimes these things go *so* badly."

A piece of chewed food fell out of his mouth and onto his T-shirt. He flicked it off and continued eating.

Zakiyyah started to say something, but Ashton interrupted. "In college, I once went out with a girl who didn't speak English," he said, his mouth full of ham and bread.

"Was that before or after drinking?" said Zakiyyah.

"During," Ashton replied. "Remember her, Jules? Maniki? Correction—Maniki did not speak *good* English, and that's *much* worse than not speaking any English at all. The worst thing a person can be when they're crap at something is to think they're good at it."

"Is that really the *worst* thing a person can be," said Zakiyyah.

"Absolutely." Ashton chewed. "It was one of the longest dates of my life."

"I wonder how *that* must have felt," Zakiyyah said, and Ashton guffawed and turned his attention to Josephine.

"How is *Paradise in the Park*?" he asked. Josephine smiled, got ready to tell Ashton something about it, but he cut her off with, "I meant, how long's the play running for?"

"A month. I can get you tickets if you want."

"Yeah, maybe. I don't know when, though. Jules and I are supposed to fly down to Cabo for the Fourth. And to be honest, Dante's not my thing. I prefer more stupid humor."

"You don't say," Zakiyyah said.

"Don't worry, Ashton, Dante is not that funny," Josephine said. "*Comedy* may be a misnomer."

"Give me a cat tied to a fan or a mediocre fart joke, and I'll laugh till I cry," said Ashton. "I'm not proud of it. It's just how it is."

Josephine squeezed Julian's hand under the table. "Cabo?" she asked him quietly.

Julian shook his head, as in *don't worry*. Another thing he had completely forgotten.

"So real life hasn't broken through your little frat party yet?" Zakiyyah asked Ashton, barely turning her head to address him.

"Thank *Christ* for that." He barely turned his head when he replied.

"Do you know what Gandhi says?" Zakiyyah said.

Ashton was still chewing. "Are you talking to me?"

"Yes," Zakiyyah said, her glossy lips tight. "Gandhi says: our thoughts become our words, our words become our actions, our actions become our character, and our character becomes our destiny."

"Hmm." Ashton swallowed and loudly slurped his Coke. "Is your intellectual snobbery designed to belittle me? Because thoughts are most certainly *not* my destiny. I know that for a fact. I'd be in jail for the things I think. But let me tell you what Ashton *says*. Because you and Julian aren't the only ones who can rattle off pithy sayings. I have a life hack, too. Want to hear?"

"Do I have a choice?"

"I call it Ashton's two-minute rule."

"Ashton, *no!*" That was Julian.

Unheeded, Ashton continued. "If you see something that needs doing and can be done in under *two minutes*, do it immediately." He paused to let the words linger. "I also call it the Ashton Sex Rule." He threw back his head and laughed.

A baffled Julian rubbed his eyes in the stony silence that followed. What was *happening*?

When the girls refused to react, Ashton baited them further. "The trouble with Julian and me being friends," he said, "is that we're opposites in many ways. Is that the same with you two? I bet it is. For example, Julian thinks he's all about the funny, while I am way more cool. But to tell you the truth, I'd really like to be both, funny *and* cool."

"I teach my kids," Zakiyyah said, "that it's always better to be realistic about your limitations."

"Your poor kids," said Ashton.

"I, on the other hand, don't care at all about being cool," Julian said, springing from the table and gesticulating wildly for the check.

"That's because Jules can go all day," Josephine said in a smoky voice. She pulled on his wrist, gazing up at him. "He doesn't need to be cool."

"And that's why," Ashton said, "*Jules* is funny."

∞

"So that was the famous Ashton," said Zakiyyah, after Ashton—who had insisted on paying—tipped his backwards baseball cap, knocked over a chair, and split.

"He's all right. No one likes to be put on the spot like that," Julian said. "We should try again. Do something less stressful."

"Less stressful than *ham sandwiches*?"

"We should go to Disneyland," Julian said. "The four of us."

Josephine clapped. "Yes, please! That would be fantastic."

"*Never*," said Zakiyyah. "I mean—no, thank you."

"He wasn't that bad," Julian said. "He was trying too hard."

"That was *trying*?"

Julian got defensive. "Look, it's not how he is."

"We are what we pretend to be," the grim young woman said, "so we must be careful what we pretend to be." She glared at Josephine, who took Julian's hand under the table and did not return Zakiyyah's scolding gaze.

13

Pandora's Box

RIGHT AFTER THE FOURTH OF JULY, WHILE JOSEPHINE struggled in *Paradise* with hypocrites and thieves, Julian met up with Ashton for a drink at Tequila's Cantina, their favorite hangout on Magnolia. Beer followed a plate of taquitos and some small talk. Well, small but pointed talk about Cabo, where Julian did not go, and where Ashton and Riley had gone by themselves instead.

Julian smiled anxiously. "Ash, I want to show you something." He took out a black velvet box from his pocket.

Jumping off the bar stool, Ashton raised his hands. "Dude, no."

"Will you look?"

"I said no."

Julian's hand was still proffered. With a great sigh, Ashton took the box, opened it, glanced inside, closed it, and stuffed it back into Julian's pocket.

"What do you think?"

"Do you really want to know what I think?" said Ashton.

"As long as it's 'that's incredible, Jules, congratulations,' yes."

Ashton was silent.

Julian waited. "Come on. I gotta go soon." He didn't want her waiting for him alone in that parking lot at the Greek. It wasn't safe.

"You're going to ask her to *marry* you?"

"I'm trying to find the perfect moment, but yes."

"How about three years from now?"

"Not helping, Ashton."

"What kind of help are you looking for? Do you want to practice your moves on me? Or do you want my advice?"

Julian studied Ashton's face. They had spent so many years together, living and working together, drinking, traveling, meeting women together, that Julian didn't need long to know how Ashton felt about anything. And most of the time, Ashton was the most chill, sunny guy despite coming from a disastrous childhood, the kind of childhood that made you question the point of existence itself. So when Julian saw the worry on his friend's face, the tension around the normally relaxed mouth, the darkened indigo rings around the light eyes, when he caught sight of the long shadow of anxiety in Ashton's expression, Julian couldn't continue to press him. He was going to have a hard enough time with his family, considering they'd never met Josephine and thought he was still with Gwen.

"I just want you to be happy for me, Ash."

"I know that's what you want." He said nothing else.

Sighing, Julian picked up his beer. "You don't like her."

"I don't know her. That's my problem."

"You're right. That's *your* problem."

"Not just mine."

"I know her," Julian said. "And you will get to know her. And when you get to know her, you'll love her."

"Yeah."

"You think I'm moving too fast?"

"Among a thousand things. And I don't *think* it. It's fact."

"What else?"

"Are you sure it's love?"

"Excuse me?"

"Have you considered the possibility that it might be something else?" Ashton said. "Something as pleasing but more misleading."

"Stop it." Julian gulped his beer.

"Do you even know the difference between love and sex?"

"Do *you*?"

"*I'm* not getting hitched, am I?"

"You want to know what the difference is?" Julian said. "Nobody dies for sex."

"Oh boy. It's already like that, is it. Also not true. The male praying mantis dies for sex. That's his whole life. Dying for sex." Ashton tutted. "What do your parents think? I can't imagine your mother approves." He paused for Julian's reply, in a way that suggested he already knew there wouldn't be any. "Have they even met her?" There was another pause. "Sweet God, Jules, do they even *know* about her?"

Julian refused to return Ashton's incredulous stare.

"Tell me, when were you planning to tell your mother?" Ashton said. "When she received your wedding invitation in the mail?"

"If *you're* like this, how do you think she's going to be?"

"What does that tell you?"

"That no one understands or cares about a single fucking thing."

"Yes," Ashton said, "that's me."

Julian regrouped, lowered his voice. "Okay, but then why are you being like this?"

"I can't fathom," Ashton said. "Have you told Riley?"

"You two just came back from Cabo! And I'm hardly going to tell her before you. Plus I know what she'll say. She'll tell me to eat more yellow food like bananas and pineapples to balance the fire in my life."

"Maybe you should listen to her for once," Ashton said. "What's the rush, Jules? I don't get it. Did you knock her up or something?"

"Don't be ridiculous."

"So why not wait? If it's real, it will stand the test of a few..."

"You want me to jump through your arbitrary hoops? And wait for what? You said stand the test of a few...few what?"

"Parsecs," Ashton said. The stress in Ashton's shoulders did not recede despite the joke. "What happened to being spooked by commitment?"

"It's not the commitment," Julian said. "It's the girl."

"Did no one tell this girl that if she wants to make it in show business, she should never get married?"

"I certainly hope not."

"Where's your common sense?" asked Ashton. "You didn't always have it, but you got it the old-fashioned way. You bought it with your life." He took a breath. "You're careful, meticulous with time, reliable, trustworthy. You're not impulsive. You don't do things like this. It's not you. It's not even the old you."

"Ashton, but she's the one!"

All his friend said was, "The one what."

Julian fell back on the bar stool. "Is that why you were such a jerk the other day?"

"Don't know what you mean."

"What I don't get is why you were rude to her friend. What did *she* do?"

"I wasn't rude, I was making small talk. What else were we going to talk about, you?"

They finished their beers.

"Have you lovebirds discussed where you're going to live?" Ashton said. "Is she going to move to L.A.? What about her career? Theatre is my life and all that? Or are you the one making other plans, like a relocation to New York, perhaps?"

"I'm not going anywhere, Ash," Julian said. "I promise." Affection crept into his voice. "Is that what you're worried about?"

"Who's worried? But why the rush? To keep her from returning east? Is her visa expiring? You do know New York is still the United States of America," Ashton said. "You can travel freely from coast to coast."

Julian peered into his friend's face. "Dude, what's going on with you?"

Ashton stared into his empty beer glass. "I don't know. I have a bad feeling, that's all," he said. "Even at Cherry Lane when I saw her perform, there was something about her that wasn't right. And I'm not the only one who thought so. Look at Gwen and Riley's reaction to her. Everybody's but yours, frankly. I can't explain it. Something's off. Maybe she's not the girl you think she is. Maybe what you've found is the Hollywood version of what you think you want. You think you've found day, but what you've really found is night."

"You're wrong," Julian said. "She is the most open, heart on sleeve girl I've ever met. She lives her life out loud."

"Yeah, okay."

"She's like a female you. Are you telling me you're not the guy I think you are?"

Ashton didn't answer. "She is trouble," he said. "I can't help it. That's what I feel."

"You're wrong."

"For your sake, I hope so."

The men fell quiet, focusing on other patrons' conversation, on the song playing on the jukebox, "Burn it Blue."

"I know how you are," Ashton said. "Quiet but ruthless. I know you won't be talked out of anything unless you want to be talked out of it. When are you planning on popping the question?"

"Soon. Waiting for the right time," Julian said.

"Oh, *that's* wise."

"I don't have much of it, though."

"Wisdom?"

"Time." Julian leaned in. "The Brentwood Country Club has a cancellation four weeks from Friday!"

At first Ashton didn't react. "Four weeks from which Friday?"

"Don't be like that." Julian rocked on his seat.

"You want to marry a girl you met five minutes ago, four weeks from this Friday?" Ashton's stunned expression was priceless.

"I'm not crazy, Ashton."

"Of course, why would I think a marriage after knowing someone not even two months is crazy?"

"You think marriage after knowing someone three *years* is crazy," Julian said.

"Am I wrong?"

"We cook together! Have you ever known me to cook with a girl?"

"Oh! Well, if you cook together!" Ashton slapped the counter. "Why didn't you say so? Holy shit. Mario! Two of your best beers, *por favor*. Our Jules here is *cooking* with a girl. He totally forgot the best piece of advice Oscar Wilde ever gave us. Mario, are you listening? Because Jules sure isn't. A man can be happy with any woman," Ashton said, "as long as he doesn't love her."

∞

First they had blood orange jello shots. When they were slightly four to the floor, Josephine asked if he had a frying pan. She was going to attempt to make him dinner.

At Pavilions on Santa Monica (to which they stumbled, not drove) she marveled at the high prices and the shiny apples. They bought steak, French fries in a bag, a mix for salad.

Things they forgot: dressing, butter, oil.

One more thing: salt.

"You don't have any salt?" Josephine rummaged through his cabinets.

"Do we need it?"

"Without salt, there is no life," she said. "What kind of Mr. Know-it-All doesn't know that? How do you eat popcorn at night?"

"I go to Arclight Cinemas on Sunset and buy popcorn. And use their salt shaker."

"Every night?"

"I don't eat popcorn every night."

When he returned after a trip to buy salt without which they couldn't live, the apartment smelled of rotten eggs. She had left the gas on and forgot to light the burner. Julian opened the windows and doors.

"Didn't you smell it?"

"Smell what?"

"They inject that terrible smell into gas on purpose," Julian said. "To warn you that you're about to die."

"Is that one of your life hacks?" She was so blasé about leaving the gas on.

"It's everybody's life hack. Your mother didn't teach you that?"

"No. Ironic, since she's a teacher and all," Josephine said. "You'd think she'd teach me how to stay alive."

"Yes, it's one of the first principles." Julian found a theme for his next morning's newsletter. "First Principles." Clearly nothing was so well known as to be common knowledge. "Your mother doesn't cook?"

"My mom is a fantastic cook," Josephine said. "She grows her own vegetables in the garden behind our house, she makes her own bread, has fresh herbs, she could write a book, she's that good."

"She never taught you about the smell of death?"

"No, because she didn't let me near the gas burners. My mother," Josephine said, "took care of everything. I danced the mambo till I felt the pain and ate her food. You want another shot?" She gave him the glass before he answered.

Like a dolt Julian stood near the cold stove. Josephine was barely dressed. She wore a thong and one of his tank tops. Her hair was bed-messy. Where was the little black box? He reached into his pocket.

"They should put the smell of death into death itself," Josephine said. They clinked and drank. "For easy detection." Instead of wiping her mouth, she let him kiss the blood orange vodka off her lips. "Have it built in, like a death hack." She giggled. "That way, everybody would instantly know what was coming."

"You'd want that?"

"To know when you were going to die? Absolutely," she said. "Who wouldn't?"

"Barring that," Julian said, going down on one knee, "they inject an odorant into gas before it runs through the pipes. Eggs is your smell of death."

"And that's no *yoke*. What are you doing?"

He took her hand. "Josephine, I want to tell you something," he said. "I want to tell you about the first time we met. You stood at the wall in silhouette, backlit by the pink lights. It had started to rain, and the man you were with couldn't be bothered to get you an umbrella. So you stood in the rain by yourself. You were a stranger to me, but all I wanted at that moment was to have the right to call your name and offer you my umbrella. I'm a regular guy, and I thought that regular guys don't fall in love like they're constantly clutching their chests and living on their knees. I never got too empty, but I never got filled up either." Julian paused. *Because the one thing that filled me up got taken away, and nothing else sufficed, not even love.* "But at that moment," he continued, "when you stood alone by the wall, I asked God that I could once in my life know what it meant, what it really meant, to love another."

"That's what I ask for, too," she said. Her hand clenched inside his.

"Josephine, I *love* you. He popped open the black box. "Will you marry me?"

There was a stunned, glazed-eyed silence. "You want to marry me?" she said. "Why? I haven't even met your mom. She's going to hate me. You haven't met my mom. She's definitely going to hate you."

"It's not for them. It's for us. For you and me."

She cried. She said yes. Her hand remained clenched.

Julian saw the sun during his day for night and all the comets blaze down, the eyes of the planets like flames, the whole world on fire, not gentle or nostalgic or soft, but an ocean, raging with the swell of one human heart colliding against another.

FIRST PRINCIPLES

FIRST, A QUESTION ABOUT GRAVITY:

If Gravity proves that the universe was created on scientific principles, then who created Gravity? Before there was matter, there needed to be a law governing matter.

Why?

The smell of rotten eggs inside your house is a warning.
Check your gas burners.
Check your furnace.

The egg falling to the floor and breaking: You can't reverse it, you can't undo it, you can't unbreak it. Without eggs there would hardly be any baking, but what are eggs if not unborn chickens? So what you have is chicken in your cookies.

- **A spending hack:** if you can't afford two of it, you can't afford one of it.

- **A vodka hack:** Vodka is good for many things besides boozing. Insect repellent. Scalp tonic. Painkiller. But primarily it's good for boozing.

- **A grammar hack:** The present tense is used to refer to timeless facts, to timeless acts.

- **A life hack:** When you hear hooves, think horses, not zebras.

- **A foundational hack:** Gravity's inverse square law means the reach of gravitational attraction is infinite.

Exit Quote:
"The most beautiful thing we can experience is the mysterious. It is the source of all true art and all science."
— Albert Einstein

14

Shame Toast

THEY WERE IN ZAKIYYAH'S APARTMENT. IT WAS LUNCHTIME.
"Sometimes, when I'm starved," Josephine said, "I make an
awesome thing. I told you about it. I call it Josephine's shame
toast."

"Does it put all other toast to shame?" He grinned.

"It puts everything else in the world to shame. It's quite a
heady mix of carbs and lard. Don't worry. It requires no gas." She
kissed him. "But don't tell Z about it. She thinks it's despicable."

"Oh, I'd blab immediately if I were to ever see her again,"
Julian said. "She *is* coming to our wedding, isn't she?"

"You're hilarious." Josephine winked. She got some bread
from the fridge and some butter from the cupboard.

"I think you have the locations of those two foods mixed
up," Julian said, sprawled at the table, gazing at her.

"Nope. The butter must be soft, and the bread must be not
green. Ergo this way. But see how the pieces of toast are skinny?
It's very important they be skinny."

"Of course," he said. "In Hollywood we're always watching
our waistlines."

"Exactly. Okay, so you toast the bread, twice if necessary,
until it's real crisp." They waited. The bread popped. "You butter
it a lot, right up to the crusts." From the fridge she pulled out a
plastic tub of potato salad.

"How long has *that* been in there?"

She smelled it. "It's potato. What can go off in a potato?"

"Well, the potato," Julian said. "And then there's the *mayo.*"

"You worry too much. It's fine. You spread the potato salad..."

"With flecks in it." He came to stand behind her, peering over her shoulder as she worked.

"It's pepper, I think. I *hope.* Anyway, you spread the salad over the toast, then you get out your cheddar cheese, sharp's best, and grate it over the potato, like this, you pepper it some more, and then you put the other piece of bread on it, and you push it down with your palm, like this, and then, well, I guess you slice it in half if there are two of you, but if you were by yourself, you'd just pick it up and stuff it in your mouth and..."

He watched her as she, her eyes closed, devoured her half of the shameful sandwich.

"Are you going to eat your half or are you just going to stand there?" she asked.

"Do you want me to eat my half?"

"If you want. It's the only thing your future wife knows how to make, so best you taste the milk before you buy the cow, I suppose."

Standing by the sink, he ate it as she watched him enviously.

"Not bad." He wiped his mouth.

"We're still hungry though," she said. "And there's not enough potato salad for another one. Or cheese. Or bread."

He nudged her toward the bedroom. "Quick, go have a shower and I'll take you to Factor's Deli, where we can ask them to make this into a custom sandwich. Who knows, maybe it'll become so popular they'll put it up on their daily specials board. Josephine's Shame Toast. Right next to the Steve Martin. But hurry. We still have to run to the Country Club for the cake tasting before your call time. And your ring is finally ready." The ring he had bought for her was four sizes too big. Who knew she had such delicate hands. She was afraid to lose it, so she never wore it.

There was a lot to do that afternoon before *Paradise*. They had to select their wedding bands. And a wedding band. They had an appointment for a cake tasting, they needed to rent him a tux, oh—and she had no dress. She had made plans to go shopping with Zakiyyah last week, but didn't. Today they were supposed to knock off half a dozen things on Julian's long list, but when he arrived to pick her up, she was still asleep. It irked him slightly that she wasn't ready, until she beckoned him into bed. Now it was two hours later, barely enough time for shame toast and a cake tasting.

While she showered, Julian sat in the chair by the window facing the street and looked over his to-do items, each day the list growing longer while time grew shorter. Choose the flowers. Drop by City Hall, apply for a marriage license. Select a wedding registry. Decide where to go on their honeymoon. (He: Hawaii? She: London?) Buy shoes she could dance in.

Normandie has a short upward slope as it heads downtown past Clinton Street, but otherwise it's straight and flat as a runway. Due north, it juts into the Hollywood Hills. Tall browning palms line its curbs like telephone poles.

It's all sunny, sunny.

Normandie is a through street. A million cars whizz by all day and night. Weekends are especially boisterous. Weekdays are quieter. Today is a weekday.

Latinos wash their beat-up cars, water their yellow petunias and red azaleas, sweep the street.

Behind Zakiyyah's house with the balcony with the yellow petunias and red azaleas, the freeway noise never stops. And across the street sits the razor-wire house. Even when Julian's mind is not in the world but on the girl, he notices it from the corner of his eye. Even now, when he is counting out the minutes left and the errands to run, the peripheral weight of the house manages to drop a chink of anxiety into his gut, where it lodges and churns.

Lowering the notepad to his lap, Julian stares at the stucco building. A chain link fence surrounds it; there's a gate to let visitors in. There are bars on the windows, bars on the gates and the doors, bars on the bars. And razor wire.

In the daytime, the two-story building looks like what it is—a fortress. Like they're hoarding the gold bullion that didn't fit in Fort Knox in one of their skanky hallway closets, either that or half of Medellin's coke supplies for Southern California.

Like: whatever's in there, you don't want anyone crawling over the fences and balconies to get.

What's there?

Who lives there?

While Julian was pondering this, a mixed-race dude emerged from the gangland house. In high tops, low-hanging jeans, and an oversized Lakers jersey, the guy locked the gate behind him, tucked his semi-automatic pistol into the back of his belt, walked across the street and hopped up Zakiyyah's stairs.

Julian closed his notebook with the wedding to-do list.

There was a knock on the door.

He stood up. The shower was still running.

The knock came again, more insistent.

Opening the door, Julian found himself face to face with a medium-build dark-skinned kid in his early twenties, big eyes, thick messy cornrows, tattoos and bling and earrings. The belt holding up his Levi's and his pistol was Gucci. The laces in his high-tops were bright red.

"Hey," the dude grunted. "Whatup."

"Hey." His right hand tightening, Julian turned his body to the left. The left hand squeezed around the doorknob. None of it went unnoticed by Mr. Cornrow.

"We cool?" he said.

"You tell me," said Julian.

"Is JoJo here?"

"You mean Josephine?"

"Yeah. That's right. Josephine."

The water in the shower was still running. Julian didn't want to say to the gangsta-boy with the insolent stare, sorry, she can't come to the door right now on account of her being naked. "She's not available. I'll tell her you stopped by."

The guy looked Julian over top to bottom, assessed his fighting stance, his stone-cold stare.

"I'm Poppa W," the young man said. "And who be you?"

"Julian."

"All right, Julian. Later. Be sure to tell her I stopped by, though. Don't forget."

"She'll know what it's about?"

"She'll know what it's about."

Julian watched Poppa W skip down the stairs and saunter across the street, where he jumped into his gold sedan with two huge exhaust pipes, turned the volume up to max on his souped-up stereo, and with Dr. Dre's "Nothing but a G Thang" blasting through the speakers, shot up Normandie and out of sight.

Things can happen, things you don't expect. One weekend you go camping with your friend, as you've gone a hundred times before, except this time rock falls out of the sky and alters the course of your life. Did you know that camping was such a risky endeavor? One minute you got plans, the next barely breath.

She came out of the bedroom in a towel, smiling and humming, not even close to ready. "Josephine, I keep meaning to ask you, who lives there?" Julian pointed across the street. He restrained himself from calling the woman he was about to marry by another man's nickname.

"How should I know?" She was drying her hair. A beat later, "Why?"

"Because a man named Poppa W just came out of there, knocked on your door and asked for you."

Josephine said something incongruous. "What door?"

Was she stalling? "I don't know how to answer that. The front door to your apartment."

"It's not my apartment."

"Zakiyyah's, then. What door did you think I meant?" Julian frowned. Even his heart frowned. "Did you think I meant your shower door?"

"No." She stopped drying her hair. "What did he want?"

"He didn't say. He just asked for JoJo."

She blinked. "He calls me that sometimes. What did you say?"

"I said you weren't available."

"Why did you say that?"

"Well, because you weren't available. Were you? And because I didn't want to tell him you were in the shower. I don't have to explain why I didn't want to tell him that, do I?"

"Ugh, Julian."

Ugh, Julian? "What *should* I have said?"

"I don't know. You're Mr. Know-it-All." She didn't look at him. "He's Z's friend, okay?"

"Okay." Julian nodded. "Except you did say you didn't know anyone across the street."

"When did I say that?"

"Literally just now."

"It's true, I don't know anyone. Z knows some people. Trevor hangs out with Poppa. I know him through Z. I owe him a couple of bucks."

"You owe that guy money?"

She shrugged. "It's fine, he's a friend."

"You just said you didn't know him."

"Jules, come on. I thought we were going out. I thought we had a lot to do."

"You're right," he said slowly. "We do. But you're still not dressed."

"I can't get dressed when you're grilling me."

"I'm not grilling you," he said. "This isn't grilling. This is rational concern. Normal curiosity. But also"—Julian kept his tone as even as he could—"I need you to be straight with me. If you know him, you know him. If you owe him money, you owe him money. But when you start by telling me you know no one across the street and it turns out that a dude you don't know is calling you JoJo, it makes me doubt the other things you tell me about him."

"It's just a stupid nickname," she said. "I didn't lie to you. I didn't know which house you meant. There are lots of houses across the street. You weren't specific."

"Yes, it's important to be specific." Julian took a breath. "Did I ever tell you I don't like guns? Never have. It's like holding death in your hand."

"Maybe what you don't like is death," she said, not smiling.

"Here's why I asked you who lives across the street," he said. "Rock falling out of the sky while you're hiking is not a foreseeable risk. But shooting by firearm is." He paused. "Especially when you live in an area where collection, outrage, reprisal, and bloodshed is the currency by which the gangs barter out their lives."

"I don't live here," she said, "and you're making a big deal out of nothing. Did rock fall on you when you were hiking?"

Julian didn't answer her. "He came to see you carrying a semi-automatic tucked into his belt and he asked for you by name."

"So? He's Z's friend. Sometimes we hang out, smoke a little. I told him I'd pay him for the weed and forgot. And he carries everywhere. You just said yourself he's not safe."

"I didn't say *he's* not safe. I don't give a shit about him."

"It's nothing. Trust me—it's less than nothing. Can I go get ready?"

"Yes, JoJo. Go get ready."

That day was the first day they were less than perfect, less than what they were supposed to be and meant to be. Julian kept trying to recreate the magic moment, the warmest night lit by the brightest stars, the ideal spot at the most romantic restaurant for sitting under the most blooming of the jacarandas. They hadn't returned to the hills of Santa Monica, hadn't climbed the steep slopes, the crystal teardrop never left her bag again, never rested in the palm of her hand. He took out the stone once when she was sleeping and he was restless. Touching it made him feel heavy inside, unwell. An electrical charge buzzed through his body again, a low-level shock.

They got going too late to taste the cakes. Or to pick out a wedding dress. They couldn't try on the diamond ring she hadn't worn yet, a ring he'd been carrying in his pocket since the first week he met her. They made up, but nothing could be perfect on a day when Poppa W was waiting for her to crawl under his razor wire and knock on his door.

During their propulsive ardor, sometimes Julian was so overpowered it felt as if her virtue could harm him, but now he wondered if he was using the wrong word for the thing that might harm him.

In her white arms and legs, he had found all kinds of promise, all good and equal to the gods promise. When his hand was under her head, she was more than California, more than America, more than the sea. She was just more. Everything she was, she was more than he ever wanted. He wasn't going to walk away from her. No matter what, no matter how many times Poppa W knocked on her door. They were going to kiss without rancor and marry without scandal. She didn't need her lover to play the lyre to get her out of hell. Her sweet husky voice could charm Hades himself into setting her free without any help from Julian.

Josephine. Every clock that had ever been struck had her name on it. She was the bell that rang in every tower. She was the seventh day of rest in every week.

Julian felt off-key but wouldn't admit it to her, or to anyone. Smiling, he left himself hidden, waiting for her to make him feel better, to make amends. She never did. In the end, that made him feel better. There's nothing for her to make amends for, he said to comfort himself and pushed on, waiting for her to get consumed by the details of shoes and jewels, of veils and flowers, by the color of the napkins and the order of the songs. That time couldn't come fast enough, though the wedding was rushing up plenty fast. She stopped humming with pleasure when he was loving her, and he stopped drumming with joy on his wheel as he drove away from her to attend to all the things she was too busy to attend to.

Julian started to notice all of his shortcomings, and every time he asked if anything was the matter, she said no, and he didn't have the stomach for a fight, for a crumbling of his most intense and aflame life. The jacaranda bloomed outside as he counted the minutes until she would finally be his wife, but the jam they were in wasn't fading or ending. One day he asked her to take a drive to Palm Springs, and she snapped at him. Are you crazy, she said, what about all the things I have to do, there's mildew in the bathtub, two auditions to get through, the mass I must go to, to pray for my breakthrough, and Z wants to get a tattoo, who's going to help her with that, you? Not wanting to hear I told you so and thus having no one to turn to, Julian cast it off as pre-wedding jitters and busied himself with the details, one foot in front of the other, one minute at a time, one task at a time, believing with his whole heart he and she were more than mere playthings of the gods, believing what she held in her hands were wedding rings, not grenade pins.

NICE DAY FOR A WHITE WEDDING

BEING ORGANIZED IS KEY

Nothing is worth a fight. Let the girl have her way. She wants a Viennese dessert bar? Fine. Tell her you get to name all the kids in return.

Don't forget to pack for your honeymoon before your wedding night, or you'll be packing on your wedding night. I do not mean that metaphorically.

And this one is so simple, I can't believe I even have to say it but:

Don't do anything at your bachelor party she'll divorce you over. You all know what that is. Don't do it.

Don't use Larkspur as your wedding flower. All parts of the plant are poisonous to human beings, especially the seeds.

- Sandpaper the soles of your shoes so you don't slip and fall.

- Ratio of celebration to photographs: 90-10. You cannot both live it and record it.

- Learn a few simple waltz moves. Better yet, learn them together. You'll look great on video.

- Stick a pack of tissues inside your tux pocket. Someone is bound to cry, and you'll seem like a hero.

- Buy, don't rent your wedding dress. Or you'll regret it for the rest of your life.

- Freeze a tier of your wedding cake so you can have a piece on your first anniversary.

- Waterproof mascara, waterproof mascara, waterproof mascara.

Exit Quote:
"The book of life begins with a man and a woman in a garden."
— Oscar Wilde

15

Charlie's Dead

EARLY IN THE MORNING ASHTON WAS ALREADY WORKING, helping an excited woman and her dogged husband load a large dining room set from *Bonanza* into the couple's Escalade, when a dusty green Hyundai pulled up and out stepped Zakiyyah Job, officious like a principal. Even her wild hair was tightly wound into a bun. Ashton ignored her while he continued securing the table, but when he was finished, she was still there, standing stiffly next to her vehicle.

Was he supposed to walk over to her? He wanted to stride back inside his store and let her take the lead. She was the one who drove up to his curb in her banger. Not even bothering to suppress his sigh, Ashton walked over to her, instantly regretting it when he saw her disapproving expression up close. A disgusted headshake was sure to follow. He was wearing his favorite gray T-shirt with the words FREE LICKS stamped on the front.

"Hello," she said formally.

"Hello..." Ashton waved his hand in a circle, pretending to have forgotten her name. "Kaziyyah?" She wore a navy suit and low-heeled shoes. Her ruffled white blouse was up to her neck. On her face she had nothing but red lipstick and black mascara.

"Not Kaziyyah," she said, already through her teeth. "Zakiyyah."

"That's what I said. What's up?"

"I need to talk to you. Our friends are in trouble. We have to help them. I don't know how much you care about *your* friend, but I care about *mine*."

What Ashton didn't *care* for was her turn of phrase. Shielding his face from the morning sun blazing down the length of Magnolia, he lamented his lack of sunglasses, wishing one of his no-good parents could've taught him how to hide his impatience. "What's going on?"

Glistening from the heat, Zakiyyah fanned herself with a map guide of Disneyland and didn't reply.

"Would you like to come in—for a *second*?" It was promising to be another scorcher.

"Fine," she said. "But only for a second. I'm on my way to work."

"I'm actually *at* work," Ashton said.

Her slow blink was like a snort. *Pfft*, the blink said. You call this work? Playing with your toys? She marched past him. Inside his gorgeous store, she said nothing. She might as well have stood inside The Gap.

As she leaned on the glass counter (for support?) and turned to him, Ashton knew it was already too late for a productive conversation. He was too ticked off. He judged all human beings by the way they reacted when they were inside his livelihood, because when they stepped inside, they were stepping inside Ashton, inside his treasure-hunting soul. So when they treated his riches as if they were nothing—the signed poster of a shining Bob Marley inscribed with his last words (*"Money can't buy life"*)—they were treating Ashton like he was nothing. And nobody reacted well to that, least of all him, the most affable of men but with a lion's pride.

"Are you going to tell me or am I going to have to guess?" he said.

"Don't be like that."

"Don't tell me what to do."

Zakiyyah raised her hand to stop him, which irritated him even more. He raised his own hand right back at her. She lowered hers. "Are you going to listen or bristle?" she said.

"Why choose?" To put some distance between them, Ashton walked around the counter, pulled out his phone and began checking his email.

"Did you know they're planning to get *married*?" he heard Zakiyyah exclaim in a faltering voice.

Her tone softened him slightly. She sounded like he felt when he'd first heard about it. Like he still felt about it, to be honest. But Ashton wasn't going to admit that to her. He didn't look up from his phone. "Of course I know about it. I'm his best man. Why are you acting as if you just found out about it yesterday?"

"Because I did just find out about it yesterday."

"Ouch." Ashton snorted. "The wedding's in three days. And you *just* found out?"

"You're not getting it," Zakiyyah exclaimed. "She didn't tell me! I'm her closest friend, and she told me nothing about it. You think that's normal?"

With silent sympathy, Ashton put down his phone. "Look, I'll admit, I was upset, too, at first," he said. "But Julian is not a kid and he's not *my* kid. It's their business what they do. My job is to stand by him. So that's what I'm going to do. What are you going to do?"

"No way," Zakiyyah said. "I have to stop them."

"Good luck with that. I can't hold your hand through it, though."

"Am I asking you to hold my hand?"

"I don't know what you're asking," Ashton said. "But I've got a meeting to get to, so..."

"If you really wanted to stand by him," Zakiyyah said, "you'd tell him that he can't marry her. That would be pretty friend-like of you."

Ashton studied her. Her huge brown eyes were about to overflow. Her red lips were trembling. He hated when women cried, even women he didn't know. All his mother did for two years before she died was cry. He leaned his palms against the counter. "Can I tell you a joke?"

"I don't think you *can*, no."

"Charlie is dead," Ashton said.

"What?"

"Never heard that one?"

"And don't want to."

"It's a perfect time for it. You'll see. A man walks into a bar—"

Zakiyyah groaned.

"A man walks into a bar," Ashton continued over her objection, "and says to another man, 'Charlie's dead.' The other man starts to wail. 'Oh my God, not Charlie! We went to school together, played stickball together, he was my best man, my best friend, what am I going to do?' A day later, a gorgeous broad with big boobs walks into a bar and says to the same man, 'Charlie's dead.' And the man says, 'Who is Charlie?'"

After a star-studded silence, Zakiyyah opened her hands. "That's a *joke*?"

"Yes. On us. *We* are Charlie. *You and me*." He winced as he said it. "The sooner you get it, the sooner you'll get on with things."

"That's honestly the least of what I'm trying to tell you," she said.

"I know what you're telling me. You think he's not right for her."

"No," said Zakiyyah. "I think *she* is not right for him."

That took Ashton aback. Nonetheless, he plowed on. "She's fallen in love, and you're not part of it. Her impending marriage is the only important thing to her. Things are changing. They always do. You gotta work out your own shit. No one can help you."

Zakiyyah crossed her arms. "You sure you're talking about me there, genius?"

"Positive." Ashton crossed his own arms. "I'm not coming to *your* kindergarten, am I, bothering you with my feelings."

"These aren't my feelings, they're facts!"

"What are you yelling at me for?"

"Because you're refusing to get it."

"I'm getting it pretty loud is how I'm getting it."

"You're not listening to me. Listen to what I'm trying to tell you…"

"Stop line-topping me," Ashton said. "You're yelling down. I'm not your guy. You should be yelling up."

"This isn't about me, or you—if you can believe anything in this world can be *not* about you," Zakiyyah said. "It's about them. It's about her. Josephine is not—"

"So go talk to her," Ashton said, interrupting. "What do you need me for, permission?"

"I did talk to her!"

"Stop yelling."

Zakiyyah lowered her voice. "You don't think I tried that first before coming here? Believe me, I tried everything first before coming here. She refused to listen. That's why I need you to talk to Julian."

"No."

"Tell him that—"

"*No.*" Ashton said it as forcefully as he could. He shook his head, raised his hand to stop her. "You have no right to tell me anything. Her secrets are none of my business. It's not your place to tell, and it's not my place to hear it. You're trying to put me in a bad spot, and I won't let you."

"But—"

"You're about to tell me something I shouldn't know and don't want to know," Ashton said. "And then I'm either going to have to keep quiet, which, as Julian's friend, I clearly can't do, or I'm going to have to daisy chain this conversation back to him. Something about Josephine that you're passing on to me to pass on to him. Don't you see how screwed up that is?"

"But—"

"If there's something she needs to talk to him about, *she* has to do it. So stop wasting my time."

"She won't listen to reason!"

"Again, not my problem," Ashton said. "It's between them. Keep me out of it. If you knew what was good for you, you'd stay out of it, too."

"I can't." Zakiyyah put her face in her hands. "They *can't* get married. I'm begging you, just talk to him. She is—"

"No!" Ashton yelled. Ashton, who hadn't yelled since he was twelve, who had never once raised his voice in three years with Riley, was shouting at a stranger. "I told you *no*," he said, quieter, "and I meant it."

"Wow," Zakiyyah said. "Just wow."

"Yeah, wow. Don't you have to be at work or something?"

"You are a terrible human being."

"Sticks and stones, lady." Ashton walked around the counter. He was much taller than she was, and he didn't want to come too close, he didn't want her to think he was menacing her. Except he was, a little bit. He *was* menacing her. "Don't insult me, just go."

"Can you really insult a man wearing a Free Licks sign on his shirt?" Zakiyyah said, glaring up at him, not backing away. "Is there anything you can say to such a man that could possibly debase him any further?"

"Ooh, are you about to, as they say in the business, *door-slam-exit*?" Ashton said. "Can't wait. But are you sure you're dressed for that?"

As she stormed out, Zakiyyah slammed the front door so hard, the Jeannie bottle from *I Dream of Jeannie*, and Marty McFly's flux capacitor from *Back to the Future* fell over in their window displays.

"And scene!" Ashton yelled after her.

16

Fields of Asphodel

"You'll never guess who came to see me this morning," Ashton said to Julian later that day when the two men met outside the Brentwood Country Club to go over the floral arrangements. Julian knew a bit about local flora and would not let anyone else choose the flowers, not even the fake Mr. Know-it-All florist who was peddling yellow lilies to Julian as if he'd gotten them on an end-of-season sale or had never worked a wedding and didn't know that yellow lilies symbolized falsehood. "Josephine's friend."

"Zakiyyah?" After Julian had ixnayed the yellow lilies he got a mouthful from the wedding coordinator about yellow chrysanthemums. No *yellow*, Julian said impatiently. No daffodils, daisies, yellow roses, tulips, nothing. Then how about red poppies, sir? the man said. I have them on special...

Lord have mercy.

Julian and Ashton strolled through the flowerbeds in the nursery adjacent to the country club. They waded through isles of delphinium while Julian tried to figure out where else he could go on such short notice to order his first choice for the wedding: asphodel, the eternal lily that grew in Elysian Fields. The asphodel was the forever flower. And this exasperating guy had none. Probably no one had it. Asphodel was rare and expensive. But it was worth a try.

Julian half listened to Ashton, half examined the short-stemmed sunflowers (for adoration, he thought with tenderness).

He decided to google some florists in Brentwood and the nearby Santa Monica. "Oh look," he said. "Flowers With Love. Wait, what?" He glanced at Ashton. "Zakiyyah came to see you? Where, at the store? What did she want?"

"To yell at me."

Julian smiled. "What did you do? Rather, what did you do now?" He opened his phone's map app and keyed in the name of the florist. Only a mile away. Perfect.

"I'm an angel," Ashton said. "It's her problem if she can't see it."

"Hang on a sec, angel," Julian said. "I have to make a call."

Ashton waited. Flowers with Love didn't have any asphodel. Julian looked for other florists on his phone, barely lifting his head to his friend. "Ashton," he said absent-mindedly, "you have to behave yourself. You're going to be dancing with Zakiyyah at the wedding. Clinking glasses, giving a toast together. You can't have maids of honor yelling at you all day long. You'll upset my bride."

"I'm hoping the girl got all the yelling out of her system at my store, but—"

"Wait, Ash, one sec."

Rococo Flowers also didn't have any asphodel. Neither did Fleur in Santa Monica. They're almost impossible to find, the woman told Julian. Tell me about it, Julian said. She knew of a place in Long Beach near the RitzCarlton by the marina that sometimes carried them. He didn't want to travel that far. But what else could he do? Get boring old tulips? Or stephanotis, which every other couple had at their wedding? Roses, for God's sake? Roses! "Ash, you feel like taking a drive to Long Beach?"

"Not if I can help it," Ashton said, "why?"

"They might have the flower I want. Hang on, I'll call them. What did Zakiyyah...wait—"

Long Beach also did not have asphodel. Julian cursed as he hung up.

Ashton picked up a colorful flower from a display bucket. "What's wrong with this one? It's nice."

Julian took it out of Ashton's hands and dropped it back in the wet pail. "Marigolds, Ashton? Please. Marigolds are for grief. Let's walk over there, look at the orchids. What did Z want?"

"She came to tell me to tell you that you and Josephine can't get married."

"I hope you told her to get in line." Julian shook his head, examining a spray of azaleas. "Get in line behind you, my parents, my brothers, my sisters-in-law, her friends from Brooklyn..."

"Oh, I told her," Ashton said. "Hence the yelling."

The two men chuckled. Julian put down the azaleas and picked up the red roses. He was feeling defeated by the paucity of his choices.

"One thing was weird, though," Ashton said.

"Oh yeah?"

"She said she didn't even hear about the wedding until yesterday."

"Really?"

"Really."

"No, that can't be," Julian said. "You must've misunderstood." He held the bouquet of roses like a bride. "Because that *would* be weird."

"Yeah."

"And impossible."

"Yeah."

"Since Zakiyyah is the maid of honor and everything."

"Yeah."

"She really needs to get on board and fast," Julian said, inspecting the rose petals for rot. "Maids of honor are supposed to make things easier, not harder. No wonder my bride is stressed. So how did you handle it?"

Ashton paused ever so briefly. "I told her Charlie was dead."

"Who's Charlie?" Julian said—and laughed. "Oh, yeah. *That* Charlie. Good one, Ash. Well, like I say, always leave them with a joke. How did she take it?"

"Door-slam-exit."

"Of course. So you made her hate you even more."

"That'd be pretty hard," Ashton said, squinting into the sun. He took out his Aviators.

"In two days you have to walk with her down the aisle, arm-in-arm. What's your plan? How are you going to smooth things over?"

Ashton adjusted the shades to cover his eyes. "I'll think of something."

"You better." Asphodel, the immortal flower. Oh, well. "I'll take the roses," with resignation Julian told the wedding coordinator, who'd been shuffling behind them, feebly gesturing to one plant or another.

"You probably should talk to your girl, though, Jules," Ashton said. "Make sure everything's okay."

"Talk to her about what? That Z doesn't want us to get married?"

"Here's the thing," Ashton said after a moment of silence. "Zakiyyah looked like trouble."

Julian smiled. "Well, like you always say, chicks are trouble."

"I do say that, but it's not what I'm saying today." Behind his sunglasses, Ashton wasn't smiling.

A ROSE BY ANY OTHER NAME

Red Poppies are for consolation. And you don't need that.

Don't use Rododendron as your wedding flower. It means danger.

- How do you know if it's love or something almost as pleasing, but more misleading?

- If you're a woman, ask yourself: If you told him the most unexpected news — not entirely welcome news — how would he react? You found a job in another city. Your mother is sick and must come and live with you. You are expecting. Does he turn, does he run, does he wither?

- Men, she tells you what you don't want to hear. A day later, are you still there?

- Ask yourselves: "Are you made to last, or made to be broken?"

Exit Quote:
"The book of life begins with a man and a woman in a garden. It ends with the Revelation."

— Oscar Wilde

17

A Rose by Any Other Name

THE NOTORIOUS JUNE GLOOM HAD LIFTED BACK IN JUNE, and here it was, the start of August, and the thick fog still drifted all over L.A. The morning after the florist, the newsletter about the roses had taken Julian too long to get out. It took him hours to write a hundred words. The new day dawns, we wake without pride, and outside is fog. Okay, yes, but we know that in three hours it will be nothin' but sky till sundown. Why couldn't he buck up? Because the clement weather was still in the future. In the present, there was unease in the muddy air, a stillness as before the Santa Ana hellstorms, a prelude to a raging fire that made you want to throw yourself into the sea to escape. The gloom weighed on Julian, made his brain and body sluggish.

He ran late. He forgot the car keys, had to return for them, and then once more for the sweater she'd left at his place. This afternoon was Josephine's last performance in *Paradise in the Park*. He was supposed to pick her up at Z's and bring her to the Greek by noon. Julian would've liked to attend her last show, but he had too many things to do. It was Wednesday and the wedding was Friday. He had to pick up their platinum bands at Tiffany's, and pay for the ruby ring he had ordered as a wedding present for her (in the right size). Then he was meeting Ashton and Riley at the country club to finalize the menu. Julian didn't think Riley would be helpful since she didn't eat food—and what if the wedding fell on a B day and all she could recommend was wheatgrass juice—but she turned out to be a surprisingly capable advisor. She understood, at least intellectually, that other people enjoyed food. Where was the list of dishes Josephine had selected? Julian had stuffed it somewhere. No time to look for it now. He was late.

He broke all the speed limits, running four stop signs on Fountain and two stingy yellows on Melrose that turned red over his head. He pulled up to the house on Normandie at 11:50 and took the stairs two at a time.

He knocked. Pounded more like.

"Josephine?"

Silence.

The sound of shoes on linoleum.

An opening door.

In front of him stood a small woman, square and solid, with a rectangle of a body and a sphere of a head, helmeted by short black hair. Her hand did not leave the doorknob as she stood in the frame. For a second Julian thought he had knocked on the wrong door. "Is Josephine here?"

"I don't know who that *is*," the woman replied in a grousy Brooklyn/Irish accent. Or was it Scottish?

"Josephine, the girl who lives with—is Zakiyyah here?"

"If you knew *anything* about Zakiyyah, you'd know she'd be at *work*." The woman inflected all her sentences upward, whether or not they were questions. It was disconcerting. It made it hard for Julian to understand her. Yes, because *that's* what made it hard for him to understand her.

The woman didn't ask who he was. She just stood in the door.

"Her call time is at noon," Julian said, trying to catch his breath.

"You're a little late for call, *aren't* you?" the woman said. "She left a while *ago*. So she could be on *time*."

Julian frowned. "Excuse me, please, but who are you?"

"Excuse me, please," the woman said, "but who are *you*?"

That he understood. Loud and clear. The same tone he had used with Poppa W. Who the fuck are you, buddy, and why are you knocking on my girl's door?

"I'm Julian Cruz."

She appraised him censoriously. "So *you're* Julian Cruz."

She'd heard about him. That was something. "Are you her mother?"

"Whose mother, Julian?" the woman said. "Whose mother am I?"

"Uh—Josephine's?" This was painful.

"No," the woman replied. "I'm most certainly not *Josephine's* mother. My name is Ava *McKenzie*. I am Mia McKenzie's mother."

For a flicker, for half a breath, Julian was relieved. She was Mia McKenzie's mother! Thank God! "I don't know who that is," he said.

"Oh, I'm certain of *that*."

"I'm looking for a Josephine Collins." He peered over the woman's helmet head.

"No one by that name lives *here*," Ava said. "Are you looking for a pale tallish girl, thin, brown haired? Likes to pretend she's *all* sorts of things she's *not*? Like a working *actress*? A good *daughter*? A good *friend*? Someone named *Josephine*? I only have one daughter, Mr. *Cruz*. Mia McKenzie is her name."

There went his brief relief. "Ava...Mrs. McKenzie, I mean," he corrected himself off her glare, "I don't know what's going on, but..." Josephine wasn't her real name?

"You don't know what's going on," said Ava.

"Can I talk to her? Is she here?"

"You said yourself she had call at *noon*," the mother said. "What time *is* it? Is it *noon*? No. It's well *past*. So you've answered your own question."

Julian stood on the landing by the dried-out pot of browning azaleas. Ava blocked the entry, hand on the knob.

"She must have changed it and not told you," Julian finally said. He kept his voice low and even. "Her name, I mean. I'm sorry, I hope I didn't upset you."

Ava laughed unkindly. She was stocky of leg, inflexible of neck. She didn't look like the mother of his bride. His bride was soft and lithe, a smiling ballerina, not a blunt-force jab of a human being. "You think it's *me* she hasn't told things?" Ava said. "Dear *boy*."

Julian stood, clutching the car keys in his hands, Josephine's red cardigan.

Ava reached for the sweater. "That's hers. I'll give it to her when she comes *back*." Was that a question? As in, was there a possibility she wasn't coming back?

Julian snatched it away. "It's fine. I'll do it."

"Okay," Ava said, "*you* do it." She began to close the door, but he thrust out his hand to stop her. The hand with the shirt in it.

"Wait, Mrs. McKenzie. Please, can I come in?"

"I don't know, young man. *Can* you?" Inhospitably she sighed. "If you must, but only for a *minute*. I just flew in, and I'm very tired. That was quite a scenic five-hour ride in the cab from the airport," she said as they stepped inside. "How many miles is LAX from here, *ten*? I flew three thousand miles in less time." On her feet she wore pragmatic thick-soled sneakers, like a nurse, not a teacher. Next to the kitchen cabinet stood a brown square carry-on, in many ways the luggage equivalent of the woman in front of him.

"You knew who I was," Julian said. "She's told you about me?"

"Not a *word*," Ava said. "Not a syllable. You know who told me about *you*? Zakiyyah."

Julian's incomprehension deepened. Didn't Josephine assure him that she had told her mother they were getting married, and her mother was fine with it?

Fine with it.

Was this what Zakiyyah had come to talk to Ashton about? That the mother was flying in? But why didn't Josephine text him, warn him, prepare him, explain, say anything? They could've gone to LAX together to pick up his future mother-in-law.

Instead, Josephine told him that her mother was abroad, visiting family in Morecambe Bay, and would not be back in time to attend their wedding. Josephine was *fine* with it, she said, her mother not attending her wedding. After the honeymoon sometime, during New York's Indian summer, she and Julian were planning to host a reception in Brooklyn for all of Josephine's friends who also couldn't make it. Her mother could come to that.

Why hadn't Josephine texted to let him know that her mother had returned from Morecambe, wherever that was? You'd think that would qualify as news, your actual mother attending your wedding. And also—don't kill yourself to drive me to the Greek on time, Jules. I'll make my own way.

Something was scratching at the back of Julian's throat that made it hard for him to swallow. Something about the name Josephine.

Her name, her name, her name, her name, her name, her name, her name.

He sat (sank?) down at the kitchen table. He felt weak in the legs.

Ava didn't sit. Her face cross, her arms crossed, she stood over by the sink where not too long ago, Josephine had plied Julian with shame toast.

"So, Julian Cruz, is it true what Zakiyyah tells me?" Ava said. "That you're planning to marry my *daughter*?" There was ice in Ava's voice, disbelief, a little grief. But something else, too, an indefinable yet undeniable whiff of condescending mockery. Like when your four-year-old nephew informs you he's planning to hitchhike from Simi Valley to Disneyland all on his own. And you pretend to take him seriously until your sister-in-law calls him down for chicken nuggets. Except in the analogy, Julian was the four-year-old with the impossible dreams.

He'd been asking Josephine for weeks to go to the Beverly Hills city clerk's office and apply for a marriage license so the official one could come in time for the wedding. It was always one of those things they had to do and meant to do and didn't get around to doing. She was sick one day, had an audition the next, wanted to go back to Disneyland another (that Disneyland again!), and then it rained so hard, the cliffs tumbled into the water.

Finally they went, just two days ago, on Monday. They presented their IDs, signed the affidavit in front of the notary. Josephine signed after him. Julian didn't look to see what name his bride had signed above the line of their *marriage license*. He didn't think there was any reason to.

That was the day before yesterday.

And yesterday was when Zakiyyah told Ashton she had just learned about the wedding. Julian had laughed. It was so farcical. Ash misunderstood. Z misunderstood. It couldn't be.

And yet…

Could Josephine really not have told her mother or Zakiyyah that she was getting married, and the only reason Zakiyyah found out was because she spotted a copy of the marriage license application carelessly left out on the bedroom dresser?

Is that why Josephine hadn't worn his engagement ring? The large diamond on your white finger is hard to hide from your oldest friend.

A stunned Julian didn't know what to say to the woman by the counter who was about to become his mother-in-law, in a future that suddenly began to seem to him as distant as the sun.

"Do you know what you should be asking *me*, Julian?" Ava said.

"No."

"You should be asking why my daughter didn't call me herself to tell me about *you*. Why did Zakiyyah have to do it? It's not Zakiyyah's responsibility, is it? She didn't want to call me, but Mia forced her hand. She wanted Mia to take care of it, but that's one thing about my daughter, which you probably haven't had a chance to discover yet. All her life it's been Mia first, Mia last, Mia *only*. What Mia wants, Mia does, and nothing else matters. Poor Zakiyyah. She's such a lovely girl. She felt like a snitch and a traitor. The girl is an angel. She's always trying to do the right thing. Unlike my daughter," Ava said, "who's constantly doing the kinds of things decent people—Just. Don't. Do. She is my *child* and believe me, I have made all sorts of *excuses* for her, but not this *time*. She's put Z in a terrible position. Z said she was advised to keep *quiet*, but I told her absolutely *not*. Friends must look out for each other. Otherwise how dare you even call yourself a *friend*? If there's truth out there that needs to be known, then your friends must help you, and your mother must help you most of all, don't you *agree*?"

"I don't know," Julian said. "I don't know anything about it."

"Yes, you don't know a great many things," Ava said. "And I can see by your face, you don't *want* to." She shook her head. "Such a *pity*. But it's like I always say—the passion for truth is the faintest of all human passions."

Dear God. Julian struggled to his feet. He needed Ashton. Ashton would know what to do.

"Who are *you*, that you think you can marry my *daughter*?" Ava said.

"We are meant to be," Julian managed to utter.

Ava laughed. "You are destined for *misery*, my boy, misery such as you have never *imagined*. Listen to *me* and run while you still can. I *know* things. Don't you know that the earth is ruled by *mothers*? With any luck, someday my Mia will be a mother—but not by *your* doing. Because she is engaged to be married to a man in New York. They've been together four years. The wedding is next May. *Save the date* was sent out months *ago*. What, you didn't get the email? Her fiancé is flying into LAX later today to take her back with us to New *York*. Enough of this *nonsense*. What a mess she has made of things, as she has pretty much out of *everything*."

Julian wasn't listening anymore. He was tumbling down the stairs.

18

Lilikoi

How Julian got to the Greek Theatre, he did not know. As he sat in the parking lot waiting for her to finish in *Paradise*, he stared with blank eyes at the menu choices she had written out by hand on his stationery and folded into his wallet. They had spent the last month planning the wedding that was coming the day after tomorrow.

Unfortunately today was a day before that day.

Cheese Stuffed Italian Olives.

Spanish Octopus.

Poached Eggs in Wild Mushrooms.

Chinese Chicken Salad.

Hawaiian King Prawns.

Milky Burrata.

Ahi tuna sashimi salad.

Maui beef carpaccio.

Lobster steamed with lemongrass and ginger.

Mango and strawberry shortcake.

Macadamia nut shortbread.

And a raw wedding cake made of chocolate, coconut, and passionfruit. In Hawaii, they called it *lilikoi*.

On the back of the menu, she had written out a phrase she wanted to use in her vows.

Neither the demons below nor the angels above can sever my soul from your soul.

He parked in the lot below the mountains they once climbed, turned his back on the stage on which she currently stood, and furiously dialed and redialed Ashton's number. Julian must have called him a hundred times.

"Where are you?" Ashton said when he finally called back. Not, you missed another set walkthrough. Not, you didn't open the store like you were supposed to. Not, you never listen to me. But where are you.

It could've been ten minutes or an hour when Ashton screeched up next to Julian's Volvo in his blue BMW. "Jules, no, this is just wrong," was the first thing he said when he jumped in. "Your AC's not working. We're going to fry in here."

"Car overheated," Julian said. "Fucking Volvos. Good for nothing."

"Why didn't you call Triple A?"

If only Triple A could come and fix things.

"Let's get in my car," Ashton said.

"How's your car better? The top is down."

"Yes, and that's insurmountable. Come, Jules."

Julian was sweating. His clothes were wet, his face. His cell phone had overheated just like the Volvo. It needed cool air before it would function again. At the moment, it was nothing but a paperweight.

After the top was up in the convertible and the AC was humming, Julian told Ashton about Mia. As Ashton listened, his shoulders turned in.

"I told you to talk to her," Ashton said.

"Talk to her about *what*? And when? She was working, you and I were getting your tux, and last night she stayed with Z. I didn't see her. I did talk to her. On the phone. She sounded *fine*. What was I going to do?"

Ashton shook his head.

Oh God.

"Chin up, Jules," Ashton said. "Mothers don't know everything. Even I don't know everything. Clearly."

"Is that a dig at me?"

"No."

"I told you all I knew," Julian said. "I didn't keep anything from you." He hung his head. I kept it for myself. So I could have this bubble of love, unburst.

"Don't get bent out of shape," Ashton said. "Calm down and talk to your girl. Who's the guy, by the way?"

"What does it matter?"

"Is it that gorilla who was in the play with her, remember him, the dude who played Moses Jackson?"

"I don't know, Ashton."

"You didn't ask? You're right, who cares. She was engaged to some asshole, so what? Obviously they broke it off."

"Is it obvious?" Julian said.

"Yes, because she can't marry you *and* marry him. That would be fraud"—Ashton's falling face took on an expression of shame and dawning realization—"and I don't know anything about *him*, but I know that *you* and she are booked at the Brentwood Country Club this Friday night, where a chef from Waikiki is making you a lilikoi cake, whatever the hell that is. Bro, eyes on me." Ashton's teal-ringed gaze was intense, beseeching, comforting. "It'll be fine. Mothers don't know everything. Friends are idiots."

"You're sure about that?"

"One hundred percent," Ashton said, flashing his killer smile. "Because I'm an idiot."

"Why didn't she tell me her mother was coming?"

"She forgot. She's busy. It slipped her mind. The way it slips your mind to open the store or meet me at Fox. You know—like that."

"Is that a dig at me?"

"Yes, Jules," Ashton said. "That actually was a dig at you."

"Why didn't she tell her mother we were getting married?"

"You don't know she didn't," Ashton said. "They may've had a blow-out precisely because she'd told her mother. I don't know much about it, but I hear mothers can do that, make you crazy, make you forget things."

"Not mothers," Julian said. "Love. Love does that."

"Like I said. As for why she didn't call you, maybe she has no signal."

"Give me a break. She's right there." Julian pointed behind him to the amphitheatre.

"Like yours, her phone may've overheated," Ashton said. "The sun beats down on all phones equally, Jules, the just and the unjust."

Julian was losing his power of speech.

"The phone is not a bullhorn to the rest of the world," said Ashton. "It's barely a whistle. Sometimes people don't answer the call."

"Yes," said Julian, "or she could've left her mother to deal with me because she couldn't face me."

"I know that's how it looks..."

"Why would she not tell me her real name?"

"Because," Ashton said, "she wants to be *this* person, not *that* person. The person she wants to be is not an Irish broad named Mia McKenzie from the old neighborhood but a duchess named Josephine Collins."

"You wouldn't tell this to the man you're marrying?"

"I don't know, Julian," Ashton said. "Have you told everything to the woman you're marrying?"

"Whatever."

"Exactly."

Julian flared up. "What does Topanga have to do with anything? How does me getting lost make me less able to marry her?"

"It's not the getting lost," Ashton said. "It's the almost dying."

"I didn't die, though. You said so yourself. Case in point— I'm in hell right here."

"Did you tell her who you were before Topanga?" Ashton said. "Who you wanted to be? I see by your pissed-off face that you didn't. So *you* didn't tell her everything. Why not? Don't flip me off. I'll tell you why not. Because now you're this person. Like she is that person. We all want to reinvent ourselves, be the new thing, not the old thing." Ashton looked into his hands. "Have I told Riley about my mother? No. She barely knows I have a dad who's still alive. That part I understand, bro. She wants you to marry her as Josephine, not Mia."

"Is she marrying Moses Jackson as Mia?"

"I thought you didn't know who it was?"

"I'm guessing," Julian said in disgust.

"Look, as far as you know, your girl has never said no to a proposal," Ashton said, "but clearly she can't marry more than one guy at a time."

"Because one of those marriages would be fake, right?" Julian shivered. Sweat was dripping off him, yet he was so cold.

"Not fake," Ashton said. "Invalid in the eyes of the law." The way Ashton said it—so carefully—made it sound as though he thought there was at least an equal chance that the invalid union would be hers and Julian's, not hers and some overbuilt asswipe's.

"Why are you using that tone of voice?" Julian said. "You just told me it was going to be all right."

"It is."

"And five minutes before that, you told me she was going to be the death of me." Julian hit the wheel. "Pick a side."

"I didn't say she was going to be the death of you." Ashton took a breath. "I said she was going to be the death of *me*."

Julian turned his head and stared at his friend. "I was joking," Ashton said, his smile non-existent. "Great. So she's made you lose your sense of humor, too, along with everything else. Incredible."

Paradise was over. People started spilling out of the theatre. "If you need me," Ashton said before he drove away, "I'm just down the road at HomeState, eating a plateful of breakfast burritos."

Julian waited for her, propped against the trunk of his car, his head curved to the pavement.

∞

She didn't speak his name when she walked across the parking lot and stood in front of him, her long face striped black and red like a grotesque clown's, the stage makeup poorly removed, the beret on her head askew, her hands knotted into her abdomen.

Julian didn't speak her name either.

"Did you get my text?" she asked quietly.

"Do you mean the text telling me not to come because you were getting a ride to the Greek," Julian said, "or the text warning me your mother was going to ambush me?"

"I'm sorry," she said. "She's awful, isn't she?"

"She?"

"It was a shock this morning, her coming unannounced like that. We had a horrible fight. She is always butting in where she doesn't belong. I ran out and forgot to text you. I texted you later. I guess you didn't get it. I told you she makes me crazy."

"How did you get to the Greek?"

She paused before answering. "Poppa W gave me a ride. I was stuck, Julian. Otherwise I would've been late."

"Poppa W gave you a ride," Julian repeated dully.

"It's no big deal," she said. "I wrote to you. I sent you an email just before curtain. It's very important. Did you read it?"

"My phone overheated." It was a hundred degrees out. His soaked shirt clung to his back.

"I'm sorry about all this," she said. "But I can explain."

Did he mishear? Can or can't? "Do you know what your mother told me?" he said.

"Julian, wait, let me go first."

He didn't wait. He went first. "She told me a few things. One thing she told me is that your *fiancé* is flying in later today to take you back to New York with him."

She dropped her bag to the ground. Her hands flew up to cover her mouth. "Oh, no," she said. "That *can't* be true. She said nothing about that this morning, nothing!"

"Which part can't be true?" Julian asked. "That you have a fiancé other than me? It is just one other fiancé, isn't it? Or that he's coming to take you home?"

"God! Why would she tell him *anything*? She knows how upset he gets. What was she thinking?"

"Ah," said Julian. "*That* part."

She fumbled with her fallen bag. The beret slipped off her head and fell. She picked it up. Her hands were shaking. "That's my mom. Always manages to make things worse. As if it's not bad enough. Jules, can you please drive me home? I'll explain everything later, but right now I *really* have to go."

"Explain now," he said.

"I have to go."

"Tell me."

"No!"

He sucked in his breath. "You're shouting at *me?*"

"Julian..." she said, wringing her hands. "You don't understand. I have to handle it my way. Not your way. *My* way." Her open face, streaked with black mascara, didn't seem so open anymore. It looked shadowed with secrets.

"I didn't know there was a *your* way," he said, his burning hands on the car, hot and getting hotter. "I thought there was just *a* way."

"Okay, I know, it doesn't—look, what do you want me to say?"

Julian said nothing.

"I told you we were moving too fast," she said. "You just broke up with that Gwen or whoever. I thought I was your rebound girl."

"Rebound girl?" he repeated. "What are you talking about? You're not my rebound girl. You're *the* girl."

She wouldn't look at him.

"Or so I thought."

"Please, Julian."

"What's your name?"

She wouldn't answer him.

"What's your name?" Julian repeated, louder. "Because you went with me to City Hall and signed a piece of paper that contracted your name to mine. What name did you put on this legally binding document?"

"Mia McKenzie," she barely whispered.

Julian was speechless.

"Don't yell at me!" she cried.

"Did I say a word."

"You're raving like the possessed!"

"Did I say a word."

"I'm in the process of legally changing it to Josephine, okay. It takes time. I was going to tell you, but it had gone on for so long, I didn't know how to."

"What had gone on for so long?" said Julian.

"The fake name thing."

"Ah."

Her lip trembled. "I have to fix a lot. I know that. Don't you think I know that? Don't make everything harder. It's hard enough."

"What about our marriage?"

"What about it?" She didn't look at him.

"What about...*you and me*?"

"What about it?"

He could only take human bites out of this abomination.

And yet the abomination was taking troglodyte bites out of him. "Are you"—Julian didn't know how he got the words out—"are you going to marry someone else?"

Her shoulders were hunched. "I *meant* to break up with him before I left for L.A.," she said, "but he got the flu and lost a job he really wanted. He's an artist. He's very sensitive. He takes bad news poorly. I didn't want to upset him by kicking him when he was down. It didn't seem kind. I thought I'd come here, work for a bit, give us some space, figure things out, and after I returned to New York, I'd know what to do, but then I met you, Julian! I met you, and *everything changed*."

"Oh my God."

"Why are you saying oh my God like that? Don't you understand? Everything changed *because* I met you."

"So not only did you not tell him about me, you never even told him you weren't going to *marry* him?" Julian was dizzy. He was losing his ability to comprehend language. "He *still* thinks you're getting married. The man you've been with for four years is flying to L.A. because he thinks the two of you are still together?"

"I didn't want to hurt his feelings," Josephine said in a small voice. "I didn't know how to tell him."

This is how the world ends. In the middle of the day, in the middle of your life, in the middle of a parking lot filled with people and ice cream trucks.

"I thought you loved me," she said, her voice shaking. "How can you be so mad at me? I was going to tell him…"

"That's why you kept me away from Zakiyyah," Julian said. "Because she knew all about you." *Be careful who you pretend to be.*

"No." She said it without conviction.

"Is that why you haven't worn my ring? So you wouldn't have to explain anything to Z?"

"I haven't worn your ring because it's too big."

"It's not too big anymore, and yet there's nothing on your finger," Julian said. "You didn't tell your mother about me. You didn't tell me who you were. You didn't tell your boyfriend you had agreed to marry someone else. Who *are* you?" Julian's voice fractured as he was fracturing. "Or do I have it completely backward? Am I the fool here? Is it *me* you haven't told you're going to marry someone else?"

"It's not like that, Julian."

"You didn't answer my question."

"It's not like that."

"Answer my question!"

"You were so insistent!" she cried. "Marry me, marry me. I didn't know what to do."

"I wasn't insistent!" Julian yelled. "I asked you to marry me, and you said *yes*. You could've said, let me think about it, and made things right and come back to me. You could've told me about him. You could've told him about me. You could've talked to Zakiyyah, asked *her* what to do. You could've even said you couldn't marry me because it was impossible. You could've done any number of things other than what you did do, which is say *yes* to me. I wasn't *insistent*!"

Tears and mascara ran down her face, raccoon tears.

"You are going to marry someone *else*!" It was a scythe to Julian's heart. His voice failed him to speak the things he wanted to say, to yell the things he wanted to yell. He pressed his hot hands into his burning temples, wanting to cave them in.

"I'm sorry," she said, "I wanted to tell you, I just didn't know how to. You were so sweet to me, so kind. No one in my life has been as good to me as you. I didn't want to break your heart."

She didn't want to break his heart.

"But eventually, what was your plan?" he said. He stopped himself from groaning. "To break it?"

"I was trying to find the right time..."

Julian put his hands up. "Stop speaking. Stop everything. Stop."

They stood in the tawdry strip lot at the Greek Theatre, the ancient mountains behind them, the food truck in the corner selling tacos and ices to mothers with kids.

He wanted to shake her, to hurt her, to embrace her, and with his embrace to crush her, to suffocate himself. He didn't trust himself to go near her. "It was all a fucking sham, wasn't it, the thing between us," he said. His fists were clenched. There were tears in his eyes. "A pantomime of Venus and Mars."

"No!" She took a step to him. "*No...*"

He put up his hands in a blocking stance. "It was. Just a sleight of hand, an illusion. Like the light on your mountain. Nothing is real. Not you, not me, not you and me." His face pulsed hot blood just under the skin. "Ashton is right. Everything you do is a fraud. That's how you can treat me like this. To you I'm nothing but a set from a cancelled show. I'm about to be dismantled for trash. You're not just acting on empty. You're living on empty. Because to you I'm not real."

"You are, Julian, *please!*" she whispered.

He turned his body sideways. When she rushed up to him, he shoved her away. "Don't come near me," he said. "Get away from me. I don't know you. I don't know who you are. My God, I don't even know what to call you. Get away from me."

"Julian, wait, please—I need to—how am I going to get home?"

"Ask Poppa W." Julian flung open the driver door. "I'm sure he'll be glad to give you a ride, JoJo."

She was sobbing, standing in the empty parking lot, her arms around herself. "What about your ring?"

"Keep the fucking thing. I hate you. I never want to see you again."

He drove away, his last words to her pounding into the scar on his head.

LAST PRINCIPLES

William Shakespeare is a big fan of plots in which horrific consequences flow from small deceptions. Think of the mischief Iago makes out of a handkerchief in Othello.

The good ended happily and the bad unhappily. That's what fiction means.

Word of the day: Torschlusspanik: Literally means panic at the shutting of the gate, or fear of being left behind.

- Never take advice from people who don't have to live with the consequences of your choices.

- Cayenne pepper on a cut will hurt but will stop the bleeding. As long as the wound is not too deep.

- To hold an open wound together, dab it with Superglue. As long as it's not too deep.

- By all means learn from your mistakes. Better yet, learn from others' mistakes. It's easier.

- You never really know a woman until she writes you a letter.

Exit Quote:
"Words spoken in deep love or deep hate set things in motion within the human heart that can never be reversed."

— Frederick Buechner

19

Mystique

AFTER JULIAN GOT HOME, HE COOLED DOWN HIS PHONE AND
read her email, read it over and over until it was engraved on
his heart. Hours later he fell asleep on the couch but only after
putting on the sports channel and watching old Wimbledon
tennis matches with the sound turned all the way up so the only
thing he could hear was the ball in its rhythmic accelerating
pattern thwacking against the grass, like gunshots through a
silencer.

∞

Julian, my love,
I'm so sorry. By the time you read this, you'll probably know
what a mess I've made. I feel horrible. I hadn't found what I
was looking for, so my poor life was littered with the leftovers
of my fruitless search. It's not my fault you came along just
as I was losing hope. What took you so long, Mr. Cruz. I'm
sorry I couldn't tidy up the chaos of my life fast enough.
Everything is spinning out of control, I know, but I didn't
think I would actually find someone like you. Who'd ever
think they'd meet him not in the kings of dirt at the Gotham
Girls Roller Derby but in the best of men like I once hoped.
I dreamed of you when I was young, but it's been a long
time since then. You and I were in the ocean together in all

our clothes, even our coats. When I see you, I'll tell you all
about it. But then when I finally found you, I wasn't ready.
I dropped the ball. I made mistakes. Despite what you think,
I'm not perfect. I'm going to try my best to fix it and hope
that when I'm done, you'll be waiting. Please don't give up on
me.

With all my heart I know there's no future for me if there
is no you and me.
Love,
Mia

∞

Early the next morning there was a new phone message from her.

"Jules, are you not picking up my calls? Come on, pick up. I told you I'd fix it. Fario came, and I told him everything. It was so hard, but now it's over. Can we meet so I can explain? I know you're upset, and you have every right to be, but I will make it better. I promise, no more secrets. Give me another chance. Meet me at noon, at our Coffee Plus Food. I just want to say...if you still want to marry me, I'm ready. I'm free. You were so upset yesterday, and I got scared and defensive, and didn't say the things I should've said. Let me make it right today. Don't be *that* mad at me, even though I deserve it. See you at noon, I *hope*. I'll be waiting."

Julian didn't know what to do. He called Ashton.

"Are you crazy?" Ashton said.

"I just want to hear her out."

"Have you lost your mind?"

Julian became hostile right back. "What about the things you said yesterday?"

"I said them to make you feel better. Also yesterday you didn't tell me the additional shit you just told me."

"I didn't tell you because I didn't know it."

"Exactly! So when facts change, we change our opinion. That's what sane people do," Ashton said. "Yesterday I had no idea that the worst case scenario would be true. Well, I suspected it might be, but I hoped it wasn't. I thought she'd be a better liar. Not: yeah, Jules, it's as bad as you thought it was. I'm really not who I say I am, and I really was deceiving you for months, and shacking up with another guy while I was shacking up with you and planning to marry this other guy while I was also planning to marry you."

"That's not the worst case scenario," Julian said. He was afraid she'd want to marry the other guy. *That* was the worst case scenario.

"You can't go back to how it was with her."

"And don't want to," Julian said. "I want to go forward, to how it's going to be."

"Now that you know the truth, there is no future with her," Ashton said. "No good future."

Julian didn't speak.

"I know you don't want my advice," Ashton said. "But you *have* to listen to me. I'm not your life hack. I read you this morning. The difference is, I'm the one who also must live with the consequences of your choices. With the consequences of *all* your choices. Just like in Topanga. I told you to wait for me, not to go on your own, and did you listen? Even then you thought you knew fucking everything. When are you going to learn? Don't you understand? What you do affects me, too."

"Okay."

"Don't fucking okay me. Don't dismiss me."

"I'm going to hear her out, Ash. I owe her that. Listen to what she has to say."

"Yes, I know. All you want is to believe her desperate lies," Ashton said. "That she loves you, blah blah, that there's no one else, and never will be. Have you called Brentwood and cancelled?"

"Not yet."

"Julian!"

"First I will hear her out, Ashton."

"Why? You know what she'll say. I'm sorry, Jules. It won't happen again, Jules. It's all bullshit. Wait for me," Ashton said. "I'll be over in twenty. We have an eleven o'clock walkthrough at the old sitcom warehouse at CBS. You know I can't negotiate without your pessimism. You can stop me from bidding on the *I Love Lucy* crap I don't need and can't afford. We'll go to Shutters for lunch. Marina Del Rey is offering a twofer sailing lesson at three. Let's go learn to sail."

"No."

"It's no good, Julian," Ashton said. "She is no good. She can't be trusted. If a woman can lie to you about this, she will lie to you about anything. *Anything.* Don't you understand? You can't be with someone like that. You *certainly* can't marry her."

"You're a fine one to talk about trust."

"Do you see me getting hitched?"

"Can't you think of something other than yourself?" Julian snapped.

"What is with everyone?" Ashton said. "I'm not thinking of myself. I'm thinking only of you."

Julian didn't know what to say. He feared his friend was right. He didn't want to hear it. He hung up.

At 11:30, Julian drove to the corner of Melrose and Gower, to Coffee Plus Food, where he parked and found a small metal table out in the street. He ordered two coffees, two morning buns, and a sausage roll. He took out his phone, went online for a bit, sat, waited.

He wished to God he hadn't called Ashton. His friend was right in the main, but wrong in the essence. Ashton's argument was an intellectual argument, not an emotional one. This was different. No one knew what truly lived in the intimacy between human beings. What some people did was no indication of what other people would do. Past experience was not evidence of future events. Julian firmly believed that. Just because a girl did something untrustworthy once did not mean she could not be trusted in the future. That thinking was a logical fallacy and Julian's mind easily refuted it, like swatting away a fly. The future was by definition unknowable.

On an emotional level? Ashton's argument didn't even penetrate the first layer of skin. Julian couldn't be without her, that's all there was to it. Whatever steps he needed to take, he would take. Whatever deals he had to make with himself, he would make.

End of argument.

End of story.

He couldn't be without her.

The coffee was getting cold. He didn't drink it because he was waiting for her.

Noon came and went.

She was late.

Three police cars, sirens on, screamed past him. Melrose Avenue was a busy street.

After a few motionless minutes, Julian began to feel not so much worry as an unformed dread freezing him from the inside out.

Did she blow him off? Change her mind? Decide not to come?

Inexplicably he began to shake, even though it was L.A. ninety. What was wrong with him? He tried to return to surfing his phone. But his vision was blurred.

He stood up, to stretch his legs, to focus on something in the distance—a life hack for those staring too long at things up close like computer screens and wedding bands—trying to get rid of the cold anxiety flooding his body.

That's when he saw Josephine walking toward him on Melrose. She had decided to walk from Normandie to meet him at the coffee shop. She was smiling, strolling, unhurried. Julian felt such relief, his legs couldn't hold him. He took a step toward her and said, "God, where have you been?"

"I'm right here," the voice said.

"I was getting so worried," said Julian.

From the next table he heard a man say, "You all right, homie?"

Slowly Julian turned. "Why are you speaking to me?"

"Cuz you fell down, brother."

Julian whirled toward where she had just been. There was nothing but empty sidewalk. Struggling to his feet, knocking over a chair, he yelled at the well-meaning stranger. "What did you do? What did you do?"

"Whoa, man, just trying to help you out. You don't look too good. Want me to call somebody?"

Julian ran. He was in no condition to drive. It took him less than six minutes to run the straight flat mile in his Mephisto loafers down Melrose to Normandie. An ambulance raced past him, then another, three fire engines, a black and white. He didn't have to turn the corner to see the emerging situation unraveling in front of Zakiyyah's house. He felt it in his soul.

And yet, the reality of the crowd, the flashing lights, the choking smoke doubled him over.

The street was barricaded by cop cars and flares to stop the through traffic. An officer tried to grab him. To help him or halt him? I live here, Julian said, ripping away. I live in that house. Neighbors poured into the street. He pushed past them, trying to get to where the crowd was thickest. He couldn't see past the backs of the people. He ran too fast. He was wheezing.

"*Como esta, mio Dio, como esta?*" an older woman was asking a young woman.

"I don't know, Mami, a shooting? An accident? No one knows. Maybe driver had stroke and rammed into tree? I was sure I heard gunfire. It's terrible what's happened to this neighborhood."

"Someone got shot? But why the car on fire?"

Another woman spoke out of the corner of her mouth. No one wanted to turn their heads away from the crowded street.

"*Chica pobre! Qué pena!*"

"*Chica pobre?*" another woman cried. "Our Poppa W was shot!"

"*Mio Dio!*"

No one could see a thing.

Excuse me please, Julian mouthed. Excuse me.

"Whoever's in that car not gon' make it. They can't put the fire out."

"The gas tank blew. Look at them flames."

"Was it an accident?"

"It was murder, Mami, I'm telling you, cold-blooded murder!"

Excuse me! Julian kept gasping. Excuse me.

"That poor mamacita. *Qué pena.* Do you hear her?"

There was wailing in the street. In the cloud of black smoke, a car was on fire. The sound of the water from the hydrant drowned out the gossip, the disbelief. Instead of sheltering in place, people left their homes and stood witness. Because it happened in broad daylight as they washed their cars and made lunches and walked to the corner bodega to buy their milk.

Shock grinds down human beings. They can't act, react, can't speak, can't feel. Sometimes they hear agony so unbearable that their minds block it out. You hear that sound, you know something terrible has happened. Someone has suffered an unsurvivable wound. Screaming like an uncontained blaze that obliterates everything. Sometimes you must close your ears and eyes to it, you must close your heart to it if you are to survive yourself.

That's what Julian had to do when he heard the soul-piercing cries of Ava McKenzie. She was held back by four officers who were trying to stop her from running out into the street and flinging herself to the pavement where a motionless Josephine lay, her red beret having rolled away, twisted in a pool of her own blood, her eyes open to the sky.

Part Two

The Tiger Catcher

"As your days are, so shall your strength be."
Deuteronomy 33:25

20

Klonopin

HELP ME, PLEASE. THAT'S WHAT JULIAN KEPT WHISPERING AS he crawled around the floor, desperately searching for a stray pill that might've gotten lost in a dark corner.

The barely furnished room on Hermit Street he rented from Mrs. Pallaver was small—a sink, a twin bed, a dresser (a bathroom down the hall). The cross of Christ on the wall. The cross had fallen down; rather, it kept falling down despite the efforts of his chipper landlady who would arrive weekly, hammer in hand, and try to nail that pesky cross into the beam.

Comedy or tragedy. It's important to know what your life is. When the gods at last reveal the beast inside, will you be laughing or crying against the ominous skies? Are you smug or melancholy in your fatuous self-pity, craven or fearless, vivid or gray?

Tonight, as he skulked on the floor, Julian concluded his life was a farce. He couldn't even rise to the comic depths of fat and vain Falstaff. He was the bitter and brainless Lavache, the Bard's least funny drunk. He was the anointed fool a writer swiped out of his final masterpiece. Case in point: he crept around the room, feeling blindly for a stray bit of dusty alchemy. That's where his magic lay nowadays, in the floorboards. Instead of sleeping, nothing but a buffoon on his knees in the middle of the night in purgatory, in a ceaseless refrain, saying please, praying please.

But then!

He found one round beige pill with a big K carved out, tucked away near the iron leg of the bed frame. Julian cried out from relief. He chewed the pill dry, threw off his clothes, fell naked on the bed, and waited on his back, eyes to the ceiling, until it kicked in. It was impossible to ignore that he only found the tablet because he was down on his knees, his forehead to the floor.

Klonopin.

Amen.

Finally he slept.

And when he slept, he dreamed of Josephine.

All clenched up, he sits in a chair at a bistro table on a wide sunny street. It's a modern city, yet there's something old in it. It's not L.A. The time feels like half an hour past the rush of lunch. A cup of coffee stands on the table. The cup is full and cold. He hasn't touched it. He never does.

He sits and he waits.

There she is. Gliding toward him.

Her dress shimmers. In her swinging hands is a pink umbrella. The red beret is on her head, tilted to the side. She wears it rain or shine. Even when it clashes with her outfit, she wears it. She used to say that a red beret went with everything.

Even a funeral, Josephine? he wants to ask.

In the dream, she waves to him, her fingers splayed, a jazz hand. She floats forward, joyous and smiling, as if she's got news she can't wait to tell him.

And despite what he knows, he can't help himself, he smiles back and for a moment feels happy, even though he is so afraid it feels like he's falling headfirst from the sky.

She is wholly herself, as he had once known her. He can hear her heels click on the pavement, beats of time on his heart. The dream is so real, it feels almost like a memory. Everything in it is as it should be, and she is alive and bouncy walking beaming in another country.

Julian thrashes about in what passes for real life.

He wakes before she reaches his table.

He always wakes before she reaches his table.

He doesn't know how it ends.

The dream is all he has.

∞

In the morning the phone rang. It was Ashton. Julian was late for work because he had spent hours calling around for a new doctor.

"Happy birthday, dude," Ashton said. "You forgot to pick us up from Heathrow."

Julian stirred. "Really?"

"It's not even fun. Look up. The word 'gullible' is written on your ceiling. Relax. There was no way I was counting on you for pick-up in your current condition."

"What condition is that, Ash?"

"Deranged. So listen," Ashton said, "I prefer to surprise you with my exceptional party planning, but I'm afraid if I'm too coy, you won't show up. Do you want to meet us at Trafalgar on King's Road? It's a beaut of a pub."

"Who's us? You mean just you and Riley, right?"

"What, if you don't like my answer, you won't come? Fuck you."

"Not the Trafalgar," Julian said. "It's too crowded on Thursday nights. And you can't reserve a table."

"How do you know? Well, I tried reserving our usual spot at the Counting House but some asshole got there first. Any other ideas?"

"The Blind Beggar on Cheapside. Or the White Crow in Covent Garden."

"White Crow. Seven sharp. And please—this time show up to your own fucking party."

Ashton hung up before Julian could defend himself with lies.

It was true, last year when they flew in for his birthday he'd been wandering and lost track of time. "For an entire weekend?" Ashton had hollered.

Longer than that, my friend. Longer than that.

Built unplanned over two thousand years, London is seventy square miles of swampy flatlands sprawled across two banks of a great winding river. In the worn Mephistos he'd brought with him from West Hollywood where they received considerably less use, Julian has walked north and south, east and west— through Smithfields and the Strand, from Pimlico to Poultry, from Mansion House to Marble Arch, to all the gates, Aldgate to Newgate, Ludgate to Cripplegate, and every crevice and alley in between—looking for the café with a small round table and a metal chair at which he could sit and order coffee and wait for noon.

He has been up and down the city so many times the geography of the streets has wound itself into his muscle memory. He is acquainted with every fish and chip shop and bookstore from Wapping to Westbourne Green. In Marylebone and Fitzrovia, the cafés look as if some of their windows might be tall enough to reflect a whole red bus in them. He has spent so long around Baker Street that the manager of Prét à Manger started greeting him by name. Every time Julian is on Baker Street, he wants to knock on number 2-2-1-B and inquire if for a small fee (or what was left of his life savings) a certain opium smoking gentleman might help him find what is missing.

To disguise himself today, on the anniversary of his distant birth, Julian shaved off his beard—three months' worth of mangy unchecked growth—for the first time since Ashton's last visit. He dressed in something that looked chosen with care. Here was his dilemma. For the new doctor he needed to be dressed like a bum in need of help. But for a birthday bash thrown in his honor, he needed to look as if he wasn't falling apart. Masquerade on all sides, yet only one man. But true to both versions of himself and hard to hide: whatever the cosplay, a strung-out Julian stumbled around like a zombie from Night of the Living Dead.

Before, when he was mainlining Klonopin, nothing got through. The drug allowed him to get up and go to work and pretend to function. But in the last few months—as his supply was threatened and then dwindled—he started getting to work later, looking worse, taking more days off, writing fewer headlines, forgetting captions and display copy, noticing fewer missed commas, all his knotted-up Klonopin-(barely)maintained order uncoiling into madness.

He would've taken today off, but though it was only March, he had no more days to take. And if he didn't show up, he might be fired. Hard to maintain the fiction you're doing fine if things are so out of control that you're getting sacked on your birthday.

He just needed a new script, and then he'd be fine.

The tube was barely moving. Julian lived near Angel and worked near Austin Friars. It took him over an hour to get to work. It would've been quicker to walk. He barely had time to hang up his coat before his manager appeared at his desk. "Oh, your highness! So *kind* of you to drop by." Graham Parry hated Julian. "My office. One minute."

"You've shaved, well done," Sheridan whispered, a punctual British lass with moist bedroom eyes and buttoned-up, overly snug blazers. "But you're still in trouble."

"Not on my birthday," Julian said.

"Just tell him you had a doctor's appointment," Sheridan said with unhelpful snark. "For you, doctor's appointments are like the American Express card. There's no spending limit."

"Funny."

"Who's being funny?"

He would've used the doctor as an excuse for being late this morning; trouble was, he was using it as an excuse for ducking out this afternoon.

Graham popped his head out. "Julian—now."

Under the glaring fluorescent lights, from behind the Formica desk, Graham stared at Julian for so long, it bordered on physical aggression. Graham was short of neck and stocky of shoulder. The recession of his inadequate lower jaw was matched only by the unnatural protuberance of his massive forehead and skull.

Today the unsightly veins in his temples were throbbing. Julian was going to sit down but thought better of it. Combat required your standing attention.

"Are you or are you not my senior staff editor?" Graham said.

"I am. Sorry, chief."

"Were you too *busy* to come to work this morning?"

Julian worked at Nextel, a local wire news agency, owned and run by one Michael Bennett, father of one Ashton Bennett. "I didn't feel well. It won't happen again. What's going on?"

In disgust Graham slapped a piece of copy on his desk. "Did you write this headline?"

Julian glanced at it. "What's wrong with it?"

"Look at it! Do I have to remind you that you're not writing for *The Onion?* GEORGE LUCAS GIVES FANS SNEAK PEEK AT HYPERREALISTIC ALIEN GENITALS."

"Seems all right to me," Julian said. "Clever. Informative."

"What the fuck do genitals have to do with the created universe?" Graham yelled.

Julian stared blankly into Graham's pulsing face. "You're kidding, right?"

Graham slapped another article on his desk. "And this? You think this is acceptable? ON MOTHER'S ADVICE WOMAN USES POTATO AS A CONTRACEPTIVE—AND ROOTS BEGIN GROWING."

"You want better headlines, give me better stories," Julian said. "I'm reactive. I write the headline for the news that's given me." THE WORLD, AND EVERYTHING THAT'S IN IT, IS IN HELL. NEWS AT ELEVEN.

"AUSTRALIAN ARMY VEHICLE DISAPPEARS!"

"It went missing after being painted with camouflage," Julian said. "You think I was out of line *there?*"

"BUGS FLYING AROUND WITH WINGS ARE FLYING BUGS!"

"Did you *read* that story?" Julian said. So now it was his fault the news was crap? He took a breath and stepped back. "You're right. I'll do better. But can we pick this up later? I've got to run out for a few minutes. Doctor's appointment."

Graham jumped up. "No! You just got here. Our new fashion section needs editor assignments and four display captions. I've got twenty gen-news stories going out without headlines. A woman fell to her death after her boyfriend proposed on the edge of a cliff!"

"There's your headline," Julian said. "You hardly need me."

"This is bullshit. Make your appointments after work."

"I can't tonight, it's my birthday."

"I don't give a shit."

"We're meeting up for a drink. Even you."

"Reschedule the doctor."

"I can't." Julian needed more magic beans. He was certain the one he found yesterday was the last bit of grace he'd been given.

"Well, I can't run my news division because you're never here."

"Sheridan will help you."

"It's *your* fucking job!" Graham said. "Sheridan is busy fixing the typos you missed. And if Sheridan can do it, then what, pardon me for asking, is the point of *you*?"

"Good question. Let's talk about it this afternoon."

"Julian, if you leave, I'm warning you, that's it. You're done. I don't care who you know."

But Graham was shouting it into Julian's back, who had grabbed his coat and was already headed for the stairs, hearing a hyperventilating Graham running behind him. "Don't you dare walk out of this office! Do you hear me? Don't you dare!"

Julian heard him. Even on the street, Julian heard him.

His head was throbbing. He stopped in a leafless square a few blocks away and sank down. He couldn't walk anymore, couldn't see. His chest was tight. Which way the tube? Which train to Peckham? Poor Ashton, who had swallowed his pride, called his dad, and got Julian a job in a foreign country. What if after the blowup with Graham, Julian would be forced to confess to his friend the reason for the desperate lunchtime visit to a private doctor across the river? Confess that he couldn't live without an anti-psychotic drug, the withdrawal from which makes people hang themselves in their backyards on balmy Sunday afternoons.

21

The Apothecary

LONDON WAS DRIZZLY AND CHILLY IN THE MIDDLE OF MARCH, especially south of the river. Everything was worse south of the river.

Julian banged on the front door until the doctor, a James Weaver, unlocked it.

"Can I help you?"

"Julian Cruz. We had an appointment."

"Mr. Cruz, our appointment was for twelve-thirty. It's nearly four. Where have you been?"

"I got lost." He had no idea where the time had gone, where he had been.

"Well, my office closes soon, and I'm with my last patient."

"I'll wait."

"I'm sorry, Mr. Cruz, was I not clear? Last patient. Call and reschedule."

"No," Julian said. "I mean—please no."

"I'm with a..."

"I need your help," Julian said. "Are you going to turn me away? I'll wait. I'll do what it takes. Whatever it takes." He stood like a post until the man waved him in.

Weaver worked at a Health and Wellness Center in the warehouses behind Peckham. In the old days, Peckham was a place no Londoner who valued his life went. Peckham entered the British lexicon just before the war, when all the school age children were taught to "pray for Peckham." And now Peckham was where it was at, where the hip private doctors worked in flash remodeled spaces.

There was no specific reason Julian had picked this doctor other than this was the doctor who could see him today. Most important, when Julian stated that he needed a new prescription for a schedule C drug, the receptionist didn't hang up.

Everything smelled of fresh paint. Impatiently Julian waited in the peach-colored room with shiny metal furniture. He drank some orange-flavored water from the cooler. He leafed through a coffee-table book on the history of British mercantile trade. He checked his watch half a dozen times to see how long it had been. Despite hearty denials to Ashton, this is how Julian knew he wasn't well. He couldn't tell how much time was passing between seconds.

Julian should've used his time more wisely. For example, he might've considered figuring out how to answer some of the doctor's inevitable questions. Even if it was just to cover his own ass, the doc might reasonably ask, um, *why* do you need Klonopin, Mr. Cruz?

Just as Julian was getting exasperated, even though it had been only fourteen minutes and he was over three hours late, the office door opened and the doctor motioned him in.

Weaver was a small nervous man with a notepad. His eyes were too close together. At certain angles he appeared cross-eyed and hook-nosed. Julian perched on the edge of the couch, trying not to stare at the man's prominent proboscis.

Sure enough, Weaver asked him questions.

Julian Cruz. Thirty-three years old. Born, raised, educated, residing in California. Correction: residing temporarily in London. Mother still alive. Father also. Five brothers. No, he didn't smoke. Drank recreationally.

The doctor glanced at his legal pad.

Julian corrected himself. "Thirty-four today."

"Happy birthday. What have you been doing in London?"

"Working."

"What do you do?"

"I'm a headline editor." Julian hoped that was still true. That he wasn't an unemployed headline editor.

The doctor wasn't impressed. "I didn't know that was a job. Let's hear a sample headline."

Julian tried not to sigh. "POPSTAR CONTINUES PERFORMING FOR 49 MINUTES AFTER BEING BITTEN BY COBRA BEFORE COLLAPSING AND DYING ON STAGE." He shivered.

"Are you cold? The heat is on."

"No." Time's a-ticking. Julian wanted to script and scram. He had a party to get to.

The doctor studied him, but he had nothing on Julian who had become quite the expert at pretending he could withstand all kinds of scrutiny. Except for an odd twitch in his cheek, a twitch he had trouble controlling since drastically reducing his Klono intake, Julian was a model of serenity. With a carefully placed hand he hid his herky-jerky face and, to lighten the mood, offered the doctor another headline. "How about... THE SCIENCE BEHIND HITLER'S POSSIBLE MICROPENIS."

"Better. Shorter." Weaver allowed himself a small smile in return. "How long have you been in London?"

"A few months." Julian corrected himself for the third time off the doctor's silence. "Six months."

Weaver studied him cross-eyed. "This morning I received your records from Dr. Fenton, your National Health doctor," Weaver said. "You've been in London eighteen months, Mr. Cruz."

Julian said nothing. What he was thinking was, *it can't be!* But he said nothing.

For long seconds the doctor also said nothing. "So what have you been doing in London for a year and a half?" Weaver asked.

Julian's been making the time fly. One Sunday, after having coffee at Victoria, he decided to take a ride to the country. Little did he know that the train terminated at Bromley because the

British liked to repair the rail tracks on their day of rest. The remainder of the trip to Dover would be by bus. Julian didn't have the stomach for a bus, so he switched platforms and waited for the train back. He waited over two hours. The clock told him. By the time he got back, it was ten at night.

That was Julian's momentous weekend excursion. He would've mentioned it to the good doctor today as an example of the kinds of things he did during his five hundred days in London, but what if Weaver followed up with a question about the seaside? What plausible genuine detail could Julian offer about Dover? If only he had looked online for a war museum there. He and the good doctor could've talked about the war. The British liked to talk about that.

What about the other 499 days? Could a rational man confess to a consumptive obsession with looking for a street in his dream and still be considered rational?

Julian had never seen lanes and courts as they had in London. A road would begin north, a narrow path with no stores, and widen into a six-lane boulevard with monuments in the parks and museums in the squares, before meandering like a river, south and west, doubling up on itself, one way, two way, past shops and outdoor vendors, ending seven miles east in a village green.

The grande dame of them all was Cheapside, the most ancient and noble of London's streets. It was formed a millennium ago in the walled City near the Bank of England, where the magnificent goldsmiths once plied their trade, and ran through central London, becoming Holborn, then High Holborn, then Oxford Street. It breezed by as Hyde Park Place, Bayswater Road, Holland Park Avenue, Stamford Brook Road, and Bath Road— ending abruptly on Chiswick Common. From the goldsmiths of Cheapside near the greatest financial institution in the world to the Puff and Stuff newsagents twelve miles away, that was London in microcosm.

And Julian had walked it all.

What could he tell the doctor? Near the Tower of London, there was a shop that sold strong drink and chips with vinegar. Julian could smell the rising swampy scent of the Thames as he sat outside in the drizzle, watching the noisy crows. He could tell you nothing about the interior of the Barbican or Westminster Abbey, but boy did he know where to get a crappy cup of coffee. He must have walked a thousand miles in his worn-out shoes looking for the thing that didn't exist. Immense London, where in the course of two millennia, a thousand souls became a million became ten million, and for the last eighteen months of this sliver of eternity, Julian had failed to discover if Josephine's soul was one of them.

He wasn't gaunt from grief. He was whittled away by pounding the pavements of an ageless city.

"Mr. Cruz? What's happening?"

Julian blinked. "Nothing. Everything's fine."

"Well, you've been catatonic and rocking for five minutes, so everything does not look fine."

"I'm good." Julian steeled his back. He hadn't been rocking, had he?

"I asked you what you've been doing, and you slumped and disappeared, Mr. Cruz." Weaver glanced into his pad. "You already have a regular National Health doctor. And Dr. Fenton, is free, so to speak."

"I'm trying someone new. Paying for someone private. I'm trying you," Julian said.

"I hope I can help. Why are you here?"

Julian didn't want to downplay it since he was here asking for *Klonopin*, not Advil, but at the same time he didn't want to seem desperate. "I need a script for Klonopin—clonazepam," he blurted. Just like that. No point beating around the bush. Time was short, the medic far from the White Crow.

"That's a serious drug. Addiction is common, withdrawal is physically and mentally debilitating. Have you taken it before?"

"What does it say in my notes?"

The doctor looked up. Julian abated. "I mean yes. Yes, I've taken it before."

"How long for?"

"Just a few—"

"I don't recommend being on it longer than seven days," Weaver said. "Ten days *max*."

Julian had come to the wrong doctor. He knew that now—too late. This was true of so many things in his life. He learned—oh he learned—but too late. "That's fine," he said. "Ten days will be fine." He'd find someone else.

"Ten days *total*."

Julian had been on Klonopin a *lot* longer than ten days total. And the National Health info didn't include a script from his doctor in West Hollywood, and another from a doctor in Beverly Hills. And from one in Simi Valley.

"Without it, I can't get out of bed in the morning," Julian said, making an effort not to turn his body inward. "I can't get on with my day. Klonopin helps."

"What about therapy?"

"Klonopin is what helps."

"Why did you start taking it in the first place? What happened?"

"Nothing." Julian made a superhuman effort to keep his hands relaxed. "I can't sleep. I can't calm down." He knew it seemed as if none of what he was saying was true. Outwardly, Julian displayed the most casual exterior, the most placid, stoic, nothing's bothering me exterior. His poker body was spectacular. This helped him in fights and interviews, on first dates and with eulogies.

But it wasn't helping him now.

Julian knew he looked like a man who needed a shot of adrenaline through the heart, not a sedative. "The girl I was going to marry was killed the day before our wedding." He didn't look at the doctor as he spoke.

"My condolences. When did this happen? Back in L.A.?" The doctor was respectfully silent. At first. "Mr. Cruz..." Weaver lowered his voice. "Answer me truthfully, how *long* have you been on Klonopin? Not...since she died, right?" The doctor gasped that out, as if not only could he not believe it, but felt himself under threat of a malpractice suit for even asking the question.

"No, no," Julian hastened to reply. "Of *course* not. On and off."

"It's wreaked havoc on people. Ruined their lives."

"Not me." You can't ruin Carthage, Dresden, Troy. Not twice.

"Out of control electrical impulses, insomnia, drowsiness. Cognitive difficulties, panic, paralysis."

"Not me."

"Muscle spasms, cramps, drooling mouth, dry mouth. Weight loss, weight gain. Loss of balance, of coordination."

"Not me."

"Death," Weaver said.

They were silent.

"Not me." Barely a voice.

"Visions? Hallucinations?"

Maybe that. "I don't have a problem with it. Really," Julian said.

"So why don't you get it from Dr. Fenton?"

Julian stayed quiet.

"Are you doctor shopping, Mr. Cruz?"

"Of course not."

"Because that's a serious crime."

"That's a serious charge, Dr. Weaver, and no, I'm not."

"So what *are* you doing?"

Clearly Julian was doctor shopping. Why even ask?

"I understand what happened to you back then," Weaver said, with an almost compassionate tone. Almost. Except for the word *then*. As if, well, it was back *then*. Like in the *past*. Over and done with. Why the malingering? "But what about *now*?"

"I'm not doing so great, doc. Can't you tell?"

After she died, Julian developed cotton mouth, a perpetual case of dry mouth that got so bad that when he was home he could make it better only by constantly sucking on a rag soaked in lemon water. And he was always home. For months after, he was frozen cold. He was cold until he left for London. When Ashton later told him that Los Angeles had gone through the worst heatwave and drought in seventy years, Julian didn't believe it. "Every day above a hundred," Ashton said. "All the reservoirs have dried up."

Because of the potent cocktail of these separate but related things—the chewing on rags, the shivering under blankets, the deadening nature of the anti-psychotic drugs, mixed in with bottom-dwelling depression and sleeping like a sick lion, and then the sudden move to London—time both stood still for Julian and ran amok.

He looked away from Weaver's gaze as he tried to beat the chaos inside his head into shape, make words out of muck, words that would get him the script he needed in the next seventeen minutes before his time was up. *Like her time was up. Did she have seventeen minutes before her time was up?*

"I haven't been on Klonopin for a few months." He'd been rationing himself, half a pill, a quarter. Like in a war.

"What have you been taking instead?"

"Ambien. Xanax. They don't help. Only Klonopin helps. I have these…" Julian broke off.

The doctor waited. "What?" he said. "Seizures? Visions?"

"No."

"Klonopin is an insanity maker, Mr. Cruz. I don't prescribe it to my patients unless I've tried them on everything else first."

"Doctor, but I have"—Julian paused to get his voice less strident—"I *have* tried everything else first." Julian didn't know what else to do, so he told the doctor the truth. He put on truth to see how it fit. "When I take Klonopin, I have a recurring dream of her."

"Like a nightmare?"

"No." Real life was a nightmare. "Like a..." Julian didn't know what to call it.

"Is this something you want?"

"Yes." More than everything.

The doctor pushed further. "If you don't mind me asking, how did she die?"

Julian's voice dropped to the back of his throat. He didn't look up.

"You don't have to tell me," Weaver said. "That's fine. Is that why you left L.A.? A change of scenery? You figured if you were in a new place, the dreams would stop?"

"No," said Julian. "Just the opposite."

Weaver said something trite, a non-sequitur. "Many grieving people dream about their lost loved ones. It's very common. I wouldn't worry about it."

"I'm not worried," Julian said. "But I'm trying to tell you something important, doc, and you're not..."

"The nightmares will go away. As soon as you wean off Klonopin, they'll go away for good."

Wean *off* Klonopin? Was Weaver crazy?

"Here's what I wonder." Julian rubbed his hands together, rubbed his knees. "What if what I'm seeing is not a dream but a premonition?"

"What do you mean, premonition?"

"Not all dreams are just dreams, right?" Julian said. "I've had disturbing dreams before." Brutally disturbing. But he'd been in a coma at the time so it didn't count. "But not like this. Isn't it possible that what I'm having is a"—Julian searched for the right word. He didn't like the way Weaver was staring at him—"a mystical experience?"

There was a long pause. "You think you've been having a mystical experience on *Klonopin*?" Weaver couldn't keep the ridicule out of his voice.

"Like an out-of-body experience, yes. It's possible, isn't it?" Julian became animated, more agitated than he felt in months, more elevated than at any time during the previous hour. "What if I'm having some kind of a transcendental projection? In the next realm, she comes to me, and I'm restored. She is not alive in spirit, doc. She's *alive* in flesh! As if I'm actually seeing her. It doesn't feel like a dream." Julian's mouth was dry. "It feels like a curtain is being raised for me on another world."

Incredulous silence ticked by.

Julian swallowed. "Maybe *love* is a consecrating bridge," he said. "Maybe that's what allows the veil to lift and the gaping chasm between life and death to close."

Weaver rocked back in his chair. "I don't know what to say, Mr. Cruz. Honestly. You've stumped me."

"I've never lived anywhere but around L.A.," Julian said. "I've never been outside the U.S. I haven't personally seen the buildings and streets in my vision. She's walking down a street I've never been on and don't recognize." *A street I can't find, though God knows I've tried.*

"Well, it is a *dream,*" Weaver said. Putting emphasis on the word Julian thought at any moment the doctor would start to define for him. You see, young man, a dream is a sequence of mental images during something we human beings like to call sleep. Sometimes these images are bizarre. Like you.

"You think it's the drugs?"

"I don't think it. I know it."

"But before I knew what happened to her," Julian said, "I saw her." He told Weaver about the apparition on Melrose, outside Coffee Plus Food. "How do you explain that? I wasn't on Klonopin then, and yet there she was. Walking toward me. Smiling. Alive." He stared down into the red and black color-block carpet.

Weaver folded his hands. "So why in the *world* would you want to continue to relive what sounds like the worst day of your life? You *are* trying to feel better, aren't you? To start fresh?"

"No," Julian said.

"Perhaps that's your problem."

"You know what my problem is? She is *dead*." Julian couldn't leave it alone because the lost girl kept calling for him. "And yet she is alive in my dream. Alive in *London*. As if she has summoned me here to search for her."

"Why would she do that?"

"If I knew, I wouldn't be sitting here talking to you. I'd be out there, looking for her."

Weaver spoke slowly and quietly as if to a mental patient with a history of violence. "Dreams are complicated things, Mr. Cruz. In psychotherapy, we are still trying to figure out the mechanism by which we dream, and what those visions mean."

"And yet you're telling me *I'm* the one without answers?"

"Clearly you don't have the answers."

"Neither do you. Will you at least allow that what I'm saying is possible?"

"No," Weaver said.

"No? Same moving image over and over, take after take, night after night, unchanging? You don't think that's strange?"

"There are so many things that are strange, I don't know where to begin. What are you doing in the dream?"

"Sitting," Julian replied. "Waiting for her."

That he was waiting for her was indisputable. But why?

Was it to recreate what had already happened?

Or...

Or was it to create something new?

Julian couldn't accept that there was no answer. Why was the doctor not getting it? Almost deliberately. *I'm trying to right a wrong,* Julian wanted to say but couldn't confess to a cold face. *A horror has happened for which I have only myself to blame. I can't let it go. And it can't let go of me.*

"What makes you think it's London?"

Julian didn't want to admit it to the reluctant drug dealer across from him, but when Josephine first started appearing to him in his sleep a few weeks after she died, he had also reacted poorly. He tried talking about it to his family, to Ashton, and then stopped. There was no point. No one got it, not even him.

Julian stopped talking about it, but he also stopped working. No more hacks, no more newsletters, no more getting up at dawn, no more walking around L.A., searching for funny advice on the easy street of life, no more website, no more Lonely Hearts. He sold his Volvo. He dropped weight—like it was an activity. He went vegetarian, then vegan, then off all food entirely. He stopped leaving his house, let the hair grow wild. He took a razor to it, became bald and bare skinned like a neo-Nazi convict with hollowed-out sockets for eyes and a Frankenstein scar on his head. Everyone panicked. Ashton moved in with him. His mother made the three-hour round trip every day from Simi Valley to bring him homemade food he didn't eat. Ashton ate it. He gained twenty pounds while Julian remained under a 24-hour suicide watch, five minutes away from being involuntarily institutionalized.

After weeks went by and he didn't die, Julian started looking inside the dream for clues. In it, the sidewalk was wet, like it had been raining. Not very L.A. He was waiting for her in a jacket. Perhaps it wasn't warm. Yet she was in a summer dress. It wasn't the dress she had died in. She died in solid yellow. Who knew that yellow was the color of death?

Julian did. He knew it.

On her head was the red beret. That's another reason it seemed more than a memory. Because in the bygone of what happened, the hat had fallen where she had fallen and got kicked away by medics and hysterics. Julian bowed down at the curb to pick it up. It was soaked with her blood. He slept with the beret now, under his pillow.

"She's carrying an umbrella," Julian finally replied to the doctor's question. "No one carries an umbrella in L.A."

"From this you got London? It could be Seattle. You could be in the wrong rainy city."

Julian nodded. The doctor was mocking him. Well, Julian could mock right back. He used to be a pro at that, before life sucked all joy out of him. He and Ashton used to be quite a stand-up act, Abbott and Costello, Laurel and Hardy, two Marx Brothers, loudest and brightest in all the bars, there all week long and twice on Sunday. "Well, doctor," Julian said. "I'm glad we both agree that I should've gone *somewhere*. So you and I are just arguing whether or not I'm in the right city?"

"No, no," Weaver said hastily. "That's not what I meant."

Julian choked down his aggravation. "Look, since I'm in *this* city, can we accept that I've already solved the geographic conundrum. Harrod's green bag. A red bus. A black cab. The most important part of what I'm telling you is that I've never been to London and neither had she. So—here I am."

"Is that what you've been doing for a year and a half?" Weaver said with concern in his voice. "Wandering around London, looking for this...café?" Spoken in a tone of someone who thought Julian was searching for a blessing of unicorns.

"No." Julian was defiant. Good thing he knew not to fidget. For many years he had cultivated an image of himself as a casual man, slightly bored with life, barely paying attention, a thin polite smile on his face, ready to make some jokey aside. Ashton used to tease him for this; he said content would soon follow form. Ashton was right. Content did follow form. Julian didn't give a rat's ass about anything anymore. Except Klonopin. Except the dream.

"Here's what I need you to explain to me," Weaver said. "Let's say you're right and this dream does take place in London. So what?"

"Maybe she's trying to tell me something."

"Yes—to get on with your life."

How banal.

"Does she ever get to your table?" Weaver asked.

Julian shook his head. "But it *feels* as if she's hurrying because she can't wait to get to me."

"That's terrible." Weaver leaned forward. "I mean that sincerely. It's terrible what you've been through. But drugs are not the answer. Let me help you—"

"Yes, by giving me Klonopin."

"Klonopin is what's wrong with you."

"*When, on this stream of darkened love, once more the light shall gleam?*" Julian said, quoting he didn't know who or what.

The doctor stared—puzzled? Troubled? And Julian glared back at him like the doctor was the one who was nuts. "*When?*" Weaver repeated, frowning. "Never, Mr. Cruz. That's when. *Never.* Your fiancée is gone. Not gone to another country, like England, or another city, like London. Gone, like dead and gone."

"So explain the dream to me."

"It's a *dream!*" Weaver yelled. Nice. Julian had managed to provoke the licensed professional into acting irrationally. Beautiful. "People dream all kinds of crazy things," the doctor continued in a (slightly) lower voice.

"Are you calling me crazy, Dr. Weaver?"

"I misspoke. Do you know what's not a dream? The reality of your present existence."

"I'm dreaming of her in *London,*" Julian said, "and you are talking to me about reality? Are you listening to yourself?"

"Are you listening to *your*self? So what if it's London?" Weaver was deeply agitated. *He* was fidgeting! "You saw the street set in a movie. You used to live and work in the capital of the entertainment industry. You must've been entertained by one or two films set in *London,* no?"

Julian gave the anger right back. "What else do you do if not interpret dreams and write drug scripts? If you can't do one of those two things, what good are you and your fancy degrees on the wall?"

"Julian, listen to me. Clonazepam has harmed your brain's neuroreceptors. It has given you deep and troubling hallucinations. Stop the drug and you will feel better. It's that simple."

"It's simple, is it?"

"Like child's play. Cause and effect. In your present state, do you even know the difference between dream and reality? I suspect you do not."

"Do *you*?"

"This isn't about me!"

"Here's what I can't seem to make *you* understand," Julian said, his fists clenched to his chest, his elbows out. "I came to London because of this dream. I'm only here in front of you, which I assume *you* think is reality, because of this dream. I had one life, I met her, she died, I came here. It's not a correlation or a coincidence. It's cause and effect. You were just talking about it as if you knew what it was. A consequence. An action and reaction. I came to London to find her." Julian rocked back.

"*Find* her?" Weaver exhaled in disbelief. "But she's *dead*, Julian."

"Then explain why she keeps appearing to me entirely alive."

Doc pummeled into silence. Bout to Julian.

After a few moments, Weaver took out his prescription pad. His fingers trembled. "I'm going to recommend a convalescent facility," he said in a flat voice. "It's in North London. Hampstead Heath. It's a wonderful place. I send many of my patients there. Patients like you."

"Oh, now you have many patients like me," Julian said. "A minute ago, you said you'd never seen my symptoms."

Weaver shook his head. And shook it and shook it. "So many like you. People who can't cope. Your reality has been distorted by the drug. One of the most serious side effects of Klonopin is that it stops you from going through the five stages of grief. Which means it stops you from getting better. You feel nothing, yes, but when you stop taking it, it's as if you've been thrown into a time warp. Emotionally you're back at ground zero—as if she died just yesterday. The whole process of healing must begin anew. If that's not *hell*," Weaver said with a shudder, "hell has no meaning."

Julian shuddered himself. "So why would I ever want to stop taking it?"

"Because you can't be on it forever."

"Why not?"

"Because you will die."

Julian laughed, a shrill mirthless cackle.

Weaver struggled for words. "I know it doesn't seem like it now, uh, but you still have a lot to live for. Hampstead Heath—"

"What's your looney bin going to do for me?" Julian said. "The girl I was going to marry was murdered the day before our wedding. Not was killed. Not died. Was *murdered*." Julian groaned in agony. In the middle of her life. In the middle of mine. "Is it going to help me with that?"

To his small credit, Weaver tripped on his words. "Yes—uh—yes, it will teach you to move on."

"As if something could."

"You have a psychoactive disorder that has gravely impaired your functioning."

"Psychoactive disorder meaning grief?"

"Meaning addiction to a controlled substance. You're in withdrawal. You haven't gotten anywhere near grief yet."

"You think I haven't gotten anywhere near grief?" Julian said in a low voice.

"Why did you stop going to Dr. Fenton? He's a very good doctor."

"How do you know?" Both Julian and Weaver fell silent. "Do you know him?" The doctor didn't reply. "After I made the appointment this morning, did you call him? Did you...*talk* to him about me?"

"Yes, but—wait!"

Julian bolted from the couch, Weaver from his chair.

"Julian, please. You are *ill*. You have pathological delusions of a deeply disturbing nature. This is not something that will go away on its own."

"You are *some* piece of work," Julian said, heading for the door.

"Did you want me to condescend to you by pretending your delusions are real?"

"What, you think you *haven't* been condescending?"

"I can't give you addictive and brain-altering medication to humor you."

"Before I stepped into your second-rate office, you had already made up your mind about me," Julian said. "You're a charlatan. You know nothing except names of the drugs you refuse to prescribe. You can't *do* a single fucking thing to help a single fucking human being."

"I can't give you Klonopin, no matter what words you use," Weaver said. "You're fragile and unstable. You've been sitting in front of me desperately trying to control your neuroleptically induced involuntary motility. You only think you've been motionless. You haven't stopped banging your knees and tapping your feet and rocking from side to side. Your hands haven't stopped twitching, especially your right. You're also presenting certain signs of abnormal posturing, which signals to me a possible brain trauma. I'm very concerned for you. You can't wean off the drug on your own. You need to be under strict supervision. My job is to keep you safe."

There was a moment—after the first moment Julian saw her dead but before the rest of his life—when there was nothing but deafening silence around him. In theatre they called the mute pantomime a *dumbshow*. It was as if he'd fallen into a black hole and kept falling. He could hear nothing. He didn't know what was happening to him, barely knew what had happened to her, but when the sound returned, he was being dragged away, his body was being dragged away, his legs folding under him, the shoes scuffling against the asphalt, the shirt yanked out of his pants, his fingers clutching her bloodied beret. But Julian hadn't been in his body when it was happening. He was outside, looking uselessly in.

That's where he still was, outside of everything, staring in.

"Keep *me* safe?" Julian said. "And who kept her safe? Middle of the day. Lunchtime. Was *she* safe? She wasn't on Klonopin, that's for sure."

"I'm very sorry. Please let me help you."

"You can't help me find a fucking cab."

"You're looking for a fix, but I'm trying to save your life. Our time is up, but come back and see me, yes? In how many days can you come back?"

"One." Julian stormed out, holding up a single finger as a reply and a goodbye—the middle one.

22

Waterloo

WHAT WAS JULIAN GOING TO DO?

He marched with all the defiance and terror of a soldier at war. He would find another doctor! There was one in Charing Cross! He would go back to National Health, no matter how shameful; he'd return to that smug quack, Fenton on Fenchurch. He would beg Ashton for help. Ashton had ways of getting things done. He'd get Julian a script. Or Julian himself would fly to India, buy the drug, smuggle it out in his—

Julian stopped. It was his *Midnight Express* moment. Because being in a virtual prison wasn't enough. He needed to waste away in an actual one.

Once he ran through his pauper passel of options, he slowed down until he was barely ambulatory. It was a long way from Peckham to the happy pub where his friend was waiting.

He hated Weaver, but could the schmuck be right?

What if he got the Klonopin?

What then?

What now.

What now, my love, now that you've left me.

Was Julian addicted not to grief but to prescription meds?

He dismissed the thought.

He wasn't addicted.

He definitely wasn't addicted.

Is that what all the people inside the ring said?

Except there was no outside. The ring was everything, and everything was the ring.

And inside the ring was the only thing he loved, the only thing that mattered.

Addiction: no job, no friends, no love, no sex, no connection, no anything, but the thing you crave and live for.

In the gloomy March drizzle, Julian resumed his sclerotic pace across Waterloo Bridge.

He stopped walking, looked around. He wasn't sure where he needed to be. Why was it so late, so dark? Where had the time gone? He looked at his wrist. There was no time to be gleaned from his bare wrist. He took out his phone. It was dead. He forgot to charge it. He did that a lot. Forgot his phone, his watch—the accouterments of his existence. There was no one on the bridge to ask. Did he carry an umbrella? Of course not. Black cabs and red buses swooshed past him through the puddles, their lights reflecting in the rainy air of the bleak and wasteful night.

Did he tell Ashton the Trafalgar, beautiful and blue, or the Blind Beggar on Cheapside, or the White Crow near Soho? Trafalgar off Sloane Square or White Crow on Long Acre off the Strand?

Stretching out his cold hands over the damp concrete parapet, Julian stared out onto the Thames, to Big Ben twinkling dimly in the mist, to the river promenade with the leafless oaks in front of the Savoy, the grand hotel. He wanted to scream.

Was he stuck in the past and unable to move on?

Was he going insane and the quack was right and the only thing he wanted was the last thing he needed? Or had he already gone mad and didn't know it?

A jogger dressed in black, running past, without breaking stride called out, "Don't do it, mate. She ain't worth it."

Don't worry, Julian wanted to reply. They put a high rail over Waterloo Bridge to stop you from flinging yourself into the water.

Somewhere in this town was the answer to the riddle inside him. But where, what riddle?

How could Julian answer it if he didn't even know the question?

23

White Crow

ON LONG ACRE, JULIAN STOOD IN FRONT OF THE WHITE Crow, letting others pass, door swinging open and closed, people disappearing inside. Through the panes of amber stained glass he could see a fragmented image of Ashton, blond and tall, in tailored slacks, trim white shirt, thin black tie, standing, raising a dark pint, telling a joke, laughing at his own hilarity, the Greek chorus crowded at three round tables in front of him, gazing up at him adoringly. Look at all the people Ashton had brought. Riley, two of Julian's brothers, Gwen, Zakiyyah, a contingent from Nextel. Every time the door opened there was a smell of warm lager, of old bitter, the din of happy people, a slot machine cha-chinging, counting cherries and number sevens.

Covent Garden, loud, drenched with rain. The West End shows had started, and the traffic was heavy and honking in the evening hour. The crowds from the bars and the cafes spilled out into the street, nearby drunken people cruising and cursing, one girl giddily repeating, "You did! You did! You did!" to her equally intoxicated lover who rejoined with "Never! Never! Never! All right, once, but never again!"

Whatever happened, tonight Julian had to pass muster. Because sometimes you live and not much happens to you. And other times your whole world stands teetering upside down on a head of a pin. You know it. The question is, did everybody else know it, too?

Julian could not describe how desperately he did not want to go inside, to pretend to listen, to make small talk, to answer unanswerable questions. He stood trying to spackle himself together, collecting slabs that had fractured and were now dangling off his person. He was doing it for Ashton. He forced himself to be alive for his friend. Taking a deep breath, he opened the White Crow door. Julian wasn't *in* a landslide. He was the landslide.

∞

"Julian!" Ashton bellowed, striding across the pub to greet him, nearly lifting him off his feet in a bear hug. "Finally! You're only an hour late. That's practically on time for you."

"Put me down."

Ashton commented on Julian's lack of tan ("Tan, dude? I'm in *London*"), his wet uncut hair, his soggy demeanor. "For fuck's sake. We didn't travel five thousand miles to see you mope. Buck up."

"I am bucked up." He glanced over Ashton's shoulder. "Gwen and Zakiyyah? Really?"

Ashton shrugged. "Riley insisted. They're all friends now, thanks to you."

"I had nothing to do with it."

"The more the merrier, Riley said, and I agree. You need cheering up."

"With *Zakiyyah*?"

"You're lucky your mother is not here, too." Ashton's arm remained around Julian. "Why are you pissing Graham off? At Christmas, everything seemed all right. Suddenly it's Defcon 2."

"He's such a hysteric," Julian said.

"He says you came in at noon, left twenty minutes later, and never returned."

"So? It's my birthday."

"Oh, now you care that it's your birthday," Ashton said. "He was *mad*, bro. He ambushed me on the fourth floor in front of my old man, screeching that it was either him or you. Said he couldn't run the news division with you *not* working there."

"What a whiner."

"I see you're not saying he was wrong. Well, my dad says to me, you think you can run things better than Graham, hot shot? Be my guest. He told Graham I might be his boss."

Julian homed in on Ashton's words. "Is he joking?"

"Dad's over seventy, Jules." Ashton grinned. "I should learn the business if I'm going to inherit it, don't you agree?"

Julian studied Ashton's cheerful face. His whole life Ashton had been on the outs with his father. After years of near total estrangement, he got in touch with the older Bennett only to help Julian. "Are *you* joking? Did you tell him you already have a job—in L.A.?"

"You had a job once, too, in L.A.," Ashton said. "How'd that turn out?" He prodded him forward. "Later for this bullshit. Tonight, we party. Don't say anything to Sheridan or Roger or Nigel."

"Like I would." Julian cast an eye over their group in the corner. "I see Graham didn't show up. And why'd you invite Nigel? You know I can't stand him."

"Now is *not* the time to be funny, Jules. Now's the time to fake being a normal human being. Mouth shut, smile on your face. Nice and big."

Julian smiled, imitating Ashton. Nice and big. Julian stretched his lips over his clenched teeth, lifted the corners of his mouth, and walked up to his friends, his face contorted. The Klonopin numbness wearing off wasn't helping. What a terrible way to live—to feel things.

Riley often came with Ashton when he visited Julian, the two of them spending long weekends in London clucking over Julian's apathy. Gwen looked good. Breaking up with Julian agreed with her. And Zakiyyah...well, what could he say. Gwen, okay, they'd known each other a long time and had become friends again, but only Riley would think bringing Zakiyyah to London was a good idea.

His two youngest brothers were happy to see him, a delegation from the Cruz family, and there was even a group of people from Nextel, no doubt invited by Ashton to prove to their L.A. contingent that look, Julian was doing fine, he made new friends! As if in any incarnation Julian would ever be friends with a dumb drunk like Nigel from sub-editing, who corrected men and insulted women and called both joking. Nigel was a skinny, gawky, rumple-haired, rumple-suited man with nicotine-stained teeth. His jacket smelled of old alcohol. Something about Nigel had rubbed Julian the wrong way since he first met him, back when he barely noticed other people existed. Nigel drank in tandem with his boss Roger, the manager of the sub-editing department, who was already too drunk to get up to shake Julian's hand. But while Nigel was a mean drunk, Roger was at least a jolly one. Sheridan, who was being all chummy with Nigel, didn't seem to mind that the man's flirting sounded like misogyny. As Julian neared, he overheard Nigel saying to her, "Do you know what virgins have for breakfast?" and she said, "No, what?" and he said, "Mm-hmm, just as I thought," but instead of slapping him, Sheridan hooted!

Julian hugged his brothers, waved at the Nextel people so he wouldn't have to shake Nigel's hand, and was encircled by Riley and Gwen who clucked and searched for something positive to say about his appearance. "My God, you've lost weight," said Gwen, trying to hide her shock.

"She's right, we've never seen you so thin," said Riley. "You used to love food."

Zakiyyah stood nearby, not approaching. Julian nodded to her, she nodded back; both kept their eyes averted. He didn't want to see what was on Zakiyyah's face any more than he wanted to show her what was on his.

"Your hair is getting so long," said Gwen, touching Julian's head. "That's so unlike you."

"Jules," Riley said, "next time you shave, stand a little closer to the razor, will you?" She smiled. "See, despite what Ashton thinks, I can be funny, too."

Julian actually smiled back at the coiffed and shiny Riley. "Look at how well you look," he said. "Does the London rain even fall on you?"

"Aren't you a charmer. Come here, come in for your therapeutic lean." She hugged him fondly, kissed him on both cheeks, appraised him. "Gwen, he's like this because he hasn't been listening to any of my advice."

"No, I have, I have," Julian said. "I'm eating yellow food. And purple food. And red food."

"You shouldn't be eating any yellow food, Jules," Riley said, "you've got no fire to balance against it." She rubbed Julian's unevenly shaved face. "You're pale like a haunting."

"I'm still looking for the sun."

"You know where the sun is?" Riley said. "Los Angeles."

"Time to get some beer into the man, and all will be well," Ashton said, pulling him away and sparing him a response. "My round."

"But Gwen is right, Jules," Riley said seriously, "you have to eat."

"Why?" Julian said. "You don't eat."

At the peninsula bar in the middle of the gold-lit pub, Ashton turned to Julian. "Riley is right," he said. "You look like shit."

"Come on, Ash, don't hold back." Julian turned away from Ashton's troubled gaze. They both stared at a nearby table with four young women.

Ashton gulped down a third of his pint while they waited for their drinks. "Do you see them?" he said. "One of them could be yours. Or even all of them. Maybe all at once—would you like that?" He knocked into Julian. "Smile, for fuck's sake. They're checking you out."

"Not me." Tall, lean, groomed, pressed, well-dressed, good-looking Ashton had always been a girl magnet. Except that one time at the Canon Gardens brunch.

"That's because I'm friendly and have a smile on," Ashton said. "Your woe-is-me look will get you nowhere. Even in London, where there's a paucity of available men."

"Yeah, like me."

"Why the hell would *you* be unavailable? Back on the horse, my brother. What are you waiting for? Isn't there a group for people like you?"

"What people is that, Ash?" Julian tried to sound less drained.

"You can't keep falling back on the moves you had when you were twenty, Jules," Ashton said, returning the women's inviting smiles. "You're no longer in your sexual prime."

"I have to join a group for that?"

"Join something. What are you doing with yourself? I know you're not working. And as Riley pointed out, you're definitely not eating. So what *are* you doing?"

"Nothing."

"Nigel says he keeps asking you to go for a drink and you refuse."

"Why would I want to go for a drink with that wanker?" Julian said.

"Oh, come on. You could use a friend."

"Not fucking Nigel."

"He's not so bad."

"No, not until you get to know him."

"You've never been out with him. You *don't* know him!"

"I know him superficially," Julian said, "and frankly that's plenty."

"He's nicer than he looks."

"He'd have to be, wouldn't he."

"Stop calling him fucking Nigel," Ashton said. "I'm not breaking up another fight. You'll never lick him, you're barely a flyweight these days."

"You don't agree that what fucking Nigel lacks in intelligence," Julian said, "he more than makes up for in stupidity?"

"You're ridiculous." They gathered their pints onto a tray.

"I see you didn't answer my question."

"You haven't answered any of mine for almost two years," Ashton said. "Welcome to the fucking club."

Back at the tables, Ashton thrust a menu at Julian and told him to take it to Zakiyyah, who was being held hostage by Nigel. As Julian got near, he overheard Nigel trying to coax Zakiyyah into leaving with him, and telling her she should smile more. "Oh, look," she said, actually smiling when she saw Julian, "the birthday boy himself."

"How you doing, Jules, having a good time?" Nigel said, less happy with the interruption.

"Well, I just got here," Julian said. "But yes."

He and Zakiyyah sat without speaking or opening the menus until Nigel joked himself out of the non-existent conversation and staggered off to the men's.

"What a guy," Zakiyyah said with a headshake. "His problem is he's got delusions of adequacy."

Julian almost smiled. "Ashton wants us to order." He handed her a menu. She pretended to look at it.

"How've you been, Julian, really?"

"Fine, thanks."

"Why do you never return anyone's calls or texts or emails if you're fine?"

"Don't take it personally," Julian said. "I don't even return my mother's calls."

"That's not a good thing," Zakiyyah said. "That's not an excuse."

"About the menu..." Zakiyyah was sharper dressed and more made up than she'd been in L.A., as if she was making an extra effort for Julian's birthday. She still subdued her crazy hair into a respectable twist, but the curls kept flying all over every time she moved her head. She looked like painted art—to other men perhaps. Julian could barely raise his eyes to her.

"When are you moving back home?" she asked. "It's all anyone's asking. Don't tell me you like living here."

"Yes, very much," Julian said. "Very much. Absolutely."

A frown marred Zakiyyah's face. "You can't possibly. It hasn't stopped raining since this morning."

"It hasn't stopped raining since 1940," said Julian, suddenly an expert on wet climates. Ironic, since there were decades in his life growing up in Simi Valley when he couldn't remember a single day full of rain. Not one. He wasn't saying it hadn't happened. He was saying, it wasn't in his memory, so it might as well have not happened. He sighed. What would people talk about if there was no weather?

Zakiyyah must have had a few pints already to loosen her tongue because she said, "Is London your penance?"

That wiped the fake smile off Julian's face. "I don't know what you're talking about."

"Fair enough, but why are you punishing Ashton, too? It's not *his* fault, is it, what happened? Why does he have to do penance? He's the happiest guy, and you're bringing him down, making him contemplate crazy things."

"What crazy things?" Zakiyyah came slightly into focus. She went from blurry to less blurry. Julian glanced over at Ashton, menus open, arm around Riley, joking with Tristan and Gwen.

Zakiyyah didn't answer, lowering her curly head into the nightly specials. "Ava is upset," she said. "She says you haven't called her back in months."

"Who's Ava?"

"Stop it. You know perfectly well who Ava is. Mia's mother."

Another kick in the gut. When Z called Josephine Mia, it was as if his Josephine had never existed. Something happened, but to another girl, another boy, in someone else's life. It was brutal. "Her name was Josephine," Julian muttered.

"It really wasn't, Julian," Zakiyyah said. "It really wasn't."

Julian hung his head.

"About Ava…"

It was true, he'd been avoiding Josephine's mother. The woman had got it into her head that Julian—who was about to become her son-in-law—was *actually* her son-in-law. She treated him as if they were fellow sufferers, travelers in grief. She called him bi-weekly, even in London, and when she couldn't reach him, which was all the time, she would call his mother and engage her in trying to find him.

"She asked about you at Christmas," Zakiyyah said. "She wanted to know if you got her shortbread."

"Yes. I thanked her for it. Didn't I? I meant to." Julian had given the shortbread to Mrs. Pallaver and her unmarried daughter. When would this ordeal be over. "Are you still at Normandie?" he said, to change the subject, to say something.

"Yes, because it wasn't Normandie's fault."

Oh, for sure, it wasn't *Normandie's* fault. Julian ground his teeth.

"It wasn't Normandie's fault," Zakiyyah said, "or your fault, or Ava's fault, or Poppa W's fault."

"Really? Not even his?" said Julian. "Because…no, fine. It wasn't anybody's fault." How about *your* fucking fault. "Do you know what you're having?"

"Or my fault, Julian."

"Do you know what you're having, or *what*."

"Julian, look at me."

He would not.

"Poppa W wanted me to tell you how sorry he is," Zakiyyah said gently.

"So he keeps saying."

"But you keep not hearing."

After he got out of the hospital, Poppa W came to Julian's apartment, Zakiyyah in tow, to explain, to apologize. He tried to save JoJo, he said, he really tried. He was so sorry. Blah. He loved her. Blah blah. They had a thing once, but it was over. Blah blah blah. Julian endured it catatonically, the weepy nonsense from an urban street soldier who lived and worked in a crack castle. But still—to think that Julian had been in a foursome instead of a twosome. Hard to accept. Hard to accept a lot of things.

Couldn't Zakiyyah see how much Julian didn't want to talk about it? How much he didn't want to talk about anything. And yet... "When you called her mother to rat her out about our wedding," Julian said, "did you do it to save her, too, like Poppa W? To save her from me?"

"I called her mother because I was worried *sick* about her!" Zakiyyah exclaimed. "Oh—I can't do this with you *again*, Julian. I just can't."

With amazing self-control, Julian pushed away from the table and stood up, leaning down into her upset face. He wanted to throw the table through the stained-glass window. "Then why do you keep bringing it up every five seconds?" he said through his teeth. *Every five fucking seconds.* That's how close to the surface it was, his outrage.

He felt a soothing palm on his back. Ashton stepped between them, glancing at Zakiyyah for a mute second, then turning and smiling at Julian.

"I tried, Ashton!" Zakiyyah said. "But you saw—he's impossible."

"And yet it's his birthday, so we're going to cut him some slack." Ashton's hand remained on Julian's back. Unlike Zakiyyah, Ashton was a pro at the manly comfort, at the open-palmed thump. "You still haven't looked at the menus? That's it, I'm ordering whatever I feel like for the both of you. You're gonna eat it and you're gonna like it. Come and help me, Jules."

As always, Ashton took care of things. He dragged Julian away, ordered bar food—Cornish pasties and steak and kidney pies and salads—and paid for it. While they waited, he drank lager like it was water. Ashton could always hold his liquor. Said it was in his DNA. He got it from his mother's side. Gin flowed through her veins when she carried him, and now it flowed through his.

"I'm going to have a stern talk with that Riley of yours for foisting that woman on me," Julian said.

"Give her a break. She's trying to help you."

"Which one? And she's not."

"Both of them."

"She's not. Trust me."

Ashton breathed a long hard sigh between the swallows. "Why are you still torturing her? Can't you see she's mourning, too?"

"She had to come all the way to London to feel better?"

"Why not? You did. You're not the only one who lost something," Ashton said. "Mia was Z's closest friend. So stop the blame game. Recall what Mike Nichols said and shut up. Nichols is *your* life hack, Jules. Did you forget your very first newsletter? It was about him."

Mike Nichols:
>Born in Berlin.
>Fled Nazi Germany.
>Related to Einstein.
>Became a comedian.
>Won more Tonys
>Than anyone else for directing.
>Owns four hundred Arabian horses.
>Has four marriages, three divorces.
>Exit quote: *"Cheer up, life isn't everything."*

Mike Nichols's Riddle on Perspective and Blame:
Premise: A lonely woman, whose husband is always away, begins an affair with a man who lives across the bay. In the middle of one night, she and her lover have a terrible

fight, and he throws her out. She takes the ferry back but
is robbed and killed by the ferryman, who throws her
body overboard.
Question: *Who is to blame for the woman's death? The*
husband, the boatman, the woman herself, or her lover?

Julian finally had an answer to a question. "Fuck Mike Nichols,"
he said.

∞

While they were waiting on the food, and Julian was catching up
with his brothers, Zakiyyah sat down across from them. Tristan
and Dalton misinterpreted their brother's glare and moved to
another table.

"Look, I'm sorry," she said. "I didn't mean to upset you."

"And *yet...*"

Reaching across, Zakiyyah patted his hand as if she'd just
learned to pat. Two slaps, like a bear, missing his hand completely
on the second go. "Ava really needs you to call her, Julian."

"It's on my list." He hid his clenched hands under the table.

"She asked me to ask you something."

"She asked *you* to ask *me*?"

"Yes. Because you never return her calls. She wants the
necklace back."

"What necklace?"

"You know what necklace," Zakiyyah said. "Mia's crystal."

"Nope. Doesn't ring a bell."

"Ava needs it back," Zakiyyah repeated. "She's become
convinced it's the key to everything."

Julian raised his eyes. "I got to keep four things from *Mia*,"
he said in a stone-cold voice. "The crystal, the beret, which was
mine to begin with, and two books. So *three* things really. Ava
got everything else. So you can tell Ava that I told you to tell her
I'm not giving the necklace back. It will never happen."

"She said she'll give you something in return for it. Some of Mia's baby pictures. Her high school diaries. Video tapes of her performing at Coney Island."

"No, thanks," Julian said. "She's haggling with me through you? Why does she want it anyway?"

"Ava says without the crystal, she can't find her."

"*What?*" Julian stared into Zakiyyah's face, suddenly at full attention. "What did you say? Find who?" His legs went numb like he was falling.

"People keep seeing Ava wandering around Brooklyn," Zakiyyah said, "and when they ask what she's doing, she says she's looking for her child. She says she's sure Mia's still out there somewhere." She glanced behind him. "Food's here. But I *know*—crazy, right."

Could Julian vanish? Fall through the floor and disappear? He didn't look up, couldn't muster even a glib reply.

∞

They pushed the round tables together. Riley put Julian between her and Ashton. As the others ate and drank and chatted merrily, Julian, who wasn't hungry or chatty, just drank, and while he was thus occupied, a million miles away, Nigel said, "If women are so much smarter than men, why do they wear shirts that button down the back?" and *everyone* laughed except for Julian, and then Nigel, encouraged by the laughter, told a limerick. *On the boobs of a barmaid in Sale, were tattooed the prices of ale, and on her behind, for the sake of the blind, was the same information in Braille.* Everyone guffawed again. Was it just him? Julian had never been great at ignoring assholes.

Not to be outdone by Nigel, Riley said to no one and everyone, "Hey, did you guys hear about the note I found under the cash drawer at the Treasure Box? On a scrap of pink perfumed paper someone had written, 'I want you to fuck me till I die.'" Riley laughed, flinging around her flouncy hair. "Isn't that *hilarious*?"

A hush fell over the ale-infused crowd. No one could tell if Riley was joking. Julian glanced at Ashton and quickly stared into his uneaten bangers and mash. Nigel roared with laughter. "Well done, mate," he said to Ashton. "But can I ask a stupid question?"

"Better than anyone I know," said Julian.

Nigel har-de-har-harred. "How did you reply?"

"I politely declined," Ashton said. "Frankly it seemed like too much effort."

"Ashton is nothing if not polite—and lazy," said Riley.

"Relax, Riley," Nigel said, "didn't Julian work there, too? How do you know the note was even meant for Ashton? Maybe one of Julian's bits of stuff left it for him—"

Julian shot up from the table. A still sitting Nigel echoed a slow beery *whoa*, Ashton a fast beery *whoa*, his hand covering Julian's fist.

"Calm down," Nigel said.

"Don't tell me what to do," Julian said.

"Try smiling once in a while."

"Don't fucking tell me what to do."

"Whatever," Nigel said. "Obviously, I was just joking around. Of *course*, no one wants you to shag them, Jules." He howled with laughter.

"*Everybody's* a comic these days," Ashton said. His face showed nothing. "Nigel, shut the hell up. Jules, come on, bud, *sit*." Standing up he forcibly lowered Julian back into the chair with the downward pressure of his hand. "Truly this is the land of no mercy," Ashton said, draining his pint and throwing Riley a scolding glare, as in *why are you starting more trouble*.

"Your favorite playwright, Tennessee Williams, wrote that *love* is nothing but a four-letter word," Riley said to Ashton over Julian's head. "That's why."

"Now *that's* funny, Riles," said Ashton.

The rough topic was changed to more genteel ones about work and new cars, to the best running shoes and L.A.'s empty reservoirs, to the stupidity of avatars and a recent earthquake that made everyone start nailing their furniture to the floor, and to the sightings of superstars.

Julian, too, tried to join in the conversation. "Hey," he piped in, "did you hear about the former Miss Venezuela who went from being a top model to spending the last fifteen years of her life living on the streets? Her body was just found in a Caracas park." The table reacted poorly; Julian didn't get why. They had just been talking about famous people! Julian tried to catch Ashton's eye, but his friend's crystal blue gaze remained in his vanishing beer. Let's have another round, Ashton said. Surreptitiously Julian checked his empty wrist and when he looked up, they were all eyeing him with a drunken mix of concern and pity, all except Nigel, who couldn't care less.

"How you doing there, Jules?" Gwen said.

"Don't ask him umbrella questions, Gwen," Ashton said. "Ask him how he's doing *today*. The more specific the better."

"I'm doing great today, Gwen, thanks for asking."

"Julian, darling, have you been to a therapist?" That was Riley.

"He's got a cot in the corner of the shrink's office at the walk-in clinic," Ashton replied for Julian. Ashton always acted as if he knew everything. Mr. Fantastic. Mr. Razzle Dazzle. Tonight, he razzle-dazzled their friends with fake knowledge of Julian's progress in the art of mourning. "Yes, he's been to a shrink. He's even been to a priest."

Zakiyyah perked up. "What did the priest say?"

"The priest asked him where his faith was," Ashton replied, winking at Julian and raising his glass. Julian raised his in reply. Ashton was always full of joy, always happy, always smiling. *How could you not love an open face of someone always smiling.* Julian looked away, the vision of another open smiling face cutting him up like razor wire.

"The priest was right," Zakiyyah said. "Julian looks and acts like a man who's lost his religion."

What could *you* possibly know about it, Julian was about to say, but she looked so sad that he kept quiet.

"Julian's also been to a faith healer," Ashton said, "and a fortune-teller. He's tried—you don't mind, do you, Jules—he's even tried electroconvulsive therapy to rid himself of painful memories."

"Did it work?" Riley asked with uncommon interest, as if considering it herself.

"It did not," said Julian.

Zakiyyah wanted to know what the fortune-teller had offered.

When Ashton became reticent, Julian prodded. "Ash? What, the cat got your tongue? You've told them everything else. Go on, tell Z what the fortune-teller said."

"She was a gypsy and she didn't know what she was talking about," Ashton said.

"Why do you even bother going to fortune-tellers, Jules?" Riley said. "To empower and optimize yourself, you should practice a cleansing regimen, like I showed you."

"Oh, but I don't go to them," Julian said. "That implies continuity. Ashton and I were walking down King Street, and one flagged us down."

"And told you what?"

Julian was amused at the pained expression on Ashton's golden face. The conversation had taken a turn Ashton resented. He wanted to convince their friends that Julian was doing everything he was supposed to, but the gypsy didn't fit into Ashton's neat narrative about Julian's alleged progress.

"She said *the time had not yet come for the Lord to act*."

There was a confused pause.

"What does that mean?" Riley said. "Act how? Do what?"

"How should I know?" Ashton said.

"You didn't ask her? Ugh. Julian, what did she *mean* by that?"

"Ask Ashton," Julian said. "He seems to know *everything*."

"It's a sin to go to fortune-tellers," said Zakiyyah. "They practice the dark arts. Black magic."

"Z is right," Riley said to Julian, rubbing his forearm like he was a genie lamp. "You must keep doing *other* things that help. Have you tried earthing, like I suggested?"

"You want me to walk barefoot in London?"

"What about an irrigation colonic?"

"Riley, Jesus, *please*," Ashton said.

"You please," she said. "I know you don't believe in it, but it really helps."

"I don't believe in irrigation colonics?"

Riley twisted Julian's face away from Ashton and to herself. "Ignore him, Jules, and listen to me. Your body must be cleansed and strong, and I promise you, your spirit will follow. How much weight have you lost? Are you drinking too much? It's so easy to do that here, look at Ashton, and it's not good for you. All that yeast running rampant in your body. It's not healthy. You should be drinking a gallon of pure filtered water. You can add lemon to it for alkalinity. It's important for your body to be alkaline, Julian, to heal properly. And you should go for a walk every day. Have you been getting any fresh air?"

"Oh, yes, Riley," Julian said, patting her and struggling up. "That's one thing I've been getting *plenty* of. Fresh air. Will you excuse me?"

∞

Upstairs in the men's where it was a little quieter, there was a sign above the mirror that said, *"No wonder you're going home alone."* Motionlessly Julian stared at his reflection.

As he was coming back through the second-floor gallery, he overheard them talking about him down below.

"He looks terrible," Riley said. "I've never seen him like this, not even when it first happened."

"He was in shock then," Ashton said. "Now it's worn off."

"Ashton, he must've lost thirty pounds," said Gwen.

Forty-seven, Julian wanted to correct her. Super featherweight.

"His eyes are bugging out of his head," Gwen continued. "He's sweating, and when he does speak, he sounds unhinged. He's worse than ever, Ashton. What's happening to him?"

"You know what's happening to him."

"But why isn't he better?"

"I don't think he's been to a shrink," said Zakiyyah.

"Well, it's a National Health shrink," Ashton said dryly.

"He needs more shock treatment, if you ask me," Nigel said.

"No one's asking you," Ashton said.

"Jules should've never come here, Ashton," Tristan said.

"Trist is right," Dalton said. "Our mom's upset with you, Ash. Why did you have to get him a job in London? He'd still be in L.A. if it weren't for you."

"Yeah, where he was doing *great*," Ashton said impatiently. "Shrink, drink, drugs, leeching, cupping. London, L.A. It's all the same. He just needs time."

"But he's had so *much* time!" said Gwen.

"Mia's mom is not doing well either," Zakiyyah said, in defense of Julian.

"But that's her *mom*!" said Gwen. "No one expects a mother to be doing well."

"He's changed, Ashton," Riley said. "He used to be such good company. Better than you in some ways. But there's something wrong with him. We all see it, why can't you?"

"You think *I* don't see it?" said Ashton.

A heavy silence followed.

"He won't get over her on his own," Zakiyyah said. "He needs someone new."

"I'm working on it," said Ashton.

Another unhappy silence followed. "He doesn't need *you*, Ashton," Zakiyyah said. "He needs a woman."

"Zakiyyah's right, Tristan is right," Riley said. "He should come home."

"Should, ought to. Says who?" Ashton said. "He's a grown man. He makes his own decisions."

"Like you, big guy?" said Riley.

"Yes," Ashton said. "Like me."

"We all want to help him," Zakiyyah said. "That's why we came, that's why we're here."

"Not me," Nigel said. "I'm just here to drink."

"Why don't you help," Ashton said, "by not talking to him loud and slow like he's backward? Help him by acting normal. Act like everything's okay."

"How do we do that?" said Riley.

"How? You *act*. Hey, Julian, there you are! We wondered if you were *redecorating* in there." Ashton threw Riley a withering look before sliding a freshly poured pint to Julian.

"Jules, Ashton has something to tell you," Riley blurted before Julian even had a chance to sit down. "Oh, yes, he's got some *great* news. Don't give me your evil eye, Ashton. No sense in beating around the bush. Party's almost over. Tell him already."

"Tell me what?" Julian sat down, looking across the table at his brothers. "Tell Mom I'm doing fine," he said to Tristan and Dalton. "Don't worry her. She's got enough on her plate. I'm an adult. I'll figure it out." He turned to Ashton. "Tell me what?"

Ashton drank half his pint before he spoke. "I'm moving."

"Moving where?"

"To London."

"*To London?*" That came out two octaves higher than Julian's normal baritone.

"Preferably to Notting Hill. With you."

"But I don't live in Notting Hill," Julian said dumbly.

"Not yet." Ashton put on his best smile. "Look, you know I don't feel right about you being here on your own. I've never felt right about it. Plus, like I told you, my old man needs help. Think of it as a father and son reunion."

"Ashton, aww, are you coming to watch over Jules?" Nigel slurred his words, his narrow shoulders quaking. "Good luck with that. You'll sack him yourself before the week's out."

"I'll be sacking somebody," Ashton said to Nigel, "but are you sure it'll be Jules?" He faced Julian. "Dude, why do you look panicked like a nun in a penguin shooting gallery? I'm not moving here tomorrow. I have a few things to sort out first. And you and I need a place to live. The girls said they'd help us look this weekend, right, girls?"

The girls mumbled in reply.

"What about the Treasure Box?"

"It's been taken care of. We're not staying in London forever, are we? Just long enough to…" Ashton trailed off. As if he himself didn't know how that sentence should end. Even Julian didn't know how that sentence should end. Long enough to what?

"Bryce will run it, you remember him." Ashton grinned. "Tristan and Dalton will help." Julian's brothers drunkenly nodded. "Your mom said she'll do the inventory, your dad the books. Riley will work on Saturdays, Gwen and Zakiyyah on Sundays. Everyone will pitch in. It'll be fine."

But it wasn't fine. No one could run that store for any length of time except Ashton, not even Julian, and everyone knew it. "Why would you leave L.A., Ash?" Julian said. "It's your *life*."

"It was your life, too," Ashton said, the shine in his eyes dimming. "It was our life. And look what happened. Plus," he added, "I *want* to move to London. Really. I'm sick of the sunshine and warm weather. I need a little rain in my life. Right, Riley? Right, Gwennie? Right, Z?"

The women tutted. "You're moving to the wrong town for a *little* rain," said Zakiyyah.

Julian wanted to back away, but there was nowhere to back away to. His chair was against the wall. "What about Riley?"

"Exactly, Julian!" Riley exclaimed in hearty agreement as to her own inconsequence. "That's what I keep saying. What about *me*?"

"You'll visit on the weekends," Ashton said.

"It'll cost me a week's salary to fly out every weekend," Riley said. "I'll be broke *and* homeless."

"Not every weekend," Ashton said. "Maybe once a month. We talked about this. And I'll come back once a month."

"Ashton," Julian said in a faltering voice, "Riley should move here, too."

"What a *great* idea, Jules!" Riley said, with fake cheer. "What do you say, Ash?"

"Stop it." He turned to Julian. "I'm not moving here for fun, Jules. I'm moving here for you."

Awkwardly Julian excused himself again and back in the men's room wondered if there was another way out of the pub. Could he climb out through the small window? Flee, leave the apartment, quit work, vanish. That was the only thing he wanted. To vanish off the face of the earth.

After splashing water on his gray face, Julian stood at the far end of the semi-circular bar, trying to block out the noise, holding on to the counter, contemplating his next move. He stared at the gold lights, the round tables, the happy drinking laughing people. Inside him was a churning void.

A gruff voice sounded next to him. "You're looking for a miracle," the voice said. "You won't find it here."

24

The Question

JULIAN TURNED HIS HEAD TO STARE INTO THE BEAKY PROFILE of an old woman in a black cloak. Her face was the color of desert dirt, dry and cracked with a million crevices. In her lizard-skin hands she palmed a dram of Scotch. Perhaps it wasn't Julian she had addressed. She wasn't looking in his direction so Julian couldn't tell her to mind her own business. He waited. She said nothing else. He thought he'd gotten off easy.

"What are you looking for?" she asked in a heavy Southeast Asian accent. "Your faith?"

Ah.

Now Julian *had* to turn to her. He wished he also had a Scotch he could palm. Instead, his empty right hand twitched on the counter. "Are you talking to me?"

"Do you see anyone else here?"

"Well, in that case," Julian said, "I don't know what you're talking about."

"Those your friends?" She gestured over to the tables. "Came a long way to celebrate with you? For your birthday? Born on the Ides of March, eh, the ancient day for ritual sacrifice and settling all debts. Well, well. That man, the ringmaster, he's been holding the fire hoops for your amusement the entire night. But instead you look like you're at your own funeral."

"Can I help you?"

"I don't need help," the woman said. "*You* need help."

"Perhaps I can call you a taxi?"

"You're the one who must hurry." Her voice was a rake scraping on gravel. "Because you're almost out of time."

What? he said inaudibly.

She leveled him with a stare from the half-hooded slits of her ancient eyes. In that crinkle of a face, the eyes burned like black fire, aware, lucid, damning, judging, and unpersuadable. As if she knew everything. Julian's hands began to shake. He squeezed them together. The fists still shook.

"I heard him say you been to priests and soothsayers, asking questions."

"I don't have any questions," Julian said. "Out of time for what?"

"That was a question."

"It was rhetorical."

She smirked. "You must be new to the English language. No, it wasn't. You know the answers to rhetorical questions."

A stumped Julian said nothing.

"Everybody's got a question, the fools and the wise."

"Not me." Who was she?

"Ask me," she said. "I've lived longer than you. The way you're going, I may outlive you. I've seen a few things. I know a few things. What do you want to know?"

"Nothing."

"You know everything, do you?" The old woman nodded. "Mr. Know-it-All. Got all the answers."

Julian gripped the side of the bar. *Mr. Know-it-All?* It must be a coincidence! It's not as if he'd trademarked his name. It was an idiom. Common usage. Many people said Mr. Know-it-All.

"How did you know my name?" he mumbled.

"Is that your question?"

Baffled, he mined her face. Had he met her somewhere and forgot? She stared back unwaveringly. She was tiny, with a tight gray body in loose black fabric. "Do I know you?" Julian whispered.

"Is *that* your question?"

"No. God, I told you—no. Look, I don't want to be rude, but I have to go. I've got to get back to my friends."

"A minute ago you stood by my side wondering how to skip out on them, and now you're rushing back?" She smirked. "How time flies."

"Were you listening to us? Did you hear what the gypsy told me?"

"No. Though some gypsies do have partial sight. What did she tell you?"

"She said the time had not yet come for the Lord to act."

"Shame," the woman said. "That one did *not* have the sight. Because the time has *definitely* come for the Lord to act. And not just the Lord, but you."

Julian swayed. He'd had too much to drink, that's all there was to it. Cha-ching, cha-ching. The slot machine in the corner was obnoxiously loud. He noticed this evening that everything in the White Crow had been unusually loud, almost agonizingly so. The slot machines, the laughter, the clinking of glasses, all of it like metal pans, jarring noises of high-strung cymbals clanging next to his ears. It had been unsettling him all night— the pub charged with electrical impulses astride the galloping sound waves—but now the decibel level had become unbearable. He pressed his fingers to his temples. "Do you really want a question?" Julian said to the old woman. Cha-ching! Bangle!

"It's nothing to me," the woman replied. "But you clearly need an answer."

Julian glanced around the pub, sought out Ashton, standing as if on a stage, telling a story. Loud. The barman at the other end, serving a family of foreigners yelling their orders at him in Greek. Loud. There was no one in their section of the pub. Since Josephine's death he had been pleading to the mute universe, hearing no reply to his shouting rage, to his red anguish.

"Here's my question," Julian said. "What is the sign by which you recognize God?"

When he was twelve and out with his parents, he passed a blind beggar on Hollywood Boulevard by Grauman's Theatre, sitting cross-legged on the sidewalk with his beastly cur, near the celebrity hands in cement, by the costumed Spider-Men. The board hanging from the beggar's neck said, "Please O Lord, give me a sign by which I will know you." Julian gave the man the only quarter in his pocket, and thought about the man's plea a long time, until he got up enough nerve to ask his parish priest.

It had taken him six years. He was afraid the priest would laugh at him. But he really needed to know the answer. He was in his freshman summer at UCLA. He and Ashton were planning to hike across the Pacific Crest Trail, through Yosemite and Death Valley, to the Black Hills of South Dakota, and then to Missoula, Montana, and Julian didn't want to be on the road and not know what he was searching for.

"If you don't know by now, young man," the priest said, "I'm afraid you will never know."

He turned away, leaving Julian embarrassed and chastised. Julian figured the answer must have been right in front of him and he missed it. In the years since, he did consider the possibility that maybe the priest himself didn't know. But if the man of God didn't know, how was Julian supposed to know? He was barely even a child of God. Sometimes he went for months without invoking God's name as anything but a swear word.

Yosemite went off without a hitch and so did the Badlands a year later and Yellowstone a year after that. But then his luck ran out in Topanga. Even after being gifted with his life, Julian continued to carry with him the sense that he was missing something, that there was something important he had forgotten, but it was a smudged sense, like an old faded print. He and Ashton graduated, opened the Treasure Box, Julian walked away from an English masters, from teaching, from a lot of things. He toiled at the store, created a website, became Mr. Know-it-All. They partied, traveled, worked hard, played hard, they had a blast, a great full life. After a parade of women, Julian found

Gwen. He got his own place. He leased a Volvo. He was golden. Everything was coming up Southern California roses.

And then—*The Invention of Love.*

And now—this.

The unflinching woman did not turn away, nor did she speak, as she sat, sipping her Scotch, either thinking or bearing the whisky burn. Julian took a step back, ready to go, and then he heard her dry, grainy voice.

"The infant in his swaddling blanket."

That was it. That was all she said. Julian thought he had misheard. He leaned in. *"The infant in his swaddling blanket?* What does that mean?"

Turning her head, she stared straight at him.

Julian staggered back. Her eyes terrified him with their black bottomless knowledge. As if she was the real Miss Know-it-All, about Julian, about everything. "Two thousand years ago, no other sign was given to the wise men when they asked your question," she said with a hacking cough. "The wisest men who lived back then. Just a newborn wrapped in a blanket. If they didn't get another sign, why should you? You're not even that wise a man."

A strangled noise left Julian's throat. He needed help so badly, and what the old woman was offering him was impenetrable and therefore useless. In response to his visible desperation, she turned away and shrunk into her robes, vanishing inside them.

Julian stumbled back to the table, gulped down what remained of his warm beer, but couldn't focus on anything except the old woman's words. He couldn't hear anyone. He jumped up, knocked over his chair—more noise—whirled around.

The woman was gone.

"What, Jules? Too much lager? Sit down." Intoxicated himself, Ashton made futile attempts to right the chair.

Julian sought out the barman. "What woman?" the barman said, pouring an ale on tap, not looking up.

Not only was she gone, but the Scotch in front of her had been cleaned up. Not even a napkin remained.

"You cleaned up her drink, but you don't remember her?"

"Don't know what you're on about, mate. Order or piss off. I'm slammed."

"Small old woman in a large black coat."

"Do you think I remember everyone who comes into my pub? Look around."

"She was a hundred years old! Drinking whisky by herself. How often do you get that?"

The fed-up barman waved his hand around the room, where multitudes clustered, young and old.

Julian examined the high stool where the old woman had sat. It was pushed in, all neat. The pub was deafening. Someone had pulled the slot machine lever and hit the jackpot, and the machine was going nuts, ringing bells and dropping round pound coins into a metal catcher, seven! seven! seven! seven! seven! seven! seven! Julian pressed his palms into his pounding head. He wasn't used to being this drunk. He must have made the whole thing up. Sometimes he did that. Dreamed things. Like Weaver said. Klonopin. Dangerous hallucinations. He had imagined a dodgy old woman, invented her unfathomable words. Baby! Swaddling blanket! Wise men!

On the bar, a white business card was tucked into the counter lip where she'd been sitting. Julian pulled it out. It was from a place called *Time Over Matter. 153 Great Eastern Road. Acupuncture and other Great Eastern rites.* That's all it said. *Time over Matter? Eastern rites on Great Eastern Road?* Was this a joke? Dropping the card on the floor he walked away. A minute later, he rushed back for it, but it was gone. Someone must have picked it up, though he hadn't seen anyone walk past. Julian grabbed on to the counter, light-headed, his chest tight.

What was happening?

25

The Widow's Daughter

THAT NIGHT AS JULIAN CABBED IT TO HERMIT STREET, HIS undimmed prayer wasn't help me or forgive me. It was, *please don't let Ashton move here.* Tomorrow, when he was sober, he would talk Ashton out of it. He couldn't let his friend ruin his life, too. He tried not to think about the old woman. His fingers kept going numb as he tried not to think of her.

When he staggered into the foyer, Mrs. Pallaver was waiting for him. Not just her. Her daughter, too. The door to their parlor room was invitingly ajar. "We wondered when you were gonna come home, love," Mrs. Pallaver said. "Come in, come in. Frieda's been waiting."

"Hello there," he said, holding on to the wall.

"How are you?" Frieda said, remaining sitting. She always sat when she was around him. He knew why. She was such a tall, broad-shouldered gal, towering over him. She was so equine in her energetic fortitude that it painfully raised the question of what she could possibly want with a slim, barely-simmering-with-life jockey like him. His old surging jauntiness had long ebbed, was washed away into the L.A. storm drains when they hosed down Normandie.

"We have a cake for you. Like last year." Mrs. Pallaver smiled. "Frieda, quick, get the candles."

"They're right here, Mum."

"It's your favorite, love." Mrs. Pallaver smiled. "Chocolate cherry. Frieda, help me light these. It's a tradition now. Frieda, I can't work this damn ignition thing, do you think it's out? Have you got plain matches?"

As Julian watched them fuss over the lighter at the poorly lit dining table—mother and daughter, a gray-haired widowed lady trying to spin off her Amazonian child on a would-be-widower who almost had a mother-in-law just like this one, and a bride, not quite like this one—the heater on low, the women having waited for him well past their bedtime, he wanted to rip open his chest to yank out the pity he felt for them, pity like piety, a pathological B-side of a love that could never be, yet which still had something undeniably human in it. Usually he would sit and have tea with them. Last year he even had cake. But tonight, he couldn't. Nothing stirred in his groin for this woman. It wasn't that it was too soon. It was that it would never be.

"I'm very sorry," Julian said, "you're too kind, but I don't feel well. Too much celebrating, I'm afraid, thank you, the cake looks very good, perhaps I can take a raincheck? But also, ahem, I wanted to let you know, give as much notice as possible, so you don't get stuck, so sorry about this also, I'm just sorry all around tonight, aren't I, but I'll be moving out. I know—it's a shock to me as well. I really like it here and didn't intend on leaving, but Ashton, I've told you about him"—*oh, stop talking, you idiot!* —"he's moving to London to help me sort out some things, and he and I are getting a flat together, we need just a bit more space than I have here, you see, we need a bedroom—I mean, *two* bedrooms"—*oh God! Will this never stop*—"Ashton wants to move to Sloane Square or Mayfair or perhaps Belgravia, he heard it was nice there, or Notting Hill, forgive me for dropping in, but I must go lie down, thanks again...I beg your pardon..."

He left them in the parlor room, standing near the little lamp and the inadequate heater and the supermarket sponge cake with the unlit birthday candles, and Julian knew with all certainty that even if he could persuade Ashton not to move to London, he would have to find another place to live. Both women condemned him in that yellow light as if Julian had been already betrothed to Frieda, as if he was no longer just the tenant or the lonely widower, but the faithless lover who broke the ungainly filly's heart.

26

Great Eastern Road

THE NEXT MORNING JULIAN CALLED IN SICK, SLEPT OFF HIS hangover as best he could, forgetting all the hacks he once knew for curing hangovers, and at noon took the overground to Hoxton. The train was decidedly *not* a hangover hack, what with the constant screeching and stopping and megaphone station naming. He stumbled down Great Eastern Road in search of 153, the number on the business card the old woman had left behind.

The roads were crowded at lunchtime on Great Eastern near Kingsland and Commercial Streets. It took him ten minutes to go half a block. Number 153 turned out to be not a holistic center for spiritual growth and material renewal as promised but a tiny take-out joint called Quatrang. Didn't specify Vietnamese or Thai like other restaurants on the street. Just said **Quatrang** in red letters with black hieroglyphics in the bottom corner. To say the place was tiny was a British understatement. It was the width of a door and a double window. The bell trilled when Julian stepped inside. The handwritten menu was scrawled on a large whiteboard on the front wall. There was room for two stools at the counter. Julian knocked one of them over as he opened the door, and perhaps that was by design, so the man behind the curtain would hear. The place wasn't meant for lingering. It was meant for getting in and getting out.

The beaded curtain rat-tat-tatted, like rice falling on the steps of a church, and a compact, solidly built Southeast Asian man came out smiling. He would have to be small to fit into a place like this. He was wiry, alert, and unblinkingly calm. He had neatly trimmed black hair and black eyes. He wore a matte black shirt and crepe-like trousers and over them a black apron, freshly laundered, ironed and starched.

"Sorry, uh, ugh, yeah, I've, I've, I've come to the wrong place," Julian stammered. "I was looking for 153 Great Eastern Road. *Acupuncture and great Eastern rites.*"

The man nodded. "You've come to where you need to be." He spoke in fluent British. "Number 153. For the perseverance of the saints. I was quoting John. Do you feel you have persevered? Never mind, we'll get to that. But let's start with lunch." He pulled out a place mat. "All things worth doing begin with a meal. It's much more pleasant that way, wouldn't you agree?"

Julian didn't know if he agreed. The man's incongruously excellent English was confusing him.

"Well," the little man explained, as if Julian had argued the point, "the way you tell is just try doing anything of importance on an empty stomach and see how far you get."

Julian stood dumbly. Had he spoken? Or did the man read his mind?

"Sit. Please."

Julian sat like a lummox.

"My name is Devi Prak," the man said congenially. "Devi like levee."

"Julian Cruz. As in, the levee was dry?"

"If you say so." Devi stuck out his wide hand. The handshake was warm and bone-crunchingly firm. "Many years ago, when I first came to this country, I called myself Devin, thinking it would be easier for the British to pronounce. But as with many things in life, the very opposite turned out to be true. The people I met could not compute the name *Devin* with the face they saw before them. They kept asking me to spell it, and even after I spelled it, still could not say it properly. They kept putting the accent on the wrong syllable. I changed it back to Devi. Everyone was much happier."

Julian appraised the man. He had smooth but weathered dark skin, an indecipherable expression on his face, cheekbones high, the black eyes sharp. Too sharp. He was neat, not a stray hair on him. Julian wondered if the man was related to the old woman in the pub. It was hard to tell how old he was. He could've been sixty. He could've been seventy. His eyes reminded Julian of the woman's, though, like bottomless pools. They were deeply unsettling.

"What does Quatrang mean?" Julian asked. "Is that a family name or something?"

"No. In Vietnamese, *Quatrang* means white crow."

Julian focused on Devi's face. The old woman from last night confronted him inside the *White Crow* pub. He had almost chosen the Blind Beggar on Cheapside. Did this mean she would not have appeared to him with her bewildering pronouncements? A flip of a coin—and suddenly nothing was making sense in Julian's life.

"Does 'white crow' have some meaning I don't know about?"

"I don't know what you don't know," Devi said, setting a white china plate rimmed in gold in front of Julian. "A white crow, among other things, symbolizes time. Past, present—and future." He gave Julian a cloth napkin, polished silverware, and a crystal glass filled with slightly sedimentary water.

Julian noticed that three fingers on the man's left hand were missing, ending in smooth nubs at the second knuckle. Only the thumb and the index finger remained intact. Julian clenched and unclenched his own fully fingered fists. He didn't mean to stare, but he did.

"What will you have, Julian?" Devi asked pleasantly.

Julian focused on the whiteboard above the spotless cast-iron Teppanyaki grill. "Is this Vietnamese food?"

"If you wish. I can make anything. I make whatever people who come to me want to eat."

"Like lasagna?"

"Oh, so you're a comedian." Devi nodded. "Very good."

"Seriously, what's the food?"

"A mix of Vietnamese, Laotian, Chinese. I'm from the Hmong tribe. From the Golden Triangle, the mountains on the northern border of Vietnam, Laos, and Burma. The area's changed hands so many times, even I can't say for sure where I'm from."

"Your English is excellent."

"Been here a long time." Devi paused a moment before continuing. "May I recommend some things? Perhaps some salt and pepper squid, freshly hawked by a reputable monger just yesterday? It's very good if I do say so myself. I had some for breakfast this morning. And then a little bowl of beef pho. It's spicy, but the broth is delicious, and I'm using twice cooked and marinated sirloin in it with a little leftover brisket. You will enjoy it."

Julian nodded. It did sound good despite his empty, singed-by-alcohol stomach.

"Anything besides my water to drink?" Devi asked. "I have some sparkling sake."

"I'll try it." Hair of the dog and all that.

"Very good. But drink the water first."

Julian obliged, despite the floating particles. "What kind of water is this? Not regular water."

"Oh, no, I wouldn't give you regular water," Devi said. "You need something stronger. This water has minerals in it. Calcium. You look as if you could use some of that. Some sinew."

The sake appeared in a crystal shot glass, and the man disappeared behind the curtain. Julian noticed he walked with a slight limp.

While Julian waited, he surveyed the surroundings, the side walls painted black and green. The only decorations on them were clocks. A Simpsons clock, a navigational clock, a digital clock with blood red numbers screaming it was 13:02, a pendulum clock whirring and ticking.

There was no calendar or other trinkets, no Asian fans, or photos of ancient temples or little grandchildren. In the ten minutes Julian was there, no one else had entered. The glass door behind him remained closed, blocking out the noise from the busy street.

The salt and pepper calamari was delicious. It was spicy and salty and tender, and there wasn't enough of it. Julian devoured it while the man watched. "Good, right?"

"Very good."

"I'm pleased. Maybe you will come back. More sake while I start on your pho?"

The pho was also good. The bowl wasn't big enough; Julian wanted more. But after he finished the last of it, he felt full and a little sleepy. Weirdly he wondered if there was a cot in the back. What an odd thing to wish for, a bed to nap in at your luncheonette.

The man brought Julian some red bean ice cream, "to cleanse the palate," and continued to study him alertly from the other side of the counter. Alert was certainly not a word to describe Julian. He was stuporous, nodding off into his empty bowl, the whirring of the clocks, the hum on Great Eastern Road, the unfamiliar combination of vinegar, lime, garlic, and coconut hypnotizing him.

He heard the man's firm voice. "What brings you here? I know it's not my food. You don't act as if you've tasted Vietnamese food before."

Opening his heavy eyes, Julian slowly explained about the old woman and the card. The man nodded with approval. Julian circled his hand around the tiny eatery. "The card said *acupuncture*." Not calamari.

"Yes, I see," Devi said, as if not seeing *any* discrepancy between the text of the business card and the reality on the ground. "Would you like some acupuncture?"

"You serve lunch *and* stick me with needles? No, needles are not what I need."

"Yet this card you speak of but can't produce promised acupuncture and you still came. Why?"

Julian tried to think. Yesterday was a liquid blur. "The woman thought you could help."

"What's wrong with you?"

"Is she your mother?"

"Will it help you to know that? Frankly, Julian, in your state," Devi said, "you should be asking questions on a strictly need-to-know basis. What did the business card say that intrigued you?"

"It wasn't the card. It was the woman. She told me a riddle I couldn't decipher."

"What riddle?"

"You're not a bartender," Julian mumbled. "I shouldn't be telling you my troubles."

"Did I not serve you sake? Twice?"

"Well, all right. But it's lunchtime."

"Do the things that trouble you go away at lunchtime? You're a lucky man. Most people who come to me stay upset right through supper."

Julian reached for his wallet. "Are we done?"

"We are not even at the beginning," the cook said.

Julian left the wallet where it was.

"You seem unusually tense," Devi said. "Like you're hiding despair inside, panic, agitation. You feel unremitting anxiety. Your fears are crippling you. You feel actual physical pain from your worry, in the center of your gut, a hole that feels hot to the touch. You have a burning ache in your esophagus that is unbearable. At the same time, your melancholy has weakened your bones, drained the blood from you. You're a mess, if you don't mind me saying so."

Julian was mute. Who was this man who saw inside him?

"How stressful is your life?" Devi asked. "Unquestionably your *chi* is not traveling across the necessary meridians. It's as if there is a ravine between what you should be feeling and doing and what you're actually feeling and doing. You are out of balance."

Julian bobbed his head. "Can you help with that? A doctor in Peckham couldn't."

"Did you pray for him? I'm joking. It's a Peckham joke."

"So, you're a comedian yourself."

"Perhaps you chose the doctor unwisely," Devi said, motioning him inside. "Come with me."

"The doc didn't help is all I'm saying," Julian muttered, sliding off his stool and following the cook.

"I heard you the first three times you said it."

Julian didn't think he'd said it even once.

He found himself shirtless in a back room on a narrow table, face down, wearing only his boxer briefs. His eyes were closed. He wondered if the real reason he agreed to enter this claustrophobic closet and allowed himself to get half-naked in front of a stranger and be stabbed with sewing tools was because he was so hopelessly tired. What was in that water?

While a hundred needles judiciously pierced the chi points on Julian's body, Devi urged Julian to confess his stories, to whisper to him tales of the living and the dead. To Julian it felt like trying to talk under a sea of ice. The mouth was frozen, the body numb, the lungs heavy with fluid. All his pointed sorrows suddenly began to feel toothless.

There was a climbing pain in his neck and down his trapezoid, pain in his forearms, in the meat of his calves, in his fingers, his brows, his cheekbones. Before Julian could react, the pain disappeared and everything else vanished, too, the troubles, the burning, almost all feeling. It was better than Klonopin. Nothing was left except a tingle in his veins.

Josephine, crystals, Ashton, inventions, Poppa W, Mia, Z, and Moses Jackson, marriage, projectiles, San Vicente, insanity, Volvo, Mr. Know-it-All, mothers on balconies, Fario Rima, blood in the street, mountains, lovers, drumbeats of grief.

∞

He blamed himself. Josephine broke up with her fiancé—because of him. Zakiyyah called Ava—because of him. The morning she died, she had a fight with her mother—about him. Because of this fight, she was high-strung and upset. When she ran out of the house to meet Julian at Coffee Plus Food, she stopped to talk to Poppa W because she was crying. Poppa comforted her. He hugged her goodbye. A few houses up the street, a car pulled away from the curb and began to roll toward them. She barely even glanced at it, but Poppa W was an old hand at cars rolling by and slowing down. In his gut he knew something was wrong. His intuition gave him an extra half a second to react, and the instinct saved his life. Thinking the short barrel of the Glock 9 through the half-open window was meant for him, Poppa shoved Josephine down to the pavement and turned sideways. Three shots rang out, two for her and one for him.

He lived.

Poppa was heavy, because he never left his compound without a piece, and despite his bloodied right arm, he yanked out his Ruger and fired four times at the screeching, speeding-away car. The injured arm trembled, the aim was for shit, and he didn't shoot straight. But he still managed to blow out the rear window, pierce a tire, puncture the gas tank—and clip the driver in the neck. The car careened, crashed into a palm tree and caught fire. As Josephine lay dying, two trapped men burned— the ill-fated driver and Fario Rima, her cuckolded overbuilt lover, whom Julian called Moses Jackson. The night before, Fario had taken her betrayal stonily but not well. He thought he was coming to California to bring his intended home to New York, not to take back the ring he had given her, yet another ring Josephine never wore. Mistaking a hug for a clinch and Poppa W for her new lover, Fario aimed to kill them both. Ava told Julian later that through the years, Fario kept repeating that he couldn't live without Mia, and no one believed him.

They believed him now.

∞

When Julian opened his eyes, he was no longer face down. Pants on but still shirtless, he was slumped in a wooden chair in the corner and the man was on the floor in a lotus position in the diagonal corner, studying him with sympathy and curiosity.

"Why are you staring at me like that?" Julian said, groggy and torpid.

"Why can't you find any consolation?" Devi replied. "Why are you treating your God-given life as if it's the greatest of evils?"

"What have I told you?"

"I don't know," Devi said. "Everything? Half of nothing? Answer me. Do you want to be pulled up by your roots and destroyed? Then keep living as you are."

Julian had no reply.

"You're suffering."

"Well, it's no secret."

"You believe that your suffering is punishment."

Julian crossed his fists on his chest.

"You think that you killed her. You think everybody killed her," Devi said. "According to you, her death has a dozen pairs of hands. You blame them all, yourself first. You fault her mother, her best friend, the man across the street who tried to save her, the getaway driver. The only one you seem to have a relatively small amount of enmity for is the man who actually pulled the trigger."

Julian had no good answer for that. Was it because he understood the pain of betrayed passion? Or was it because Fario Rima was also dead?

"You feel that you've pushed her into a marriage she could not enter into, and that her death is punishment for your obsession. Julian, look at me." Devi shook his head. "None of this is true. It's your ignorance talking."

"Is ignorance another word for conscience?"

"Ignorance of the Divine Law. You think you're being punished because the God you don't believe in is displeased with you?" Devi tutted in his corner.

"Who says I don't believe in God?"

"*You* do. By your despair. To live without hope is to reject the possibility of God's mercy."

Julian thought about that a long time. The words tolled and resonated and finally faded. "I don't see much mercy or hope here, Devi Prak, whoever you are."

"There you go again, proving my point. When you wallow in self-pity, you wander away from God. How can He help you when you're this far?"

"I don't need help."

"You've literally been begging strangers for help."

Julian stayed quiet.

"Do you know what one of your problems is?" the cook said. "You're deluded. Not just you, of course. Many men."

"You?" Julian thought he was being clever.

Vigorously, Devi nodded. "Very much so. I know what it means to blame yourself. I learned the hard way. Harder than you."

Julian scoffed.

"Yes, deride—it's the refuge of skeptics. Do you want to know what your greatest delusion is?"

"Even if I say no, I fear you'll tell me."

"You have two," Devi said. "One is you think the things that are out of your control are in your control. That's your hubris, your irrevocable pride talking. To think *you* can control whether another human being lives or dies. It's the most difficult lesson for us to learn." Devi looked into the palms of his hands.

Julian didn't want to hear it.

"And two—you have limited your access to her by perceiving her only as mortal."

Julian blinked.

"It's true, her body is mortal," Devi said. "But her soul is not."

Julian said nothing.

"You do believe she has a soul, don't you? Or do you think this is all there is?"

"I don't know," Julian said. "And what does it matter?"

"Your cynicism is alarming," Devi said, "but fortunately, your delusions are temporary. You still have a chance to discover your own irreducible immortality. I don't know about her. Do you have something of hers with you? A relic that belonged to her? I'll be able to tell you better then."

"I don't usually carry her things with me." Julian put a hand on his heart where she lived. "What's the point," he said. "She's gone, and I'm eternally damned."

"How can a soul made in God's image be eternally damned?" Devi exclaimed. He stretched out his arms, cracked his spine, twisted his neck. "This is what number 153 represents. The lie of your premise. Erase it from your thoughts. John 21. You are not the fish that got away. And neither is she." Devi was firm. "No one is beyond salvation."

"What have I told you?"

"You told me she led you into her aura in the mountains," Devi said. "She held a crystal in her hands and you both vanished. She showed you a timeless realm."

"It wasn't a realm, it was a reflection."

"Call it what you will. Did you *feel* in this reflection or did you not? Do you have the crystal with you?"

"What's it to you?" Julian was exhausted and hostile. Now Devi wanted her stone, too?

Devi tilted his head, observing Julian's twitching body. "When you're not on Klonopin, do you stop dreaming of her?"

"Yes." He didn't like this man's questions. They were starting to remind him of the shrink's. "Look, I have to get back to work." Julian only imagined getting up. "My boss hates me as it is." He struggled to his feet, feeling faint.

"Because you keep vanishing?" Devi said. "Who wouldn't hate you for that? But you don't need a shrink." The man paused as if ambivalent about continuing. "You need a shaman. Sit down."

Julian sat down.

Rising to his feet, Devi approached Julian. "First, you must let go of your anguish," he said. "You're not a murderer. You're not the man who killed her."

But he was. He was.

"A killer burns with a terror in his sleep," Devi said. "That's not you."

The shaman was wrong. It was him. Julian would never forgive himself for abandoning her in her last hours. He pressured her before she could defuse the ticking bomb that was her life. His last words to her was that he never wanted to see her again. He told her he hated her. His last act was to shove her away. There was no forgiveness for that. There was no redemption. He couldn't look at Devi for fear he would cry in front of a stranger.

Devi almost reached out to comfort him, Julian must have looked so demolished. "It wasn't her time," Julian said, barely audible. "She was only twenty-eight."

"It *was* her time," Devi said. "People have the gift of death, as well as the gift of birth. She wasn't punished. The punishment you talk about, that's man's unforgiveness. *Man's* merciless nature, not God's."

Julian shook his head in disagreement.

"Did you love her?" Devi asked. "Answer me. What did that feel like inside you? It felt like light, didn't it? Not darkness. Where does your love for her spring from, if not from a divine source?"

"So what?"

"Just think," Devi said, "why would He who made you and made her, who gave your heart the capacity to love and your soul the capacity to change run through you with hell-fire?"

Julian collapsed inward.

"You are not made *only* to suffer," Devi said gently but firmly. "You are made for other things."

"Like what?" A downtrodden Julian waited. "Is there a single thing you can say to actually help me?"

"That depends. Can you give up Klonopin?"

"No."

The man said nothing.

Julian peeked outside. With shock he saw it was dark. He jumped up. "How did it get so late? Ashton is going to report me missing." He fixed the little man with a suspicious stare.

The man stared back, stern and mute. He adjusted his black sleeves, rebuttoned them, brushed off the dust from his sleeves. "I may be able to help you," Devi said. "I don't know. Bring me her things, whatever you have of hers, and then I'll tell you. But—and it's a big but—there is one non-negotiable condition."

Warily Julian braced himself for what it could possibly be.

"You can never take Klonopin again."

Julian blanched. "I told you, I can't do that."

The man slid open the noisy curtain. "Suit yourself. Then I can't help you."

"You don't understand. I need it to function." Julian was plaintive, like a child begging.

"It isn't true. The opposite is true. The Peckham man was right. You *can* function. You just don't want to. Not only is the drug not the solution, it's its own problem. You take a pill so you can dream of her? How does that help you? How does that help her?"

Julian was reeling. How could anything help her now?

"I'm telling you how it is," Devi went on. "You don't want to hear it, I see that. But if you stick with me, you're going to hear a lot of difficult things. This is one of the easiest."

In vain Julian searched the back room for his discarded shirt.

"Klonopin is a life-threatening drug," the man said. "Gradually you will lose your mind—what's left of it. Klonopin, like Ativan, like Fentanyl, like Propofol, like opium"—Devi paused for a breath—"separates you from life."

Julian thought her death had done that.

"Is it effective?" Devi continued. "For a time. Then you stop eating. Then you stop breathing. Then you stop wanting to eat, wanting to breathe. And then you die. There's a reason that during war morphine is given only to the hopeless."

"Klonopin is not morphine."

"Eventually it's meant to kill you."

"It takes away my pain."

"Oh, sure," the man said almost cheerfully. "The same way death takes away your pain. Because it takes away your life."

Julian didn't agree. But he listened.

"What you still don't know," Devi said, "is that your suffering is not meant to destroy you. It's meant to show you a way out. And Klonopin is a trap door over your conscious self. There is no way out."

Julian knew this to be true.

"The trick is not to take Klonopin so you can see her. The trick," Devi said, "is to see her without it."

"I can't see her without it," said Julian.

"Stick with me, doubting Thomas. I will show you how."

Julian shook his head. "I've tried. I can't."

The Vietnamese man was unimpressed by Julian's low tone, by his defeated demeanor. "You have *not* tried," he said coldly. "You have done *nothing*. You know the drug is there, like crutches in the closet."

"No," Julian repeated stubbornly.

One blink and the man held Julian's shirt and jacket in his hands. Another blink and Julian was being ushered out.

"Go home," Devi said. "If you don't come back, I'll know you've found someone else to give you what you think you need."

"You think *you* can give me what I need?"

The man's face did not change its school-principal expression. "Do you yourself even know what that is?" He shook his head. "If you want meaningful communication with the dead, you cannot do it while unconscious. Have you considered that maybe she never reaches your table in the dream because you stop her with your opiate wall?"

Julian had not considered this.

Unceremoniously, Devi shoved him out into the street. "Julian Cruz, what if I told you there was a way you could see her again?" he said. "In this world, not the next, and not in your dreams, but in real life. Would you stop taking Klonopin then?" Before Julian could take a questioning breath, Devi shut and locked the door.

27

Red Beret, Take Two

WAS DEVI PRAK A SNAKE-OIL SALESMAN OR A WIZARD?

Was he inventing tricks to fool a desperate man? And frankly, how hard was that? Before the bell sounds, you're already down for the count, while the other fighter has fled the ring clutching the victory belt.

It was after eleven when Julian banged on the door of Ashton's suite at the Covent Garden Hotel on Monmouth Street near Seven Dials.

"Where the *hell* have you been?" Ashton said, flinging open the door as if he'd been on alert for hours. "I was about to call the police."

Riley was asleep in the bedroom, so they went up the road to Freud Bar in a concrete basement.

Even if Devi *was* the great deceiver, what other options did Julian have? Admit himself into Weaver's sanatorium? Bathe in mud as Riley had suggested, get his grief stung out of him by bees? Join a bereavement group? Dive into online dating as Ashton kept advising?

"I hear you didn't come to work again today," Ashton said. "By all means, Jules, make my job harder."

"I was hungover," Julian said. "That's your fault. Too much celebrating. I took a day off, is that not allowed anymore?"

"How many days off is that since January, thirty? And why are you twitching? Is that DTs or something?"

"Course not," said Julian.

"So what the hell is wrong with your hands? You look like you have Parkinson's, dude. Or you're on crack."

Through sheer will, Julian forced his body into a pillar-like posture. He didn't want to upset Ashton with the reality of his addiction. His friend had had entirely too much of that in his life. "What do you know about the Hmong shamans, Ash?"

"The who?"

"The Hmong. A mountain tribe from Vietnam."

"Nothing."

Julian knew how Ashton worked, so he waited, his hands knotted together. When they were on their second pint, Ashton cleared his throat. "Black Hmong?"

"What other kind is there?"

"Shut up. Many of them were converted to Christianity by the missionaries. Some conflated the New Testament with their ancient shamanic rites."

"What sort of rites?"

"Ancestor veneration. Healing rituals. They burn a lot of incense," Ashton said.

"What for?"

"To ward off sickness. To summon the dead."

"Do they do that a lot?" Julian asked carefully. "Um, summon the dead?"

"Why? Are you thinking of going to a shaman? Sometimes they summon the dead with the help of newborns, I believe. But you can only do that if you're one of the strongest Hmong."

"What makes someone a shaman? I mean, how can you tell if someone is a real shaman or—a fake one?"

"Well, I suppose you know because a real one would either heal the sick or summon the dead," Ashton said. "I mean, that'd be the first fucking clue, don't you think? His results."

Too invested to be baited, Julian downed his beer, leaving his hands on the glass to steady them. "Riley burns incense. That doesn't make her a shaman."

"Yes, because Riley," said Ashton, "is not from mystical mountains nor does she act as an intermediary between the spirit and the material world during soul-calling rituals. Go to the library, dude. Or check out this thing on your computer, it's pretty neat. It's called, wait, the name will come to me—the internet!"

Stifled and trite, Julian was ground down and at the same time floating a mile above Londontown. Was Devi a shyster, a trickster, a liar?

Or was he the real thing?

"This soul-calling, it's not devil worship, is it?" Julian asked super casually. "Like to ward off sickness, or, you know, for the other thing, you don't have to sell your soul, do you?"

"I don't think so. But sure, the soul can definitely be hijacked by an evil force. Look at Johnny Blaze. Why the sudden interest in the Hmong?" Ashton asked. "You think the hill men from 'Nam can fix you? They might have the power over numbers and cards. But trust me, not in your favor, bro. I've seen it time and again in Vegas. While you're at the fights, I'm at the tables. Never sit at a Hmong table. They'll pick you clean. They don't bust, and they always have an Ace in the hole. Is that what you wanted to know?"

Julian didn't know what he wanted.

They continued drinking, sitting at the bar side by side, listening to Counting Crows "Daylight Fading," watching rugby highlights on mute.

Usually he stayed with Ashton and Riley when they visited. But tonight Julian begged off. He said he wasn't feeling well. Which wasn't a lie; look how his hands were shaking.

Julian barely closed his eyes that long and rainy Friday night. Early Saturday morning, still in Friday's clothes, he was on the train to Hoxton, carrying her things. The red beret. Her crystal quartz necklace, now wanted on two continents. The playbill she had signed for him at *The Invention of Love*. The two books by her bedside: *A Chronicle of a Death Foretold* (how Julian wished he hadn't read it. He couldn't get the image of the mother trying to break down the door to get to her son being murdered on the other side out of his head); and *Monologues for Actors*, the book she had bought when they first met. Ava McKenzie had taken everything else.

The door to Quatrang was locked. The sign said closed. Devi was busy with someone else. Through the mirrored glass windows that made it difficult to peek inside, Julian spied another man, a burly hirsute bear, folded into thirds at Devi's counter.

Did Devi serve his customers one at a time? How could he possibly stay in business? Julian banged on the door until it opened, barely.

"You are obnoxiously loud and now is not a good time," Devi said through the crack.

"I was thinking about what you said."

"Still not a good time, despite you trying to lure me into conversation."

"I agree to your terms," Julian said. "Whatever you want. I won't take it again. Klono. Ever. Just…help me."

"I have to go. I'm busy."

"Please help me." Julian tried to get a foot inside the door, but Devi wouldn't let him. His strength belied his size. He could knock out twenty Julians with a flick of a finger.

"Now is *not* a good time," Devi repeated. "Though it's true— you have almost no time left." He sighed. "Do you have her things?"

"Yes." Why did Julian feel such relief? He took them out of his pocket one by one.

"Whoa," Devi said when his hands touched the beret. Their eyes met. "The spirit of your life is on fire in this thing."

"You mean *her* life," Julian said.

Devi's eyes didn't leave Julian's face.

"She died in it. Her blood is on it."

"I feel it. I feel a lot." Devi nodded. "Come back Monday. I'll talk to you then." He moved to close the door.

Julian stopped him. He didn't want to go. He wanted to stay in Devi's stern, soothing presence. "Wait...her things...you're only going to borrow them, right?"

"As opposed to what? Selling them on eBay?"

"I don't know why you do anything you do. Maybe for some weird voodoo."

"Mr. Cruz," Devi said. "I'm a Hmong man. I come from North Vietnam, South Burma, from an ancient civilization of shamans. I told you this. I am many things. But one thing I'm not is a Creole Haitian black man. You're confusing your mystical rituals and your dark-skinned foreigners, which is understandable, given your ignorance on a wealth of subjects, this in particular."

"Your voodoo needles confused me," Julian said.

"Come back Monday."

"Wait, what did you mean when you said I could be with her again? Like in a séance?"

"Monday, Julian."

"Wait! Why not Sunday?"

Devi spoke slow. "Because it's *Sunday*." He slammed the door.

28

When We Were Kings

JULIAN SPENT A RAINY SATURDAY HANGING WITH HIS brothers and Ashton, while Zakiyyah, Riley and Gwen shopped at Harrods. At night the seven of them met up for dinner at the Savoy Grill and saw Noel Coward's *Blithe Spirit* at the Savoy Theatre. *Time is the reef upon which all our frail mystic ships are wrecked.* On Sunday, they got together for brunch at the Bar Brasserie in the lobby of the Covent Garden Hotel.

Ashton pored over the Sunday paper for apartments to rent and carried on a running argument with Julian over Notting Hill that sounded like a stand-up routine. It amused the girls, and perhaps that was the point.

Ashton: "Why do you say Notting Hill is too far from work?"

Julian: "It's a geographical fact. Plus it's too expensive."

Ashton: "What else do *you* have to spend your money on? Notting Hill is young, eclectic, the girls come in all shapes and sizes, and to the one they love themselves a Yankee wid"—he stopped himself—"bachelor."

Julian: "How do you know this?"

"Yes, Ashton," said Riley. "How *would* you know this?"

"Yes, Ashton," said Zakiyyah, and for the first time Julian saw Zakiyyah's genuine smile. Her teasing face lit up. "How *would* you know this?" Aha, Julian thought. Okay, so a little bit like a beauty queen.

Ashton: "I researched it for *him*, baby. Notting Hill—bars, nightlife, great food, music, shopping, a Saturday street market to die for. There is nothing wrong with the place, not one thing. Jules, surely we can find a Hermit Street for you in Notting Hill. You can't be living on the only Hermit Street in London."

Julian: "Why do we need to find another one? I'm already *on* one."

Ashton: "Because I'm not living in Whoreditch or wherever it is you've been hiding."

Julian: "Highbury."

Ashton: "Same difference."

Julian knew he wasn't worthy of Notting Hill with its princely terraces. To live there, he needed to be the kind of man who could lean against a posh black gate and sing "On the Street Where You Live."

"It goes without saying *you're* not worthy," Ashton said with his razzle-dazzle smile. "But I am."

After brunch, everyone but Ashton flew home. They all had to be back at work on Monday.

Julian and Ashton spent the rest of the crisp and windy mid-March day together like it was the good old days in L.A. They walked around Hyde Park with about a million others who were grateful it wasn't raining.

They had dinner at Dishoom, the best Indian in Covent Garden. They waited an hour for a table, drank at the bar downstairs, ate late, and were fully in their cups by midnight.

An exhausted Julian walked quietly by Mrs. Pallaver's ajar parlor door on his way upstairs. She didn't call out to him. *Where you been, love. Frieda, look who's home.* It was just as well, though demoralizing.

He was wiped out from the sun and wind, and from talking— Julian hadn't talked so much since before Josephine died. He was showered and naked in bed—without Klonopin—unwell, dry-mouthed, and for the first time without her things to cling to. He couldn't sleep. Tomorrow Quatrang. What would it bring?

It was quiet in his third-floor walk-up facing the rear. His whole life here was like living in a dumbshow.

Once in a while, back in L.A., Julian would stay with Josephine on Normandie. With no AC, they'd leave their windows open, and all night through the screens they'd hear music blaring, dogs yelping, cars on the freeway burning by. After hours of this, even wine didn't help, and white noise became black noise, "Wrecking Ball" and "Dang" jangling against "Hard Out Here for a Pimp," honking on Clinton, sirens on Melrose, bodega alarms, Kendrick Lamar flow-rhyming his life, dogs barking and barking, Julian humming "When We Were Kings," wishing for ear plugs or drugs or a wife.

If it wasn't for her and her gentle face in their brief soliloquy, a face that didn't belong across the street from a house fenced with razors, Julian would've never set foot in that hood.

Yet now, when it was soundless every day and night in his monastic room with the fallen Christ, a room he rented from a sweet English lady out of central casting, all he wanted was what he would never have again. His nerves charged and his heart on fire.

Then: grinding discomfort with being alive.

Now: every silent minute longing to be electrocuted with life.

29

Zero Meridian

Ashton wanted to have lunch before his flight on Monday. What could Julian say—no? Can't, Ash, I'm busy with a shaman? He said yes.

He took off work, again—unconscionable really—and returned to Great Eastern Road first thing Monday morning, March 19. It was a brittle, gusty, terrible day.

Inside Quatrang Julian was hit with a sharp smell of pungent incense, and other unfamiliar scents—chalky milk, fermented fruit, ashes.

"Sit," Devi said.

"Am I eating?"

"Too early." Devi slid a goblet of murky water in front of Julian. "Drink."

Sit. Drink. Julian sat, drank. The dusty water looked unappetizing but tasted strong and sweet.

On the counter between them, Devi laid out Josephine's things. Julian watched warily. The crystal, the books, the playbill. Seeing the beret on display turned Julian's stomach. There was no way to see it without seeing it on the street, rolled away to the curb where she would never need it again.

"Tell me more about the light in the mountain," Devi said. "What time was that?"

"With her? Noon. Why?"

Devi was mouthing something, touching the beret, the crystal. "What happened to the stone here? Looks chipped."

"It's my fault," Julian said. "I took it to a jeweler. I wanted to cut it in half and drill a hole in it so I could wear a small piece of it around my neck. But the crystal broke two of the guy's diamond drill bits." Julian kept the pieces of the chipped-off crystal in a glass jar by his bed.

Devi nodded. "That's the thing about crystal. Some crystals you can reface. And others you can't. It all depends whether the crystal wants to be drilled into. Clearly this one does not." He caressed the stone. "It has a very powerful *chakra*. Compressed energy."

"Yes."

"Her mother let you keep it?"

"At first, she gave it to me gladly. Said it was cursed."

"Cursed why?"

"It's not obvious why?"

"So why would you keep it if you thought it was cursed?"

"My whole life is cursed." Julian reached for the beret.

Devi Prak, compact like a Derringer, disagreed. "You think you're cursed?" He laid his hand on the hat. "Do you even know what that means? That someone has cast evil upon you. Like who?"

"I don't know, but—Devi, why do you keep touching her beret? What's wrong with it?"

"Nothing," Devi said. "Her presence overwhelms it. It's an ancient rite of many cultures to keep sacred the property of the dead because their spirit remains in the material things they've left behind. Their things become holy relics."

Julian took the beret from Devi's hands.

"I was wrong," Devi said. "It happens so rarely that I freely admit when it does. From what you've told me about her and from her actions, I perceived her soul as new. But it's not. Her soul is old. That's unfortunate for her, but in some ways, it may be a blessing for you."

"Why unfortunate, why a blessing, what are you trying to do, summon the dead?"

"I see you've read up on Hmong shamanism," Devi said. "Just enough to be truly ignorant. No, she is far beyond that now. You need deeper magic than a séance."

"Like what?"

"First tell me what you want, Julian."

Julian squeezed the beret in his hands as if he wanted to squeeze her life from it. What he wanted was to summon another sonnet for her out of the dust. He couldn't put what he wanted into words.

Watchfully, Devi took him in. After a few minutes he pulled up Julian's shirt-sleeve and used an edge of a silver coin to scrape off a patch of skin on the inside of Julian's left forearm.

"Um—ouch?"

"Hush," Devi said sternly. When a few droplets of blood seeped from the skin, Devi applied a salve into the lesion.

"You know," Julian said without rancor, "if you didn't peel me open, you wouldn't need to apply the ointment." He didn't mind. Devi could do a lot to him. He felt a flow of unspoken compassion from the gruff cook that was intensely comforting.

"If I didn't peel you open, how would I release your toxins?"

Devi and Riley were birds of a feather. "What's the grease you're putting inside me anyway?"

"Tiger balm," the man replied. "Stop fidgeting. You really do need another week or two, a month even, to rid your body of the poison you've been taking. Look at you." It was true. Julian was unusually jittery, his fingers tapping on the counter, sliding back and forth, his shoe banging against the foot rest. He kept itching his elbow and the back of his neck. He was a ticking mess.

"It's not Klono, it's you," Julian said. "Just tell me what you want to tell me and be done with it."

"Turn your attention to the tremor in your right hand," Devi said. "Focus. Tense your fist, clench as tightly as you can, take a breath, take a drink, then relax. And repeat. While you do that,

I'm going to make you food. But until tomorrow, I want you to eat nothing but warm white rice, boiled chicken, a little lemon grass and salt. Nothing else."

"What's happening tomorrow?"

"All in good time. No beer with your friends, no coffee, no donuts. No Indian food."

"Okay." How did Devi know what he had to eat yesterday?

"You don't need to be Sherlock or a shaman to know you smell of chicken tikka, Julian," Devi said. "Cumin is hard to hide."

Julian clenched his fist. As soon as he unclenched it, his right fingers quivered. Devi's back was turned while he was at the grill. "You're not focusing," Devi said, as if he had eyes in the back of his head. "Clench, breathe, relax, repeat. And look around you. Because you're only minimally observant, you think I have nothing but clocks on the walls, but do you even see my wallpaper altar? It's in front of you. Take a moment to bow your head."

Julian looked up at the wall above Devi. There was a vague design. He thought it was blotched paint.

Devi put the chicken and rice on a plate and poured Julian another glass of foggy water. "I feel the power of her red and formidable aura," Devi said, backing away to the grill. "But I have to be honest with you, Julian, I also strongly feel the fading of her soul. I've pondered your dream and examined her spiritual situation. You are right, the dream is quite mysterious. Because you should not be able to see her, and likewise she should not be able to see you. Eat. Unfortunately her soul has remained in disharmony with itself to the very end. Disharmony causes suffering. And suffering makes us blind."

"I'm not blind," Julian muttered, defensively rubbing his left eye. "I see her."

"Hence the mystery. Suffering separates us from love. During our life, it separates our souls from our bodies since the two are intimately connected. And after we die, it separates our souls from divine love. This girl brought great harm to herself and those who loved her. She spread anguish into every life she touched."

Julian lowered his head in pained assent.

"Eat," Devi said. "A temple cannot be healthy when its sustaining force is ailing."

Julian was sick in both body and soul. "Are you sure her soul is old? New would be so much better."

"Better for who?" Devi turned his back. "Some souls *are* brand new," he said quietly. "Because the world is constantly being reborn even as we perceive it as old."

"How do you know so much about her?"

When Devi spun around, impatience burned in his dark eyes. "Save your questions for the big things," he said. "I know because of the intensity and desperation of her suffering that's present in her life's blood—and because when I reach for her in the spiritual realm, I cannot find her."

How could Julian eat when he was being told such things.

"Here's what I know," Devi said. "Each of us has been given a soul, and we get several tries on this earth to bring that soul closer to the divine fate that was bestowed on us at birth. That's the mystery and majesty of the grace that's being offered us. Despite the pain we cause others, we are given a second chance, and a third, and a fourth. The struggle for our soul's perfection is our main purpose in life—or should be. To bring it as close as we can to its ineffable glory, so that eventually," Devi said, "we might have life and give life, and live well, and maybe, if we're lucky, become citizens of paradise. When our souls are new, many of us don't know how to do this. Like infants don't know how to smile. But most of us learn." Devi turned his head as if he didn't want Julian to see inside him before the next obvious question. *Did Josephine learn?*

"How many chances do we get?" Julian asked.

"Some of us only need one." Devi raised his eyes and regarded Julian, saying nothing. "And some unfortunately need more than seven." He lowered his gaze again. "We never get less than one. And we never get more than seven."

Julian couldn't bear to ask about Josephine. He held his breath.

Devi told him anyway. "When you met her," Devi said, "she was on the very last of her journeys. That was it for her."

For a few minutes, Julian wobbled miserably on the stool. "Devi..." he whispered, "please say you have the power to bring her back."

"I told you, I have no such power," Devi said grimly. "No one has."

"But you told me there might be a way I could see her again," Julian said. "Was that a lie?"

"I do not lie."

"So what did you mean then?"

Devi didn't reply.

Julian couldn't take a breath.

Devi pushed the plate forward, pushed the drink forward. "You need strength. Here."

Each grain of rice getting stuck in his throat, Julian ate and drank.

"Do you want to change your life, Julian?"

"*Desperately.*"

"You will never change it unless you change what you do every day."

"What would you like me to do, get a hobby?" Julian said. "Perhaps eat more greens?"

"Change what you do right now, and you will change your future. The consequences of every act are contained within the act itself."

Julian had no future. He didn't want to say this to the diminutive shaman.

Devi watched him for a few moments, shaking his head.

"What?"

"And conversely, do things exactly the same, and guess what will happen? Let me tell you about yourself, Julian. Did you know that in the English language, there's no such thing as future tense?"

"Of course there is."

"You love to argue, don't you. No, there isn't. Our verbs describe the things we do and the things we have done. They describe our *actions*. There is present tense and past tense. That's it."

"I came here Friday, I am here today, I will come here tomorrow," Julian said.

"You have no idea if you will come here tomorrow," Devi said. "You might. Then again, you might not. All future tense is either necessity or possibility. We *must* do it, or we *could* do it. All action in the future is either implied or wished upon. What's another word for action? Movement. And without movement, there can be no change."

Who was Julian to argue. He had been living as a catatonic.

"The future is the one part of our existence that stands outside time," Devi said. "Because without something that time can measure—like action or movement—time has no meaning. Julian Cruz, you of all people know this. Eternal London has swallowed you. Your inert grief has swallowed you. You've lost years of your life to the shapeless void. Two years have passed, but if someone told you it was ten years, you'd hardly be surprised. And soon, it *will* be ten years. And then twenty. It will be the rest of your life—unless you *act*. Unless you act *now*."

"Act and do what?"

Devi waited, his black eyes absorbing Julian's downward yet anxious demeanor. "Do you know what a meridian is?"

"What does it have to do with what we're talking about?"

"Do you always answer a question with a question?"

"It's a line of longitude," Julian replied. "It crosses a line of latitude. It's a way to measure distance."

"It crosses many things," Devi said, "and yes, one of the things it measures is distance. As in how far something—or someone—is from you."

"*Someone?*"

"Yes. What else does a meridian measure?"

"Well, time, I suppose."

"Be more certain, Julian, be precise in your speech. Does it or does it not measure time?"

"Yes."

"Yes. Because time and distance are inseparable."

"Okay?" It came out as a question.

"In our universe there is a galaxy," Devi said, "and in the galaxy many stars, and one of those stars is our sun, and our sun has planets orbiting it, and one of the planets is earth, and on the earth there are oceans and continents and islands, and one of the islands is England, and in England there is a river called the Thames, and on the southern banks of the Thames there is a town called Greenwich, and in Greenwich there is a hill, and on this hill may lie the answer to the question you're asking."

"What question?" He had so many. Or did he only have one?

"Many years ago, the King's best men built an astronomy pavilion in Greenwich to help British sailors navigate the seas, to discover the most accurate and reliable method of determining where they were going."

"Okay. What does it have to do with me?"

"Do you know where you're going?"

Julian shut up. Devi went on. "George Airy, Britain's Astronomer Royal, built his famous telescope, and with it for many years he studied the path of the stars and the planets. He called the invisible line that his telescope pointed at the *meridian*, a word that means midday. And what's another word for midday?"

Julian tilted his head. "Um—noon?"

"Why do you sound so hesitant? Yes. Noon." Devi emphasized *noon*, as if he was teaching Julian a new word. "Airy observed the sun as it crossed the meridian at noon. Eventually, the line became known throughout the world as the Prime Meridian or zero meridian."

"I get it, Greenwich Mean Time is based on it, but…"

"Another word for the meridian is *transit line*. That's why Airy's telescope is called the Transit Circle."

"Okay."

"And what does transit mean? No, don't bother," Devi said. "It means passage. It means *journey*."

"*Okay*."

"The Prime Meridian is a channel that separates how far everything is from everything else. It's the grid, and all our miles and minutes are to the left of it or to the right of it. It measures how far Karmadon is from me," Devi said cryptically. "And how far Josephine is from you."

"Who is Karmadon?"

"You're asking the wrong questions," Devi said. "Not who is Karmadon, but what happens on zero meridian at noon. Not to the left of it or to the right of it, but directly on it."

"I don't know, what happens?"

"Things that go beyond the linear nature of time is what happens. Don't look at me like that. You know there's an unreality to time, an illusory component. That's never more obvious than on the meridian as the sun passes overhead. Time is a contradiction. There's an essential conflict built into time's very nature—that each and every event was once future, is now present and has since passed. Every moment is all three, and neither, and all at once."

Julian opened his mouth to disagree. To *vehemently* disagree.

Devi didn't let him interrupt. "Think before you argue. Even as you're opening your mouth, the first part of your sentence is gone, bye-bye. Before you so much as finish measuring the location of the sun, the sun is elsewhere. The hurricane doesn't stand still, Julian, nor the earth, nor a single atom on it."

"Exactly," Julian said. "But what's past is past. Nothing can change it."

"You're sure about that?"

Why did Julian blink before he said yes, one hundred percent sure.

"You don't think the past could be like England, for example? A foreign country, where people do things differently. A place you can go, just as you've come here?"

"Yes," Julian said. "One hundred percent...sure."

"From the way you're slumped, I can see why you'd think so," Devi said. "You are deeply myopic."

"Nothing can change what's already happened," Julian said. "That's pretty much a first principle."

"Listen to me very carefully," Devi said. "Take your assumptions about what you know and throw them all out the window. All of them. You need to learn a new language. The language of the meridian, of universal time, of hope, and of faith. That's your missing first principle right there." Devi drew his finger in a straight line along the counter. "One of the many fallacies in your thinking comes from drawing time with a ruler on a flat surface. That's not what time is. That's not what the meridian is." Devi formed his hands into a ball. "In the spacetime beyond this earth, the meridian is not a line but a celestial sphere. What's another name for celestial? Heavenly. Spiritual. Otherworldly. Godly."

"Or planetary." Trying to be scientific about it.

"Yes," Devi said. "Pertaining to planets. By definition, outside our known world. To make sense of the physical contradiction that is time, certainly *to alter it* requires an observer and a mover, like an axle in a wheel. It requires a soul. It requires you."

Julian sat hunched and slightly trembling.

"Think of yourself as the hub inside this sphere, with the meridians crossing through you like spokes in every direction, north and south, east and west. You turn, and the lines of perspective turn with you. Every point on which you stand has an infinite number of zeniths and nadirs, of horizons and meridians," Devi said. "It all depends on where you look. It all depends on where you step. Within yourself, you contain an infinite number of possibilities." The small man paused so the broken man could absorb this. "You are the essential wave *and* particle in the immensity of all creation."

The clocks whirred. All was quiet.

"And it just so happens," the cook continued, almost as an afterthought, and so low that Julian had to stretch across the counter to hear, "that at the Royal Observatory in Greenwich, there's a spot on the Prime Meridian that once a year forms a small tear in the fabric of time and space. When the brightest star in our sky is crossing the highest point above your head, that is when you must act."

"Forms a *what*?" Did the man just say *tear*?

"Once a year," Devi said, "on the vernal equinox—when day and night are of equal length—a portal at the Transit Circle can open, and if you have heart enough and are strong enough, you can travel through this gate and search for Josephine in the past when her soul inhabited another body."

Julian was silent for several rotations of the beating clock.

"Her quartz crystal will catch the sun and the chasm will open, just as it did for you in the mountains," Devi continued. "It opens to its widest aperture a picosecond past twelve and closes a picosecond before 12:01. Every second that ticks by and the sun is in motion, the portal gets narrower and narrower until it squeezes shut. You have 59 seconds of motion, of action, of the future to change your life. Can you do it?"

Julian let out a heaping breath. He didn't realize how long he'd been holding it. His lungs filled with new air. "Devi, what are you *talking* about? What portal?" He stammered in incomprehension. "I thought you were going to, you know, burn some incense, call up her spirit, act as an intermediary. But you're saying you've found a *time machine*?" Julian laughed. The knot in his body loosened. It didn't help that Devi wasn't smiling, but clearly the man could set up and carry a joke a long way for a payoff.

"Have you ever been to Greenwich?" Devi asked, putting on a clean black apron. "It's worth a look. It's got a wonderful park, and for maritime history, the *Cutty Sark*. And my good friend Mark, owner of Junk Shop, sells all kinds of stuff out of his yard." He brought out white plates and stacked them on the counter.

"Don't change the subject."

"Why not?" Devi said. "You have no faith. What more is there to talk about?"

"What you're saying is impossible."

"Like your dream of her is impossible?"

Julian inhaled. "More than that."

"Like when you told the Peckham man about your predicament, and he said it was impossible?"

"Yes, like that," Julian said, a shade less convincingly.

Uninterested in persuading Julian further, Devi got busy laying out the cooking utensils he needed for lunch.

"Is that it? You're done talking?"

"Do you want me to tell you more things you refuse to believe?"

"Yes," Julian said instantly. "I want you to tell me more things I refuse to believe."

Coming closer, Devi spoke intensely. "Under the Observatory, there's a void where the bedrock has been dissolved by slightly acidic water. Rock and soil have been washed away. The structural integrity of earth has been breached. A sinkhole has formed. The vertical sinkhole is what leads you to a quartz cave. It's a plumb line."

"*Quartz* did you say?" The slow wheels in Julian's brain were grinding. "Where does the cave lead?"

"To a river."

"You're a joker. There are no caves and rivers under London."

"You've been here all this time and haven't bothered to learn the history of our underground rivers?" Devi tutted.

"I know the city was built on a marsh flat."

"That's only part of it. The Londinium of two thousand years ago was a swamp of rivers and volcanic caves. Human development, irrigation, rechanneling of the water has made many rivers disappear and others recede underground, but some are still there, invisible to the naked eye. Like *time* is invisible to the naked eye," Devi added pointedly. "Yet you're still pretty sure time exists, aren't you?"

Julian wouldn't be baited. Also he was sure of less and less. "Where does the river lead?"

"To Josephine."

Julian's teeth started to chatter. A shiver misaligned his spine.

"Think of time as an overflowing river," Devi said, "that runs through all things and all events and all souls. There is a point on this river when she was alive. Maybe you can steer your dinghy there."

"How would some river know where she is?" Julian muttered.

"Her beret and crystal will take you to her."

He was roiling inside. This was preposterous! How did he get himself into this lunatic conversation, inside this lunatic joint, to this lunatic man?

"What are you worried about?" Devi said. "Either I'm right, or you're right. It's really quite Kantian."

"Kantian? No, no, don't explain. Tell me," Julian said, "when does this magical event occur?"

"I told you. Tomorrow."

"You never said this."

"I did. I said vernal equinox. Do you not know when the vernal equinox is? What kind of a know-it-all are you?"

"Tomorrow?" Julian emitted a dry laugh. "As in twenty-four hours from now?"

"Correct," Devi said. "You know—like in the *future*."

"Well, you're not giving me much *time* to think about it, Devi." He was humoring the cook.

"You think *that's* where your time crunch comes?" Devi said. "That you have twenty-four hours not to act but to think? Try getting down a narrowing spiral in 59 seconds. Or finding a moongate. Or navigating a black river in darkness, knowing that the human body can only be without food for forty days. Think about *those* things, why don't you."

"I'm going to be without food for forty days?"

"I didn't say that. I'm helping you assign priorities to this thinking you're about to do."

Julian jumped off the stool. "This is crazy. Look, I have to go. Ashton's waiting. How about this. I'll go get some books on the meridian, on the history of the Observatory and this Transit Circle. I'll go to Foyles on Charing Cross Road. They have a whole section on astronomy and navigation. You've given me a *lot* to think about. I'll come back when I have more info." He reached for his coat.

"Take all the time you need," Devi said. "You've been taking your time so far. Why stop now?"

"Settle down," Julian said. "When is the next time this supposed thing opens?"

"March 20."

"I don't mean tomorrow. I mean the *next* time."

"How many times do I have to repeat myself?" Devi said. "A year from tomorrow. March 20."

"It only opens for 59 seconds once a year?"

"*Finally*, I'm making myself clear."

Julian weakened.

"So you see, you have plenty of time to get your head around it," Devi said brightly. "Instead of searching for your lost love, you can take a year to read all about the meridian."

Devi was an immovable force. He would not be swayed. Could Julian be swayed? One man was a post and the other was flung about like a sapling in a storm. Julian perched on the stool for support, listening to the ticking of the clocks, the dripping of the faucet, the breathing of the little man, his own conflicted constricted gasps. There was a vacuous ringing between his ears.

Devi tried again. Opening Julian's palm and placing Josephine's translucent stone into it, he said, "You had magic in your hands all this time and you didn't know it. What's the crystal made of?"

"Quartz," Julian dully replied.

"Yes. It has light reflecting, light absorbing properties. It becomes charged when heated. Because it's *quartz*, Julian. The second most abundant mineral found on earth. A major component of granite, which is nothing less than the earth's core that's been melted and cooled and hardened. And what does quartz do? It changes heat—another word for light—into electromagnetic energy. It focuses and amplifies this energy. Quartz is piezoelectric, which means it stores energy and discharges it when shaken or squeezed. And what do we use quartz for?" Devi opened his hands to the ticking clocks on his walls. "To measure time. And to heal the sick."

Julian's breath was shallow.

"I am your healer," Devi said. "Go to Greenwich, my boy." The cook lifted Julian's hand to the ceiling. "Hold her quartz up to the sun. See if it might alter time."

Julian couldn't explain to Devi that until Josephine came along and showed him what real magic was, he had been a rational man, jaded by years of working behind the curtain in Emerald City, no longer taken in by the optical illusions and special effects of moving pictures. While living in the land of enchantment for sale, Julian turned away from the make-believe of Tinseltown while he looked for practical solutions to everyday problems. How to simplify jobs. Reduce stress. Ease life. Clean stains off clothes. Marinate steak. *How to find a non-poisonous plant in the wild to tame your raging head wound.* A man who searched for household uses for honey and vodka while ignoring the dream life reflected in the fake windows of Technicolor backdrops was not a man who could easily see mystical power in arbitrary lines of navigational utility.

Ashton—who believed good-naturedly and superficially in everything—mocked him for this. How can a man like you, Ashton would say, who was lost and then found, not believe in miracles? It wasn't that Julian didn't believe in miracles. But he was certain he'd been allotted his lifetime supply in Topanga Canyon.

Today that man stared into Devi's impassive face with disbelieving eyes.

"Let's say for a second, for a hypothetical, that I can...that this thing is real," Julian said. "Can I come back?"

"No," Devi said. "You cannot. But finally you have asked a worthy question."

The impossibility of what Devi was telling him banged on the fear drum of Julian's gut. He wanted to laugh, but a slasher-movie laugh. It's not real! his raw senses cried. It's a trick. It's just another backlot.

But what if it is real, a small voice inside him whispered.

And what was more terrifying?

That it wasn't real?

Or that it was?

30

Notting Hill

A DAZED JULIAN STUMBLED TO THE TRAIN. BY THE TIME HE got out at Moorgate and ran through the rain to the Gallery in Austin Friars, where Ashton was unhappily waiting, it was well past their appointed hour.

"Sorry, man, I have no watch," Julian said, "and my phone's never charged."

"Whose fault is that? Why do I have to suffer because you can't get your shit together? I have to be at Heathrow by four."

They ordered fish and chips, but Julian couldn't eat. Devi told him not to. How ridiculous! He was so agitated, he didn't know how Ashton didn't notice his hyperactive body.

"What's the matter with you?" Ashton placed his hand over Julian's arm. "Stop twitching. What the hell?" So perhaps he did notice. "Are you on drugs or something?"

"Not anymore. Don't worry," Julian added when he saw Ashton's face. "I'll be fine in a day or two."

"Will you find us a place by May 1?"

May 1 was the *future*. "Sure."

"You inspire zero confidence. Can you try not to get fired?"

"Absolutely."

"That would entail you actually going to work."

"First thing tomorrow morning I'm there." That was also the *future*. Julian grabbed the arm of his chair.

"Do not write any more headlines like FREQUENT SEX ENHANCES PREGNANCY CHANCES."

"Why, is it not true?"

"Graham's so pissed, Jules. Like *so* pissed. He says he'll never forgive you for tricking him the other day."

"What did I do? Oh." Julian actually laughed. "I didn't do anything wrong! I simply asked him if *first hand* was two words or one. I sought his wise counsel. He told me either way was correct. So I followed his advice and wrote it as two words. How is that my fault?"

"Because of the headline you wrote, that's how," said Ashton. "INTERNS WANT FIRST HAND JOB EXPERIENCE."

Both men laughed.

"You're making a mockery of journalistic practices," Ashton said, cheerful and light-hearted. "I'm going to reassign you when I take over. I can't have you making a fool of me, too."

"Can't wait," Julian said. "To where?"

"Since you can't do the job you've got, obviously I'm going to have to promote you," replied Ashton. "Graham's been moved to the basement, to records, the poor bastard. I'm giving you his old job and putting you in charge of the editorial department." He whipped open last Friday's *Evening Standard*. "Now check this out." He showed Julian a circled ad for an apartment. "Bright airy furnished two-bedroom flat near Notting Hill on Cambridge Gardens. Look at the price. Not bad. Go rent it. No questions asked."

"You don't want to live there," said Julian.

"Yes, I do."

"No. The higher numbers on Cambridge Gardens are under the A-40 highway. You'll be in a nuthouse in a week from the noise." He mushed around his mushy peas.

Ashton showed him another place on Elgin Crescent.

Julian shook his head. "Not there, either. There's a pub on Elgin Crescent, one of the loudest in London," he said. "Every Friday night someone's getting arrested. Recently a bloke got killed."

"How the *hell* do you know?"

"It was in all the papers," Julian said calmly. "Why are you shouting?"

"Oh, now he's calm."

"I'm always calm. Also, Ashton, I told you that Nextel is nowhere near Notting Hill. How do you plan on getting to work every morning?"

"Hop on the Central Line, baby." Ashton grinned. "Get off at Bank."

"Yeah, okay," Julian said. "You'll be letting three jammed trains go by before you can squeeze your ass on a Central Line train. Might as well take the Circle Line. Either way, it'll take us over an hour to get to work. Is that what you want?"

"No, Jules, what I want," Ashton said, "is you back in our beautiful L.A., living your life and getting jiggy with the babes. But since I can't have that, yes, I want a ritzy flat in Notting Hill with a palm tree outside to remind me of home. Hey, we only live once."

Did they only live once? "You'll never hear a Hindu say that," Julian said lightly. "But seriously, Ash, what about Riley? She didn't seem too happy with the idea of you on your own five thousand miles away."

"I won't be on my own. I'll be with you." Ashton slapped the newspaper closed. "Did I tell you we're in couple's therapy?"

"You and Riley are in therapy together?"

"Crazy, right? Everybody in L.A. is in therapy, you know that. Even Riley's Yorkie. Lucky for me the dog has his own therapist. But yeah. She wants to make sure we can work out our shit before we get married."

"What shit?"

"Oh, you know. I'm not serious enough about life, love, work, *et cetera*. She calls it my Peter Pan syndrome. Says it's time to grow up."

"Ashton." Julian shook his head. "Dude, trust me on this, if you're going to therapy *before* you get married, the next move is to break the fuck up, not get hitched."

"Imma tell Riley you said that. She gon' be mad."

It was time for Ashton to catch a cab to Heathrow. Both men were reluctant to part ways.

"Do I seem all right to you, Ash?" Julian asked.

"No."

"I mean, do I seem better than before?"

"No."

"Like I'm sane, but depressed?"

"No."

"What, do I seem like all the wheels are about to come off?"

"No." Ashton got up. "Wheels came off long ago, brother. They came off that fucking night at the Cherry Lane in New York. I will never forgive Nicole Kidman's driver. I haven't seen the real Julian since."

Julian got up, too. "How do you know this isn't the real Julian?"

"That's the worst thing you've ever said to me," Ashton said. "See, I'm still hoping for a revival." They bumped fists, shoulders. Julian was going to hug him but stopped himself.

"Dude, chill," Ashton said with a friendly slap. "I'll see you in a month."

The *future*. "I hope so," Julian said as they left the Gallery. "Without you, I can't do anything right."

31

Time Over Matter

Thirty minutes after saying goodbye to Ashton, Julian was back at Devi's counter. He extended his hand for the dusty water even before it was offered.

"You're back."

"Like I've got so many more attractive options," Julian said. The cook was quiet. "Is it wrong for me to say I don't believe you?"

"Do you think I'm lying?"

"I didn't say you were lying, Devi," Julian said. "I said I didn't believe you. There's a difference."

"You won't get far with disbelief."

Devi had prepared a plate of cold chicken and white rice for him. Dutifully Julian ate it. When he was done, he sighed. "I'm in no shape to argue this," he said. "But I'm not ready to take your word for it either. Mostly I'm a hundred times not ready to carry it out. I'm not the guy to go into the fray for you."

"Not for me," Devi said. "For *you*. Decide if you're going to stand up or wait for another chime of the hour. Remember, like all of us, you wake up to a new day. Decide if it's actually going to be a new day, or exactly like the days you've been having. It's in your hands, Julian. And the work of one's hands is the beginning of virtue," the cook added. "You think you're having a bad day? Well, why not say instead that today is going to be one of your best days yet?"

Julian took a breath. He had a million things to ask, but memory for barely a dozen answers. "The river only flows one way, no?" he said. "Forward. So I would be going into the future. But you said I'd be going into the past? How can it be both at once?"

"I told you, because time is all things at once," Devi replied. "Also, you're not the flowing river. You're not even the rocking boat. You're the man in the boat. You don't know how to row, and the boat has no oars. That's you."

"I'll ask again. Am I going into the future? Technically, isn't it in my hypothetical future and to my hypothetical future that I'd be traveling to?"

Devi assented. "You can only go into her past because there is no future in which she exists. But since you haven't acted yet, it *is* your future self and your future actions you're contemplating. It's all just possibility as you sit on my stool."

A voice stopped Julian from his knee-jerk cynicism, the same voice that reminded him that Josephine came to him as he slept, walked to him in a new dress, in a new place, blooming with life. It was only because she was so vividly real when she appeared to him that he listened to the Hmong cook now. At least on the outside, he didn't want to be like Weaver, the hectoring skeptical disbeliever of miracles.

"The universe doesn't give you many second chances," Devi said. "But it's giving you this one."

"Why?"

"Maybe because you were asking so loudly that even my deaf mother heard you."

"I knew it! I knew she was your mother."

"Well," Devi said, "you are Mr. Know-it-All."

When Julian attempted no reply, the shaman persisted. "I feel the possibility," Devi said. "I feel it in Josephine's things, and I feel it in you. I feel it in the new moon and in the rain that's been falling, and in the cold wind. The earth is swirling into a new order."

Draping his elbows on the counter, Julian listened to Devi's low voice, like on a distant radio. "I can't do it," he said quietly. "Honest. I can't. I can't go into a cave. The truth is, I'm afraid of confined spaces."

"It's not forever," Devi said.

"Forever or five minutes, it doesn't matter." Julian chewed his fingers. "What else happens there?"

To make Julian feel worse, Devi told him about some other things he could expect. "After falling down the well," the cook said, "you'll meander. You'll feel lost. Try not to despair. There is an end. When you find the moongate, you'll know the river is close. From your gloomy demeanor I gather you've been inside caves before?"

"Sort of. It might've been a talus cave," Julian said. "Scary as balls."

"Well, balls *are* scary," Devi said. "But a talus is not a real cave. It's just rocks piled up."

"Yes, like after an earthquake or some other seismic event that shifts the earth under your feet," Julian said. "I may have disturbed them, I don't know. They collapsed on me. It took me a long time to dig myself out. I lost my way."

For many minutes, Devi was silent, studying Julian, appraising him, measuring him against some unfathomable internal thing.

"This will be something else," Devi finally said.

"What's a moongate?"

"Oh, Julian."

"Oh, Julian what? Is it a gate that looks like a moon?"

"Yes. It's a gate that looks like a moon. A talisman. It allows you to live inside the mystery."

"Is it manmade?"

"How can it be manmade? You're in a *cave*!"

"Don't get impatient with me, shaman. Just explain it."

Devi's expression was severe. "To get to the moongate won't be easy," he said. "You may have to jump. You may even have to leap."

"I'm not a leaper."

"I reckon you'll have to become a good many things you're not," said Devi, refilling Julian's goblet. "Once inside, there's no turning back. You can't change your mind. The portal is not a revolving door. It only opens one way. The only way out is through it. The only way out is forward."

Julian was pensive. "You said L.A. was her seventh and last time?"

"Yes."

"So to which of her seven lives would this river of yours take me? Is it random? Or do I get to choose? I hope it's back to L.A. That way, I can kill Fario Rima."

Devi looked at Julian like he was ashamed of him. He picked up a cleaver and took out two heads of cabbage from the lower cabinet. "Just once, can you think before you speak?" Devi said.

"Why? If I have to travel anywhere, why can't it be to L.A.?"

"Oh, good God, Julian!" Devi took a few deep breaths. "If you want to go to L.A., American Airlines flies there twice daily from Heathrow."

Julian tutted. "You think you're so smart."

"Only by comparison." Devi relented slightly. "I'm not certain, but you might make your way to her beginning, when her soul was a fledgling."

"How will I know if I get to the right place?"

"Because she'll be there."

"Will she be young or old?"

"Her beret and necklace will take you where you need to be," Devi said by way of answer.

"But at what point in her life will they insert me? When she is two? When she's fifty-two?"

"Her relics will guide you," Devi repeated.

How could the faith healer dangle such tattered rope in front of a drowning man? Julian's frightened face must have betrayed his turmoil. Devi put down the cleaver, gazing at Julian almost kindly.

"Are you a mirage?" Julian asked weakly. "Is this nothing but my grief playing tricks on me?"

"Would that I were a mirage." Devi displayed his hand with the fingers missing. "I've had real pain to make me real."

"I don't think I'm very good at grieving," Julian said. He had grieved for only one other thing before Josephine.

"No one is good at it." Devi did not look up.

"First grief is like first love," Julian said. "All consuming. Maybe that's why it's so hard to let it go." That was bullshit. It was hard to let it go because Julian began most days with his body lowered up to the neck in a tub of wet Klonopin cement that hardened as the day wore on.

"Have you ever heard the saying that nothing can be accomplished without fanaticism?" Devi asked. "The flip side of that is that nothing can be enjoyed without serenity. Unfortunately, you don't have enough of either. You need fortitude. You need perseverance. You need silence and patience. Do you know how to fence? Do you know how to joust? I'm starting to worry."

"*Now* you're starting to worry?"

"Perhaps waiting another year is not the worst idea," said Devi.

Julian let that hang in the air as he thought of other impossible things. If he was never coming back, what about his family, his mother? "My God, what about Ashton?" he said, his voice cracking, as if just realizing what going and not coming back would mean.

"If you don't want to be spooked by the answers," Devi said, "stop asking scary questions."

"But Devi, next month Ashton is moving to London—for *me!*"

"So don't go."

"Be serious."

"You don't think I'm being serious?" Devi said. "*What do you want, Julian? Answer me already, answer yourself.*"

A chill went through Julian's body. *What do you want?* That's what Josephine had said to him on the darkened stage at the Cherry Lane.

"Look at that," Devi said with a smirk. "You've managed to answer your most pressing question. Knowledge is so liberating, isn't it? When the alternative was before you, you reacted with dread. I watched you. You started to shake. You went white. That's how you know what you want. You don't want to wait another minute. You desperately want what I'm offering you to be true."

At last, one true thing.

For many minutes, Julian studied Devi with doubt, with fear. Then he wrote down Ashton's phone number. "If by some chance you're telling the truth and I do vanish, will you call him and tell him what happened to me?"

"And he'll believe me?"

"Probably not. Since I don't believe you, he might not either." Time ticked on. "Will I be alone in the cave?"

"What's more frightening?" Devi said. "To be alone? Or to know that there are others there with you, desperate people desperately longing?" He picked up the cleaver. The only sounds in Quatrang were the ticking clocks and the razor-sharp blade slicing through the cabbage. One head. Then another. There was a hill of cabbage on the wooden board before either of them spoke again. Devi's little place was warm, the oven in the back was on, the yellow light was pleasant, the thwack of the cleaver, the soft thumpy ticking of a dozen quartz clocks, the colored beads of the curtain, refracted light, smell of garlic and vinegar, the shimmering shade. It *was* hypnosis. Julian gradually stopped shivering, became heavy lidded. His shoulders slumped. His naked anxiety weakened. Drained of energy, he struggled to keep his eyes open.

"What is in this drink you keep giving me?" he muttered. "It's like I'm being drugged."

"You're being strengthened."

"What's in it?"

"Tiger," Devi replied. "Would you like to lie down for a few minutes?"

"Please," Julian said, slurring his words. "What do you mean, *tiger*?"

"I don't know how I can be more clear," Devi said, helping Julian off the stool.

Julian let himself be led to the back. Behind the small room with the acupuncture table, the stainless steel refrigerator, the cast-iron stove, and the gleaming metal counters, there was a narrow door, and behind it a space big enough for a hard cot. Is this where Devi slept? But why? It was like living at Mrs. Pallaver's, like an ascetic. Julian knew why he lived like that, but why would Devi live like that? Julian barely took off his jacket before his head lowered, his body fell, and he was unconscious.

And when he slept, he dreamed of Josephine.

32

A Boy Called Wart

WHEN JULIAN WOKE UP, HE STAGGERED OUT FRONT. IT FELT late, as if he'd been asleep for hours.

"Good morning," Devi said. "Are you hungry?"

The whirring clocks said it was nine. Outside was dark.

"After you eat, you should go home." Devi put cold chicken and boiled rice in front of him. "You might want to change clothes. You're not really dressed for cave travel." The goblet of murky water appeared.

Julian stared at it. "What's in this?"

"Minerals. Calcium."

"You said tiger before I fell asleep. Did I imagine that?"

Devi shook his head. "Is it delicious? Yes. Is it good for you? Yes. Does it have medicinal properties, healing properties, mystical properties? Yes, yes, yes."

"Come on, what is it really? Coconut water?"

"Tiger water. It's an ancient Hmong custom. Tiger bones are ground up and made into a beverage. When you drink it, you're taking on the tiger's endurance, his patience, which you desperately need, and his perseverance. You're taking on his stealth and his strength."

Julian pushed the goblet away. "Please be joking. You're like Ashton. I can't tell with either of you."

"Do I look as if I'm joking?"

"Your face always looks like that. Also, I don't know you. You could be."

Devi poured himself some sake into a tumbler and perched on a stool across the counter from Julian. "I'd offer you sake," he said, "but you're at half-strength as it is. The Klonopin has really done a number on you."

Julian ate slowly, drank the potion even slower.

"We are not just shamans in my family," Devi said. "I come from twenty generations of tiger catchers. Trust me, you need to have a lot of faith in yourself to succeed in *that* line of work."

"*You* catch tigers?"

"I used to."

"Um, is there much call for that in the middle of Hoxton?"

"Some," Devi said. "Probably as much as there is for caving."

While Julian ate, Devi talked to him about the art of catching tigers.

"You must be quiet and motionless. A tiger is a fearsome, awe-inspiring, lethal force of nature. To catch him will require everything you have. You must become fearsome and awe-inspiring yourself."

"And I seem fearsome to you?"

"You must mirror the tiger in action and character as best you can. Never forget this about the tiger: he is smarter than you. He is faster than you, he's stronger than you, he's much more dangerous than you. Yes, you can bring a gun to balance out your strengths, and you can kill him, but if you kill him, you haven't caught him. And what is our name? Is it tiger catcher or tiger killer?"

"Since I'm drinking ground up tiger bones," Julian said, "I'm guessing killer."

"The bones of one tiger last one Hmong tribe a thousand years," Devi said. "From the tiger, I've learned to sit quietly and observe the world. I watch him for a long time, and that's how I know when to catch him. I know when his guard is down, because mine is never down. I catch him when he's just had a big meal and gone into the water. I catch him when he is slow and sleepy, I catch him from behind when he doesn't know I'm coming."

Julian pointed to Devi's three missing fingers. "Sometimes he knows you're coming."

Devi gulped down his sake. "A different kind of tiger took those. I lost my fingers to frostbite when I was looking for my son. And all the toes on my left foot. That's why I limp when I walk."

"You have a son?"

"I had a s-s-son."

Julian waited. Devi's face became distorted. He didn't look up. He disappeared in the back, and when he returned, the face was smooth stone again and the voice didn't stammer. Julian diverted the conversation to other imponderables. "How can my body, all blood and bone and muscle, travel through time?" he asked.

"You are matter, and all matter is energy," said Devi. "Like the soul, it was created, but it can't be destroyed. You will take a different form."

"My body can't be destroyed?" Julian became a little excited.

Devi shook his head. "Do you bleed like the Lord, thirst like the Lord? Do you feel pain like the Lord? Watch out for falling rocks, Julian, for swords, pestilence, fire, ice, bad water, evil men. Watch out for the hangman's square and for black rain. Don't make people more powerful than you angry. You'll still be matter, but you'll be dust. Yes, your body can be hurt. Like Josephine's. Your flesh is mortal. Be careful with it. As the breath leaves your body, so all your plans perish."

"I guess I'm going, right?" Julian said.

"Everything is a question with you."

"Guess so. Right?"

And Devi almost laughed.

"Tell me something, Julian. Are you head or hands?"

"I guess these days I'm mostly head." Julian stared at his hands, clenching and unclenching his fists. "I know a little about plants. My *abuela*, my father's mother, insisted on sharing with me everything she'd learned from her own grandmother who grew up in Salina Cruz in Mexico."

"So you know how to garden?"

"No," Julian said, "just how to tell plants apart."

"What good is that?" Devi sounded deflated.

"What do you mean? You're wandering around and see a green thing, you'll know what it is."

"Why is that a skill *anyone* would want?"

"You wouldn't want to know what a flame tree is called, or the different grasses, or when strawberries are in season, or whether you can eat the poison berries off a yew tree?"

"No," Devi said. "And you won't either. To plant something in the ground, now *that* would be worthwhile."

"You got the wrong guy for that."

"It's not me who's got the wrong guy," Devi muttered, pulling out a stack of journals and peering into pages of copious notes in a tiny exacting hand. "Do you know about horses?"

"A little."

"Let me rephrase," Devi said. "I don't want to know if you can tell an Arabian from an Andalusian. I want to know if you can dress a horse or ride a horse."

"Um, no, Devi, why in the world... Also, I know we're supposed to be talking about my strengths," Julian said, "but I confess I'm a little afraid of horses. What I mean by that is—they scare the shit out of me."

Devi allowed himself a look of judgmental frustration. "No horses and no caves. Got it. Do you know how to build a platform, a simple box?"

"Build? Like with a hammer and nails?"

"Do you know how to paint?"

"Pictures?"

"Houses."

"No. To both."

"I know you don't know how to cook. Do you know how to count money?"

"I kept Ashton's books at the Treasure Box. So yes."

"On a computer?"

"Yes."

Devi sighed. "Would you know how to count money on paper or an abacus?"

Julian's entire skillset was being called into question!

"So the answer is no," said Devi. "And you can't fence. So you can't be a knight. You can't fence and you can't ride. Can you carve up a whale or a seal?"

Julian nearly retched.

"Have you ever been inside a church?"

"Devi! Of course. My dad's family was from the old country, devout Catholics."

"You yourself seem to have shallow theological knowledge at best," Devi said. "So you can't work for a monastery."

"Why do I have to pretend to be something else? Why can't I be myself?"

"And what is that?" Devi closed his journals and folded his hands. "Unless all of Josephine's incarnations are clustered into the twentieth century for your convenience, you'll likely be heading into a time and place where there are no cars and no computers and possibly even no iPhone."

"I told you I wasn't ready," Julian said, filled with alarm and self-doubt. "You're the only one who's surprised."

"Were you a history major in college at least?"

"Ashton was."

"Is Ashton coming with you?"

"English, okay," Julian said. "I was a double major. With Phys Ed."

"Why, so you could be a gym teacher?"

Beat. "Among other things."

Devi groaned.

"What? I received a well-rounded liberal arts education."

"Good for nothing. I was half-joking earlier, but do you actually know how to row a boat?"

Julian didn't answer. How hard could *that* be?

Devi threw up his hands. "Why," he said, "tell me, *why* didn't you learn at least one thing, one thing you could do except write ridiculous news headlines? You were Mr. Know-it-All. And yet you don't know how to do *anything*. Can you sing?"

"I can be paid not to sing."

"I know you're not funny," Devi said, "so you can't be a court jester."

"I can be funny!"

"Not on purpose."

"Well, you better think of something, smart guy," Julian said, "because in your grand plan, I have twelve hours to learn to be funny."

"It's not me who has to think of something," Devi said. "*I'm* going nowhere." He said that almost regretfully.

Am I going somewhere? Julian wanted to ask. Am I *really*? He chewed his lip. "When I was a kid," he said, "I used to play a naker, a small kettle drum."

"Now nothing can hold you back."

Julian struggled. To reveal other things about himself or not to reveal? He had put them so far away. He hadn't spoken about them to anyone, not even Josephine. He took a pained breath. He was probably never going to see Devi again, either way, no matter how this turned out. "In my other life, I used to be a boxer," Julian said. There it was. The unvarnished truth.

The little man wasn't surprised by much, but he was surprised by this. "You *were*?" He put his cleaver down.

"Yes." Julian didn't meet Devi's gaze. "Super middleweight. I was an undefeated amateur. Thirty-four knockouts. I was headed for the qualifiers for the Sydney Olympics before I changed my mind and decided to go pro. I was undefeated then, too. Had my nose busted twice, one split decision, but never lost a fight. I was pretty good." Julian smiled with soft pride at the memory of himself the way he used to be. "Until—" He stopped. He *hated* talking about it. Since he was eight and watched a video of Muhammad Ali defeating George Foreman in Zaire, a boxer was the only thing Julian wanted to be. Boxing was his high-wire, his passion, his stage. It was a crushing, embittering body blow to him when he was forced to stop. He returned to school for his masters, but his heart wasn't in it. His heart wasn't in anything. He substitute taught—scrambling to find a substitute life. Eventually he found whatever. It was nothing but consolation. Boxing was all there was.

Devi nudged him. "Until what?"

"Until life intervened," Julian said. "Just to fuck with me and my small dreams. I suffered a traumatic head injury. I had to have a craniotomy, and then they put me into an induced coma. I was never the same after. I partially lost vision in my left eye. It affected my balance, my ability to see right hooks. Oh, I tried to keep at it. I retrained myself to fight southpaw, but it was no use. I kept getting creamed. I lost some fights—like all of them. I had to retire before I got permanently retired."

"Was the brain injury from a fight?"

"No. It was from half a mountain falling on my head." Julian *really* didn't want to talk about it. To this day there was much about what happened he didn't understand.

Devi stared at him, a storm swirling in his usually emotionless eyes. "Ah, the looming talus cave," was all Devi said and remained quiet for many minutes. "Well, it's great that you used to fight. But so what? You can't fight today." His tone was considerably gentler than before.

"I didn't say I couldn't fight," Julian said. "Just not professionally. You said I'm going into the past, right? Why can't I go into the past when I can still fight?"

"Are you even *pretending* to listen to me?" Devi said. "You're not going into *your* past. You're going into hers. And you're bringing your feeble body with you, with all its head wounds and blind spots and drug addictions."

Julian reached up to rub the long, ridged scar on his skull. "How will I know it's her?" he asked. He sounded so sad. "How will I recognize her, what will her name be? Will she look the same, be the same?"

"Relax, Julian, practice control over yourself like I just taught you. Inhale, clench, exhale, release. Even if you don't know the name for a tiger, you still know it's a tiger, don't you?"

"Not if it doesn't have stripes."

"Nothing will change the tiger's essential nature," Devi said. "And nothing will change hers."

"What do I do when I find her?"

"Do you really need my advice on what to do when it's your turn in the field with the goddess?" Devi asked. "Do what you like. I'm giving you a shot, that's all. And I'm promising you nothing. You may have another Fario Rima to deal with. She may be lying in a bed of thorns. She may be stained with blood."

"She's already soaked in blood," Julian said, falling silent, afraid to ask the real question.

"I'm saying the return of your girl might not heal the very real loss of your girl," Devi said. "You should be prepared for that. You should prepare yourself for a lot."

"But will she love me?" Julian whispered.

Devi sighed, and then took mercy on him. "Does she love you in your dream?"

Julian admitted it felt as if she did.

"There you go. Often you can answer your own questions. You should try that more often."

It was time to go.

"The girl is the gravitational irregularity around which your own timespace has formed," Devi said. "She is the planetary mass through which you must travel if you are to live again."

They were both speaking quietly. All outward anguish had leeched out of Quatrang.

Tomorrow was a new day.

"God. I wish I had even another week," Julian said.

"You have it," said Devi. "You have another year."

Julian rolled his eyes.

Devi patted his shoulder. "A week isn't a scientific measurement," he said. "A week is the only time unit that doesn't spring from astronomy. It comes to you straight from the Bible."

"*That* makes me feel better about not having another week," said Julian.

"I'm saying you don't need a week. Don't get hung up on time. Get hung up on action. We talked about this. Time is a secondary feature of our existence, not a primary one. Time is a mystery, like much else in our world. We measure it, but we don't understand it. It's an elusive thing, yet a concrete thing. You can't see it, you can't feel it, you can't use your senses to explain it. It flies against reason. And yet you know it exists. Ten to fifteen billion years, the age of the universe. Five thousand years, the span of recorded human history. Two thousand years since a new dimension was introduced into the life of man. Forty-five minutes in a boxing match. Three minutes per round," Devi said. "And one second, the average time between the beats of a human heart."

Not hers. "Do you know how fast a bullet travels?" Julian said. "Three thousand two hundred feet a second. And Fario Rima was thirty feet from her when he shot her."

Devi's hand remained on Julian's shoulder. "I don't know how to vanquish death," the shaman said. "If I knew, trust me, I wouldn't be standing here, yakking to you. But I do know how to give you that leap second back."

The clocks chimed in midnight. Soon the tube would stop running.

Julian clutched her red beret in his pocket.

"Be not afraid," Devi said. "Remember the boy called Wart."

Julian squinted. How did this mystifying man know so much? Wart, an average boy with average skills, pulled the sword from the stone and became King Arthur. "I'm no king," Julian said. "I'm a beggar." Which is why he was in Quatrang, which is why he was going to Greenwich. Because he had nothing to lose, or so he thought.

"The portal won't open unless your soul is aflame," Devi said. "Do you have the power to pull out the sword? I don't know. Your friend Ashton doesn't know. Your dead lover doesn't know. Even you yourself don't know. It's *your* future. By definition, it's unknowable. But if you get to the Transit Circle in time and wait for the sun to cross the meridian and open up the infinities of your cynical heart, then you might get to see what you're made of. We should all be so lucky as to discover who we are."

Julian stood at the door. Was he really not going to see this man again, this life again? Like matter contemplating its own extinction, it was impossible to accept.

"The day of the cave is upon you," Devi said. "This is your one chance. Make it count."

They shook hands.

"Don't let go of her things. You can't get to her without them. And keep them on you, even if you think you don't need them. And for the love of God, do *not* be Orpheus. Do not disobey the rules of the universe."

"I don't know what those are."

"You'll learn." Devi unlocked the door. "When you were a kid, who did you think you'd grow up to be? Besides a boxer. A hero in your own story, right?"

"Nah." Julian buttoned his coat. It was blistering cold outside. And windy. "Back then I loved the movies. I wanted to grow up and work on a movie set."

"There is real magic out there, not just movie magic," Devi said. "Godspeed, Julian. Go catch that tiger."

33

Dumbshow

THE NEXT MORNING, A WARY, ANXIOUS, AND SLEEP DEPRIVED Julian alighted in Greenwich, England. Before he left his room, he left a note for Ashton on his dresser. *"Please forgive me,"* it said. *"I know you'll be all right. I wish I weren't leaving you behind."*

He jumped off the train, and then was barely able to put a foot forward. He limped down the station stairs, through a short alley, and stumbled out onto a busy high street at morning rush hour. Uncertain which way to go, Julian picked a direction and started toward it. He didn't know what he expected. He didn't expect Greenwich to be such a large bustling town, but he didn't want to stop and ask for directions. He wished to be invisible.

Before he could become invisible, when he was just plain ridiculous in his black clothes like he was about to perpetrate a bank heist, someone asked *him* for directions! A man and his daughter stopped him on the street; with a heavy foreign accent the man said, "Excuse me—"

Julian tried to walk on.

"Excuse me," the burly bloke repeated, blocking his path. "We're trying to find the Observatory and the Prime Meridian—"

Julian opened his hands. "I know nothing."

"Ah," the father said, nodding vigorously as soon as he heard Julian's American accent. "Of course. An American."

Before Julian could become offended, the man and his child vanished.

Or did Julian vanish?

Past a bookshop and a hotel, past everything with green awnings (not gold from his dream), up ahead on Nevada Street was a Rose and Crown pub, advertising the best fish and chips since the 1800s. Beyond it, Julian glimpsed some park-like greenery and lost his nerve. He decided to duck into the Rose and Crown, Devi's warnings about food notwithstanding.

Though High Street had been teeming, the Rose and Crown was quiet and empty except for the barman, and one patron who soon left. The barman greeted Julian with a peculiar hello. "How *are* you today?" the man said.

That was odd. How was he *today*? It was as if the barkeep had spoken to Ashton about how to properly address the bereaved.

When he approached Julian's table, he said, "What will you be having?"

"Do you have any plain chicken and rice?"

"Of course. As always."

Julian ordered coffee and an ale. Both came at a temperature called room. He drank neither.

He sat in the farthest corner, near the fireplace, with his back to the wall. Red heavy-cloth curtains lined the windows. Red leather benches, dark wood tables, a mahogany bar. "I Want to Marry you," by Train pulsed through the overhead speakers. Someone wanted to marry another someone.

The chicken was bland and unsalted. Julian chewed it without enthusiasm. He spent a while with the food as if he didn't want to part with it, as if he didn't want to walk toward the next inconceivable step of his life.

He had told Devi the truth. He didn't like caves. The feeling of suffocating under rocks was always with him.

But an insistent voice in his head was telling him that all his dreams were but a kiss away.

Was it true? It seemed so unlikely.

All your dreams are a meridian away.

One hundred and two meters to the east away.

All your dreams are a moon away.

Julian sat for over an hour, maybe longer, staring out the window. No one else came in. Finally, he paid in cash and left.

Go find your blue chance, he said to himself as he walked out into the cold windy sunshine. Stand under it. Fall into it. Swing off your one blue chance.

Let's try it one more time.

All your dreams, a Great Eastern Road away.

A continent away.

A sea away.

A bullet on Normandie away.

The River Styx away.

All your dreams, a death away.

All your dreams, away away away.

I should've kissed you.

∞

In the Royal Observatory, in the Transit Room at noon, the light of the cloud-covered sun passed through the crosshairs of the circular golden dial, and a magnified ray of light struck the crystal in the trembling palm of Julian's outstretched hand.

Nothing happened.

He waited for the phantasmagoria of color that had washed over him in the Santa Monica Mountains with her by his side to wash over him now.

That didn't happen.

The stairs flanking the telescope stayed black-painted metal, the telescope remained as it was. The crowd of foreigners outside continued to gambol on the brass line bolted to the cobblestones. Sweeney, the impassive rotund guard, sat as he was, at the table behind Julian.

But something was different. All sound had gone. Julian was in a dumbshow, a pantomime without words. He couldn't even hear the whoosh of his inhale.

A few feet away from him, by the base of the telescope, beyond the short iron gate, at the bottom of the black spiral staircase appeared a swirling electric blue hole, vivid like the borealis streaking across the sky.

The adrenaline flood of *Oh my God* and the pressure-cooker of the clock paralyzed Julian. He couldn't tell if a second had passed or thirty. Quickly he hopped over the railing, stepped down into the well and put one foot over the blue light. He couldn't feel the floor under his foot. He didn't wait another moment. His arms by his sides, he straightened out, made himself into a human projectile sliding down a water flume, took one tiny step, one enormous step, and leapt into the blue vortex.

Part Three

Medea

"That man that hath a tongue, I say is no man,
if with his tongue he cannot win a woman."
William Shakespeare, Two Gentlemen of Verona

34

Moongate

IN THE DARK JULIAN COULDN'T TELL IF HE WAS FALLING.

His eyes couldn't adjust to the blindness. No, he definitely wasn't falling. He was stuck, confined on all sides by ragged walls. Or maybe he was oscillating so fast, he couldn't tell he was moving. But it didn't feel like it. He'd been trapped before. He knew what trapped felt like. First shock, and eventually panic. Julian tried to feel above his head but couldn't move his pinned arms. The shaft was too narrow.

Because he was compressed, his breathing was labored, and he became anxious. Running out of oxygen anxious. Why did he jump with his arms at his sides like an idiot. Now what was his plan? In four minutes, was there going to be no more air? Maybe he should take little gulps to conserve it. Perhaps in two or three days he'd lose some weight and drop dead to the cave floor—one way of getting down.

Julian opened and closed his eyes, trying to see, to hear noises, maybe Sweeney overhead? This wasn't claustrophobia. It wasn't an irrational fear of confined spaces. He was squeezed into a canister and unable to escape. Seemed rational to be alarmed. He counted to sixty, to feel time passing. Everything stayed the same.

But there had been action. There had been movement.

There had been a *change*.

There was joy.

There was. There was.

Devi didn't lie! The conduit that wasn't there at 11:59, opened for Julian at 12:00, and let him in. He had life. He had hope.

Because he was in the future.

That's when he realized he wouldn't run out of air. Because he wasn't in an airless canister.

He was on a magic carpet.

He just had to learn how to fly it.

His heart rate steadied when he decided to approach his predicament with Holmsian logic. He could not be stuck with no way out. Therefore, there must be a way out. He wriggled his shoulders. He twisted his pelvis. Why did he wear such a heavy jacket! If it weren't for the jacket and all his sweaters and jerseys and tees underneath, he'd be slimmer. A good thing he had lost all that weight. Forty extra pounds of Julian wouldn't fit into this tube, *wide enough for one man but not all men.*

Couldn't gravity help him just a little? There was still gravity in the magic cave, wasn't there? Gravity came to the known universe before all matter. Before there was matter, there first was a law governing matter.

Why did there need to be a law governing matter before any matter existed?

Why did there need to be a law governing something that didn't yet exist?

And why couldn't this first principle of gravity help him now? Was he no longer part of the known universe? He wished he could squirm out of his jacket. Devi had given him contradictory instructions. The cave is cold, he said, wear something warm. Well, here he was. Man enough, warm enough, and stuck.

His shoulders were wider than his pelvis, and the top of his body wasn't moving. What could Julian do, short of dislocating his arms? A lot of good he'd be to himself, alone in a black cave with his limbs out of joint.

Little by little he managed to fold his upper body inward. He hyperextended his turned-in feet. Weaver, the Peckham quack, had noticed that Julian presented with abnormal body posturing. Hell, yeah. Good thing, wasn't it, that his old brain injury made his limbs bend and contort and flex in unusual ways when he was stressed. Hooray for old brain injuries. He moved his hands and then his arms in front of him. This allowed his shoulders to narrow. His body inched down. Progress! The longest journey through time began with a single wormy slide.

Julian wriggled and twisted, painfully slowly. Belatedly he thought that maybe he was Ralph Dibny after all. How disappointing, a rubber contortionist. Josephine would approve.

He was barely moving, constantly getting speared on the ragged walls. He lost all sense of how long it had taken him to descend even a few feet. The darkness was deeply disorienting. Nevertheless, he persisted. The few things he knew about caves helped him. Caves were coal mines under the surface of the earth. Long shafts led down. He was inside such a shaft now. Eventually he had to hit the cave floor.

And eventually he did. His feet and legs dangled. Another twist or two from his flexing torso, and he fell—maybe ten feet—landing gracelessly on the hard ground. He sat for a few moments, getting himself together, feeling relief but also rising tension. It was black like the bottom of the ocean. There was no visual imprint of any kind. But there was sound. Water was dripping.

Julian was about to turn on his flashlight but was stopped by another sound—distant flapping. He remembered that bats lived in caves. Were they in this one? Would they attack him? He was reluctant to turn on the light and see their tiny rat bodies, grotesquely large eyes, cartilaged fanning wings. Drip, drip. A flap or two.

He twisted on the Maglite, bought brand-new at Boots that morning. Without it he wouldn't be able to find his way. Unlike the webbed flying mammals, Julian didn't travel by sonar, he had no echolocation. The flashlight was cheap but would do. It had variable settings, was slim, used a non-replaceable lithium ion battery and was rated to stay on for 100,000 hours.

He wouldn't be in the cave for 100,000 hours, would he? Before Julian grew discouraged from dividing that number by the hours in a day, he got up and got going.

He didn't know what was more eerie: to sit sightlessly in an ebony space with no shadows or to see the narrow beam reflected off the low-hanging stalactites as he moved forward. His earlier excitement had dimmed and was replaced by gnawing worries. He found a long stretch of tunnel, an underground corridor that he hoped would lead him to a moongate. Isn't that what Devi had told him? You'll meander. You'll feel lost. When you see a moongate, you'll know you're close. The river is just beyond.

His tentative footsteps echoed off the walls. Slowly he made his way through a dripping, flapping tunnel filled with cascading lime, a dark labyrinth, an unmarked haunted house, every curve and choice between left and right jolting his anxious heart. Other than bats, what else lived in caves? Bizarre troglodytes like salamanders, the decomposers at the bottom of the food chain, were they waiting for Julian around the next turn?

Was he the bottom of their food chain?

And what if he made the wrong choice and went left when he should've gone right?

Case in point: he didn't get far before he came to a dead end. He brought nothing with him to mark the walls or leave a crumb trail like Hansel. He returned to the previous fork and tried again. When he didn't watch where he was walking, he tripped over a stalagmite. When he didn't watch his head, he butted into a stalactite. Julian decided to watch out for the head, since he knew from bitter experience he couldn't do without it, though breaking a bone was also less than ideal—as he also knew.

In frustrating fits and starts, often doubling back and repeating his steps, he made his way through the subterranean maze, grateful for every turn that wasn't a dead end and didn't have bats swinging from the ceiling.

How long had he been walking? He took out the watch he had bought from the flirty girl at the Observatory and checked the time.

It read noon.

Damn piece of junk. He threw it against the wall. It echoed as it broke.

But at last, something new was happening.

The tunnel deepened, widened, lengthened. The noise of dripping water echoed louder. The stalactites got longer. Beneath them, the stalagmite hills that towered like termite houses grew taller. The passageway emptied into a vast underground chamber webbed with dangling rock.

The drugstore flashlight exposed the immense space a fraction at a time. Julian examined it foot by foot.

Bisecting the enormous room was a spine of jagged stalactites uniting with calcium columns and flowstones. Amid the spectacular asymmetry Julian found a perfectly formed circular opening in the stone. Was that the moongate? It was silver white, lit up by the blue LED from his Maglite. A smiling Julian took a step forward, aiming the light at the tamped-down dirt at his feet, taking care not to trip.

Instead of dirt, a few feet in front of him the cold beam found nothing but blackness.

Julian stopped smiling.

Julian stopped walking.

He couldn't take one more step.

The ground underneath his feet had ended.

∞

His eyes had to be deceiving him. Looping the lanyard of the flashlight around his wrist, Julian inched forward and pointed the beam into the black void. The light was swallowed up by the darkness. His legs pulsed from standing too close to the edge. Backing away, he walked up and down the chamber, shining the light at the segmented blackness hoping to find a way across. But it was no use. The void split the cave in half, a canyon between him and where he needed to be.

The echo in the hollow space amplified every drop of falling water. Acoustically it sounded as if the water was gushing not dripping.

Was the chasm his imagination? It had to be, right? Nearing the edge, Julian knelt on the ground for stability, just in case, not wanting to crouch and, in his unbalanced desperation, topple over as he once did into the backyard pool. He lowered his hand into the black space, fingers wiggling. Nothing but air.

Rising to his feet, Julian stood, mouth ajar, lungs shallow, the flashlight drooping from his fingers.

And there he had been, thinking that what he disliked most was cramped spaces and things that lived in them. Spiders, crabs, silkworm, blind fish. The creatures that adapted to a world devoid of light, that evolved to inhabit blackness, how could one not be afraid of such things? Yet here in front of him was something even more frightening than cave dwellers.

Across the chasm, the giant cavern was full of shadows and inky forms, a city of statues sculpted by the cave itself, abstract and colossal. Everywhere Julian pointed his light, there was extraordinary ominous beauty of strange creation. If the divide was real, Julian could not cross it. He knew that. It was thirty feet wide, maybe more. What could he do, scale the side wall like a salamander? Vertical caving, like vertical mountaineering required special equipment for humans to ascend and descend. It required special skills. Julian had neither the skills nor the equipment.

Deciding to test his reality, he broke off a small piece of a soda straw stalactite, hoping it wasn't a weight-bearing crosspiece. Would the cave come crashing down on his head again because he had touched something he wasn't supposed to?

When that didn't happen, Julian proceeded to test if spacetime was real. He lobbed the hard chunk of calcium into the ravine. It fell and fell. He never did hear the sound of it landing.

He prayed he'd gone deaf. He broke off two more pieces from a different soda straw. One as a control, one as a test. He threw the control against the wall, like his useless watch. *That* made a sound. So he wasn't deaf, alas. The test went into the hole in the earth.

It fell and fell.

In a small corner of a giant room, he sank to the ground, his legs numb from fear.

Just like before, in the open wild, Julian became certain he was going to die.

Devi hadn't prepared him! He told Julian much would be required, but he didn't say what it would be. He said the cave wasn't a revolving door. There was only one way out. Forward.

But there was no way forward! Damn that Devi.

What was the cave called? The Q'an Doh Cave, Devi said. What did Q'an Doh mean? Why hadn't Julian asked? Maybe it was important. Maybe Q'an Doh meant Cave of Illusion. Julian was so hung up on the meridian and the portal, and the impossibilities of it all, he forgot to ask the Hmong man about impassable divides.

Eventually he calmed down and tried to think—by no means as easy as it sounded. Nothing in his thinking could grasp the physics of an ill-trained terrified man long-jumping thirty infinite feet.

Okay. Assuming Devi hadn't sent him here to die, what else did the Hmong cook say?

So many incongruous things. It *was* like hearing a foreign language. The familiar words stuck. Everything else fell through the sieve of incomprehension. Devi hoped Julian wasn't afraid of heights. Julian had ignored him. How could you be underground and worrying about heights? But maybe this is what Devi had meant. The dizzying height of leaning over an underground crater.

What else did Devi say?

He said Julian would have to learn to do many things he had not done before.

You will have to jump, Devi said.

You might even have to leap.

Julian got up and walked cautiously to the lip of the canyon.

Indisputably, Devi said that to get to the river, Julian had to walk through the moongate. Undeniably, Devi said Julian would have to learn how to jump.

This was insane! Julian wasn't an Olympic jumper. Hell, he wasn't even an Olympic boxer. Not that boxing skills would help him now. He shined a light across the blackness to the milky entryway. It was so tantalizingly near, yet so unreachably far.

What was real, what was illusion?

There is magic out there.

You might even have to leap.

Oh my God.

It was impossible.

Like a coin coming up heads for eternity impossible.

No.

Simply no.

In a panic Julian called out. Called to the dripping walls, to the rocks full of chilly humidity. "Anybody out there? Is there anybody out there?"

His voice came back, an unrecognizable high-pitched echo. *Theretheretheretherethere…*

"Help," he yelled.

Helphelphelphelp…

"Please. Somebody help me."

He sank to his knees. "Please," he whispered. "Somebody help me."

Memememememe…

Maybe Devi didn't tell him the truth. Maybe the portal did reopen. Julian could climb up the shaft, return to his life. The old woman, Quatrang, Devi, all of it a wretched grief hallucination. Weaver had warned him. Withdrawal from Klonopin was dangerous stuff.

But…if this was a dream, you couldn't get hurt in dreams. Julian pinched the skin on his hand. It hurt. He began to rationalize. Maybe you *could* get hurt in dreams. Maybe what you couldn't do is die in dreams. He was ready to conform all knowledge to his present reality—anything so long as he didn't have to jump.

How much time needed to pass before he got desperate enough to do it?

How long was that other man trapped in the canyon before he cut off his arm and lived? Julian should've bought the guy's memoir that fateful day at Book Soup, read it, memorized it. He might know now how to save a life.

One thing for sure: it would take more time than this before he jumped. Perhaps a hundred thousand hours—until the Maglite died.

How many of those hours had he already spent down here? Julian couldn't tell. He wasn't three days thirsty, or forty days hungry. What he was, was afraid.

He lay down on his side, curled up in a corner, and fell into a dreamless sleep.

When he woke up, he flicked the light back on. Was it his imagination or was the flashlight dimming? Turning it off, he closed his eyes and tried to remember things.

Gravity bends both light and time.

The gravity field inside a black hole is so intense that not even light can escape or penetrate it.

And if there's no light, there is no speed of light. And if there is no speed, there is no movement, and if there is no movement, there is no time.

Inside the black hole, time stands still.

What does that tell you, Julian?

There is no speed. There is no time. There is no distance.

There is only space.

And in space you are weightless.

Oh my God.

There is only one way out. Forward.

He opened his eyes and flicked on the Maglite.

You will see what you're made of.

Nightmare formations, dripping water.

Ask yourself—what is the deepest desire of your heart?

If you know the answer, then leap.

Julian stood up.

He measured out how many of his running strides it took to get to the edge of the canyon from the wall of the cave.

Fifteen strides.

And then he practiced counting and running with the light.

He shed his two sweaters and his sleeveless tank, shed them like skins to remake himself into a being light enough for leaping. He left on his jacket because it had her beret in it.

He practiced counting and running with the light. He wished he'd worn his sneakers instead of the thick waterproof shearling boots.

Carrying the flashlight impeded the forward thrust of his arms. He attached the lanyard to one of his belt loops and practiced running the steps another hundred times with it bouncing against his hip. That also turned out to be cumbersome. It was easy to get distracted and misstep. But he couldn't run in the dark.

Or could he?

What if he miscounted? Did he leap on fifteen, or did he run fifteen and then leap?

Julian stuffed the Maglite into his pocket, closed his eyes, and took three tottering steps in the darkness. Was it better to see or not to see himself falling into the abyss? Why didn't Devi tell him to bring a catapult? A long pole to run with, to vault off, to help him get across. What was he going to use as a pole vault now, his heart's desire?

Water dripping, dripping, dripping. His heart beating, beating, beating. Two hundred times a minute it pummeled in the chamber inside his chest and echoed in the chamber of the cave. When he couldn't take it, he waited out his terror on the ground, rocking back and forth. And then he would get up and practice the fifteen steps again.

And again.

A hundred times.

And then a hundred more.

He wanted the running and the counting to be committed to memory, one, two, three, four, five, six, seven, eight, nine, ten, eleven, twelve, thirteen, fourteen, fifteen—jump.

He grew exhausted of running and from running. He curled up in the corner, closed his eyes, and slept, or only thought he closed his eyes, only thought he slept. Blackout. He couldn't even feel himself blinking.

How many chimes of the hour will you let pass before you stand up and take the wheel of your life?

The time has come for you to act.

Julian stood up, stood straight.

One last time, he shined the Maglite across the floor of the cave, stared at the cold beam of light skirting the ground, ending in blackness, and resuming across the divide at the silver shimmering moongate. He put away the flashlight, felt for her necklace above his hammering heart, for her beret in his pocket, crossed himself. It was for her. For her. *Why are you afraid, ye of so little faith.* Help me, save me, carry me. He ran.

1,2,3,4,5,6,7,8,9,10,11,12,13,14,15—

Julian leapt into the black air.

35

White Lava

WOULD HE KNOW IF HE WAS HURTLING THROUGH SPACE?

Without sight or sound or light or time, or gravity, how would he know?

He opened his eyes. Darkness. But solid ground underneath him. He wasn't flying but lying on his side. There was a liquid pain in his calf. He must've landed on a sharp rock. He fumbled for the light. His hands were weak from fear, and it took him a few tries to click it on. He lay in front of the moongate, the edge of the black canyon barely behind him. If he shifted his body, he'd roll right into it.

Crawling away and sitting up, Julian shined the light over the maw. Did he really make that otherworldly leap? He marveled at it briefly, his body too sick from an overload of adrenaline to feel genuine relief.

He was across, that was the important thing. The hard part was over. Now to find the river. Pressing down on the wound on his calf, his fingers smudged with blood, he decided he was well enough to get going. He dusted himself off, wobbling on spindly legs like a fawn, and stepped through the moongate.

Julian didn't know what he expected. Marigolds and sunflowers, troubadours and minstrels? None of that happened.

But past the quartz and limestone gateway, things were different. The hanging speleothems vanished, the ground became hard and smooth, the off-white walls of the passage circular and ropy. It also got colder. On the one hand, the bleeding cut in his leg coagulated. On the other hand—fucking cold.

Zipping up his jacket, he limped on. The tunnel made a sharp right turn and then narrowed so much that Julian could no longer walk it. He had to get on his knees and crawl it. He almost smiled. Crawl on his knees like he was searching for Klonopin. Then, as now, with the same goal.

The tube became moist, then wet, then had standing water in it. What he needed was a headlamp. Damn Devi. Julian was forced to hold the flashlight between his teeth to see ahead as he crawled through cold water.

When the cylindrical walls around him widened, he felt a momentary relief, like maybe he could stand up soon, stretch his legs. He should've known by now that widening caves spelled nothing but trouble. The passage ended abruptly, high above another chamber of horrors.

Two stories below him was a grotto of swirling water.

In disbelief he put his head in his knees.

Was the water below deep or shallow? Oh, what did it matter. If it was shallow he would die jumping in. If it was deep, he'd be swallowed up by the undercurrent. There was no shore, just cave walls and water. The walls were striated but free of mineral deposits, nothing for Julian to hold on to, to attempt a controlled descent. At the far end of the grotto, the water streamed into a black tunnel, as if the grotto was the headwaters of an underground river.

Was this *the* river? The river of death, the river of life, of mystical rings, of black magic things, of sorrow, of fire, of heroes and thieves, was it the River Styx? Would he become invincible like Achilles? Or would he drown like a sinner? Would he ferry across to where she might be, waiting for him on the banks, his very own Persephone?

Shivering, his shoulders hunched, Julian tugged on the leather rope around his neck to make sure the crystal was secure and zipped tight the pocket with the red beret. Was it too late to point out how much he hated detested loathed being wet in his clothes? Another fall, another letting go. He could stand still and die. Or he could dive to where she might be.

Julian was rootless and stripped of his life. If he were a poem he'd be the blank space between the lines. If he wasn't living inside her death, he'd be nowhere.

And she'd be nowhere, too.

He sat with his back against the wall a moment or two longer.

He couldn't remember if he ever told her how much he loved her. There was so much he never told her. They ran out of time.

One more second, one more chime. He took a deep breath and let go.

36

Black River

BETWEEN HIM AND HER WAS A COLD WIND WORLD. A COLD wind world made of whirling ice.

Julian swirled round and round, through rocks and rings and crater moons, pieces of this world and another floating by as he bumped into hard things he couldn't see.

Starlings, cutwaters, flotsam, all hazard for the wherryman. What if he was the flotsam? A discarded marginalized thing tumbling without any hope of stopping, floating until the river propelled its debris to a jetty, where he would get stuck with the rest of the discards.

The air was heavy like he was under water. Oh, that's because he *was* under water. He was in a cold fog and shivering and then in a fire and burning up. He preferred to be part of the hot sky fever, it was better than the piercing crystals of frost. Some of it was bright red, but most of it was inky black, with air so heavy it felt solid, like glass or trees, the sound of his own labored breathing above the aqueous rush.

When he hit the water, he was shocked by how cold it was, like a slice of a shiv. He knew what that felt like: he had angered a mislabeled bantamweight once by a knocking him out in the fifth, and the dude was waiting for him in the alley, swollen eyes and all, brandishing a knife instead of his gloved ineffectual fists. Let's see who's the champ now, champ, he said. Before Julian could counsel the boy against punching above his weight, he stabbed Julian in the upper left shoulder. The knife still lodged in his arm, Julian got to knock the kid out one more time.

That's what it felt like now, the stabbing, except all over his body.

In the madness, the lanyard came loose, and Julian was thrown into blackness, the beam of light vanishing underwater. It probably wouldn't have worked for long anyway. Like him, the Maglite was water resistant, not waterproof. How long had he been gasping for breath? Crashing into a cutwater, he grabbed onto one of the things stuck there, a ragged barge of corrugated wood, a log. Julian climbed on top of it. It wobbled but didn't sink. Keeping his arms and legs as far away as he could from the cold water, Julian lay face down on the makeshift raft and let the river carry him away.

It was unquiet. The noise of the cold wind, the shrieking in darkness of colliding metal things, churning through the heavy air, solid things in the void crashing into each other and dragging one another down river. He heard piercing shrieks in the distance but not a far enough distance, and the wind carried other things spinning past him, other animate desperate starving grieving things like him, all trying to get to somewhere else. It felt bottomless and vast and fast, like skydiving at night without light, seeing nothing, but fearing that his mortal body might crash against stronger atoms than him. The enormous terrifying things out there that he couldn't see made him feel like grit in the eye of the universe. How could he drift like wood and not know where he was flowing? How could he go and not know where he was going? There could be a beheading where was he headed. That's how the wind screamed, like a scorned lover witnessing the death of his loveless queen. Is this what he sounded like the day she died? The merciless shrieking, was that him? The bled-out memory was at his hooded lids, bright like day, white like noon, shrill like the guillotine. They had to pull him away, cover him with a blanket, turn him away from her, lay him down, administer alms to him.

She wasn't the only one who died.

She died, but he was the one who could remember nothing. And without memory what was he but a smudge, barely alive. How he left the street, how he got home. Ashton and he flew east where her mother lived, where she was buried. Julian knew this only intellectually. He didn't remember flying, not then and not even now when there was nothing in front of him or behind him except the things he had lived through, his immovable regret about losing her, about losing a life with her he had yet to live, squeezed in like boulders between his shoulder blades.

Dreams of purple minivans, kids playing patty cake, Andromeda naked in his satin sheets, all gone, and then chaos. Julian was no one on a river of nothing on the way to nowhere, all because a Hmong shaman said, you want to see her again? Then this is what you must do. You have a second and a spit to leap. To run, to jump, to crawl, to shiver in rivers, you have much less time than you think. An eternity in icy suffering, a picosecond in bliss.

London, the city of art, the city of poverty. The city of rain, of wealth, of poetry. London, the city of souls. A few hundred years ago, a woman was murdered by her boarder, a painter from Switzerland, a country not normally known to produce coldblooded butchers. The little man cut up her body, threw the guts into a swamp, and carried the rest of her in parcels, out and about on the London streets. The bloodshed and terror were downwind from Julian's floating dinghy. After he died, the Swiss painter hid in hell from his landlady, and the shrieks Julian heard was her finding him and dragging him out. That's what it sounded like. The murderous artist preferred to remain in hell rather than face the dead woman's vengeance.

37

Dead Queen, Take One

HE HEARS CHURCH BELLS RINGING, NEAR AND AFAR.

Julian lifts his head off the sandy slope. He must have passed out after his log ran aground. It's warm and murky and smells like a swamp. Light filters in from somewhere. Sitting up in the pebbly grit, he examines himself. His clothes are damp but not soaking wet. How long has he been out? He touches his calf. Oddly it doesn't hurt. Has he had time to heal—or has the River Styx healed him? His body is not sore, nothing hurts, as if he had not just been inside a dank nightmare with bats and black holes and screaming souls.

He looks for an exit to his small enclosure, following the diffused beam of sunlight filtering through the rocks. He hates how familiar it feels—the confined space, the lightseeker in a half-panicked daze. Climbing up a slope, Julian finally crawls out of the hole into fresh air in a small wood. For a few minutes he sits, getting his breath and his bearings.

Past the trees and the brook, there's green open land. Julian stops at the crossroads of two unpaved rural roads. In every direction, he sees rolling fields and gentle hills, sees low stone walls dividing properties and hedges between the knolls. He doesn't recognize it, but he doesn't *not* recognize it. It's not familiar, but it's not unfamiliar either. The fields and hills are colored with the greenest grass. The damp weather is certainly familiar, as is the mottled sky.

The thing that's uniquely different is the sound of the relentless bells. They've been ringing non-stop, from a sea of belfries.

Julian doesn't know where to go. What if he starts walking in the wrong direction? Crippled by indecision, but also relieved to be out of the darkness, Julian folds and unfolds her beret in his hands, kneads the red leather, inhales the leafy air, tries to figure out what to do next. Where is he? The river and the cave clearly took him somewhere. He is no longer at the Greenwich Observatory. Something has worked, but what? Julian wishes Devi were here to answer his questions. He presses the beret to his chest.

Behind him he hears the steady clopping of horseshoes. He turns just in time to leap out of the way of a horse and wagon. The driver nearly runs him over.

"Hey!"

"Hey, yourself, move yer arse," retorts the man behind the reins. "Don't stand in the middle of the bloody road."

Definitely England. But where? And when…?

Warily, he and the driver eyeball each other. Julian doesn't know what to say. The horse scares him. Horses kick people in the head. They throw people off their backs. They don't come when called. The horse and an open wagon is odd. But the bearded driver is looking at him as if Julian is the one who is odd.

"Where am I?" Julian says.

"Every man must answer that question for himself, mate," the driver says. "What you looking for?"

How do you answer that question?

"Are you seeking a position?" the driver asks impatiently.

A position? "You mean work?" Julian finally says.

The driver cracks the whip. "Farewell, fool."

"Wait!" Julian takes a careful step forward. "Yes," he says. "I'm looking for a…position." He pauses as he chews his lip. "I heard they were hiring…nearby."

"Yes, it's easy to get lost 'round here," the man says. "Well, hop on, then. I know where they be hiring. Got a farthing to pay me with?"

A farthing? Who talks like that? "No, sorry," Julian says. "But if I get work, I'll pay you. Do you live around here?"

"Oh, just climb on! I ain't got all day."

Julian scrambles into the open wagon with the dirty straw, and they're off.

He is pitched from side to side. Not all the hay is dry, and it stinks of rot. The horseshoes clop rhythmically, the church bells ring, and the dogs bark.

"Why are the bells going off like that?" Julian asks.

"Where you been?" the man says. "Them bells is ringing because the Queen is dead."

"Oh, no," Julian says. "Queen Elizabeth is dead?"

"That's right, mate." The man cracks the whip. The horse jolts forward.

"What happened?"

"She died, that's all. She was old."

Peeking over the side of the rocking wagon Julian sees a street lined with tall narrow thatched-roof tenements that look like—odd that he would know this—whorehouses. They all have white walls, and he's read somewhere that per London ordinance, all houses of bawd had to be painted white to be clearly marked in every neighborhood. It made them so much easier to find. They're shuttered because it's day—or maybe because the Queen is dead—but regardless, every tavern, ale house, and dicing house on a street marked Turnbull is white-limed. Does London have brothels in the present day? Julian hasn't seen them, not that he's been looking.

They pass an obligatory church adjacent to the dissolute quarter, take a right, and make their way up another meandering street.

The geographical windings of the streets are oddly recognizable, like a dream version of something Julian already knows.

Now that they've left degenerate row, the houses become better kept and more sparse. Every half field sports a stone manor or a stately Tudor. A pub stands on a corner of a hilly dirt-road intersection. Julian squints, struggling to remember. It's *so* familiar. At the moment, it's called the Spotted Pig, but it sure is shaped like the narrow corner pub he's walked past a hundred times at the bottom of Islington Green where Essex Road splits off from Upper Street.

If he's right, there will soon be a large monastery on the left-hand side. Right on cue, the imposing rectangular structure appears. It's Clerkenwell! Julian is keenly disappointed in his location. He didn't travel very far, did he? Mrs. Pallaver's terraced building on Hermit Street is just south of where they are.

But if this is Clerkenwell, it's Clerkenwell as Julian's never seen it. There are no streetlights or bistro pubs or beautifully appointed terraced homes with black doors, no green posh squares, no universities. They hadn't passed a Hermit Street because it doesn't exist. None of the roads are paved, and next to his chugging wagon women walk wearing hooped skirts that scrape the ground and carrying pails of water that hang from the yokes on their shoulders. One pulls an obstinate pig. Another an obstinate child. It's as if he's landed in a museum village, laid out like Clerkenwell from the old days. Is it really the past? It's hard to believe.

"Excuse me," Julian calls to the driver, "that church we passed a while back, was that...was that St. Mary's?"

"St. Mary's? Are you daft? The nunnery hasn't been called St. Mary's since the Dissolution. That was St. James."

Julian stops speaking. He can't remember what the Dissolution is. He tries again. "The street we were just on, was that St. John's?" Because that would be *unbearable*. He lives off St. John's Street.

"It was." The man stops the horse. "Off you go. This is where they're looking to hire."

Reluctantly, Julian jumps down into the road. He's in front of a long country lane at the end of which stands a solemn gray manor. "Who lives there?"

"It's Collins House."

Collins? As in...*Josephine*? The adrenaline rushes in. "What's the date?"

"I believe it's a Monday."

"No...what year is it?"

"Oh, God's teeth! I regret ever letting ya get in me wagon. Lady Collins'll hang me." The man cracks his whip. "Anno Domini 1603," he says, driving off.

1603!

But didn't the man say Queen Elizabeth had just died?

Oh my God—he meant Elizabeth I.

A stunned Julian stands in the middle of the road, his mouth open. He puts his hand on his chest to quiet his heart, to feel for her beret in his jacket pocket.

He's in 1603!

The church down the road is called St. James to this day. He walks past it when he takes the Thameslink train at Farringdon. Why did he call it St. Mary's? And what does he know about Clerkenwell in 1603?

Next to nothing is what. "Clerk's Well" used to be known for making watches. The best timekeepers came from Clerkenwell.

Now that he knows he's in Clerkenwell, Julian wonders if the River Fleet brought him here. Before the Fleet became a ditch and sewer, it was called the River of Wells, and the wells supposedly had healing properties. He's read this on a plaque, so it must be true. Maybe that's why his calf healed so fast, it wasn't Styx, it was the River of Wells.

Uncertainly Julian starts down the long lane lined with overhanging oaks. The countryside is barely populated, the weather lukewarm, the sun in a haze. At the end of the road, the graystone, two-storied gable-roofed manor stands amid sprawling but unkempt grounds. As he nears the house, Julian overhears two female voices arguing behind a row of hawthorn hedges and beech trees. He slows down to listen. One voice is breathy, angry, whiny, grating, unmodulated. The other is maternal and cajoling.

"Now, pear…"

"I don't care, I don't care, I don't *care*!"

"Now, darling, that is *not* a nice thing to shout. Where are your manners?"

"I've been nice my whole life and where has it got me?"

"Plummy, you're jeopardizing everything we've worked for. After your fit of hysteria last week, Lady Falk has expressed grave doubts that you are a suitable match for her son."

"I am a terrible match for her son, Lady Mother! I can't stand him!"

"As *always*, you're being overly dramatic. You're not up on a stage. Stop acting. You and Lord Falk are old friends. You've known him since you were children."

"And have hated him since then. He is cruel and stupid. I do not desire to be anyone's wife, especially Lord Falk's. I'm going to join the Lord Chamberlain's Men, and I don't care what you have to say about it. I'm going to get another part in one of Will Shakespeare's plays."

"Never, pear! Only beggars and thieves become actors."

"Mother, you're hopelessly old-fashioned. This is not the fifteenth century anymore. And soon we shall have a new King! Who, I hear, loves the theatre. The Globe is having a renaissance."

"Oh yes," the older woman dryly replies. "A renaissance right next to the bear pits and the brothels."

"There are brothels everywhere, Lady Mother," the younger voice says. "Many are down the road from us on Turnbull Street. I pass them when I go for a stroll with Beatrice."

"You must never walk down there, blossom. That street is not for you. Neither is the theatre."

"To perform on the stage is the only desire of my life," the younger voice cries.

"Ladies don't perform on stage—or have desires. Also, your Shakespeare is a hack."

"He wrote for the Queen! The Queen herself sat on his stage and watched *Romeo and Juliet* performed in front of her."

"Be that as it may, *you* cannot be on stage like a strumpet."

"Why ever not? The Queen was!"

"Are you the Queen, my darling?"

The girl emits a groan of outrage.

"You can never be on that stage if you are to marry Lord Falk. He is a knight."

"Oh, bollocks to that, he most certainly is not a knight. A nightmare, maybe."

"What's gotten into you? Don't be salty. You know his father was a—"

"Mother, Lord Falk has never in his life picked up a sword except to hand it to his lord father."

"Cornelius! I can't bear this anymore, come here. Cornelius, can you hear me?"

Julian hears shuffling across the grass and a reedy tired voice. "Of course I can hear you and Lady Mary, madam. The dead can hear you."

"Fetch me my fan and my salts, it's too warm, and for some reason I'm starting to feel poorly."

"Very well, madam," the man says. Julian crouches behind the hedge, trying to pry open the thick gnarly branches so he can peek at the women. The younger voice has a timbre to it that has weakened his legs. It must be his imagination.

"Have you calmed down, pear?"

"Yes, Mother. Very calmly, I will not marry Lord Falk. I will sell my body on Turnbull Street first."

The mother gasps.

The girl's strident voice forges on. "Forget selling. I will *give* my body away to all men, including Lord Falk's swine herder, if it will stop that wretched man from marrying me. I will give it away to the first man who walks down our road. That is how serious I am. Oh, come now, Mother—don't faint. This isn't the Middle Ages."

"Darling..." The mother's voice trembles. "You *must* be married before we have a new King. You know about our dire financial situation. Otherwise, the coronation tithe will impoverish our family."

"There will be no wedding. There are methods to stop it, you know."

"O the Word of the Lord! What methods?"

"There's Falk's death. And if that doesn't work, there is always mine."

"Cornelius!" the mother cries. "Salts—please! Now, my precious darling, you listen to me. At eighteen, you are almost past marrying. I had three children by the time I was your age. And you see what happened to your friend Beatrice. She used to be such a catch. But now she is twenty, and no man wants her as his wife. You're nearly past your prime child-bearing years yourself." For some reason, there's a dense silence between the two women before the mother hurriedly continues. How Julian wishes he could see. "Lord Falk demands and requires a male heir." The mother lowers her voice to an anxious hiss. "You know very well what can—and does—happen to ladies of the court who can't produce a male heir. What will you do if you're now too old to bear him children? You'd best get started, my love. There is no time to waste—"

Someone kicks Julian in the ribs. He loses his balance and falls over.

A tall, thin, gray-haired man stands over him like Lurch from *The Munsters*. "Who are *you*, good sir? Announce yourself!" The man has a tough face, a strong frown.

Scrambling to his feet, Julian stammers. He has not prepared an answer to that most simple of questions. Who is he, indeed?

"Are you a vagrant?" The man looks over Julian's black attire. "An alien? Are you from the Low Countries?"

Julian shakes his head.

"The government allows mad beggars to wander around," the tall man says, "but not able-bodied men. Which are you?"

The formulation stymies Julian. "With all respect," he says, "I'm an able-bodied man, but I'm not wandering around. I heard you had a position…"

"You've come for the gardener job? Why didn't you say so?" Lurch motions Julian to follow him. "I saw you examining our hedges. Have the thrip mites destroyed them?"

"Uh—spraying the bushes with water should knock off the mites," Julian says, lagging behind the tall man, unprepared to face the women.

The man leads him through an opening in the privet hedge. On a wood bench near an untrimmed and sickly looking yellow hazel two ladies sit, a mother and a daughter.

The gray-haired mother, in mourning attire, looks like a once attractive woman grown old before her time. On her head is a black hat like an elaborate beekeeping hood. Under the sheer black veil of this contraption, her white-painted face staring at her child is both exasperated and adoring.

The daughter is in mid-pause, peeved at her tantrum being cut short. She wears a long, embroidered silk gown with a white lace collar starchily fanned out like a plate at her chin. Her face is painted white. Her dark hair is curled, swept up and half-covered by three hats: a bonnet and over it another bonnet and over it a hood. Feathers, pearls, and colorful beaded stones adorn the hair and the hats. Her red lips quiver and her dark eyes—a moment ago trained on her mother and glistening as if she was about to cry from her frustration—now turn on Lurch and Julian.

"Pardon me for interrupting, Lady Mary," Lurch says sonorously. "But your lady mother must know: a man has come for the gardening position."

"A man, Lady Mother!" the girl exclaims. "A *man* has just walked up the road to our house!"

"*Shh*, plummy!"

Julian looks around for something to hold on to. He's afraid he won't be able to remain standing.

It's impossible.

It can't be.

But it is.

It's *her*.

Devi was right. Julian would recognize her anywhere. In disbelief, he stares into her face. Unconsciously, his hand stretches out to her. She is a mirage borne of grief. He has lived too long haunted by the ghost of her snuffed out life.

"Good God, sir," Lurch says, "are you...*weeping*?"

Tears run down his face. Julian swipes at his cheek. "A speck in my eye, that's all." He looks away, stares at his feet, at the mother's face, at Lurch's suspicious glare, at anything but her. It *can't* be true.

Can it?

"I didn't catch your name, sire," the older woman says, rising from the bench.

"Julian Cruz, madam." He must sound almost normal to them, for they do not react to his accent.

"What an odd name," the tall man says.

"Don't worry, Cornelius, he's not an alien, he's a foreigner!" The mother visibly relaxes. "Listen to his English. He must be from Wales. They speak most peculiar over there. I am Lady Aurora Collins, sire, and this is Master Cornelius Grysley, our steward. And here is my daughter, Lady Mary."

Did the mother say the steward's name was Grizzly? That's almost better than Lurch. Without lifting his head, Julian gives a sideways bow in the women's general direction. He wishes he had a hat to take off or knew how to kiss a lady's hand. They didn't teach you that in Simi Valley. "I'm from the unknown forest," he says, mentioning the only place in Wales he's vaguely heard of. He can only imagine what his black Gortex jacket, cargo pants, and waterproof Uggs must look like. He doesn't dare meet the girl's eye.

"Where's your hat, sir?" the mother asks.

Before Julian can answer, Grizzly cuts in. "I don't know about Wales, but in London, it's against the law for men over the age of six to be seen in public without a hat, even on Sundays, unless you're a nobleman. Is today Sunday, sire, or are you under the age of six? You are most certainly not a nobleman."

Julian doesn't know if today is a Sunday.

"He's a gardener, Cornelius," says the mother, as if that explains anything. "But if you are a gardener, sire, where are your gardener's clothes? They usually wear skirts, low shoes and trunkhose. And hats."

"I'm a man of many trades, madam, not just gardening," Julian says, his voice unsteady. "I lost my hat over yonder."

Animated, the mother stands up. "A man of many trades? What luck, Cornelius! Just what we need. My daughter is getting married—"

"No, she most certainly is *not*," the daughter cuts in.

"Pay no attention to Lady Mary, sire," Aurora says. "She *is* getting married, and we're in dire need of help with urgent household tasks in preparation for her wedding day."

"Let this poor man be on his way, Mother," Lady Mary says. "You're wasting his time. Unless you'd like to employ him for that other thing you and I were discussing—"

"Mary! Excuse my daughter, please, Master Cruz." Lady Collins smiles anxiously at him, as if afraid he is going to change his mind and leave. "I've heard that on the continent they grow flowers, especially for weddings. Do they do that in Wales? Some of the Dutch traders have been bringing their flowers to sell at our street markets. Daffodils. Orchids. What do you think?"

"We can try, madam. When is the wedding?" Julian is hoping to hear an actual date.

"Never," Mary says.

"The end of June," Lady Collins says with a sideways glare. "What other services do you offer? Mary—quiet!" Aurora yells at her daughter before she can speak.

With cruel mockery, Mary twirls her parasol.

"Are you a ditcher, by chance?" the cranky Cornelius asks.

Julian's never held a shovel in his life. "What do you need dug?" Isn't he ambitious.

"A deeper moat around the house. Dunham can show you."

"Who is Dunham?"

"The gong farmer."

Julian doesn't dare ask what a gong farmer is.

"It hasn't rained in a month," Cornelius adds, "and our moat has gone dry. None of your flowers will take. The soil is rock solid."

"This is still England, isn't it?" Julian mutters, then, louder, "It won't be a problem. I'll divert the stream."

"Oh, he'll divert the stream, how marvelous!" Aurora exclaims. "Do you hear that, Cornelius?"

"Yes, madam, another one with promises he won't keep."

"One way or another, the flowers will go into the ground, Lady Collins," Julian says.

Gratefully she steps closer to him. "Also, our chandler has run off."

Cornelius: "Water is more important, madam."

Aurora: "Hush, we cannot have a wedding without candles."

Cornelius: "Nor one without water, madam."

Aurora: "Master Cruz, we are woefully low on candles. Is that also something you can help us with?"

"Of course."

Aurora beams. Lowering her voice, she says, "Cornelius was my husband's butler for twenty years, but now that John's dead, he refuses to do any actual work."

"I can hear you, madam," says Cornelius.

"I know. It was said for your sake, Cornelius." Aurora smiles at Julian as if they're old friends. "When can you begin, sire? Please say immediately."

"Sooner, madam."

Finally Julian allows himself an earnest gaze at the girl on the bench. Buxom she sits in layers of flowy and tight-fitting fabric, her hands clasped on her lap, sublimely irritated by the world. Her painted face is fuller than when he knew her and her form shorter and more rounded. Through the blazing brown eyes fixed on him with tempestuous whine, Julian sees as if through an opaque window the soul of the girl he had loved, pressed against the glass. *Josephine*, his mouth inaudibly forms the truth of her name even if the truth is a lie. *Josephine, it's you.*

"Do you know my daughter, Master Cruz?" a frowning Aurora asks.

Get yourself together, Julian, or they'll skin you.

"I do apologize, madam," he says. "Lady Mary looks very much like someone I once knew."

"I can attest, Mother," says Mary, "that I have never seen this vagabond before in my life."

"Mary!" A tall, stalwart woman marches toward them from the house. "How many times have I told you not to speak to anyone in that tone, not to your lady mother and certainly not to our guests?"

"Yes, Aunt Edna."

The no-nonsense woman comes to stand at attention in front of Julian. "I am Lady Edna Emmet, Lady Aurora's sister," she says. "I am also Mary's governess." She's in all black, except for the white collar to match her white hair and face. Her eyebrows and eyes are as black as her skirt. She faces her charge. "Lady Mary, when you behave this poorly, it reflects on me for teaching you poorly, on your mother for raising you poorly, and on this great and noble house. Is this how you choose to *act*?"

"No." The girl rises to her feet, chastised but rebellious. Her white parasol falls to the ground. Instinctively Julian bends to pick it up. So does she. Their heads graze together. A material part of her, her bonneted skull, collides with a material part of him, his once-fractured skull. Rudely she snatches the parasol from his hands.

"Lady Mary!" Edna booms.

"Oh, fiddles—may I be excused, Lady Mother, Aunt Edna? Thank you ever so much." Without waiting for permission, the young woman spins on her little heels and storms to the house, her skirts puffing around her.

Wait! Julian wants to yell. Don't go. He takes an instant loathing to Edna for nagging Mary away.

In an awkward silence, the grownups remain under the hazel. The shearling inside Julian's Uggs is moist and itchy. The adrenaline drop after Mary's departure is like a pin in a balloon. The air is sucked out of him. He wobbles.

Edna studies his attire. "What is that metal zig zag line on both sides of your jacket, sire?" she asks.

Damn it. Why did he unzip his jacket? He was warm. He's still warm. When were zippers invented? "It's something called a zipper," he replies. "A trader from Italy brought several of these jackets from the Alpian goat herder region." He stretches his mouth into an unctuous grimace.

"What trader?" Edna says. "And brought to where, to Wales?"

"Just a trader selling exotic cargo," Julian replies. "Fine carpets, some pine wood, a camlet made from goat. I opted for the jacket, having no need of the other items. His name was Bernard Bondymer. He sails to Blackfriars twice a year with his wares. I can take you down to the docks for his next visit, if you wish, which I believe will be in August." While waiting for Weaver in Peckham, Julian had leafed through a coffee table book on the history of merchant trade in medieval England. Incredible. Turns out the charlatan *was* good for something.

Stupefied, his new compatriots stare at him. Edna is suspicious and unmollified. She whirls to her sister. "Why do you allow the girl to talk to you like that, Aurora?"

"All right, Edna, let's not…not in front of…"

"Why won't you listen to my advice? Ignore her. It will pass. Like all foolishness. Act. Women can't *act*! The girl has gotten all the wrong ideas from what little education she's had."

Neutrally Julian studies Edna's imperious face.

"I told you, Aurora," Edna continues, "we should've never taken her to the Fortune, as you insisted."

"I didn't see the harm," Aurora says, leaning on Cornelius for support. "How was I to know she'd start entertaining these ludicrous notions? The play we saw was harmless fluff." She addresses Julian. "It was called *The Blind Beggar.* Have you heard of it, Master Cruz?"

"Yes, *have* you, Master Cruz?" says Edna. "It's about a swindler and a fraud who pretends he is a duke to seduce an unwitting queen, and after he is banished to Alexandria, he deceives a passel of women there, too." She glares at him.

Julian stares calmly back. "But at the end of the play, the blind beggar becomes the King of Egypt, doesn't he?"

"Yes, but only by corrupting innocent women!"

The four of them start toward the house.

"Mary has always been a willful child, madam, don't mind her," Cornelius says. "She takes after her father."

"Sir John was an honorable man," Edna says. "The child is petulant and selfish. You want to know how to stop her, Aurora? You tell her she cannot have what she wants, that's how." Edna sounds like a drill sergeant.

"Easy for you to say, sister, but she's all I've got left."

"Then you have no one but yourself to blame."

Can Julian tell Edna to shut the hell up or would that be rude?

Aurora pats his arm as if she can read his thoughts. "Master Cruz, I'm ever so sorry I've put you in the middle of our family squabble. Would you mind if Mr. Grysley showed you to your room? Ask Krea to prepare him a plate, Cornelius. And show him the chandlery. Oh, and get the wagon ready for him to go to Borough Market tomorrow. You can drive a horse, of course, can't you?"

"Most certainly, madam," says Julian without a blink.

"Thank you for giving me more to do, sire," the steward hisses to Julian. "Because I've been so idle lately."

"You *have* been idle, Cornelius," Aurora says, "but your indolence reminds me—how's Cedric?"

"No better."

Aurora tuts. "Such a shame. I hope you don't mind taking the horse by yourself across London, Master Cruz."

"Of course not."

"Cedric is our hostler," she says. "Normally *he* would drive you to the market, but he's developed a terrible rash on his eyes. Pus is dripping out. We fear he's near death. You wouldn't happen to know something about pus, would you?"

"Very little, madam."

"We're close to the stables, shall we take a peek at our poor groom?"

One glance, and Julian immediately sees what Cedric's problem is. The hostler's brain appears to be oozing out of his blood-red eyeballs. Cedric lies on a bed of straw in a vacant horse stall and moans. Julian doesn't come too close in case (in case!) Cedric is contagious. He thought maybe he could improve Cedric's condition with some saline solution, but there's no remedy besides prayer for what ails the groom.

"What do you think it is, Master Cruz?" Aurora asks anxiously.

"I can't say for certain, my lady."

"A barber surgeon came the other day and pulled out two of Cedric's teeth," Aurora says, "but that didn't work."

"*That* didn't work?"

"Not at *all*. Would you like to taste his urine, to diagnose him more accurately?"

"I—uh—no, that—that will not be necessary," says Julian.

"Are you *sure*? Our doctor is good but too expensive," Aurora says. "It's cheaper to replace Cedric with another hostler than to hire the best doctor. He frequently tastes the urine of the sick to diagnose illness."

"He's clearly a more thorough medical man than I am,"
Julian says.

Cedric keeps moaning.

Julian tells Lady Collins there's one thing he can try. He can
boil some common leaves in water with honey and wash out
Cedric's eyes once the tincture cools. There is boric acid in the
plants, Julian says, which can help with some eye rashes. Honey
is good for many things, including disinfecting wounds.

Cornelius and Edna snort and balk, but Cedric nods
vigorously. Try it, try it, he whispers. Aurora orders Cornelius
to collect a barrow full of leaves from the nearby laurel bushes.

Edna whispers something to Lady Collins, who looks Julian
over and frowns. "My sister makes a good point," she says,
suspicion creeping into her voice. "Where are your things? You
couldn't have come all the way from Wales without any baggage."

Julian must think quick. "I had two large cases with me,"
he says, "but would you believe it, at the last inn I was in, I was
separated from them by a migrant victualist, who saw me put
my head down on the tavern table and promptly relieved me of
my belongings."

"Pray tell—what *was* the name of that infernal inn,
Mr. Cruz?" says Edna. "Because that's *terribly* inhospitable."

"The Star Tavern," Julian replies. It's the only pub in West
London he knows. "A welcoming enough place but filled to the
rafters with unsavory characters. I actually overheard some
patrons planning what sounded like a great train robbery." Julian
says it to amuse himself. The great train robbery *was* planned at
the Star Tavern, according to the eponymous film.

"The great *what* robbery?"

"Grain robbery," Julian hurriedly amends. He must stop
joking or it'll get him into real trouble. "But I was in my cups and
could've misheard."

"Poor man!" Aurora says. "Cornelius, have Gregory help
Mr. Cruz choose some items he can wear from the wardrobe
of the departed. Without delay, sire, let's get you out of these,

whatever they are, and into some trunkhose. We'll all feel better once you're in trunkhose. Oh, and Cornelius, tell Gremaine to bring some fresh water from the well. Gremaine is our ewerer. But ask him to rinse out the bucket first—after all, Master Cruz is our guest." Aurora chuckles. "Sometimes Gremaine forgets to rinse out the water bucket for weeks at a time."

38

Chandlery

JULIAN DOESN'T SEE MARY ANYWHERE INSIDE THE WELL-appointed house, all stone slab floors, thick plaster walls covered with wood paneling, and large tapestries. He is introduced to Gregory, the keeper of the wardrobe, and to Catrain, his wife, who is the seamstress, the housemaid, *and* Lady Mary's lady-in-waiting.

"Are you also the matchmaker?" Julian smiles.

The nearby Cornelius, who is possessed of something called a reverse sense of humor, reacts poorly to Julian's question. "The reason Catrain fulfills several positions in the household, sire," he says through his teeth, "is because our housemaid and lady-in-waiting have recently died. Our acater has also recently died. Because of that, Farfelee, our cook, has no food. Does *that* also amuse you? I don't remember Lady Collins hiring you for the position of a jester."

If Devi were here, he'd tell Cornelius it's because Julian isn't funny. Devi might also explain to Julian what an acater is.

The narrow room Cornelius gives to Julian is off the kitchen. In the buttery, next door, a half-dozen vats of odorous grease stand on the floor around a long wooden work table. Gremaine twitches non-stop, not the best trait for a man who carries murky water in a drought. Looking at the ewerer, Julian wonders if this is how he himself appeared to people in his previous life. He suspects Gremaine did not heed Lady Collins's instruction to wash the bucket.

In an upstairs room filled with organized piles of discarded clothes, Gregory allows Julian to pick out a few things to wear. Gregory is a slow-moving gentleman with an unseemly amount of facial hair like a Russian monk. (Oh, yes. The men sport copious facial hair in this old new world. Everyone but Julian. No wonder they mistrust him, him with his zippers and his infernal clean-shaven face!)

"The clothes in this room belong to members of our household who have died," Gregory tells Julian. There is nothing funny about that, especially after what Devi had told Julian about clothes carrying the spirits of the dead. The man finds Julian some breeches, trunkhose, an itchy tunic which Gregory calls a skirt, a coarse white shirt, a capotain black hat, and torn black gloves. The one decent thing Gregory shows Julian is a short silk cloak, offering it to him with pride. The cloak is red satin on the inside and pink linen on the outside. It's embroidered with gold and silver stitching and has tassels and a silk fringe. Julian doesn't know what to do. To not accept would be a mortal insult, but to accept means he might have to wear it.

He accepts.

"Don't you feel fortunate," Gregory says, handing it over. "Thank the good Lord for the dead, wouldn't you agree?"

A few minutes later, dressed in itchy but more appropriate attire, an exhausted Julian sinks on a bench at the kitchen table, and Farfelee, an exceedingly large cook, orders Krea, his exceedingly small scullery maid, to bring Julian some household loaf and sausage with onions. Krea whispers to Julian that she is also the baker since the baker has died.

"Thank the good Lord for the dead," Julian says, mimicking Gregory.

"Oh, I thank God for the dead every morning and night, sire," Krea tells him. "I only wish there was more of them."

Julian suppresses a laugh. "Krea," he says, looking the maid over. "Does it rhyme with Medea?"

"I don't know what that is, sire."

"Medea, the Greek sorceress who takes revenge on her faithless lover by killing her own children?"

"Oh, that most certainly sounds like some people I know." Krea is minute and homely, a skeletal antlike bird. Her face is ruined with smallpox scars. Along with the bread, Krea brings him a half-gallon jug of ale to drink. Julian gulps from it thirstily. Thank goodness, the ale is weak.

"Have you got a fork for me, please?" he says, pointing to his sausage. The maid has given him a pewter spoon.

"I don't know what that is," Krea replies.

"You don't know what a fork is? What do you eat your meat with?"

"The spoon."

Julian looks deep into the sausage and picks up the spoon. The sausage is shoe-leather dry, but on the plus side it's unconscionably salty.

"People from foreign parts make everyone nervous," Krea tells him after Cornelius steps out for a moment. "That's why Master Cornelius is like that. We never know who is carrying the pestilence or is about to rob us."

"Well, robbing I don't know about," Julian says, "but as far as the plague, you need to look inward for causes of that, not outward." When Krea stares at him obtusely, he changes the subject. Do they still not know what causes the plague? "Krea," he says, "it seems an awfully big staff to take care of just two women."

"We had more but they died. The pestilence came last year, real bad. It spared some. It spared Lady's daughter," Krea says, in the tone of someone who's critical of the pestilence for its value judgments. "It spared Lady's spinster sister, Lady Edna." The tone is only slightly warmer. "Also the useless Gremaine. He is Lady's nephew, which is why she refuses to let me put a pillow over his head. I've offered to do it—but Lady is kind and says no."

This Krea is quite a character, Julian decides, just as Cornelius returns. "Have you finished eating and yapping? I need to show you the chandlery before I hurry to prepare your horses."

In the room with vats of grease, Julian gags, the little food he's eaten and the gallon of ale repeating in his throat.

"What's wrong?" the steward asks.

Julian breathes through his mouth. "What is that putrid smell?"

"I don't know what you mean," Cornelius says. "I smell nothing untoward."

"What's in those buckets?"

"That," Cornelius replies, "is the suet from which you will be making tallow for your candles." The steward eyes him. "As a chandler, you *are* familiar with the process of candle-making, are you not?"

"Of course." Julian sifts through his brain for anything he knows about candles. "I usually make them with—beeswax."

"You come from a part of Wales where they're ignorant of the law, sire?" says Cornelius. "Because all beeswax production and sale in London is controlled by the Guild on behalf of the Church and Crown."

"There's a candle-making Guild?" Julian thinks he's being funny.

"That is precisely the case." Cornelius can barely contain his contempt. "The Wax Chandler's Company, established by Royal Decree two hundred years ago. Is this, perhaps, news to you as a chandler?"

Julian can't continue to converse because he is retching. The meaty gristly buckets of fat stink so bad. It smells like an animal dying.

"How many candles do you think we'll need, Grizzly?" Julian asks, as Krea carries in another vat of fresh grease, not fully solidified. The bucket is heavy, yet she carries it and sets it down without trouble. Krea is strong despite her size. In many ways, she is insect-like.

"A thousand candles," Cornelius replies. "Of varying thicknesses and lengths to fit our candlesticks."

Julian balks. He will be stuck in this rancid room for eternity, while out there in the sunlight, Lady Mary will be sewn into her wedding dress and have daffodils from Holland placed in her ringlet hair.

"Can't we just buy the candles?" Julian asks. He can load a wagonful tomorrow.

"Have you *any* idea how much candles cost?" Cornelius says. "Lady Collins has a wedding to pay for. We have seven vats of suet for you—the chandler—to make into candles. And pardon me, sire, but what would be the point of you if we could just buy the candles?"

Why does everyone keep asking what the point of him is? Graham there, Cornelius here. Julian is sick of it, frankly. "But Grizzly, if we're making tallow candles, why can't we also make some beeswax candles?"

"Do you want us all to hang?" the steward says. "And even if this was a good idea, we have no bees, because we have no flowers. So where are you going to harvest this beeswax from?" Cornelius tuts derisively. "Oh, and one more thing," he adds. "I don't know about the unknown forest, but here in Clerkenwell, if you steal anything over a fivepence, it's the gallows for you. Newgate is a mile away as the crow flies. You *are* familiar with Newgate prison, aren't you, sire?" He turns to go. "You have much to do, jack of all trades. Best get started."

39

Medea

"KREA, WHAT IS THIS NASTY POTTAGE MADE FROM?" SIDE BY side she and Julian stand, staring into the vats.

"Cow drippings, lamb drippings, pig drippings," Krea replies. The grease from the things she and Farfelee cook for the house. The buckets have stood for weeks, the fat waiting to be made into tallow.

"Did the last chandler die of disgust?" Julian asks.

"No, sire."

He has no choice but to confess his incompetence and beg the scullery maid for help. "Can you teach me how to fish, Krea?"

She shakes her head. "I do not know how to fish, sire."

"Please call me Julian," he says. "I mean, can you show me how to make tallow?"

"Of course," she says. "But why did you say fish if you meant tallow?"

He makes a mental note to only be literal from now on. "We don't have time for this, Krea. The wedding is in—I mean, how long do we have before the wedding exactly?" If only he knew the date Elizabeth I had died.

"Less than two moons, sire. Seven Sundays." Krea smiles as if pleased with herself. "That's how I measure all things," she says. "By the day of rest. I got seven of them before Lady Mary is married and gone from this house."

Julian squints. "Do you want Lady Mary to be gone from this house?"

"No, sire. I'm just counting the Sundays until she is. All things come to those who wait."

"That is true. But...Lady Mary doesn't seem happy about the upcoming marriage."

"Lady Mary," says Krea, "is never happy about anything. No time for idle chit chat. We have work to do."

They drag two of the vats into the side yard by the kitchen and heat up the coals. Krea says it's easier to cook the suet outside over low heat coals. Julian doesn't understand. Hasn't it already been cooked?

"You got meat in the suet," Krea replies, "pieces of gristle and bone. You're not making meat candles, are you?"

Oh, so not completely humorless. The gnome makes the wry comment into her shoes. "I suppose not," Julian says. "Krea, look at me."

The little woman lifts her eyes. She is an aviary creature, beaten down and plain and pocked of face, but there is fire behind those pale gray eyes, and smarts.

And something else Julian can't quite put a finger on.

Something unkind.

"I'm not Lady Edna," Julian says. "You may look at me when we speak."

Krea's hard face softens. "Let's render the fat before the sun goes down. I need to hurry. I must make pandemain for the morrow."

Julian nods. He will not ask what in the devil's name is pandemain.

"Lord's bread," Krea says.

"I didn't ask."

"You didn't look as if you knew."

Krea pours some grease over the spread-out coals, throws on a little tinder, and brings a lighted wick from inside the kitchen while Julian stands and watches. When were matches invented? God, how is it possible that one man can know so little.

"Krea, how did you light that?"

She looks at him as if he's touched in the head. "From the fire in the kitchen."

"What if the fire in the kitchen goes out?"

"It's everyone's job to make sure one of the fires is always on in the house. Or it's the old-fashioned method, I suppose. Flint and steel. It's only happened once in the twelve years I been here."

She's known Mary since the girl was six. "Flint?"

"Like a piece of quartz."

Julian flinches at the word *quartz*. Of course. Fire was discovered by the first men from striking quartz, the most abundant element on earth, an element with electro-conductive properties. Fire transformed mankind, made civilization, made life possible. And the first spark came from quartz—the thing Julian holds in the palm of his hand when he ignites the sun to make love possible. He trembles.

Krea instructs him to simmer the pots of suet, stirring frequently and adding more coal as needed. "It's called *rendering*," she says. After the oil is separated from the solid matter, Julian must strain it into a clean pot, over a fine metal grate lined with cheesecloth.

"And then I pour the clean oil into a Mason jar, place a linen wick in it, wait for it to harden, and I'm done?"

Krea frowns. "I don't know what a Mason jar is. But the wick must be braided for strength. Also, Master Grysley needs tapered candles. Make jar candles only if you wish to face the consequences for disobeying."

"Krea, I can't make tapered candles. The grease won't harden enough to hold their shape."

"Of course not, sire," she says as if he's an imbecile. "You need to add potash to the grease for structure."

Potash? "Where do I get that?"

"You can buy some at the market, but Lady would prefer you make your own."

"Make my own potash?" Is the gnome joking?

"It's not difficult. The greens you collected for Master Cedric's eyes, the leaves and plants and flowers, use them. Burn them down to ash."

"Okay," he says. "That doesn't sound hard."

"Then you leach the ash. That's not hard either. It takes time. But what else have you got to do?"

"Nothing." Julian says, imagining Mary somewhere in the house. "How do I leach the ash, do I dilute it with water?"

"Yes." Krea looks pleased he knows something. "The stuff that rises to the top is the stuff you want. The stuff that sinks you throw away. You won't get a lot of potash, but you'll get some. After you mix it into the rendered suet, your tallow will harden. Of course, that's when the real work begins. Because every time you dip your braided wick into the grease, you must wait for the tallow to harden before you can dip again. You will probably have to dip and harden six times to make one tapered candle."

"How many did Master Grizzly say I had to make?" He hopes he's misheard.

"A thousand."

What a disaster. Why did he let Lady Collins think he could make candles?

Krea must see it on his face because she says, "Patience is a virtue, Master Julian. You must learn it." She leaves him in the yard, dejectedly stirring the suet with a wooden spoon. He must be wiped out because his eyes won't focus. Making his hand into a fist, he peers through the tiny opening between his clenched fingers. It's a life hack. He forces his eye to focus on one piece of gross gristle at a time, and this is what he is doing when he raises his head, with the fist still at his little eye and spies Lady Mary standing next to the coals, impatiently tapping her heel on the hard ground.

40

Lady Mary

HE IS SO SURPRISED TO SEE HER, HE DROPS THE SPOON INTO the pot of grease.

"Well done," she says.

"Lady Mary," he stammers. Where's his poker face?

"Do *not* address me," she commands, speaking low. "Do *not* look at me. I have but a minute. Is it true that you're going across the river tomorrow morning? To Borough Market, in Southwark?"

"Yes—"

"That was not a question!"

"My lady, um…"

"Do not speak to me, you impertinent clot! Tomorrow morning you will take me with you. Do you hear me?"

"It's difficult not to hear you."

"Do *not* address me!" But she lowers her voice. What's extraordinary is how her voice raises the hair on his neck, sending a wild elated tremble through his body. It's unmistakably her voice, breathy and dewy, even though the words she is saying with that remarkable voice are so fractious. She sounds as she did on stage at *The Invention of Love*—British but ornery. "I heard Cornelius and Aunt Edna discussing you. They think you're a swindler. If you don't take me, I'll tell Lady Mother they're right, and how you had to ask Krea how to make candles."

Julian stays silent, eyeing her from behind his impassive face.

She redoubles her efforts. "I'll tell her you're a Catholic! Do you know what we do to crooks and swindlers and Catholics?" She mimes a rope knot around her neck and yanks it up. He can't take his eyes off her. She is so beautiful, even when she's acting heinous. "You'll be thrown into the bear pit."

Julian remains expressionless.

She quadruples her efforts. "I'll tell Lady Mother you were eyeing me in the garden, brazenly and lustfully, and it'll be the rack and gallows for you, a commoner and a vagabond ogling with lascivious intentions a soon-to-be-married noble lady."

His head cocked, Julian, who's been forcing himself not to blink so he could continue staring at her, straightens out. With every word she speaks she looks more agitated, and more alluring. This is a new and unfamiliar Josephine, one who hasn't learned to smile yet. *Like a newborn soul.* Julian can't help himself. He smiles.

"You don't have to threaten me," he says. "All you have to do is ask." And not even ask that nicely.

Mary is only slightly shamed. "Just have the carriage ready to go tomorrow at dawn. Say nothing to anyone. Do you understand?"

"Yes," Julian says. "But I won't have a carriage. I'll have a wagon."

"Ask for a carriage!"

"To go to the market? I'm going to fill your family's carriage with flats of flowers and sacks of potatoes?"

"Don't argue with me!" she says. "I don't know what flats are, nor potatoes of which you so impudently speak. I don't care how you do it, just do it."

"Where are you headed, may I ask?"

"You may not," she says, swirling and giving him the back of her head.

"Are you planning to audition for the Lord Chamberlain's Men?" The Globe Theatre is in Southwark, near the market.

She starts toward the house.

"Wait!" Julian calls after her. She stops at the door. The hem of her dress has gotten dusty in the yard and her curled hair has fallen out of its bejeweled pins. He takes a few steps to her. She glares at him so rudely that she probably doesn't notice how he's gawking at her. He wants to touch her. He wants to lay his unsteady hand on her warm skin to prove to himself that she is really real.

"Pardon my impertinence—are you wearing whiteface makeup?"

She brings her gloved hand to her cheek.

"The paint you put on your face is made with vinegar and ground up lead," Julian says.

"I know what it's made of," Mary says. "I'll thank you not to talk to me about it. You're not allowed to notice either my face nor what I have on it."

"Please don't wear it," Julian says. "Lead is poison. In the old days"—he regroups—"I mean, women have been known to die from it."

"Pfooey."

What can he do to keep her talking, to keep her with him? "Your mother is right about one thing, though—women can't perform on stage."

She waves him away. "Shoo, eavesdropping fly," she says. "Mind your own tallow. Why don't you continue to pretend you can do what you do, and I'll continue to do what I can do, and we'll see at the end of the day which one of us will be fed to the bears."

Why does it have to be either? She walks inside before he can say another word. But she says another word. "Don't ask Cornelius for the carriage," Mary calls back to him. "When you really need something, ask Lady Mother."

The sun goes down and the house is plunged into darkness. The stove is alight in the kitchen, and the embers are almost out in the small fireplace in the chandlery. Outside, the stars are obscured by clouds and the moon is new. There is a gusty wind that swirls through the trees. As Devi said, the earth is swirling into a new world order. How right he was. Julian's miniature room—a narrow bed, a bed stand, a small table—doesn't have a candle. It has a casement window with a broken latch. The panes of the latticed glass flap open and shut in the hard wind. He ties the latch with a piece of twine he finds in the kitchen and lies down on his bed. The pillows are plentiful but hard as quartz. The wool blanket is itchy, and the sheet is like sandpaper. It reminds Julian of Mrs. Pallaver's. But Mrs. Pallaver's didn't have Josephine in it, except in his dreams, where he never collided with her skull while fetching her umbrella.

And the hard bed there has prepared him for his hard bed here.

Julian lies on his back, clothes loosened, not off, his arms crossed on his chest, looking up, wading through the wonder.

Josephine is *alive*!

There is more of her.

She is not done yet.

And because of that, Julian is not done yet.

His clocks were stopped, and all his worldly goods dismantled; he was a pile of rocks, and yet new life has been breathed into him because there is life left in her.

Thank you. Oh God, thank you.

She had been separated from him, dispersed and scattered. Yet on the Other Side he found her and called out to her by name. Not the name of grief—*Josephine*—but by the name of truth. *Mary* is *Mia*. Relieved to not be cold or in water or in the black cave, heartened to be anywhere at all with her, even a place where he must breathe through his mouth not to smell the rendered tallow outside his door, even a place where she's preparing to marry someone else, Julian barely gets her good name past his lips before he falls asleep. *Mary! Mary...Mary—*

41

The Italian Merchant

TWO UNEXPECTED THINGS HAPPEN THE FOLLOWING MORNING. One, it pours. And because it rains, the trip across the Thames with Mary gets postponed.

And two, Cedric gets better. Instead of dying, he lives. He opens his eyes, now crusty instead of goopy, sits up in the straw and calls for Julian.

Julian doesn't know this at first. He spends the morning holed up in the chandlery, straining the batch of clarified suet, the grease splashing over his tunic and face. Wiping his chin on his sleeve, he turns—and there's Lady Collins in the doorway.

"Master Julian, what an amazing thing you've done for our family," Aurora tells him. Julian demurs. The boric acid and a little honey did most of the work. Pleased that something he had learned from books and his *abuela* has solved a real-life problem, Julian heads to the stables to examine the weepy and grateful hostler. Julian wishes he could tell Devi that maybe the stuff he knows about plants is not entirely useless. It's come in quite handy in keeping his head attached to his shoulders.

Immediately things change for the better. Gregory offers Julian a new wardrobe made of linen and silk. He is offered breeches that don't itch, suede doublets and leather jerkins, given bleached linen shirts with leg-of-mutton sleeves and puffy white collars, soft leather belts, excellent felt hats, a long black cloak, fine woolen hose, and slip-on leather shoes. Amazing how slightly

nicer clothes elevate his stature not only in the estimation of the
household but even in his own eyes.

Gremaine brings him actually clean water, and Krea boils it
any time Julian asks. Dunham the gong farmer offers to help with
the candles. Julian refuses. Dunham is the family's latrine cleaner.
He's got a doughy face, a snouty nose, round, too-close-together
eyes, greasy hair with blunt-cut bangs that fall halfway down
his forehead and a misshapen body, angly in the shoulders and
stodgy in the middle. Also—any time of day or night—the boy
smells worse than a dog kennel that hasn't been cleaned in weeks.

Aurora invites Julian into the great hall with the family,
introduces him to her enfeebled Uncle Henry and Aunt
Angmar, and places Julian by her elbow at the massive
dining table. After supper, he's allowed to sit in the well-made
armchair, one of only two in the hall. Everyone else perches on
benches and stools. Aurora herself pours him a goblet of red
wine. She begins calling him Julian. He is served lamb and beef
and pork with beans and bread, and honey cake for dessert.
His spoon is no longer pewter but polished silver. Aurora tells
him he has brought good luck to the family because it hasn't
rained like this since March. When has Julian heard that before,
that he has brought someone good luck? From Mary when she
was Josephine. He glances at Mary now. Sitting far away at the
polished oak table, Mary ignores him.

What did Aladdin's genie say? You cannot force anyone to
fall in love with you. And making himself lovable so the girl
falls in love with him is not as easy as it sounds. Mary, Cornelius
and Edna have formed a trinity of hostility with which they
shade every word they speak to Julian. But if his goal is to have
Mary's mother love him—done! Keeping them both plied with
wine, Aurora regales him with family stories, starting with the
minutest details about the deaths of her loved ones. Now she
runs the estate herself, does all the things Sir John used to do.
"But no matter how hard I work," she says, "I still carry a terrible
foreboding that I won't be able to keep death from my door."

Warmed by the wine, Julian gets cold when he hears this. "Wash your hands, Lady Collins," he counsels. "Stay healthy." The water is carried in filthy buckets. "Add a little vinegar to your water to disinfect your hands."

Aurora says she does wash her hands. "I wash them every morning."

"You must wash them more often than that, my lady," Julian says. The things Gremaine and Dunham touch cannot go near a human mouth. Aurora listens to him as if he's a priest giving a sermon (complete with wine). Curing Cedric seems to have put her completely in his thrall.

Julian suggests other ways to keep contagion at bay. Dunham can't be allowed to saunter through the house after cleaning the pit latrines. "You wouldn't let a pig from the pen wander through your halls, would you, dear lady?" Julian says. "Think of Dunham as something filthier than a pig. Tell him to soak himself in a tub of vinegar before he enters your—or your daughter's—chamber."

Aurora laughs as if he's joking.

Julian hails vinegar as an easily available, first-rate disinfectant. He instructs her—"and her loved ones"—to drink a small diluted amount every day to clean their insides. He tells her to use it to soften her skin and as an antiseptic for cuts. She listens to him open-mouthed. Finally!—someone appreciates Julian's fondness for vinegar.

"Do not use whiteface," Julian says, "even though it has vinegar in it. It also has lead in it, and lead will make you sick. Over time it will kill you."

"Over time, everything kills you, my dear," says Aurora.

Julian segues from lead to Lord Falk. As in, speaking of poisonous things, dear lady....

"Mary's feelings are immaterial," the mother says, pointing to the family coat of arms in the center hall by the fireplace. "Ancestral honor must be preserved. The house needs a male heir." She tells him the Collins family once owned half of

Clerkenwell and helped build all of its Catholic monasteries, including St. Mary's (so it was St. Mary's once!) before they were taken over during the Dissolution and all its tithes confiscated by the Crown. "My husband named our youngest daughter after that glorious convent," Aurora says with sadness.

"Clerkenwell is a very good town," Julian says. "It was built to last. The churches will stand. So will the parks, the markets, the theatres. It will grow and prosper. Don't worry."

"How do you know?"

"I have a feeling," Julian says, tapping on his chest where the crystal hangs.

Aurora dabs her eye. "My husband's father was a great noble of the royal court," she says. "He fought for Henry VIII, and his father fought for Henry VII. My husband and his ancestors were all part of the chivalry. And now, I have no sons to send to fight for the new King. Our coat of arms is rusting. I know my daughter doesn't want to marry Lord Falk. But do you see why she must? We must have an heir. Otherwise there will be nothing left of our family."

What can Julian say? She *cannot* marry another. "She seems quite determined not to," is what he says.

"Yes, she's obstinate like the mules in our stables." Aurora pours them more wine and lowers her voice. "She's always been such a willful child. Whatever she wanted, she was determined to get." She glances around to see if anyone's listening before proceeding. "I tell you as a trusted friend, but a few years ago she even dallied with an Italian merchant who sailed through London and caught her fancy. Don't look so shocked. She told me she wanted to marry *him*!" Aurora lowers her inebriated voice to an embarrassed whisper. "Imagine the dishonor!"

"The dishonor of marrying an Italian?" Julian asks with a small smile. "Or marrying a merchant?"

"You jest, but it could've been a terrible scandal." Aurora is divulging deep confidences. "Mary was sixteen. She said she was in love. Bah! Did she not understand that she was a noblewoman and he was a peasant? I told her the decisions she made when she was sixteen only seemed trivial. In reality they would affect her and her family's life forever."

"What happened to the Italian?"

The mother sighs into her wine. "He turned out to be faithless, like many Italians. Unlike Clerkenwell"—she smiles—"Mary and Massimo weren't made to last. He sailed home. Mary went through a rough patch, became ill—with some female things." Aurora coughs and says no more. "Lord Falk's mother and I arranged this marriage to help her out of her melancholy. Despite what Mary thinks, she and Lord Falk are quite well suited. The Italian had little to recommend him besides his looks. I told her it's best to stay away from the Italians and their seductive ways."

"I couldn't agree more," says Julian, and in bed that night prays that tomorrow it'll stop raining, and he'll be allowed to take Mary to London. He doesn't have a concrete plan, but he needs to find a way to get close to her before her wedding to someone else fast approaches. Devi was right. He said, *you might have another Fario Rima to deal with.* Well, at least this time around, Julian knows the truth right from the start. He will deal with Lord Falk. In the shining city that's Clerkenwell in 1603, Julian has only one road, and her name is Mary. Wherever she leads, he will follow.

42

Fynnesbyrie Fields Forever

IT RAINS FOR FIVE DAYS STRAIGHT. ON THE ONE HAND, THERE'S no need to divert the stream. On the other, Julian will go insane. No one can leave the house. The family can't even go to church on Sunday, a first in seven years. The horses' hooves and the carriage wheels sink into the quicksand mud on Collins Lane.

Julian busies his hands while his soul climbs the walls.

Together he and Krea roll empty barrels out onto the lawn to collect rainwater and then roll them full into the buttery. They boil plants, leach them, add potash to the clarified oil, fill thick glass jars with wicks and tallow. Krea teaches him how to braid the wick to make it thicker and stronger and how to dip the braided wick into the grease, though she cannot teach him how to wait for it to harden before he dips and re-dips. Julian must learn patience on his own. She teaches him how to make mash for ale. It takes forever, like candle-making; there are a dozen steps, and like the candles, the ale is gone in a day or two, and in any case doesn't keep, so the process must begin anew.

No one drinks the water, as if they know it's sewage. They drink ale for breakfast, dinner, and supper. Ashton would approve. Poor Ashton. Julian hopes Devi has told his friend about what's happened to him. Sometimes it's hard to believe the other life is gone. Julian tries not to think about it.

He can't find one private minute alone with Mary. During the day while he toils by Krea's side or sits with Cedric at the stables,

Mary stays by the corner window in the great hall and reads, always in the presence of one or two members of her family. Occasionally he hears her singing or performing bits of plays in front of them. In the evenings, while Julian and Aurora spend time entertaining themselves with cards and conversation, she remains by herself near the fire or in the library next door.

Edna refuses to join Julian and Aurora in their frivolous games since she disapproves of cards only lightly less than she disapproves of Julian. "Correct me if I'm wrong," Edna says to him, "but education in Wales is quite poor, isn't it? Non-existent, really."

It's no wonder Edna is suspicious of him. Every time Julian opens his mouth, he says the wrong thing. His one pithy *King Lear* quote falls on confused ears. *"You have begot me, bred me, loved me. I return it back to you."* *King Lear* must not have been written yet. His careless defense of Shakespeare as a genius *sui generis* who helped write the King James Bible is met with the same troubled reaction. James, the first of his name, has not been crowned yet. "Which King James Bible could you possibly mean, Master Julian?" Edna asks.

Even beverages are not safe. A few days ago, he asked if there was any tea, and Edna said *tea*?

The British didn't have tea in 1603? It's the end times.

Julian is afraid to say anything lest his ill-chosen words betray him. Krea has told him how the witches and the insane are treated in Elizabethan London. "Equally, sire," she says. "Both are burned at the stake."

Lady Collins often talks about the crackdown on Catholic priests in post-Reformation England. One could be hanged for harboring a Catholic priest, she tells Julian. Edna, who isn't even part of the conversation, pipes in with, "What about harboring just a plain old Catholic? What is the punishment for that, dare I ask?"

"Oh, the Catholics are also burned at the stake," Krea tells Julian.

Correction to those who are burned at the stake: The witches, the insane, and the Catholics.

In the manor's dark paneled library, the books are bound between ornamented gilded covers and proudly displayed. Nothing is spined. This isn't Book Soup. The covers, like the books themselves, are works of art. They're all in color, gorgeously illustrated, elaborately inked and typefaced, they are precious jewels. Julian is awed by their craftsmanship.

One evening after supper and wine, Julian follows Mary into the library and pretends to browse alongside her. They're not alone. Blind Uncle Henry is by the window, his wife Angmar by his side, and Edna is by the fire, close to Julian and Mary, listening in. Mary has picked out several volumes, pressing the books against her bodice. She wears a starched puff collar like a white Frisbee around her neck. Her arms are hidden with oversleeves and undersleeves, she is laced up through the waist and hooped out with a farthingale skirt, whalebone rings rippling out, keeping her at an untouchable distance from him. He can still gaze at her bored annoyed face, her luminous skin, curls expertly arranged, adorned with pearls and a gold-fringed bonnet, a whole life burning behind her large brown eyes that try to maintain a glassy composure.

He wanted a sonnet out of the dust?

Here she is.

Casual as all that, Julian asks Mary what she's reading. (*Is that for your one o'clock? No, that's for my 4:30.*) She thrusts at him the three tomes in her hands. A blue velvet copy of *The Book of Hours.* An exquisitely embossed and illustrated *Canterbury Tales.* And *The Art and Craft to Know How Well to Die.*

"Why would you ever read such a book?" a frowning Julian asks about the last one. He doesn't give it back to her.

"Why does Lady Mother say a prayer of Extreme Unction over me each time I leave the house?" Mary asks, scanning for other books on the shelves while Julian continues to hold hers. She sighs theatrically. "Because death is never far away. It's in every soup pot, every mushroom, every hoof of the horse. Isn't that right, Aunt Edna?"

"That is correct, child," the eavesdropping Edna replies. "Now choose your books and get on with it. It's almost time for bed. Catrain is waiting to bathe your ladyship."

The briefest blink passes between Julian and Mary after the word *bathe*, as his mind fills up with the image of *bathe* around the image of *Mary*.

"Death is the reality of life," Mary continues. "Last week our baker got the sweating sickness in between dinner and supper. He was gone by sunrise."

Julian blinks. "What's the sweating sickness?"

"It's a sickness where you sweat," Mary replies as if talking to the village idiot.

She promptly drops the books he's just handed her and waits for him to pick them up and hand them to her again. His hand brushes against her silk glove, underneath which there's a fire-breathing dragon of a real girl. *The life of the dead is placed in the memory of the living.* "Shun death, Lady Mary," Julian whispers. "That's my advice."

"Thank you for your invaluable counsel, Master Julian," Mary says, "I simply don't know what I'd do without it."

For the first time, her golden voice has spoken his name out loud. *Julian.* Yes, her words were cutting, but her throat has summoned his name from her lungs, from the breath that rises and falls around her heart.

"It's time, Mary," Edna says. "Say good night."

"You regale Lady Mother with so many bits of knowledge about vinegar and lichens," Mary says. "Tell me, good sir, do you know anything about when the rains will stop?"

So she still wants to go to London! Julian's heart jumps. The hellish rain. "Judging by the sunset this evening, possibly tomorrow," Julian replies. "Though I fear the ground will still be too wet for me to take the wagon." The wheels sink into the mud. He knows this from bitter experience. He has tried the past two mornings. He and Cedric spent hours afterward, digging out. There will be no travel until the road dries.

"You've done this," Mary says in a hiss, and before he can protest, adds, "Lady Mother keeps saying the rain is because of you, and it's ill-bred to argue with one's mother." She marches away in haughty disgust.

What if she's right, and the rain doesn't end until the day of her wedding? Did Julian come all this way to be the man who doesn't even take part in the race?

The only reason he endures the rain half as well as he does is because of Cedric. He has made a friend in the grateful and reverential hostler, who enjoys Julian's company and has taken the bad weather as an opportunity to teach Julian everything he knows about horses. Cedric is not Krea. He teaches patiently and pleasantly.

In the stables, with the rain falling, Cedric shows Julian how to handle the horses and the wagons. Cedric never asks why Julian doesn't know these things. Cedric is just happy to be alive. He shows Julian how to tie up a horse, and how to lead it to water, and how to make the carrot pulp to feed it. He teaches Julian how to jump up on the driver's bench, how to stop a horse, how to slow it, how to make it go. He teaches Julian how to saddle and pack a donkey. After all the instruction, Julian still doesn't care much for horses or donkeys or the rain, but he likes Cedric.

Though the rain stops, the lane out of the manor remains impassable. While he waits for the ground to dry, with Cedric's help Julian harnesses Alastor and walks the beast to the nearby market at Smythe Field. The family needs food and Julian needs plantings. The soil is finally soft; it will take seedlings well. The woman meant to be his bride but betrothed to another lives in an empty orchard where the flowers have not yet taken root.

Holding Alastor by the reins and yanking him through the gloppy earth, his workman boots covered with mud to his calves, Julian heads across Fynnesbyrie Field, where despite the recent flooding, women are laying out their washing on the wet grass to dry in the sun. Little boys run in puddles with their dogs, water carriers bobble rods on their shoulders, while a dozen men practice archery.

The laying out of the clothes on wet grass amuses Julian, but the arrows that are shot indiscriminately through the air do not. Where do those land? It doesn't seem to trouble anyone else, not even when one of the arrows whistles down and lodges in the squishy ground three feet ahead of a woman carrying a baby.

At Smythe Field market they sell cabbages and beets and leeks and onions, they sell wild garlic and soapwort plants for bathing. They don't sell potatoes. No one's even heard of potatoes. (How is that possible?!) Julian buys other things a mule can carry, things to protect Mary.

He buys lavender to keep moths away from her in the coming summer, and flea bane to repel ticks and mosquitoes, and marigold to comfort her hands sore from work, though he is relatively sure this novice soul Mary has never done a real day's work in her life. Julian doesn't buy anything just for esthetic value. Everything has a dual purpose. If it's attractive, so much the better. Aside from its medicinal benefits, marigold is a sturdy plant and pleasant to look at. But Julian's priority is keeping disease away. He loads up the donkey with calendula and cinnamon, with dried cloves and yarrow flowers, with grain to make ale, and apples for cider vinegar.

Pleased with his purchases, Julian is less pleased with Alastor. The mule walks slow with a heavy load, and at one point, the ass halts and refuses to budge. Julian must stop and rest until the beast chooses to lumber onward. His hand kneading the crystal stone around his neck, Julian watches the meadow, the children running around, the couples arm-in-arm, mothers and daughters arguing, two friends competing in a friendly archery game. Julian gazes at the two friends a long time. Ashton will be all right. He'll move back to L.A. He'll be fine.

The field is tranquil. This particular field doesn't exist in the land of the future, having been replaced by streets and buildings, but something like it does exist. Julian knows this firsthand (not first hand), having grown up with five brothers in a little house with woods for a backyard, and a mother who was always home when her kids were small.

Slowly he walks his purchases back home. Julian doesn't know how any of this turns out. What will happen to him and her? He can live here with her, he knows it, he feels it. He will live with her anywhere. The question is, how does she learn to live here with *him*?

43

The Boy and the Boatman

THE NEXT MORNING BEFORE DAWN THERE'S A KNOCK ON HIS latticed window. It's Mary, though Julian scarcely recognizes her in the dim blue light. She wears a long brown tunic with a black belt, and a black overcoat. He can't see her hair; her head is covered by a man's cap with a long hood over it. Her face is free of white paint. In her hands she holds a large wicker basket filled with clothes and food.

"What time is it?" He is so happy to see her.

"Is your head broken?" she replies. "You can't look up at the sky yourself? It's before sunrise. Why aren't you ready?"

"I am ready. What did you do to your hair?"

"Don't question me, don't evaluate my appearance. Hurry before someone sees me. I'll meet you by the stables. Did you get the carriage? I have to put my basket in it."

"We have the covered wagon—"

She stomps off without waiting for the rest. It's glum and soggy out, but at least it's not raining. Cedric has already woken up, harnessed Bruno to the wagon for Julian, and gone back to sleep. Julian guides the animal carefully down the narrow lane, walking alongside it, holding the reins, the way Cedric taught him. In her male cloak and hood, Mary looks like a boy. A boy with a soft face.

The face is the only thing soft about her.

"Why are you walking?" she says. "Why don't you get up here and drive the horse? Are you going to walk the horse like it's a mule all the way to London? We should get there in a fortnight, then. At this speed, we might miss my wedding, so perhaps your plan is sound, if hellish. Look at your boots, they're filthy, they'll never dry, you can't walk inside any establishment with footwear that awful, unless it's inside a shop of dirt, is that where you're taking me, to a shop of dirt?"

Julian has been wishing all these days to hear Mary's voice. Well, here it is. He trudges on in silence, hoping St. John's Lane is drier and he can actually sit next to her, awful boots and all.

St. John's Lane is drier. He sits next to her. She remains extraordinarily cranky. Nothing Julian does pleases her. Her rounded features are sharpened by the constant stream of complaints piping forth from her lovely mouth.

She didn't like how slowly he was walking, and now she doesn't like how slowly he's driving, but when he drives faster, she doesn't like that either. She is unhappy with his inability to navigate potholes, which jostle the wagon and cause commotion to her insides. At one point she loses the cobbler's cap in her hands, and Julian has to jump down and retrieve it from a puddle. She scolds him for the wet cap, for the mud it fell into, and for how long it took him to bring it back to her. "Take your time, by all means," she says. "It's not as if I have anywhere to be."

He says nothing.

"This is all your doing," Mary says, "the rain, the mud. I hope you're happy."

Julian is not *un*happy. He wants to talk to her. He wants to tell her about how familiar some strangers can be, as if you've known them forever, about the music of destiny, about the smoke of stars through which she shines so bright. But she's impossible to speak to. He can barely concentrate on keeping the horse from galloping and killing them both, he can't also respond to her harangues. To be fair, she doesn't really require a response, except occasionally when she asks, "Are you even listening to me?" to which he replies, "Of course, Lady Mary, please continue. You were saying how the horse is a thousand times more valiant than I."

She is not wrong. As Mary is a novice to her soul, Julian is a novice to the horse. As she is new to herself, he is new to this life, which has in it horses, not Volvos. He either pulls on the reins too hard or loosens them too much. It's like learning to drive a stick shift in rush hour—with a live, half-ton animal, next to a beguiling heckler, riding shotgun. He can't get the horse to maintain a steady walk. Conversation is thus awkward. "So, what play are the Lord Chamberlain's Men staging, Lady Mary—Bruno! Go!"

"Are you deaf as well as blind?" she says. "I don't want to speak to you. I must practice my lines, and I can't open my folio because your driving is making me want to vomit. Look over there"—she points to the horse's head—"One of its blinders has come off. That's why it's so jittery. It can see the wagon."

"What should I do?"

"What should you *do*? Am I the driver? Am I the yeoman? I don't bloody know. Do what you want. I suppose you jump down and fix it."

Julian fixes it, but now the horse is running. "Whoa," Julian says. "Whoa, horse. Bruno, steady on, girl."

"Does Bruno seem like a female horse's name to you?"

He wants to place a hand on Mary to keep her safe. His driving is about to topple her over.

"You're majestic with a horse," Mary says. "You must be a knight. Where's your coat of arms? Where's your noble sword?"

She's not wrong, but she is beastly.

This continues for a long painful while, but somewhere on Goswell Road, Julian finally manages to get the horse to walk. Good thing too, because Goswell Road is the worst. None dare call it a road. It's one pothole after another. The wheels are going to fly off his wagon the way they've been flying off the conversation with the moody beauty by his side.

As the horse comes under control, Mary also comes under control. She likes talking about herself. She tells him she hopes to get the role of Katherina in *The Taming of the Shrew*. A couple of years ago she auditioned for *Twelfth Night*. It was staged at the Fortune, near Fynnesbyrie Field. Julian knows where it is; he has walked by there with Alastor. It's not far from Collins Manor. He has even met Philip Henslow, the irascible man who runs the theatre. "*Oh!*" Mary exclaims, "*Let me be boiled to death with melancholy.* Yes, I was very good. I managed to dress like a boy and get a part as Viola, but unfortunately Mother caught me sneaking out of the house with one of the Italian spicers." She sighs dramatically. "He used to drive me to the playhouse. He was ever such a nice man. Not like you. Massimo was polite..."

"I'm not polite?"

"Not even slightly. He was handsome."

"I'm not handsome?"

Mary says nothing. "But when I was caught riding with him..."

"Like you are with me?"

"Nothing like this, believe me. Mother assumed the worst."

Julian has heard this story from Aurora, but from a different perspective, the perspective of a mother. He becomes distracted by the horrifying condition of the road to Cripplegate, one of the main gates through the Roman wall into the city of London. It's a gulley of mud and filth. He's certain if he fell into it he would drown. He really wants to put his hand on Mary; she is sitting too close to the edge. "Are you sure your mother wasn't worried about other things?"

"Well, yes," Mary says breezily, "she did advise me to keep my devil's portgate shut before a terror befell me."

"Um—devil's portgate?"

"I do not wish to discuss it further. And perhaps you should be less distracted by me, you don't seem to know where you're going."

"I know where I'm going." *And I know I'm going with you.* "I'm not distracted by you, my lady. That is, unless you wish me to be. I'm trying to find another way inside the city to avoid this blasphemy of a road. But don't worry, soon we'll be at Cripplegate. Maybe we can stop somewhere and have lunch?"

"Have what?"

"Dinner, I mean." Julian is never going to get used to lunch being called dinner.

"We have no time for dinner," Mary says. "We have to be on the other side of the river before 12:30."

"We have plenty of time." Julian glances thoughtfully at the sky, as if he can read the ancient scrolls on it. They left the house at sunrise, how late could it possibly be?

"You're about to turn into Turnbull Street," Mary says. "Do you call that avoiding filth? That's the brothel quarter, where the bawdy houses are."

"Thank you," he says. "I know what a brothel quarter is."

"Oh, I'm sure you do."

"Lady Edna enlightened me."

"Yes, she does like to discuss the topic of brothels at some length."

"And in great detail."

Mary almost giggles. "Not enough detail, obviously," she says, trying to keep a straight face, "for, a minute ago, you didn't know what a devil's portgate was."

"I knew what it was," Julian says. "I was being polite, as you had requested. Continue with your fascinating story. What did you say after your mother told you to keep the, um, gate closed?"

"I told her—too late, Lady Mother."

"You should stop joking with her. You know how literally she takes you."

The girl says nothing at first. "That's when Mother decided to marry me off to save me. But not to Massimo, of course." Mary sighs. "There are so many things Mother doesn't understand."

"I think your mother's trouble is that she understands them too well," Julian says.

"She doesn't know where my heart lies. It's not with Lord Falk."

"Is it with the Italian?"

Mary shrugs. "He was entertaining. Like a play. A diversion. But I don't want to be some silly lady dying a slow death in a fusty house." She presses her hands to her chest and lifts her face to the sky. "I want to be on the stage, in the open air, in an amphitheatre! I want to hear the people in the galleries applaud and the groundlings laugh and cry and cheer!"

"But they still won't be cheering for you, Lady Mary," Julian says. "They'll be applauding for the thing you're putting on for them, for someone else. Don't you want to be loved for the young woman you actually are?"

"Don't speak to me so presumptuously about love," she says. "And no, I want to be loved for the woman I pretend to be."

Indeed, *Josephine*, indeed. "Which is what? A girl playing a boy playing a girl?"

"Precisely!"

Julian pulls up on the reins, slows down the horse and turns to look at Mary's pearl-skinned face, her full, red, decidedly un-man-like lips, her white neck peeking through the loose black twill of a man's cape. "You'll never look like a boy," he says, his voice lowering. "You won't fool any man."

"More fool you that you think this," Mary says, throwing off her hood under which she proudly displays her dark crew-cut hair. He gasps. She is delighted by his shock. "Yes, Master Julian, the *lady* is the pretend part. Every day, I wear a wig to fool the world. I fool you, Lady Mother, Edna, everyone. This is the real me. A girl with boy hair." She smiles with gritty satisfaction. "Stop gaping and drive. Time's a-ticking."

"Does your mother know you have no hair?"

"Make an effort *not* to be constantly foolish," Mary says. "Of course she doesn't. Only Catrain knows because she helps me bathe."

Julian drives on, his mind whirling. "Katherina is a big commitment, Lady Mary. How will you explain your day-long absence to your mother? To be at the Globe by call time, you'd have to be away from home six days a week. Are you going to head back across the bridge at night, by yourself? Or have a boatman ferry you across? It's not safe for a lady, even one who's dressed as a boy." Julian is just dreaming out loud. He will be the one to take her to the theatre, he will be the one to never leave her side.

"I don't feel like explaining myself to you, Welsh rabbit, foreign scullion," Mary says. "Since you clearly can't do two things at the same time, stop speaking and drive."

Julian drives and Mary goes on speaking. As they pass the gatekeeper at Cripplegate and enter the northern part of the city of London, she tells him if she becomes an associate member of the troupe, she will run away from home.

"That's your solution," Julian says, "to run away to the Globe? Your family will find you instantly. Take you home by force if necessary. They'll alert the Master of Revels that one of his Lord's Men is not a man, and Richard Burbage will sack you."

"They've heard of our Richard Burbage in Wales?" Mary says. "I didn't think the Welsh knew how to read."

Richard Burbage, Julian wants to tell her, is one of the greatest and most beloved actors in the history of English theatre. The mourning after he died was so intense, it overshadowed the death of an actual queen. He is buried in Shoreditch, at St. Leonard's, near Devi. Julian has read Burbage's short bio on a plaque while walking by. The words on his long-lost tombstone had been: "EXIT BURBAGE."

"Do you know what running away is?" Julian says. "Running away is leaving early in the morning before anyone wakes up and traveling to a place where you can't be found. It's changing your name. It's finding a different stage." He turns his head to her. "It's finding a different life."

Mary stares into his face. Julian doesn't care about the turmoil she must see in his eyes. He lets her see it.

"Change my name to what?" Mary says, frowning, slightly trembling, dreaming of the possibility.

"Anything you want." Julian wants to press the red beret to his chest. "How about Josephine?"

"Josephine Collins?"

"Why not?"

They sit suspended in time.

Julian snaps the reins, and they continue down Vine Yard to Cheapside. The roads are slightly better inside the city walls, because many are cobbled, but they're also narrower. In front of them on a hill stands an enormous red cathedral without a spire. "What church is that?" Julian asks Mary. Has he lost himself geographically? Vine Yard is where Aldersgate Street is. He is usually so well oriented. He thought they were in the center of the walled city, but he doesn't recognize the rectangular colossal church.

Mary is back to being peevish. "You don't know what church *that* is? It's St. Paul's."

That dark rambling building that stretches for blocks is St. Paul's? Julian stops the horse. They're on Ludgate Hill? It can't be. "Where's the dome? Where's the steeple?"

"What dome?" Mary says. "The spire was destroyed by lightning forty years ago. The Protestants and the Catholics both saw it as proof that God was displeased with their wicked ways, so the Queen ordered that the church remain unrepaired until we got ourselves in spiritual order."

"How's that going?"

"Slowly."

The church is a town in itself.

"Is there a gallery inside?" Julian asks, marveling at the massive red cathedral. "There used to be a gallery in the nave called Paul's Walk."

"It's still there," she says. "It's for gossiping beggars. Would that be you?"

"And there's a roof walk. Let's tie up the horse and climb up, look at the city. The view must be astonishing."

"Are you dim in the head? Am I a human or a pigeon?"

But Julian is excited. "Come on, let's go. We can stretch our legs, walk down to Paternoster Row. You love books, don't you? Back in the old days, Paternoster was home to the largest collection of booksellers and publishers in the world."

"What old days?"

Julian can't remember the heyday of the printers on Paternoster Row, Thomas Nelson, T. Hamilton. All the days, past and future have become one unbroken forest. This is what happens when a lost girl's eternal splendor is your balm and your wound.

Mary refuses to walk with him, but graciously allows a short break for food. They tie up the horse in a corner by Ludgate, pull out some pandemain and ale from her wicker basket, get some carrots and a bucket of water for the horse, and perch at the back of the covered wagon. He's tailgating with Mary, Julian thinks with amusement, chewing the bread hungrily. Pandemain, the bread for the wealthy, is baked into a size of roll that fits into a lady's hand. It's made from well-sieved wheat. Krea bakes the *panis Domini* but doesn't eat it herself. The servants get their own, much rougher "household loaf," stale remnants of pandemain mixed with un-sieved wheat and acorns and peas.

If Julian and Mary wanted to talk, they wouldn't be able to hear each other without shouting. London is abominably loud. And the stench from the streets is strong. Julian is not used to the stink or the spectacle. The streets inside the walled city are mazes, narrowed by tall Tudor houses, whose second-floor jetties overhang the cobblestones as if entire buildings are about to topple. Crowds of filthy busy people jostle their carts and pull their donkeys, carrying yokes and barrows down the winding lanes over broken stones. Men stroll with pipes in their mouths. "The holy herb," Mary calls it. "It was brought over from the New World. Have they heard of the Americas in Wales?"

"Yes," says Julian.

"Well, apparently tobacco from the Americas is good for your health, or so Aunt Edna says."

Julian refrains from comment.

After lunch, it takes Mary and him a long while to make their way down to the river, even though it's only a half-mile. There's too much foot and beast traffic. Children keep chasing pigeons in front of their horse. At the corner of Thames and Farringdon, a brawl has broken out involving a dozen merchants and one fishmonger. It stops traffic in all directions for at least a half-hour.

The Thames doesn't look familiar. Julian hardly recognizes it. Fast-flowing and opaque, the river is twice as wide as the Thames he knows. To get across to where the Globe is, they can drive the wagon over London Bridge or tie up the horse right here at Blackfriars and hire a boatman. Julian must admit, he's a little bit curious to see the bridge in its current incarnation. People live on it. Tall, smashed-together houses line the bridge's parapets. Would his wagon fit between the homes? He'd rather not risk it. It's over a mile away, and time is short. Still, it would be amazing to see.

They leave Bruno near the embankment and carefully make their way down the muddy slope to the leaden shore. The River Fleet is broad and fast as it empties into the Thames at Blackfriars. The crossing doesn't look easy. The river banks are swollen. Is the Thames a tidal river? Everything worries Julian, every decision is so precarious. He's afraid of making the wrong choice.

The little boatman readily agrees to take them across, though he charges them extra, saying that the current is strong with the river at high tide (!), and it will take over an hour. He even jokes with them, saying it's a good thing they didn't try to cross the day before, because London was a lunatic asylum. "The new King rode in from Scotland with his entire contingent and entered the city at Temple Bar," the boatman tells them. "It was absolutely terrible, the mess, the noise, the crowds."

But as soon as Julian offers Mary his hand to help her into the dinghy, the boatman swears and hurls the half-shilling

Julian had given him into the mud. He shouts at Julian not to set foot into his boat, to take his dirty money and leave. Perplexed, Julian backs away and stares anxiously at Mary. Something is happening, though Julian is damned if he knows what it is. But it's dangerous for her. He feels it. "Let's go," he says, trying to pull her behind him.

"No!" She wriggles free. "We paid for a ride, we're getting a ride."

"There's yer money!" The boatman points. "In the filth where yer buggering lot belong, you sodomizing pederasts! What you're doing is punishable by death. I don't take your sort 'cross the river. Death is too good for the likes of ya. Get away from me and me boat before I knife ya. You're swine herd, you'll burn in hell. You need an arrow in yer nuts, not a boat ride!"

"What are you on about, old man?" Mary says, with genuine incomprehension.

Raising his oar, the boatman lunges at Mary and swings. Julian steps between them—as if offering the faux boy his arm wasn't an egregious enough breach of public etiquette. Now he, a grown man, has just made it worse by defending the young boy's honor. He moves his head out of the way, and the flat of the oar cuffs him on the shoulder. Needles spring to his eyes. But before the boatman can swing again, Julian grabs the oar by the paddle and yanks it out of the man's hands. "All right, now," Julian says in a calming tone, as if the man is a wild dog. "Settle down. No sense in flying off the handle—"

The man is incensed. He grabs the other oar and swings it. Julian blocks it with the oar he's got. They fence for a few grunting thrusts, a few misplaced parries. "Put it down," Julian says, panting and trying to knock the oar out of the man's hands. "It's fine—we'll go somewhere else."

"No, we need a ride!" Mary cries behind him. "You got it all wrong! I'm not a man. See? I'm a noble lady!"

She throws off her hood, showing him her monk-cut hair and her makeup-free, milky and hairless face. For a moment, the irate boatman stops trying to bash Julian's brains in and gapes at her in utter confusion. Julian shakes his head. How does she manage to make a bad thing worse? There's nothing Mary can do to prove she's not a man, short of being imprisoned for indecency. It's hopeless.

Empowered by his righteous anger, the wherryman swings again. Julian blocks and jabs him in the solar plexus with the oar handle. The man loses his footing, staggers, and tumbles backwards into the brown slime. Julian stands over him, the handle at the man's throat.

"Are you going to stop this nonsense," Julian says, "or am I going to have to beat you senseless?"

"Beat him senseless, beat him senseless!" cries Mary.

"You heard the lady," says Julian.

"Don't hurt me!" the man squeals.

"Oh, you're not so brave now when you don't have a filthy oar in your hand," Mary says, pitching the oar the boatman has dropped into the river. Julian throws his after hers. They float in the shallow water, as the man, cursing and yelling, chases after his paddles, without which his boat is useless.

"Quick, let's go," Julian says, not daring to take Mary by the elbow to help her up the slope, lest they be hanged, two men touching in public.

She refuses to budge. "No. We're getting our ride." She's as stubborn as the wherryman.

"Not from him."

"Well, there's no one else here. Do *you* have a boat?"

"Mary," Julian says, stepping close to her to impart the gravity of their predicament. "Did you hear what he said? He thinks you're a man. You must now face the consequences of dressing like a man. You didn't think this part through, did you? The man in the water is about to yell for help, and soon there'll be a dozen oars pounding us on the head. And then the constable will arrive. Are you ready to explain yourself to the police?"

"It's your fault!" she cries, shoving him in the chest. "Why did you have to touch me?"

"I didn't touch you, I offered you my hand."

"You don't go around offering men your hand!"

"Well, you're not a man, so there's that," Julian says. "But in a minute, we'll both be at Newgate. So, how about if we resume this argument while we're driving away?"

"I'm not driving *anywhere*," Mary says through her teeth, "unless it's to the Globe."

"Not today."

"Yes, today!" It's a despondent, high-pitched wail.

"You don't sound like a boy right now," Julian says. "You sound like a petulant child that needs to be spanked and sent to bed."

Mary slaps him across the face and squelches uphill, mud covering her hose to her knees. She swears under her breath. "Do not ever speak to me again," she says. "Near the horse or anywhere. I hate you. As soon as we get back, I'm telling Mother everything. I'll get into a little trouble, but you'll be at the gallows. You're a despicable man."

Julian hurries behind her, relieved she wasn't bludgeoned by an oar and also relieved Mary won't have to provide evidence to the London police of her irrefutable sexual assets.

At the carriage they continue to spar, but they can barely hear each other. A large loud family walks their giant pet pig past them on Thames Street. Grocers, bakers, fruit sellers, fishmongers shout at the top of their soot-filled lungs, drivers yell at their horses, dogs bark, and Bruno makes his throaty horsey chuffing noises as if he's about to kick the shit out of both of them with his hind legs.

Julian's had enough. "Stop it," he says, loudly enough for her to hear, yanking her away from the rear of the horse so she doesn't get kicked in the teeth.

She rips her arm away. "Don't you dare put your hand on me!"

"I don't want to argue with you anymore," he says. "You want to go to the Globe? Fine, I'll take you." He thrusts his finger up at the bells of St. Paul's, ringing in the hour. Panting, they count. There are eleven interminably slow gongs. "It's eleven. Do we have time to get to London Bridge from here, get across, and ride another mile to the Globe? If you think we do, then let's go."

"We do!" She crosses her arms.

"Then let's go."

She climbs into the seat by herself, he grabs the reins and they're off. They don't speak down Fish Street. Irritated and stressed out, Julian is halfway across London Bridge before he even realizes he's on it. The tall houses and shops are so densely jammed together, they hide the river from him. Look at that, he's on London Bridge! *In the 1600s!* And he's too busy fighting with Aphrodite to even lift his eyes. It's shameful.

The bridge is not just a water crossing, it's a narrow city. It stinks of old cheese, sweat, fish, and horse manure. It takes a long time to silently drive the wagon across the river to the south side. Horse and foot traffic is at a near standstill. Pedestrians, carriages, wagons, and pack mules all must share the path between the tall homes. The bells ring in noon while they're still crossing. "I could walk it quicker," Mary says through her teeth.

"You're welcome to, my lady," Julian responds through his teeth.

When they finally clop under the grotesque severed heads at Great Stone Gate on the south side of the bridge, the bells ring in one o'clock. None of the Londoners gawk up, so he doesn't either, playing it cool, as if a dozen heads with open bulging eyes is nothing to him, a trifle.

The Borough Market is up ahead, red and yellow florals glowing invitingly under the green awnings, but they turn on Clink Street instead, an alley of prisons and white-walled brothels. The area is not fit for a lady. It's barely fit for a man. The toxic fumes emanating from the tanneries and dyers over on Maiden Lane are overpowering.

By the time they arrive, sweaty and fed up to the slate-colored spherical Globe Theatre, it's nearly two o'clock in the afternoon.

And wouldn't you know it—the Globe is closed!

(*Wouldn't you know it, Nicole Kidman had an understudy!*)

Silently the round magnificent theatre rises on the shores of the wild river, in the midst of primordial ooze, surrounded by muddy ponds, marsh fields and Bankside brothels. The Cardinal's Cap house of bawd is just across the road from the theatre, next to the bear circus. On wide display the swollen Thames flows, peppered with barges and shallops. London billows on the opposite bank. Though the Globe is built from ordinary wattle and daub—sticks and clay mashed together—it's been painted the color of silver-gray to look like a Roman forum, and when the afternoon sun hits it, it shimmers like a jewel.

A quiet jewel. There are no auditions, no plays, no other people, no sausage or walnut sellers as there were on Throgmorton Street. The wooden doors are shut. The sign on the chalk board on the door reads that the Globe is closed—as is apparently every playhouse in England—to observe the twelve-day mourning period after the Queen's funeral. Next to it is a list of the three plays the Lord Chamberlain's Men will perform when the theatre reopens. *Sir Thomas More*, *A Midsummer Night's Dream*, and *All's Well That Ends Well*. Three plays a day? Julian is impressed. While Mary stands stunned, he counts the days. Finally, he knows exactly what day it is. The Queen was buried on April 28. The Globe will reopen on May 11. Today is May 8.

He would like to tie up the horse and wander around the theatre (it's the *Globe!*) but there's no time for marveling because Mary bursts into tears.

"There, there," Julian says without touching her. "We can come back when they reopen. Maybe we can stay and see *All's Well That Ends Well*. How would that be? *The mightiest space in fortune nature brings, to join like likes and kiss like native things.* We'll get here early. I'll take us another way into the city. Just wear your girl clothes next time. We'll cross by ferry at Temple."

"By wherry!" she cries, blowing her nose into a handkerchief. "Welshman...you don't even know how to speak."

"I know how to count the minutes in the day, though," Julian says. "Let's hurry to Borough Market. There are probably no flowers left."

"I'd rather burn in hell than help you," she says, a true Persephone. "I'd rather marry Lord Falk than help you."

His heart squeezes. He makes his face impassive. "Did I ask you to help me?" he says, jumping up into the seat and grabbing the reins. "Just sit quietly and say nothing. That'll be the biggest help of all."

"I wish I were a man," Mary says as she watches him load up the wagon with purchases from Borough Market: cheese, smoked meat, vinegar, soapwort, lye, flowers. "Look at the freedom you have, and yet you're nothing. You come and go as you please, and no one says a word. But me!" She sniffles. "Plus, it took me five minutes to put on a man's clothes this morning. Some britches, some hose, a loose shirt, a jacket, a coat. It will take me over an hour to get back into my dresses in your idiotic wagon before Mother sees me. I've got petticoats and underskirts and overskirts and aprons and corsets, and blouses and overcoats and three layers of bonnets on my head. I'm a magpie. A patch of everything. And the Globe is closed. Everything's awful!"

"I consider this not your finest performance, Lady Mary," Julian says with love but without sympathy. He wipes his brow. "You want to be one of the Lord Chamberlain's Men? Then act like one. Stop crying. Do what you must do. Be gracious. Start with that. See how you do."

"I hate you," she says.

"So you keep telling me. How can you be an actor, how can you turn into another human being if yourself is all you see?"

"Myself is not all I see, unfortunately," she says, almost spitting. "I see *you*."

"Do you think you're the only one suffering?"

"I'm certain you are not suffering enough."

"You're blind to other people, Mary." Julian hears Devi saying this about the L.A. Josephine and tries not to hang his head.

"I wish I were blind and deaf right now," Mary says.

"Lift your eyes," says Julian. "Everywhere you look, people teem with anguish. Go visit the Black Friar Pub on Queen Victoria Street. Old men in wrinkled suits sit in the garden, glasses of beer long empty, hearts full, not wanting to leave, watching the world, trying to find their best selves. As you should try to do."

Mary glares at him with fury and worry. "Shut up, you demented Welsh lout. Who in the name of all that is holy is Queen Victoria?"

Julian is wiped out. Why is it so hard to drive a horse, to say the right things, to be reunited with her in this old new world? His shoulder is sore from being pounded with the oar.

They don't speak the rest of the way. Leaving his side, she climbs into the covered wagon. After driving past the aptly named church of St. Giles Without Cripplegate, just outside the Roman wall, Julian lifts the canvas flap to check on her. She has changed into her normal clothes. The wig is loose on her head, pinned to her bonnet, she's in a smock and a gray ladies' coat. She has fallen asleep curled up on her side on the floor of the wooden wagon, surrounded by his recently bought purple heather and white asphodel.

44

Josephine and the Flying Machine

MARY DOESN'T SPEAK TO JULIAN AS THE NEXT FEW DAYS PASS filled with dripping candles, ale mash, and flower plantings. She doesn't speak to him, but she also says nothing to her mother about their misadventure or his vile nature, as she had threatened. Her silence heartens and encourages him. If she really wanted to harm him, she could've done it with a word.

The morning the theatres reopen, he hears a rapping at his casement. He's been up, anxious she wouldn't come. But there she is, her wig on, wearing her white bonnet. She looks like a lady this morning, albeit a lady in a man's dark overcoat.

"Are you sleeping in again, princess?" Mary says. "Hurry up. Because today I'm not turning back. I don't care if the pillory awaits you. In fact, I would find that rather enchanting."

It's unseemly how happy Julian is to be insulted by her.

He takes her a different way to London to avoid the bad roads and the crush of the inner city. Instead of going down Farringdon through the congestion at Cripplegate, he makes a right on Clerkenwell and heads west down a country road that becomes Theobalds Street. He has set his sights on the other church of St. Giles, the better known one, on top of the hill on Holbourne. He won't deny it, he too wishes he could take her in a carriage not a wagon. She is too lovely to ride on a bench with him.

They clomp down a country lane. He still struggles to control the horse. "Please sit a little closer to me, Lady Mary," he says. "Or with the next pothole you're sure to fall into the street."

"I'd rather be trampled by a horse than sit closer to you," she returns cheerfully.

Julian has lost his game. He can't stumble into a flirtation even by accident. How did he manage to charm her at Book Soup, or any girl, ever? How did he manage to have sex with anyone? Excalibur indeed. He can't even control a horse!

"For someone who's supposed to be from some Welsh forest," Mary says, "you seem to be quite an expert on London gates and country lanes, and how to get to the Globe the roundabout way. How is that possible?"

"I lived here some time ago," Julian replies. "I had lost something and spent a long time on these streets trying to find it."

"Did you find it?"

"I did, yes." He doesn't look at her as he hurries the horse. *I don't know how, but somehow I found it.*

There are few people around them, mostly water carriers and milkmaids. Holbourne is a rural road, no shops, no buildings, no statues, no museums, no squares. The sun rises behind them, lighting up the rolling meadows. It's May, and warm. Bluebells and bugle line the fields; heather blankets the grass with its pale purple blooms. Wild cherry trees, the broadleaf ornamentals, are bursting with white buds, and meadowsweet grows tall in the long grasses. Up in the distance Julian spots the long graceful white spire of St. Giles, cloistered behind the stone walls of a Catholic priory and a leper hospital. The monastery has been shut down, but the church still runs the hospital. The air is so crisp that Julian's nose hurts and his eyes water.

Before he turns south to begin their descent into London, Julian stops the horse at the crest of St. Giles High Street and Drury Lane. His breath catches in his throat. He hopes Mary's does, too.

There is no Shaftesbury Avenue, Charing Cross, Seven Dials, Covent Garden, St. Martin in the Fields, or Long Acre. They don't exist. There is nothing but a dirt path that winds down through the meadows to the gate at Temple Bar near the shimmering river.

There is nothing around them but springs of asphodel. Every growing thing they gaze upon is purple, white, or green. Laid out in the low-lying valley, as far as the eye can see, is the sprawling, barely awake London. Cheapside and the Strand connect the old city with the Parliament towers and abbey spires of Westminster. In the city, the red brick monolith of St. Paul's towers on its very own hill among the haze of a hundred pale church steeples, needled against the packed Tudors. All the bells are ringing.

Julian waits for Mary to hurry him along, but she says nothing. He has no words, and she has none either. Silently they sit side-by-side, reins in his hands, bedazzled by the sun, gazing at the city before them, their horse grazing.

"Did you know," Julian says to her softly, "that long ago St. Giles had the freshest air in the city?" He is using the wrong tense, but he doesn't care.

"Oh, no, is this the church of St. Giles in the Fields?" Mary exclaims, returning to her old self. "Lord Falk lives around here. Take me from this revolting place at once. Why did you come this way? What if he or one of his men sees us? You could've ruined everything. If I get chosen by Lord Burbage, you need to promise me you'll take me the normal way from now on."

Julian snaps the reins and the horse lurches forward. "Yes, Lady Mary," he says. "From now on, I'll take you the normal way."

She blushes before recovering. They clop downhill on Drury Lane. "Did you know that St. Giles is the patron saint of lepers?" Mary says.

Julian does know that. "Lepers and cripples."

"There's a leper colony back there, by St. Giles." Her voice rises and falls on the word *leper*. "Mother says I shouldn't be afraid of them. How does one become a leper, I wonder?"

"Well, first, one has to say: when I grow up, I want to be a leper."

"What?"

"I'm joking," Julian says. "Lack of hygiene is how. You are right to be wary. Leprosy is incurable, unfortunately."

"No, it's not," Mary says, frowning. "What are you talking about? You're cured through Christ."

"Well, I don't know if Jesus is wandering around Holbourne," Julian says, "looking to heal the lepers."

"Yes," Mary says, "they didn't think Jesus was wandering around Palestine either. I'm surprised at you, Julian. Baffled, really."

"Why?" Julian smiles. "Do you find my lack of faith disturbing?"

"I suppose I do," Mary says, not understanding the smile and not returning it.

The dogs bark. The church bells ring.

At Temple, they tie up the horse and wagon, and hire a boat to take them across the full-bodied Thames. They ride without incident. Mary lets him help her into the boat by leaning on his proffered arm, and no one beats them with oars because today he is a gentleman and she is a lady.

This late morning, the shining slate-colored Globe is a hive of activity. Vendors hawk sausages and candied apples, while inside the wooden multi-tiered playhouse men stand in the sandy dust under the open sky, waiting their turn to audition. Because they've left their wagon on the north bank, Mary must slip into a nearby alley to change into her hose and tunic and pull off her wig, while Julian keeps watch nearby.

It becomes quickly apparent to him that Mary is far from the only woman pretending to be a man at the Globe. A dozen others mill around the groundling gallery, waiting to audition, soft of body, their skin creamy, their eyelashes long. These "men" wear baggy coats and long tunics to hide their breasts and hips and slender necks. Do they really think a man won't be able to tell? These women do not know men.

Mary gets ready to take the stage, her lips mouthing the Katherina monologue.

"Stop ogling me," she says. "Do you want somebody to hit you with an oar again?"

"You're doing great," Julian says. "But slow down. Why are you speaking so fast?"

"That's how everyone speaks on stage," Mary says. "Have you ever seen a play?"

Julian is skeptical. "When you get up there, act as if you already have the part."

"What?"

"Yes. Don't audition. Rehearse. That's the trick."

"Oh, suddenly you know things."

"I'm a Mr. Know-it-All." He smiles.

"Well, no one likes a know-it-all," Mary returns.

She acquits herself well with her speedily recited memorized monologue. "*The more my wrong, the more his spite appears. Did he marry me to famish me?*" It sounds like *themoremywrongthemorehisspiteappears.*

The unkempt, gray-haired man who, Julian assumes, is Burbage, doesn't blink at the haste with which Mary delivers her lines. He asks her to read something else, maybe from Bianca? Mary doesn't know Bianca's part. Julian encourages her silently from the ground. The producer hands her a folio with her new lines in it, which she reads once to herself and once out loud. She does okay. It's the right line but the wrong reading. "*Believe me, sister, of all the men alive, I never yet beheld that special face, which I could love more than any other.*" She rushes through the words as if she hasn't yet beheld the special face she can love more than any other.

Despite this, Burbage doesn't send Mary away.

She returns to Julian in the archway, where they await the decision in silence. He wishes it weren't so late. He wishes they could stay, see the next performance. And the next. He's at the *Globe*! But it's going to take them hours to get back home. Maybe they can come back. Maybe—

Mary doesn't get the part of Katherina. But shockingly she gets the part of Bianca. When Julian looks around, he realizes that most of the female roles—Katherina, Bianca, the widow wooed by Hortensio and the hostess of the alehouse—have been given to the women posing as men, while the parts of Petruchio, Hortensio, Lucentio and Haberdasher, have gone to men proper. It's as if everyone is aware of the crossdressing farce and is all right with it. The question is, will Lady Collins be all right with it when she discovers what her soon-to-be-married noble daughter is up to?

Burbage invites the auditioners to stay for the two o'clock premiere of *All's Well That Ends Well*. "We think you'll love it," he booms from the stage. "It's never been performed before."

Mary turns her head. Julian catches her staring at him. "Did you hear that?" she says.

"Hear what? We can't stay—unfortunately. Wish we could. Let's go."

"That's not what I mean." Her tone is mischievous. "Master Burbage just announced the play has never been performed before."

"I heard him. Another time, perhaps." He takes her by the elbow. Any opportunity to touch her.

"Yes, of course. And why should we see it, in any case? You said you've already seen it. Why, days ago, you read lines to me from this play. *Join like likes, kiss like native things.* Do you remember?"

Julian hurries her out of the playhouse. "Who knew you paid such close attention to the things I say, Lady Mary?"

"You were reciting the words so slowly," Mary returns, "I couldn't help it."

Nothing is safe!

On the ride home, an exhilarated Mary talks non-stop, but Julian detects an underlying anxiety about the practicalities of her future at the Globe. He tries to nudge her in a different direction.

Two Gentlemen of Verona is being staged at the Fortune, he tells her, "near your house." After Mary finishes scoffing, he continues to hawk caution like a champion. The Fortune is every bit as big and beautiful as the Globe, he says. Okay, not quite, but she doesn't have to know that. He can sell it. "Maybe more so," he says. He's seen it with his own eyes. It has amazing flying machinery that even the Globe doesn't have, a special effect contraption for the winged entrance of angels and apparitions.

"I care not one whit for angels and flying machines," Mary says.

"But you know who might care? Josephine. Josephine and her flying machine." Julian smiles. *"Come Josephine in my flying machine,"* he sings, *"up up, a little bit higher, to where the moon is on fire."*

She is unmoved. "I don't know why that deserves a smile," she says.

Julian persists. Philip Henslow who runs the Fortune is an old friend (a brand-new acquaintance, he means), and the theatre is walking distance from her house. Over her relentless derision, Julian tells her that *Two Gentlemen* is perfect for her, since it's about a girl who dresses as a boy.

It's rated poorly, Mary argues. It's considered by many intelligent people, "outside of Wales," to be one of the bard's worst.

They bicker pleasantly as they ride. It's not terrible, Julian says. Yes, it's immature, but it's a comedy. It's funny. It makes people laugh. The audiences love it. Lance and his dog Crab bring down the house. "Wouldn't you like to make the people howl with laughter, Lady Mary?"

What's the stupid play about, she asks grumblingly.

"It's about two best friends," he tells her, "Ashton and Julian." He smiles. "I mean Valentine and Proteus." Valentine wants to go to Milan and asks Proteus to go with him, but Proteus is in

THE TIGER CATCHER 367

love with Julia and refuses. When he is forced to go anyway, he and Julia swear eternal love to one another. Of course, in Milan Proteus instantly falls in love with another girl. Meanwhile, Julia dresses as a boy named Sebastian and travels to Milan to win back her lover. "You could audition for the role of Julia," he tells Mary. "It would be a wonderful role for you. Even so, you'll need to get your mother to agree. I could maybe help you with that. It won't be easy. But it will be easier than the Globe."

Mary remains outwardly unpersuaded. "You think you're clever," she says. "But I'm cleverer than you. I don't need your help. I'll figure something out. You'll see."

Julian sleeps like the dead and is awake at dawn. First thing he does is check on his growing seedlings. It has rained overnight, and the ground is sopping wet. Because of his efforts, she will have beautiful flowers for her wedding.

He spends the afternoon mixing clarified suet with potash and dipping thick braided twines into it. He dips, lets it dry, dips, lets it dry. It's painstaking work and it takes up his entire afternoon. He is hidden away in the buttery, busy with this monotonous task. But without his labors, come end of June, there won't be enough light for the betrothal of his beloved to another man. Black humor. His right side aches from the repetitive movement of his right arm moving the hardening and enlarging candle up and down into the tallow, up and down, up and down.

He looks up from his throbbing reverie—and Aurora stands in the doorway, wringing her hands. She exhorts him to continue as she approaches. "I know you have much to do, Master Julian," she says, "but I need your help with a delicate matter. I hope you don't mind the personal nature of my request."

Welcoming the opportunity to rest his limb, he wipes the warm wax off his hands, and they step outside for a stroll in the gardens where Krea can't hear them.

Aurora begins by returning to the story of Mary and Massimo. Julian tells Aurora not to fret, that it wasn't Massimo Mary wanted, it was what he was offering her—which was freedom. Lady Collins looks genuinely perplexed as if she doesn't know what Julian means by the word *freedom*. "But some weeks after the man left, she started to feel very poorly. She took to her bed. We almost lost her, Julian!"

"Please—don't tell me anymore, Aurora," Julian says, slowing down and glancing at the house, wishing for Krea's interruption. He doesn't want to hear it.

"You're right, of course, I shouldn't be telling you this. I'm merely pointing out," Aurora says, "that I don't want to take away another thing she wants. I need her to marry Lord Falk at the end of next month without fuss." She informs Julian that yesterday Mary confessed to a lie. Apparently, she wasn't visiting with her friend Beatrice as she had told her mother. "She says she and Beatrice sneaked off to London together, so Mary could audition at the Globe! She chopped off her hair, Julian! Her glorious beautiful hair! I got the vapors when she showed me. It's hideous, simply hideous. I said to her, what's Lord Falk going to say when he finds out on his wedding night that his bride looks like a little boy?"

"And what did Mary say?"

"Well, she is an impertinent trouble-maker is what she is. She asked if I was certain Lord Falk didn't prefer little boys." Despite herself, the mother chuckles. "Sometimes she can be so wicked. But her haircut is not funny in the slightest. Nor is being accepted into the Globe troupe. I told her what she was proposing was impossible. She replied that not being in the actors' company was the impossible part." The mother blows her nose. "She told me to come talk to you. She said you've helped me with many things since you've been here, and maybe you can offer some advice. Or even a solution. She is right. You are very wise, Master Julian."

"Yes, I'm like a little Yoda."

"Like a what?"

"Never mind."

"I'm going to wring Beatrice's neck next time I see her. She has absolutely no common sense—like all old maids."

Julian nods with fake understanding.

"Tell me what to do," Aurora says. "Something that doesn't involve her being on the stage."

"I don't know what that might be," he replies. The stage is her life.

"Well, she can't go to London, that lepers' colony! It's all plague and fire down there. The city spits out black skeletons. Is there anything else she can do? Think! Anything at all?"

Julian suppresses an incredulous whistle. Wow. Mary *is* good.

"As a matter of fact," he says, after a judicious throat-clearing, "did you know that the Fortune is auditioning for new members to join the Admiral's Men to be in a production of *Two Gentlemen of Verona*? There is a role in it that's perfect for Lady Mary. Philip Henslow is casting it now, to premiere in June. I know Mary is supposed to be getting married at the end of June—"

"Not supposed to be. Is."

"Yes, well. I assume Lord Falk cannot know of this?"

"He can never know!"

"Then tell her that's the condition of your approval. She can join the troupe but must leave the production before her wedding day. And," Julian adds, "if you like, I can drive her to the Fortune. I can wait for her, watch over her. The flowers are growing nicely, I can do my gardening and chandlery work in the morning, and go to Smythe Field to pick up the things we need while she rehearses. There's a butcher's near there and an adequate apothecary. And, I happen to know Sir Philip. I could put in a good word for your daughter. Last week, I rid him of a rather unsightly facial wart by a light application of the usnea lichen shrub boiled in a tincture. He is ever so obliged to me."

Aurora embraces Julian, her eyes watering. "Oh, Julian! It's a *wonderful* plan. You're simply a Godsend. I'll go and speak to Lady Mary at once. I hope she'll approve."

"Yes," Julian says with a straight face, "her approval is key." That Mary!

Aurora rushes inside the house, past a motionless Krea, watching Julian like a fearful owl. Krea doesn't know what the two of them have been plotting, but she knows they've been plotting something. "Poor lady," Krea says. "In childbirth, all grief begins. Lady's daughter has learned that lesson well. A shame Lady herself has not."

"Lady's daughter has not learned that lesson well, what are you talking about," Julian says, his smile fading. "And Lady Aurora doesn't see it your way, Krea."

"Oh, but Lady will," Krea says. "She will."

45

Sebastian

THAT NIGHT JULIAN WAKES FROM A DREAM SO VIVID IT MAKES his loins ache. He dreams Mary's bare flesh is in his hands, and she is on top of him. Jerking awake, he opens his eyes, but it's black outside, and there's no moon. It's like being in the cave. There's a breeze from the flapping window. Did he leave it open?

There's a weight on top of him. A soft hand touches his face. He exhales.

Shh, Mary whispers. Often Krea sleeps in the kitchen.

Not a dream then? Julian tries to reach up to touch her face, but he can't move. Her knees are pinning his arms to the bed.

Your beard is growing in, finally. Why was your face shaved when you first came to us? Don't they know in your Wales that the longer the beard, the more virile the man? She caresses his face from forehead to jaw.

Mary?

Are you expecting someone else? Krea, maybe?

He tries to move his arms. What are you doing?

You don't know?

Her hands rub his chest under his shirt, play with the quartz stone. Her soft lips graze his mouth, his bearded cheek, his closed eyes. The scratchy covers have been pulled off. Now he's covered with crinoline and silk chemises. He yanks his hands free and reaches up to touch her—and groans. She is bare from the waist up. Shh, she says, fussing with his nightshirt. Her head lowers to his head. Her lips kiss his lips. How is he supposed to stay quiet? Let me take off my shirt, he whispers, tearing it off. He circles his arms around her back, presses her breasts into his bare chest, loses his breath, emits a sound somewhere between agony and ecstasy. Are you a mirage, he whispers, or are you my lost and true girl?

Shh, Mary whispers back.

You too, he whispers, cupping her full breasts. It's the first time he has touched a woman since she died.

My love, I found you again.

Thank you for helping me with my mother, she says. You gave me what I want and made it seem like it was all Mother's idea. She now *insists* I audition at the Fortune, she's practically ordering me to! A day ago, she thought death was preferable to me being on the stage and now it's the only thing I must do. You did that, Julian. I don't know how. She rubs her breasts, her hardening nipples back and forth against his chest.

Mary, he haltingly whispers.

Don't say my name.

Mary.

What, you don't want this?

His silence is her answer.

I don't hear you, Julian.

Mary. His voice breaks.

They kiss a long time, her arms under his neck, his arms around her. He fumbles with her starched petticoat, with her chemise, he is trying to find her naked hips. Their breath grows short, their two bodies frantic.

What are you doing.

What does it feel like?

Stirring up a cauldron of trouble is what it feels like.

Then that's what I'm doing.

She is deliverance, soft and warm. Maybe in her riding discourse with him she is all sharp edges, rocking on a hard bench on top of the world in public, but here in the dark, she is hot flesh in his hands. Her contours may be different from the girl he had known, the clavicles and the hair shorter, the hips and thighs rounder, the breasts heavier, but her full lips kiss him the same, if slightly more wildly, and she moans the same, if somewhat more mildly, and now it is he who's begging her to be quieter. She swings her breasts against his face, smothering him. They dry mill against each other, their bodies in rhythmic motion, but Julian knows how this ends—the milling won't remain dry for long.

The other day I watched you wash in the river, Mary says. Did you see me hiding?

No. He can barely hear her. I think it's supposed to work the other way, he says. I'm supposed to watch *you* washing naked in the river.

I'm a lady, not a vagrant, she says. I take hot baths, I don't wash naked in cold rivers.

Aha. His eyes closed, he imagines seeing what's in his hands. I touch, therefore I am. I feel, therefore I am. I love, therefore I am.

You were so slim, so handsome. Your shoulders looked strong, your arms. *Everything* on you looked so strong.

His breath is shallow, his hands more ardent. Her body squirms on top of him as he grinds against her, her breasts in his hands, her nipples in his mouth. Like most men, Julian is a visual creature, and he likes to see his women, and especially he would like to see this woman, *the* woman, but tonight, the blackout is a fourth dimension. He sees her fully, flying and audacious. He has forgotten about the cave and the dark omens. He has washed in the River of Wells and has been healed by its waters. In her honor he has grown his hair long, worn rags on his body and red satin jackets, his grief and loneliness have been washed away, and she has pierced through it all, a fireball in his pale night.

It's not true that love returns strongest only to the broken.

Though maybe it is.

I didn't think I would ever hold you again, Julian whispers, his voice cracking, barely stopping himself from saying *Josephine.*

He doesn't trust himself. If he holds her any closer he might suffocate her. Yet, it's not close enough. Julian needs to be inside the space where there is no inside and no outside. But it's not where Mary is yet. How could she be? She is drawn to him only for this moment while he is coupled to her for four hundred years of empty beds. Once again, they are not in balance.

How far are you taking me, Mary? he whispers. Because I don't have far to go.

I wish I could take you all the way, Julian, where you want to be, and where I want to be, but I can't, Mary says. We can't get that far, I'm sorry.

Is it the wrong time of the month? I don't care about that.

She pulls away from him in the pitch-black night.

Why would you say that? Her body stiffens.

Julian pulls her back to him, skin on skin, breath on breath. I don't care about anything.

Yes, you're like all men. But *I* care about things, Mary says. We can't do the thing you want because bad things can happen, and I can't have them happen to me. She breathes out, a wingless damaged thing. I can't have them happen to me *again*.

Even in his ardor Julian is knocked down by her words.

He holds her head in his hands. I will be careful. I promise.

That is what all men say.

His shiny desire dampens.

All men have said this to you, Mary?

Furious rustling is his response. The weight of her open corsets and billowing skirts slides off his body. He is light again, and heavier than ever. The latticed casement creaks and swings. Wait, he pleads, but in the black night it's all gone, the dream, the girl, the noise, the breath, the lust, the comfort.

Only love remains.

The next morning, with Aurora's hearty approval, Julian gets Cedric to harness the carriage instead of the wagon and takes Mary to the Fortune. It's just over a mile from the house, but Mary refuses to walk because she is not a commoner. This, after riding with produce in the back of his wagon like a peach or a plum. She is curt with him, won't look at him. They leave early, before Edna can fire off her shrill questions. The only ones up are Cedric, who never says anything, Dunham, who is too busy carrying buckets of filth to care, and silent Krea, who watches them leave.

Julian sits on the driver's bench without Mary, the reins in his hands. Mary is in the carriage, a cloak over her man's clothes, a wig on her head. They've stopped being equals. He's now her driver.

"*Mary*," Julian says when they're near Fynnesbyrie Field.

"I don't want to talk to you."

"After last night, you don't want to talk to me?"

"After what you said last night, yes. Quiet. Mind the road. I'm trying to learn my lines." She pulls the folio in front of her face, as the carriage bounces over the potholes. "*Poor forlorn Proteus, poor passionate Proteus*," she recites.

She auditions for the Admiral's Men as Julia. The long-haired wig serves her well. She pulls the wig off when the time comes to read for the boyish Sebastian. The short hair serves her even better. She gets the part before they leave the theatre. Henslow himself announces her admission into the troupe as he shakes Julian's hand. The rehearsals will last two weeks. She'll have almost four weeks with the play before her wedding, just as she'd had with *Paradise in the Park*. Except this time it's the wrong wedding.

On the way home when Julian tries to talk to her, she shuts him down. But in the black of night, she comes to him again. "You upset me so much with your words," Mary says, after climbing through the window and on top of him.

"I'm sorry." He wraps his arms around her. "What you said upset me."

"I don't know why it should. I don't know why it would. Was I faithless to you? Were you my betrothed?".

"Yes," Julian whispers. "I *am* your betrothed. Do you feel how I hold you? Like you are mine. Like I am yours."

"Why do you want to touch me at all if you think I'm such a soiled creature?"

"I don't think you're soiled, Mary." He pulls her loose flowing gown to her stomach. "I wish I could see you," he says, her body in his gripping hands. "You feel so beautiful."

"You've seen me during the day," Mary says. "I am beautiful."

He kisses her throat, breathes into the space between her breasts as if to animate her. He sits up in his hard bed, pillows propped against the wall, and she straddles him, wriggling in his lap. Julian wants to lay her down, wants to be on top of her. He is breathless and rapacious. What a heady cocktail she is in his monastic bed off the buttery by the kitchen. She has awakened his body. She has his soul. She holds it in her careless hands, the hands that wave mistreatment on Henslow's stage as her lips ask, *how do I prevent the loose encounters of lascivious men?*

Do you want me to touch you? Julian whispers.

You *are* touching me. You've been caressing me top to bottom since I've come through your window.

Yes. I mean...do you want me to touch you to make you fly?

I don't know. Are you saying what you mean? Or is it like always with you, a play on words?

I'm saying what I mean.

How can you make me fly?

Lie down, let me show you.

Yes, but...I don't want you to do that thing, the earthly thing...

That earthly thing is the most sublime flight of all, but okay. Climb down from me and lie on my bed. Lie flat on the bed and open your legs.

She winces and retreats.

I won't do anything you don't want me to do, Julian says with regret. But lie down. I'll do other things. We'll have *happiness without consequences*. It hurts even to say it. Because he doesn't believe it. He is a fraud to her, even now. For he knows too well what follows happiness without consequences.

Consequences.

All you want is more.

She lies down in his tiny bed. He lies on his side next to her, kisses her, and with his eager fingers brings her happiness in the black night, without seeing her, yet seeing only her, his eyes wide open, his heart wide open, he brings her happiness again and again, responding to her arching body, to her clutching hands, flying drunk himself on the wings of her stunned expressive moaning.

What you have is a magic carpet.

You just have to learn how to fly it.

Oh, he's learned.

And the next night.

And the next.

And then, finally, without him having to ask, she says, Julian…do you want me to touch *you*?

God, yes.

He lies on the bed, and she wedges in between him and the wall. Her soft hand clutches him. A gasp of happiness escapes her throat, and then his throat. I like how it feels. *Yes, Mary, me, too.* It's so smooth, so hard. I'm sorry I can't give you the other thing.

Don't be sorry while I'm actually in your hands. But make me last, Mary. I don't want it to be over. Go slower, softer, steadier. Yes, like that.

She brings him lasting happiness.

The next morning, Julian takes her to the Fortune, and waits for her for three hours in the dust like a groundling, watching her rehearse. The Fortune is quite a theatre, a noble competitor to the Globe. The crowds come to watch even the rehearsals because the only event in London more popular with the public than the theatre is an execution. "Never show the wires" might be a Hollywood axiom. But here at the playhouse in 1603, the special effects contraptions are in full view for all to see: the flying machinery, that ostentatious *deus ex machina*; the fire and smoke; the pig's blood for passion and revenge in ready buckets by stage exit right; the trap door in the floor as the mouth of hell. And just over the trap door, on center stage, on display for all the masses, his one and only Mary stands, a scant and lavishly costumed soul.

The stage is for all things under the sun, for all humanity, for all life.

And at night she comes to him again, bringing him joy between her slick hands and pushed-together breasts.

They begin to leave the house earlier, they forego the horse and carriage like commoners, they walk to the Fortune and back to prolong their minutes together. Mary tells her mother that Julian is helping her memorize her lines, and they need the length of the walk to rehearse them. Aurora can't thank Julian enough for helping Mary.

In the idylls of Fynnesbyrie Field, away from archer's arrows and boys chasing pigeons, they sit in a leafy corner on the grass and have a picnic of pandemain and ale. He reads lines with her. They argue over her delivery.

She dreams of him that has forgot her love, she recites.

You dote on her that cares not for your love, he recites back.

She counters with, *that man that has a tongue, I say is no man, if with his tongue he cannot win a woman.*

I can win a woman with my tongue, Julian says, if only she would let me.

Julian!

I can win a woman with other things, too, if only she would let me.

Julian!

What light is light, he murmurs, *if Mary be not seen.*

He is fed upon the shadow of her perfection, she murmurs back, their heads pressed together.

It's warm and June and everything blooms. They pick purple orchids from the meadow and take the long way back, between country homes and farms. The bluebells and meadowsweet carpet all their fields.

Rain or shine, the groundlings and the gentry arrive for their daytime entertainment. Sure, the performance is speed-read as if the actors are going to be late for the four o'clock beheading, but Julian was right about *Two Gentlemen.* The laughs Mary gets are worth the occasional rain, and the way she lights up when she takes her exuberant final bows is worth everything.

She climbs into his window every night, and in the darkness they learn to see.

46

Consequences of Happiness

THE BED THEY SHARE IS A MONK'S BED, NARROW AND HARD. Julian is not himself narrow. Neither is Mary. They take up all available space. The horsehair mattress shifts under their bodies.

I don't want it like this anymore, she says, groping for him in the dark, her hands seeking him out, grasping him, freeing him from the shackles of his life, both new and old.

What do you want, Mary.

What do you want?

All I want is you.

It's good that Julian finally has an answer to his most pressing question.

He wants to say to her some other words he carries on the tip of his tongue. You can't marry Lord Falk. You cannot bear his children. But Julian knows he can't make an offer of marriage to Mary until he can support her. She can't ever feel that she's wasting her time on him. He needs to execute a plan, because the days and nights are racing by in bliss and fear.

In response to his fractured silence Mary says, I shall hang myself if Lord Falk ends up being my fate.

Don't say that. Julian turns his head to the wall. Please. Even in jest.

Do I sound to you as if I jest? Why do you keep saying no, Julian? No to me, no to Cornelius. The only one you say yes to is Krea. She asks you for something, and you're always ready to help.

But why is your first word to the rest of us always the cautious n-n-no? Can't you say yes to something for once? Say yes to me, say, yes, Mary, you can't marry another man and have his children.

Yes, Mary, Julian whispers inaudibly. You can't marry another man. You can't bear his children.

When will they trade his stony mattress for her feather bed? Every blessed day they are together draws her dreaded wedding day nearer.

Julian grows consumed with figuring out a way to get them out. He travels to the Thames docks past London Bridge and talks to the seamen. When do the merchant ships come? Where do they go? Can he buy a passage for two? How much does it cost? He saves every shilling Aurora pays him. He needs a few months and then he'll have enough to get them out of London. But he doesn't have a few months. He has weeks. He needs another solution to the crisis they're facing.

They can't talk about it, even lightly, even in hypotheticals. It's too real. They withdraw from the impossible and talk about what they can. They hide behind the gentlemen and ladies of Verona. They hide behind Krea.

"You're quite chummy with Krea," Mary says.

Julian demurs. Not chummy. He owes her. She has taught him well. He has skills because of her. He can get work elsewhere. Soon he will tell Mary of his plan. He and she can hide south of the river until he can make enough money to buy them a sea crossing to far away.

"Krea is a peasant, Julian, remember that," Mary says. "They live by a different code than noblemen or merchants or even yeomen like yourself. When Krea was a child, a pig wandered into the hut they lived in, in the middle of London, no less, and took her baby sister. In my opinion this event has made Krea emulate the pig in her dealings with people. She can be vicious."

"And though she be but little, she is fierce," Julian recites. "I agree, Krea can be a tough old bird, but she's been nothing but helpful to me."

"She's fattening you up," Mary says. "The shambles is just down the road." The shambles is a street in Clerkenwell with the butchers and slaughterhouses.

"So, in your scenario," says Julian, "is she the pig or am I the pig?"

Mary laughs. "Both," she says.

As their time together shortens even as the gloaming June days lengthen, she finally invites Julian to scale the wall trellis to her bed chamber after everyone has gone to sleep. But that night, Krea is in the kitchen so long, cleaning, making bread, and drying out the sprouted grain for the ale mash in the warm oven, that Julian himself falls asleep before he can climb through Mary's window.

In recent weeks, Julian has noticed that Krea has become less friendly with him. He doesn't understand why and doesn't want to. The seeds of suspicion Mary has planted inside him about Krea have taken root. The little maid acts as if she's no longer his friend. She refuses to help him boil the potash, refuses to braid the linen into wick for his candles. She claims she's too busy. She used to help him gladly. No more.

The following evening when Julian sneaks out, he collides with Dunham who is splayed on the ground below Mary's windows, smoking a cigar and drinking mash. When Julian asks the latrine boy why he isn't in bed, Dunham replies that this is where he sleeps. "Why aren't *you* in bed, Master Julian?"

"You sleep outside near the refuse moat?"

"This is where I sleeps," Dunham repeats, puffing away. Julian is forced to return to his room, climb through his own window like a thwarted thief, only to hear Krea in the next room, scrubbing the suet off the stone tile.

Mary can't believe Dunham sleeps outside her open windows. Apparently, no one else can believe it either, because when Mary confronts her mother about it, who confronts Cornelius, everyone acts surprised that Dunham sleeps outdoors. But also—everyone is surprised that Lady Mary would care a whit where Dunham sleeps. Cornelius is surprised the lady knows Dunham's name. Mary and Julian drop it, and Dunham continues to loiter outside her windows.

Notwithstanding their frenetic pettings—two teenage lovers in the backseat of a car fumbling toward ecstasy—they still haven't been *together*, and just when they need each other most and when their time feels like it's running out, they begin to have an increasingly difficult time getting together at all, even in Julian's bed. Krea stays awake into the midnight hours, either in the kitchen or in the chandlery, carrying the suet to and fro.

Her constant wakefulness gets so frustrating that Julian talks to Aurora. To his surprise, Mary's mother defends Krea! Krea is preparing for the wedding, Aurora says, and knows how much ale needs to be made, how many candles need to be hardened, and how much meat needs to be smoked. Julian doesn't know what's happening in the topsy turvy world in which Lady Collins takes the scullion maid's side over his.

He tries talking to Krea directly.

"We used to be friends, Master Julian," the aviary woman says to him, "and now you're tattling on me to Lady because you think I work too hard?" Aurora has told Krea about Julian's request? Wow.

"I didn't tattle on you, Krea," Julian says. "I'm concerned for you. You are working too hard."

"Why do you care how hard I work?"

"Because you're always banging the pots, spilling grease, swearing, cleaning up in the dark. I also work hard, and I can't get to sleep because of you."

"Are you sure it's because of me, Master Julian?"

He squints. Darkly she squints back.

"What do you mean by that?"

"Just askin' a question."

"Yes, I'm sure it's because of you, Krea."

And to Mary in the fields the next day Julian says, "Krea knows about us."

"She's a half-wit, she knows nothing."

"She may be a half-wit. But she's smart enough to know what's right in front of her face."

"Are you saying she's smarter than Mother?"

"Oh, your mother also knows," Julian says. "She just pretends not to." Perhaps that explains Aurora's cooling toward him.

They pass a house on Golding Lane they've passed every day, but today, on the wooden frame above the entrance, a dripping blood-red cross is sloppily drawn and below it on the door the words: *"Lord have mercy upon us."*

Mary rushes past, eyes to the ground.

"What happened there?" Julian glances back.

"Catastrophe." She takes his arm. "Avoid that house like the *plague*." Under the oaks she stops him and pulls him close. "Julian," Mary says, "Dunham will not decide for me how I choose to live in my last free days."

"These are not your last free days." Julian's heart tightens.

"Will the gong farmer choose for *you*? Will Krea choose for you? Come to me tonight. No matter what. After supper, I'm telling Mother I'm taking a bath early to get ready for tomorrow."

"What's tomorrow?"

"Julian, have you not been paying attention?"

"Literally to nothing but you, Mary." And to the termite hill Julian is building lint by lint, penny by penny for their future together. "What's tomorrow?"

"Tomorrow Lord Falk is coming to stay the weekend."

"What? No! Why?"

"It's tradition. The groom comes a fortnight before the wedding to make sure all is well in the house of the woman he is about to take as his wife."

Julian's spirits fall. That's why the entire staff has been like dervishes, the servants polishing the silver and oiling the floors.

"Of course, that's why. Mother's been anxious about it for weeks. How could you not have noticed?"

Oh, he noticed. He just didn't want to see.

"You will finally have the pleasure of meeting him. You can tell me if you think I should marry him."

"I don't need to meet him," Julian says, "to know you should not."

She kisses him. "Tonight, Julian," she says. "I'll be in my bed, waiting. You want me? Come and take me." After saying that, she barely manages to wrest herself away from him, out in the open, in Fynnesbyrie Field, under the linden trees.

Not that anything could keep him from her bed, but that night he is in luck because Krea either exhausts herself or has an inordinate amount of fermented mash; either way, she vanishes. She usually sleeps in the far corner of the kitchen, but Julian can't see her anywhere. Instead of going outside where the rancid Dunham is lounging in the mud under the trellis, Julian tip-toes through the nighttime manor in stealth, takes the servants' stairs to the second floor, creeps down the darkened corridor and feels his way to Mary's bedchamber. Hers is the seventh door on the right.

He comes in without knocking. She is lying on her four-poster bed. There is no light, not even a candle. Only the moon outside, almost full, shines a silver beam to illumine the room, the decanter full of wine, Mary under the canopy, wig off, naked in the white sheets, the soft quilt thrown to the side.

Here, finally, is the consequence of happiness.

The consummation.

Are you going to take off your necklace?

No, it never comes off.

Why did you bring the beret with you? Do you want me to wear it?

Yes—and nothing else.

But when she puts it on, the red beret looks black, like blood in darkness. Unsmiling she falls back on the bed when she sees the bottomless expression in his eyes. Julian takes the beret off her before he can touch her.

He traces the outline of her body with his fingers. He proves to himself she is real and alive through his five senses. He can touch her: his passionate palms caress her, her curved back, her round hips, her ample thighs. He can hear her: they're panting, her moaning body stretching over his. He can feel her: her elbows as they squeeze his head in a vise, the weight of her body as she moves up and down on him, slides back and forth as if she's rowing across the river. He can smell her: rosewater and lavender, meadowsweet and clover. He can taste her: his lips kiss the salt on her neck, on her breasts, in the center of her heart, at the softness of her belly. The guardian angel shows him living water in the delta of life.

He has much to offer, much to bestow. His love is soft and diamond hard. He is open mouthed at her response to him. He fears the precipitous end.

But the end doesn't come. Not even now when relief and lust and love is crystal cut across his body. He turns her onto her back. He holds her wrists above her head. She is wrapped around him, as he lowers his weight on her, presents himself to her like a gift of gold and myrrh. Belatedly he realizes that myrrh is a wrong word, a bad word. Myrrh is what they give to Jesus to prepare Him for His burial. To remember that, at this most alive of moments, upsets Julian, upsets him just enough to stop him from finishing. To regroup, he slows to kiss her, to give her a chance to catch her breath.

Come night, come, come day in night.

"Julian," Mary whispers, "who are you? Where did you come from?"

"Why do you ask?"

"I'm dreading the day you'll return to that place and I'll be left here dreary and alone without you."

"I won't leave you," he says. "I will never leave you." He struggles with himself—to ask or not to ask? "Did Massimo leave you? Did he break your heart?"

"A little bit." She shrugs. "He acted as if he wanted me, but he only wanted the part he could see. Nothing else. I was more angry than anything." Mary's arms bind around Julian. "But I tasted the thrill of the stage because of him," she says. "And then just like that—it was all over. Him, the stage, everything. And worse, he left something unwanted behind with me." She emits a cracked moan of anguish. "I won't deny, I was devastated. I boiled up some plants, I prayed. Then the blood came. It was such a relief. I was *so* grateful that it wasn't to be. I couldn't even feel guilty for being grateful. It was as if the good Lord had answered my prayers. Mother said that the Lord didn't answer those kinds of prayers, to do away with the life growing inside you, but who does then? I had prayed so fervently. And someone most assuredly answered." She pauses through Julian's silence. "Do you know how many women die in childbirth? I didn't want it to be me. I wanted to live, live! I wanted to dress in finery, stand above the world on a stage with my arms outstretched, take another bow, and another. I didn't want to be a mother."

Julian's head is buried in her neck. It's painful for him to hear.

"I want nothing less," she says. "I'd rather be stoned three times than suffer childbirth once. But enough about it. What's gone is gone." She opens her arms. "Come here."

Julian loves her until she can't take it anymore. Julian, she whispers. I'm going to fall into ruin. I'm going to cry and moan and scream and everyone will hear me, everyone, not just Dunham, but even the Camberwells the next manor over.

He holds her shivering body to his.

You have swallowed me, you have slayed me.

Who says this, Julian? Mary?

They quench their thirst by the light of the watery moon. They haven't slept. Soon it will be time for him to go. But that's in the future. In the present Mary speaks. "Why did you come to me? Am I your plaything? From the first moment you saw me, you were locked into me, why? I'm such a fool! I thought I could control you, manipulate you. But you can't control what you don't understand. Did you always know that if I gave you half a chance you'd have this power over me?"

"Mary," he whispers, "you are the brightest of all the stars in my sky."

"Why, Julian, why?"

He caresses her. "If I ever say words to you that sound less than words of love," he says, "it's because I want real life to live up to my dream of your perfection. That's all I ever wanted. Do you understand? Promise me you'll forgive me. Forgive me if I ever say loud cruel things I do not mean."

"Like what?"

"Words of anger or even hate," Julian says. "Sometimes words can set things in motion in the human soul that cannot be undone."

"You want me to forgive you for what you haven't done?"

"Who knows what might happen," he says. "The future is unknowable. Please promise me you'll remember this night if we should ever come to combat and forgive me."

"Likewise, will you forgive *me*?" Mary cries. "I *have* to marry Lord Falk, Julian. Oh! Despite all my bravado, it's true. That's just me railing in fury against the injustice of my fate. That's just me struggling in vain to take charge of my one brief life. But Mother is right. I do know what's at stake. I loved my father. And I love my mother. There's nothing I can do."

"There's plenty you can do," Julian says. "You said you would never marry him."

"And yet I must."

"No. You mustn't. There's another way." He holds her face in his palms. "Come with me." His thumbs wipe away her tears. "Come away with me."

"Come away with you where?"

"Away from here. Where we can hide and live. Somewhere you and I can have a life."

"Is there such a place in all the world?" Mary says, closing her eyes.

"There is," Julian says. "Mary! We'll hide across the river. I need to earn a few more shillings, and then we'll sail down the Thames to the English Channel and around France and Spain. We'll sail to Italy, beyond the Alps, where it's warm and the sea is green. We'll get married, and we'll sell wine or grow grapes, and we'll find a new stage for you to ply your trade."

She puts her fingers to his lips. "Stop speaking."

He kisses her hand as if she is a princess.

"I can't dishonor my family, Julian."

"It's not a dishonor to marry me."

"I'm noble-born."

"What does that even mean?"

She pulls her hand away. "Don't demean it. Just because you don't understand it. I don't understand what it means to work like you do, to scrape by for a living, not to have your own home, to be a migrant, a wanderer. Not to own a horse, not to know how to ride a horse. I don't understand it, but I don't demean it."

They sit up in her four-poster bed. Some conversations are too difficult to have lying naked face to face.

"Look," Julian says, "if I could change myself into a duke or a prince for you, don't you think I'd do it? I'd do it instantly." I changed myself into a gardening chandler for you. "But I can't move up."

"Right. Only I can move down."

"Being with me is not moving down." Julian frowns at her words. He needs to persuade her, not sound desperate.

"Whatever you call it, it's not staying where I am," she says, "and it's not moving up." Mary shakes her head. "We have sumptuary laws in this country. Do the Welsh know what those are? It's when you can't wear certain fabrics like silk or fur if you're not landed nobility. If I gave up my name, I'd have to wear rough wool—and cotton, heaven forfend! I couldn't be seen with veils of lace on Sunday."

"Italy is the heart of the Renaissance," Julian says. "In Italy, no one will give a toss about your titles and your lace."

"You want us to milk goats together?"

"If need be. Or play the piano."

"Play the *what*?"

He sighs.

Mary watches him—an unconvinced and unimpressed lady—twist himself into new thoughts and words. She's not buying what he is selling. "You prefer marriage to Lord Falk to being my wife?"

"I didn't say I prefer it. I have to think about it."

"You're running out of time for thinking. The wedding is in two weeks."

"Don't you think I know that, better than you?"

She's just trying to buy some time until he is out of her bed. He watches her parched mouth, her sweet face, her half-closed eyes. If only he could confess to her what she needs to sacrifice to buy some time. Everything.

"This is so easy for you," Mary says, her voice rising, "you don't have to give up *anything* to be with me!" She's misread his thoughts, heard day instead of night.

Julian folds his hands. He takes deep breaths, to count through fifty-nine seconds of impossible infinities. "I know it's hard for you to believe, Mary," Julian says, "because on the surface it looks as if I have nothing, but the reason I have nothing"—he gathers himself together to keep his voice from rising or breaking—"is because I gave it all up to find you."

"What do you mean, *find* me?"

"To be with you. I gave up my family, my home, my work, my friends, my things, my future. My own future. I gave up my life to be with you."

Mary crawls to him on the bed and wraps herself around him. I'm sorry, my love. Let's not decide impossible things right now. I need my Julian back, his light and wild caress. Let's not squander our priceless seconds with idle words and empty tears.

They're not idle and they're not empty, Julian says.

There's so much sadness in the sweet sticky air when he makes love to her again.

Am I the face that launched a thousand ships, she moans.

No, he says. You are the face that launched just one.

They intertwine their lips and limbs. Their skin burns with the friction of their bodies. All that I have is my soul. Will you ever give it back to me, Mary, Julian whispers. Will I ever have it back from you?

He closes his eyes, and the next thing he knows, Mary's shaking him awake. "Have you gone mad? The sun's coming up. You can't sleep here! Leave before we both lose our heads."

Naked, he presses himself against her one last time, kisses the softness between her breasts.

It's almost dawn; the house is stirring. Hugging the wall, Julian runs down the back stairs and outside. He heads for the healing river—to clear his head and to wash his body in the damp chilly morning.

As he's crossing the lawn to return to his room, he sees a tall, odd figure making his way down the narrow lane to Collins House.

It's too early for visitors, yet there he is. The man is not in a carriage or on a horse. He's on foot, and his body is covered from head to toe by dark robes and tall boots. He wears a tightly wound scarf and leather gloves. Julian can't see his face because the man's head is hidden behind a black hood and a ghoulish black mask with a long white beak. He's an upright walking bird. He is terrifying. An anxious tick lodges in Julian's chest. He drags a barely awake Cedric out of the stables. "Cedric, who is that?"

"A doctor," Cedric replies, rubbing his eyes.

"Why that awful mask?"

"To keep death away," Cedric says. "The mask is filled with bergamot oil. The doctor douses himself with vinegar, and he chews the angelica weed before entering a home. Someone inside must be contagious."

That can't be, Julian thinks, hurrying to the manor. At supper last night, everyone looked fine. He can't speak for anyone else in the night, but he knows he and Mary were burning alive in flames. The masked man fills Julian with a sickly foreboding.

Lo and behold, it's a mistake. When the doors are thrown open and Lady Collins with Cornelius run through the house, yelling for an explanation, it turns out the doctor had walked down the wrong lane. It's not a surprise. The lanes are barely marked. It must be the poor Camberwells, a field and a hedge over yonder.

The doctor leaves, but the house remains in turmoil. It's not only Julian who sees a bad omen in the doctor's visit. Lady Collins, superstitious to the last, orders all the bedding stripped and boiled. She commands Catrain and Krea to wipe down Mary's bedchamber with vinegar and hot water, to wash Mary's hair again with lye, and to scrub her body with soap.

"Out there," Lady Collins says, as overwrought as Julian has ever seen her, "there is a slew of pestilence!" She has gathered the entire household into the great hall. "Out there is nothing but a festering carbuncle of grief and death. We must protect what we have remaining in this house with every thread of our being. I don't have a husband, I've lost five of my six children, my one remaining child has lost her father. We hardly have any servants left. At any time, the reaper can snuff out our existence. When we saw that man, none of us was surprised. We said, who's next? Yes, it was an error on his part, but nothing is a coincidence. It's a terrible sign. Master Julian, I don't want you to go to London anymore until after Mary's wedding. If there's something we need, get it at Smythe Field. London is a sickbed. The kites that fly overhead, feeding on dead flesh and refuse are healthier than the masses that walk London streets." Kites are buzzards, carrion eaters. Lady Collins lowers her voice to a distraught hiss. "We have forgotten we're in the middle of an epidemic. The errant doctor reminded us of this. Nothing will be better until winter. We must prepare for the worst." Aurora twitches with anxiety.

"The newly released inmates, full of disease, roam the roads and ask for quarter at any house that will take them. We must turn them away. The foul air taints us all."

"The air is not foul, Lady Mother," Mary says, carelessly. "It's alive with life! The roses in Julian's garden are not for our graves, they're for a wedding." She gleams at him from across the hall.

Julian inclines his head but doesn't dare speak. He's not the actor she is.

Aurora stares in grim silence at Julian and at her daughter. "Enough out of you," she says to Mary in a lowered voice. "You heard what I said. Watch yourself. Go get ready. Your bridegroom is coming."

Lord Falk is a hideous human being. He arrives later that afternoon in a four-horse-drawn carriage, followed by an entourage of riders. Most noblemen ride their own horses. Not him. He brings with him a butler, a steward, his own cook (immediately casting Farfelee aside), and a wagon full of meat and wine. He orders Cedric to clean his horses' hooves, supervised by his own men, of course. He commands Cornelius to show his men to their rooms and to fetch him the cleanest water from the deepest well, supervised by his own men, of course. He brings a gift of fine Italian silver cutlery for the mother of his bride, and then drones on ceaselessly about how expensive it was.

He is overdressed, overloud, overbearing. He wears a maroon velvet tunic tied with a gold-studded thick and showy leather belt. Fur drapes over his shoulders, even though it's June. He kisses Aurora's hand as if he is doing *her* a favor. He barely acknowledges Edna, and doesn't glance at Julian. To his credit, he becomes slightly less pompous when Mary descends the stairs, for she is a vision in an abundant champagne-colored lace dress. She wears pink silk gloves and a gold bonnet. Her ringlet curls are decorated with flowers and pearls. She is rosy and healthy, her skin flushed, her dark eyes shining, her lips red and full, the swell of her breasts prominent in the tight embroidered bodice.

Even Lord Falk is momentarily thrown off the pedestal of his own making at the sight of her. Having finally found the occasion to don Gregory's flamboyant pink and scarlet coat, Julian stands in the back of the hall with the rest of the servants and watches Lord Falk slobber over Mary's silk-gloved hand. This isn't the moaning nude girl with the pixie-cut hair whose body Julian had so thoroughly loved the night before. She has transformed herself into a genteel princess who is forced to sit next to a man in fur and velvet, forced to listen to him list the joys of watching a bear be chained to a post and ripped apart by dogs. "Bear-baiting is far more entertaining than those silly plays Lady Mary once dragged me to. Isn't that right, my dear?"

If there's any justice in the world, Black Death will infect him. Falk manages to be both pompous and stupid. He may be well-born, but he is actually ill-bred. He is pretentious and fraudulent. Julian doesn't know if the man is trying too hard, or if he's always like this. Julian is pleased to see that Falk's relative attractiveness falls on blind eyes. Mary clearly can't stand him. Falk is oblivious to her real feelings, as he's oblivious to much.

In many ways, he reminds Julian of Nigel. When Aurora counsels hiring wise women for simple illnesses because wise women are less expensive than doctors, Lord Falk says, "And more rare," and guffaws at his own joke.

Falk laments the absence of soft linen rags when he needs to use the jakes and continues to showcase his fascination with all matters egesta by telling a tedious story about a man named John Harrington who, a few years earlier, in 1596, invented a flushing lavatory that drew water from a cistern and funneled it into an underground chamber. Though Queen Elizabeth had superficially liked the toy, Harrington has since gone broke because his ridiculous idea didn't catch on. "And why would it?" Falk says. "A flushing toilet! What nonsense. What could possibly be better than a hole in the ground, isn't that right, my darling?"

Julian keeps his mouth shut. He prefers not to discuss such things in front of ladies, though in this world everyone—nobles and commoners, men and women—talk about all manner of subjects considered off-limits in Julian's day.

It's Lady Collins who casts aside her recent unease with Julian and invites him to destroy Lord Falk, if only with words. "Master Julian," Aurora says, motioning him to sit by her side, "what is your opinion on this delicate subject? Lord Falk, you've met our Julian? He's a very good friend of the family, my lord. He's a yeoman from Wales, who happens to be an expert on many matters."

"Though not an expert on many others," says Edna.

"Like horses and candles," says Cornelius.

Lord Falk scrutinizes Julian. "When a stranger rises too quickly through the ranks of an unfamiliar house," Falk says, "it often means that he's misplaced in his origins. That's Aristotle's opinion, not mine." He sneers. "Well, let's hear it, *expert*. What say you about the pit latrine?"

"I have just one question, my lord," says Julian. "The waste inside the hole in the ground, where does it go?"

"Who cares? It's in the ground!"

"But the ground is porous."

"Who says?"

"We do," Julian says. "By our actions. When we plant and water and fertilize and farm, we say it."

"I do none of those things," Falk says. "Get to your point, yeoman."

"I don't have a point," Julian says. "I have a question. I'll repeat. Where does the waste from the pit latrine go?"

"This matters why?"

"Because it pollutes your groundwater," Julian replies. "It contaminates the wells from which you draw the water with which you wash your face and hands, and with which you cook your food. Because the waste spreads fatal disease. That's why."

"Nonsense. What disease?"

"Diphtheria, dysentery, tape worms, typhoid fever, hepatitis, and cholera," Julian replies calmly.

There's a chilly silence in the great hall. The wood on the fire crackles.

"Why do you argue with me, yeoman?" Lord Falk booms, scanning the embarrassed faces of the gathered.

"Because I think you are wrong, my lord."

"It's irrelevant in any case," Lord Falk says. "There's no defense against the illnesses you mentioned."

"Harrington's flushable lavatory with a cistern is one such defense, my lord." Julian speaks the words *my lord* with disdain.

"You naïve Welshman," says Lord Falk. "No one cares about those trifling diseases. The plague is all that matters, and the cistern is not a defense against it. No one knows what causes it. Could be anything. Foul air. Cats and dogs. Unwashed lepers. Welshmen wandering about."

"Bites from fleas that live on infected rats," says Julian.

Lord Falk hoots. "Well, *that's* absurd! Fleas don't bite human beings. And rats don't get infected." Frowning, he sits up in the oak chair, the most honorary chair in the hall, the chair where the great Lord Collins himself had sat when he would come home and remove his armor after fighting in the name of the Crown.

"The rats die first," Julian says, wishing he were a nobleman and owned a sword and knew how to fence. Lord Falk is insufferable. "That's how you know the plague is coming. The rats die first."

Lord Falk spits. "Where did you hear such tripe?"

"Probably in Wales," Edna pipes in, and Cornelius heartily agrees.

Lord Falk and Edna and Cornelius laugh. "Of course! Listen, boy," Falk says, "why don't you stop talking and run along. Tell

Krea to bring me some wine from the cellar. Unless you'd like to fetch it yourself. My dearest Mary, I'm ever so sorry you had to hear such drivel. I hope you weren't offended."

"Not in the slightest, my lord," Mary says, her eyes glistening. "Master Julian may be correct about the plague. He's told us that the bubo that swells and bleeds under the skin is the last symptom—not the first—as we had all thought. By the time you spot the buboes on your body, it's already too late."

"I hear you well, my lady!" Lord Falk exclaims. "I will examine your body for buboes beneath the skin." He grins and clucks his tongue. "Very soon I will examine your body thoroughly for all sorts of things, including your virtue." He horselaughs, motioning to Julian to scurry. "Shoo, bubo expert— go fetch me my wine."

In the kitchen, Krea doesn't reply to Julian as he passes along Falk's request, doesn't even raise her eyes to him. "Are you all right, Krea?"

"I'm very well, Master Julian," she replies into her shoes. "But I have no time to banter with you. The lord needs his wine."

Unsurprisingly, Julian doesn't get invited to dine with the family. He has some household loaf and old fermented ale with Farfelee. Side by side, they eat silently, discarded and glum. Krea is nowhere to be found. The tiny woman has been underfoot for weeks, but now that Julian wants to talk to somebody, she's MIA. Only the fire is on. Collins House is saving all its candles for the upcoming wedding feast.

It gets dark later and later these June nights. Tonight is the summer solstice. It's still light out after supper when Mary enters the chandlery. "We would like to read some poetry," she says to Julian, lifting her skirts off the greasy floor. "Mother is asking for four tapered candles."

Without saying a word, he hands her a stack. Mary's gloved fingers graze his hand as she takes the candles from him. She nudges him to turn his gaze to her.

"Do you now see?" she whispers, looking up into his face.

"I saw it all before."

Behind Mary, Krea reappears in the kitchen. Julian watches as the maid crouches and begins to scrub the threshold in the doorway.

"Can you give us a minute, Krea," Mary says, without glancing back.

"The entry is filthy, m'lady."

"It's not going anywhere. But you go somewhere else."

Krea doesn't move. Mary turns and steps toward the maid. "Leave, Krea. Go scrub the stove for Farfelee, go fetch more wine for Lord Falk."

"But the sill's filthy now, m'lady."

"Leave, Krea!" Mary looms over the insubordinate maid who is still on her hands and knees. Krea creeps away in reverse, not raising her gaze from the floor.

Mary comes back to Julian. "What did I tell you? Her contempt for me is a bottomless cup."

Julian stands quietly, taking her in. His eyes shine with his love for her. Her mother is wrong to sacrifice her last remaining child at the altar of the unholy.

"The proposal you made me last night, did you mean it?" Mary asks in a trembling voice.

His heart leaps.

"You know I did."

"I will go with you." She speaks in muted tones. He strains to hear her even though she stands at his chest. Their hands intertwine over the candles. "You said the mountains?"

"I said the sea. But let's go where there's everything."

"We will have to leave soon."

"How about tonight? Too soon?"

She chuckles. "We have to wait until he's gone. But let's leave the very next day, before dawn. Prepare to go. Pack your things."

"I'm ready now, I have no things," Julian says. "I have nothing but you."

"I don't have money, Julian, but I have jewels," Mary says. "Lots of them. Gold rings and pearls. They must be worth something?"

"They're worth a lot." He wants to embrace her.

"If we sell them, we won't have to hide out in London. We can set sail at once."

"That's a good idea," Julian says. "The gold dealers on Cheapside will gladly take your rings off our hands."

"Mary!" Aurora's voice sounds from inside the kitchen. "Where are those blasted candles? We can't read the words on the parchment."

"Memorize the poems, Lady Mother, as I do," Mary says. "Then you won't need the candles."

"Don't be cheeky, Mary. Come, your lord is waiting."

"*He* is not my lord," Mary whispers to Julian, making a soft kissing sound with her lips. "I'll try to sneak down to see you tonight."

"All right, my love," says Julian.

"Mary!"

"Coming, Lady Mother!"

After the house has gone quiet, Julian lies in bed naked, aching and waiting for her, kneading her red beret, playing with her necklace. He reaches through the air to caress the shape of the invisible girl, so close he can feel the outlines of her hips in his hands.

He waits a long time, and then he falls asleep.

And in the night, he dreams of Josephine again.

He sits at the familiar table under the gold awning, and watches her walk toward him, a smile on her face, the red beret on her head, carrying the pink umbrella, her dress sashaying. He frowns in both the dream and in life and grips the beret. There's an incongruence he can't reconcile. How can one beret be in both places at once, on her head and in his hands? *Josephine*, he mouths, *why are you here? Mary and I are running away.*

For the first time Josephine speaks to him in the dream—actually speaks—but he can't make out what she's saying because the lunchtime crowd is obnoxiously loud. A man's rough voice is shouting, another voice is pleading. He can't pay attention to the pleading voice because he's trying to lip read Josephine's words. God, shut up! he wants to yell at the shouting man.

"It's not true!"

"If it's not true, then what are you doing here?"

"She hates me, she's always hated me, it's poisoned her soul, she's lying to you!"

"Do you think I believed the ugly words of a scullery maid? I beat her for her impudence. She is lower than a pig to me. This isn't about her!"

In his sleep Julian feels pressure on his chest like concrete. He's having trouble breathing.

"I was trying to get to the kitchen. I was hungry!"

"How could you do it, how could you!"

"It's not what you think, please—stop..."

"You have disgraced the House of Falk—"

O my God. It's not a dream. Julian opens his eyes. He's still on his back. It's dark out, there's a mere glimmer of a moon behind the fast-moving clouds. The wind is fierce. The pressure on his chest is crushing him.

"Forgive me, my lord. I made a youthful error. No one has to know."

"If Krea knew, it means everyone knows. You've made a cuckold out of me!"

Julian tries to jump up. He will run to the window, leap through it, kill Falk with his bare hands. He welcomes the chance.

The nightstand topples.

He takes one step and falls.

"I promise you, my lord, no one knows!"

Julian hears commotion outside. "Aha!" Lord Falk yells. "She was right—it *is* a wig! Oh, what have you *done*, you brazen harlot." There's a sound of flesh being slapped, a mighty struggle.

Julian tries to stand up, but he *can't*.

Something bizarre is happening to his body. It feels as if it's falling asleep. Not part of him, but all of him, from his feet that won't hold him to his mouth that won't scream. His body is falling into paralysis, the nerves and veins and muscles replaced with a million piercing needles.

"Let go of me, my lord, let *go* of me!"

Julian crawls to the window on his weakened elbows, on his buckling knees. He tries to shout, but no sound comes out.

"Not only do you dress as a man to act on a stage like a whore off the streets, but you've been fucking a peasant who insults me when I'm a guest in your mother's house!"

"You're the fucking peasant!"

By the force of his fighter's will, soaked in adrenaline-fueled terror, Julian pulls himself up to the ledge and headbutts open the casement. Any moment his circulation should come back, any second now.

But it doesn't come back.

The very opposite happens. His body weakens, the pain from a million stabbings becoming more fierce. Though Mary and Falk are in a brutal struggle right next to his open window, their voices grow muffled, as if he's going deaf. He can barely see.

"Julian!" Mary screams. "Help me!"

I'm coming, Mary! But he's not coming.

He hears Falk's growling and Mary's gurgling cries. Are the two of them falling quieter or is Julian losing his senses, one by one? She is gagging as if she's being choked. It can't be! But Julian can't breathe, can't speak, can't fight. It's as if he is being choked himself. He's terrified she will die if he doesn't get to her. The problem is, he's dying, too.

"*Julian...*"

"You've ruined me!" Falk yells. "You've made a laughing stock out of me. There goes the clown whose wife pretends she's a man by day and lets another man fuck her by night!"

Mary, I'm coming. With a superhuman effort, a naked Julian hurls himself over the window ledge and out onto the ground. The beret falls from his crippled fingers.

The needles that stab his body from within become boiling hot. He is being electrocuted and burned. He grasps for her beret. A flash of lightning illumines the yard. He sees Mary, pinned against the wall, slide lifeless to the ground, her hands dropping away from Falk's hands around her throat.

No! Julian wants to yell. His mouth opens in a silent scream. The current inside his body is set on fatal. He is frying from the inside out.

Lord Falk turns to Julian and draws his sword. "There you are," he says, lunging forward.

Julian wants to stand up, to fight, to kill him, as he knows he must, as he knows he once could. But Falk, the house, the garden, Mary are fading from Julian's view.

*Mary...*he whispers in his last breath, the hand holding her beret stretching out to her, as Lord Falk's raised sword flashes silver over his head like lightning and slices down through the air. *Mary—*

47

The Coat

JULIAN OPENED HIS EYES, WITH HIS ARMS RAISED DEFENSIVELY over his head, the red beret still clutched in his fingers. But it wasn't Lord Falk looming over him. Julian was on the floor looking up into the flummoxed face of Sweeney, the guard at the Transit Circle. Julian was surprised he could open his eyes at all. He thought he was dead.

Clearly, Julian's hearing had come back. With no difficulty he could hear Sweeney yelling. "What—are—you—doing? Why are you crying? Sweet Jesus—why are you *naked*? There's decency laws, they're gonna book you for public exposure! Get up. Are you some kind of a performance artist? They come through every once in a while, act all crazy. It's not funny, mate. When did you grow a beard? Hey, what's going on here? Stop shaking!"

Julian couldn't speak. He remained on the floor, his body, every bone in it feeling flattened as if by a concrete spreader. He was in agony.

Sweeney grabbed a trench coat from the nearby closet and threw it over Julian. "That's my coat over your filthy body," the corpulent guard hissed. "Get up and get on out of here. You want me to lose my job? We got kids coming through on class trips!"

Julian felt around his neck for the stone, clenched his fist around the red beret. He couldn't get up. And didn't want to. He squeezed shut his eyes.

"*You'll* be arrested," Sweeney said, "but why should *I* lose me job because you can't keep your knickers on? This is the Royal Observatory. A historical place built by kings. Have some respect. Take your shenanigans elsewhere. Well, what are you waiting for? *I* can't help you up, I got a bad back. Come on now, before I call the police. Take my coat and bugger off. Get up!"

Grabbing on to the railing, Julian finally managed to pull himself up. He barely swung the coat closed before a family of grandparents and small children filed through, stopping near the telescope. A tyke sandwiched himself next to Julian's hip, struggling to sound out the words above the open door. PRIME MERIDIAN OF THE WORLD the boy read off the plaque. Julian stood with his head bent until they left. What was wrong with his body? He felt deboned.

Sweeney resumed his rant. "What do you plan to do about paying me back for the coat? I can't afford to give it to every souse that staggers in here. What's wrong with you, drinking like that? It's *noon*. Write your name and address in my book, I want you to send me cash for the coat, seventy quid it cost me at Marks and Spencer." Sweeney stared into Julian's face. "Oh, for the love of Christ. You're gray, mate. Don't pass out, I can't lift you. And don't vomit, they'll arrest you for sure. Indecent exposure, vagrancy, vandalism in a historic building. Nice start to your God-given day. Oh, hell, just get out of here. Get yourself to the loo. What the bloody hell happened to you? One second you were standing fully dressed and the next you was down on the floor, hairy and naked. That's not funny, mate. Not funny in the slightest."

"Did I vanish?"

"Oh, so he speaks!" Sweeney said. "No, you didn't vanish. I blinked and you was down." The guard squinted at him suspiciously. "Why, were you…trying to vanish?"

Julian couldn't breathe. "Can I borrow a twenty?" he said finally. "I swear I'll pay you back."

"You take my coat and now you want money, too?"

"I promise I'll pay you back, a day or two, but—please."

Julian threw up in the bathroom.

Sweeney found him in one of the stalls on the floor.

"In my coat?" he thundered. "This is how you behave yourself in another man's coat?"

Without the guard Julian couldn't have gotten down the hill. Sweeney took him the back way, where the deliveries came and went, down through the Royal Garden to Crooms Hill. He hailed a cab, stuffing Julian inside. A ride to Great Eastern Road was forty pounds. Sweeney cursed loud and long before handing over another twenty to the driver.

Julian didn't remember getting to Quatrang. He got out of the cab and staggered inside, where a stunned Devi, serving another man, dropped the bowl of pho when he saw Julian—his hair overgrown, a full beard when just yesterday he was clean shaven, an exhibitionist's trench coat, an expression of mania and despair on his face.

"You're *back*?" Devi said in shock. His jaw went slack.

Julian fell and passed out.

48

Side Effects of Electrocution

How could you do this to me, Julian said to Devi that night and the nights that followed. I thought you were supposed to make it better. I thought you were supposed to help me. Before I met you, I was getting better...

Devi cleared his sympathetic but skeptical throat.

I *was*. I was getting over things.

Devi made another noise.

Look what you've done to me. I had an unhealed wound before but now it's raw again like it just happened. It did *just* happen. Do you have any idea how that feels?

Devi was hidden in the corner, and Julian could almost swear he could hear the little man crying.

Or was that strangled sound coming from Julian's own throat?

How could you not tell me she would die again?

How would I know this, Devi replied.

I don't believe you. I don't believe no one's not come back and told you.

There was a pause before Devi spoke. If they did, they didn't return to me.

Only a lunatic would come to you in the first place, Julian said. A madman. How desperate I must have been. You took advantage of my weakness.

I gave you hope.

How could you send me when you didn't know it would work?

"But Julian," Devi said, "it *did* work."

Julian stared back defiantly and then closed his eyes. "You're lucky no one's come back," he said. "Or someone would've killed you by now for sure."

"Like you want to?"

"Yes."

"Something's wrong with your body, Julian," Devi said.

Julian lay naked on the table in the back. "That's the least of what's wrong with me."

But by Devi's expression, it wasn't the least of it.

Basted with ointment, a towel thrown over his groin, Julian slipped in and out of consciousness, dozens of long healing needles puncturing his body. Devi washed him down with a sponge soaked in hot tiger water, held the glass filled with hot tiger bones to Julian's mouth. Pungent incense was burning, the candles were lit. The tiny room was warm, quiet, the air heavy with grief, with wishes unfulfilled.

After he told Devi what happened, Julian lay motionless while on a low stool in the corner, the cook twisted like a mute epileptic.

"What, the tiger got your tongue?" Julian said, his gray eyes condemning. "Now that you need to explain things, you've taken a vow of silence?"

"Maybe you should explain things to me."

Julian stared at the ceiling. "You're so blasé. It's all part of some larger whole to you. You're indifferent to my suffering."

"Stop harassing me, Julian," Devi said. "I'm well acquainted with the sorrow at the heart of life."

"Yes, just not with the sorrow at the heart of my life." A brief silence followed. The harangue resumed. "You think everyone else has succeeded where I failed?"

"As is often with you, you've got it exactly backwards," Devi said. "You succeeded where everyone else has failed. They could've died in the caves. Or not made it over the Black Canyon. They couldn't navigate the river. Got impaled, injured. Drowned. Never made it out. And on the other side, a thousand more things could've gone wrong. As far as I know, no one has survived the return trip." Devi touched Julian's body with his fingers as if he couldn't quite believe the man in front of him was real, the man he had sent into the abyss from which there was no return. "I don't know how you did it. It's incomprehensible. Like conception. A thousand things could've and should've gone wrong."

"Or," Julian said, "just one thing could've gone right. She could've lived."

"But she does live, Julian," Devi whispered from his corner, his voice filled with barren longing.

"I didn't wash in urine or wine," Julian said. "I didn't wash in the blood of the lamb. I wasn't sanctified or baptized. I wasn't sacrificed. I wasn't"—he broke off. "I wasn't enough."

The debriefing continued, the unpacking, the going over every word, every choice. "How could you have sent me so unprepared? I should've brought three sources of light, three! I had one. At the first sign of water, the light died. My piece of shit watch didn't work. Got stuck on noon. I wasn't warm enough, I wasn't dry enough, I couldn't climb, hold on to anything, the boots I never should've worn never dried, my jacket was too thick, but I couldn't leave it because it had her beret in it. Devi! My God. I didn't know I had to keep track of time."

"As do we all," Devi said. "And yet do we?" He paused. "And how would it have made a difference?"

"I didn't know to look for evil inside Falk, inside Krea."

"And if you knew?"

Dunham could've been the one. Or the boatman. There was danger everywhere. There was plague and dirt and oars. How did Julian know he was supposed to be looking out for such swift death? He raised his arm to cover his eyes so Devi wouldn't see his devastated face—and stabbed himself in the cheek with the acupuncture needle impaled in his forearm.

Methodically Devi fixed the needle, wiping the blood off Julian.

"You know what would've made a difference?" Julian said. "A headlamp. You sent me into a *cave* without light. You didn't tell me I had to leap over a black hole. Do you even know what the world record is in the long jump?" Julian thought he was ranting, asking a rhetorical question.

"Thirty feet," Devi instantly replied.

Julian frowned—at what, at Devi's insolence, at his ready response? "So you do know some things. How, because you've gone yourself, you've leapt over that canyon? And you're here, so you came back. You knew it was possible!"

"No. It's not what happened to me."

"What happened to you?"

"Something else, and I do not wish to discuss it."

"If you knew, why didn't you tell me?"

"Tell you what?"

Julian groaned. "How unattainably far I had to leap."

"And what would you have done if you knew?"

"Would that I'd had the opportunity to find out."

"Well, now you know," Devi said.

"What good is it now."

"Now you've learned how far you can leap."

"Not far enough."

"Farther than anyone I've ever known."

"Not far enough."

∞

Eventually he had to leave Devi's, put on Sweeney's coat, take a cab home. Devi gave him money. Julian forced himself not to look through his taxi windows at Old Street, at Goswell Road, the roads where he had just walked with her, a second ago, an infinity ago. He lay half sunk in the backseat waiting to turn off St. John's. Hermit Street was clean and treeless, neat well-kept brick terraced houses with black doors, just like always. Nothing out of place. Except for him.

"Where you been, love," Mrs. Pallaver said, opening the door and smiling. "Forgot your key again? You been gone for days." She patted his arm as he limped past and then stared at him uncertainly. "When did you grow such a beard? And what happened to your lovely hair? I've never seen it so messy. Well, as long as you're back, my dear."

"I'm back." He started up the stairs, holding on to the railing.

"Are you still planning to move out?" she asked. "Cause I have somebody interested in the room."

"Yes, Mrs. Pallaver."

"Are you all right, love? Would you like a cup of tea?"

"Yes, Mrs. Pallaver, please." The kindness got to him.

Julian's room was just as he'd left it. He ripped up the farewell note he had left for Ashton on the dresser. He sat on the bed. He lay on the bed, curled into a fetal circle of grief, clenching her red beret to his chest.

He had spent so many hours of his precious days in a dark buttery with buckets of suet instead of with her. He had lived through a miracle. He thought he had time. Nothing ahead of him but possibilities. He spent hours walking the mule back and forth from the market, gazing at the Fortune, getting stuck in the mud, harnessing, reining, loading, packing, unloading, unpacking. Planting her wedding flowers. Rolling barrels of water back and forth, empty, full, empty. And then exhausted he would sleep, and another day would begin and end, same as before, except for a few minutes when she was with him. They walked through Fynnesbyrie Field. He laughed at Lance and Crab. When she was Sebastian, she would rip off her wig and fling it at him, and he would catch it and hold it to his heart. With joy they waded in the River Fleet, trying not to slip on the wet moss stones.

Sweeney told him there was no break between the moment Julian was dressed and clean shaven and the moment he was undressed and bearded. Time remained at noon at zero meridian, and yet time had passed in the life of her soul, in the life of his soul.

She *lived*. And Julian lived with her.

Was it the past? Was it the future?

It was in another country. Time and space were coordinates of the material world. The place where Julian was with her had no material dimension. It just was.

∞

He returned to work—for a day. It felt longer than his time in the cave. When four o'clock came, Julian went to human resources and asked for a leave of absence. He promised that when he got better, he'd be as good as new. They must have thought he was going to rehab, because Eleanor in HR signed his papers with fiery enthusiasm.

Julian was broken and needed to be repaired. Devi was unable to help with the unmistakable injury to his body. Reluctantly, Julian had to admit he needed a real doctor. He went to the National Health Walk-in Clinic. When they couldn't help him—because they couldn't find anything wrong with him—he went to St. Bart's.

In the emergency room, he said there was something the matter with his heart. That got their attention. They triaged him stat, and then couldn't find anything wrong with it.

I may've been hit by lightning, he said.

They took that seriously. After admitting him, they ran tests, asked questions. Trouble is, to get to the truth, you must know which tests to give, which questions to ask, and they did not. For example:

Why do you think you were hit by lightning?

I could've been electrocuted.

Why do you think that?

Because I feel an electromagnetic disturbance in my body.

You feel it right now?

I feel it right now.

They examined him. We can't find any Lichtenberg figures on your skin, they said. Lightning burns, we call them, they look like black-and-blue flowers. They're our first clue to the scope of the damage. The more flowers you have, the worse you got hit. You don't have any. You have some burst capillaries around your hands and feet. You may have had some internal bleeding which healed on its own. Did you fall?

I didn't fall. I told you what happened.

But *were* you hit by lightning? You said you *think* you were hit by lightning. Wouldn't you know if you were?

I can't remember. It may have zapped my memory. Something doesn't feel right. Fix it. I'm moving apartments. I need to return to work. Just—fix it.

They did an EKG, a stress test. His heart was fine, no tissue damage, as often happened after an electrocution. When did this supposed event supposedly occur? they asked. We've had good weather in London, no storms, no thunder. In our medical opinion, you did not sustain a direct hit from a bolt of lightning. You would've melted from the current. You would've been carbonized.

"Perhaps I *was* carbonized," Julian said, staring out the window at the black and red rooftops, the tips of the trees just greening. "Carbonized, and then reformed, but put back together not one hundred percent correctly."

Julian regretted saying that, because the stream of doctors returned not only with his medical file two inches thick, but with Dr. Fenton and Dr. Weaver in tow. Notes were exchanged, discussed, examined. They had meetings at the foot of his bed. Suddenly everything became about the girl.

Well, it was only right.

Everything *was* about the girl.

"Julian, why do you think you were hit by lightning?" Dr. Weaver asked, all pretend concern.

The grumpy but benevolent Fenton was actually concerned. "Julian, is this another one of your tricks to get me to prescribe more Klonopin? I've heard so many excuses from you, but this one, I must say, is one of your best."

"Am I asking for Klonopin?" Why, why, why, why.

Intense heat from electrical current damages your lungs, they said. It expands the air inside them. Your lungs stretch. Sometimes they burst. We don't see anything like that in your chest.

What *do* you see in my chest? Julian asked. Do you see my heart? Do you see my soul? Run your tests, tell me what you find.

"We see a man who is having hallucinations," Weaver said.

Julian demanded that Weaver be taken off his case. He had a right to a different doctor. Weaver was making everything worse. Julian called for the hospital administrator. He was strapped to a blood pressure machine, and his vitals bore him out. Whenever Weaver spoke, Julian's blood pressure spiked, and his heart rate shot up. They took Weaver off his rounds. A vindicated Julian felt better, rejuvenated by his anger.

The elderly and ineffectual Fenton stayed. Are you suffering from amnesia maybe? What year is it? What day is it?

Julian didn't know what day it was.

Why, Julian, why do you think you were hit by lightning?

Because I feel there is no strength in my bones. There's something in me that feels broken. Not a lot broken. A little broken. I used to be a boxer. I know about these things.

Fenton laughed. He thought Julian was joking. Then he turned serious but skeptical. Where does it feel you're a little broken?

Everywhere, said Julian.

You sound confused, Fenton said. Were you hit on the head a lot when you were a boxer?

Finally, they found something. Julian had a ruptured ear drum! This was exciting. It would explain his pervasive dizziness, why he stumbled when he walked. They got excited, too. They took more X-rays and found hairline cracks in the navicular bones of his feet, the boat-shaped bones that connected the feet to the toes. That's why it hurt so much when he walked. He remembered his friend Cedric in the stables telling him that horses frequently got this type of injury and had to be put down. Julian felt less grateful than he should've been that he wasn't a horse.

He checked himself into a convalescent home in Hampstead Heath to recuperate. It was a live-in rehab facility for old people with broken hips and stroke patients who couldn't manage on their own. They had a wellness counselor on premises, to help the elderly adapt to their permanent physical limitations. By far, Julian was the home's youngest resident. The counselor, a well-meaning youth named Kenyon Reece with two years of vocational social services training diagnosed him with fibromyalgia!—a largely psychosomatic disorder of the central nervous system.

Julian slept fifteen hours a day, sat motionless in the garden.

After two weeks, with his body almost healed, he left but didn't feel any better.

∞

He needed to get himself together. Ashton was arriving soon. Julian had to pretend to be plugged back to life. So the shell that was Julian searched for new digs for him and his friend. Ashton wanted Notting Hill? Julian would deliver Ashton Notting Hill. It was the least he could do; after all, the guy was moving continents for him. He and Devi went looking together and found a spacious, renovated two-bedroom, two-bathroom flat on the third floor of a posh white townhouse. It had a large open-plan living area and kitchen, with a balcony overlooking a *My Fair Lady* street, three blocks from Portobello Road. There was even a palm tree outside to remind Ashton of home.

Julian's appetite came back. He ate as if he hadn't eaten in eight hundred years—four hundred there, four hundred back. He inhaled Devi's Chinese chicken salad, soy garlic Korean beef, coconut rice. Pho. He ate and ate. "Had I stayed with her, honestly, I don't know how I would've survived."

"How long were you there? Was it years?"

"Why years?" After lunch Julian was back on Devi's acupuncture table, his body slathered with balm and pierced with needles, frankincense burning around him. Devi was chanting, singing, praying.

"You look older."

"Well, I'm not. It wasn't even two months."

Devi's mouth got twitchy.

"What? Why are you looking at me like that?"

"I'm not looking at you."

"You are literally staring at me with your evil eye. What?"

"Nothing," Devi said. "Sometimes you get upset when I tell you things you don't want to hear."

"Fine, don't tell me."

"Why did you ask if you didn't want me to tell you?"

"Fine, tell me."

"I was thinking," Devi said, placing a calming palm on Julian's chest, "about how permanent the love is inside us, and yet how temporary our time is with it."

"As always, you're not helping." Julian returned to his disquisition. "They had never heard of King Lear, Devi. They'd never heard of the King James Bible. They didn't know what caused the plague. They painted their faces with lead. And my God, the way they dressed! Their collars were starched like plates around their necks. No one had buttons, everything was tied together with ribbons and rope, and there I was wearing a jacket with zippers on it. They might have burned me for witchcraft for the zippers alone. I was ridiculous. They made candles out of animal fat, have you any idea how disgusting that is? There isn't going to be anything in my life more disgusting than that."

"Famous last words," Devi said.

"I did nothing but arouse suspicion. I didn't know who the King was, who the Queen was. I didn't know what day it was."

"You still don't."

"They didn't have potatoes, they didn't have tea or corn. Everything I said was wrong. And I should've brought a backpack."

"Would a backpack have helped you?"

"It wouldn't have *not* helped me. You should've warned me, Devi. The long-jump record is thirty feet? I'm sure that jump was longer. I don't know how I made it. By all rights, I should be dead. You didn't tell me what was ahead of me. I wasn't ready. I didn't have enough time." Julian closed his eyes.

"Enough time for *what*, Julian?" Devi said, his tone parental.

This time Julian ripped out the needle before covering his face with the crook of his arm. He railed about the idiotic bearable things because he couldn't rail about the unbearable ones.

Oh, Mary.

He didn't save her. He thought all he had to do was keep her from a terrible marriage and everything else would work itself out. But it didn't. There was nothing else that mattered, nothing else that made one softened heart of difference.

His lamentations continued. "What do I know about the long jump? What do I know about how to approach a jump, the vital importance of the last two strides, how to take off properly, what to do with my body in the air, how to land? I impaled my calf on a rock, but I could've impaled my heart on a stake, jumping blind, flying blind, landing blind. I power sprinted in darkness. You should've told me to bring a retractable flexible pole for the vault. Am I Carl Lewis? Am I Jesse Owens?"

"Did you do it, or did you not do it?"

"Just dumb luck. I tried to run as fast as I could, thinking like an idiot that the speed at takeoff would propel me over the insurmountable distance."

"The speed at takeoff *is* the single most important thing in the jump," Devi said.

"I didn't jump, Devi," Julian whispered. "I *flew*."

Okay, he didn't bring a headlamp, but he held her in his arms again. He had glimpsed the immortal, had righted the bitter wrong of L.A. His faith had been answered. Why didn't that feel like enough? There was nothing to be done about it now, but Julian couldn't help but feel in his dank depression and occasional mania, filled to the brim with both ardor and sorrow, that if only he had brought three lights as he should have, if only he had made other decisions, tiny adjustments in his free choices, they might've accumulated into a different destiny for Mary. And therefore, into a different destiny for him.

49

The Lady, or the Tiger

JULIAN WAS WAITING FOR ASHTON AT ARRIVALS IN Heathrow. Ashton was tanned, blond, happy. He was wheeling a suitcase and a duffel.

"Jules, you showed up at the airport!" Ashton said with a delighted grin. "Are you trying to prove you're not deranged?"

"Yes, or as it's called everywhere else in the universe, being a friend, but whatever." Julian smiled back.

"Same difference. Are we taking the tube? Fine, let's go. I'm starved." The men made their way to the people mover. "So what have you been doing with yourself?"

"Oh, you know," Julian said with a shrug. "A little bit of this, a little bit of that."

"What the hell is that on your face?"

Julian hadn't shaved off the bushy facial hair that now curled and twined halfway down his throat. He stroked his beard. "You like it?"

"Are the razors being rationed again in London like during the war? Shaving cream, too? Scissors? No, it's a good look for you. Perfect. You've heard of insect repellent? Well, what you've got going is a babe repellent."

If only. Julian didn't know why but the girls for some reason dug the crazy-ass beard. Nearly every day he had random women strike up conversations with him on the tube and in the street. Maybe he looked like he was in need of salvation, and they were just the ticket. Julian appraised Ashton's luggage. "This is all you brought to live in another country? Two bags?"

"What else do I need? A suit, some jeans, a toothbrush, and a duffel full of condoms."

Julian shook his head. His friend was incurable.

"Just kidding," Ashton said. "I solemnly swear there's not a single condom on me."

"Aren't you the eternal pessimist."

"Okay, okay, just one"—Ashton grinned—"but I brought it for you. I was hoping your terrible streak with women would end now that I was here, but by the thing on your face I see that even one condom was shockingly optimistic. Oh, and why did you sign a year lease instead of a month-to-month? You think we're still going to be in London in a year? Nuts to that. Not me, baby. I only brought two bags."

"It was only available on a long-term lease." But Ashton was right. There was no reason to stay in London for an entire year. Julian just had to get himself sorted, and with Ashton here, that would be easier, and then their time would wind down and another life would beckon, and things might actually get better. "Wait until you see the apartment," Julian said, trying to sound upbeat. "You're not going to want to leave."

Indeed Ashton liked the new spread. "And I *love* what you've done with the place, Jules!" There was an air mattress in each bedroom and linen from Marks and Spencer. In a kitchen cabinet stood two water glasses and two shot glasses, and the fridge was stocked with a 12-pack of Heineken and a bottle of Grey Goose. The pantry contained a box of Corn Flakes and a tin of raspberry Pims cookies, which Ashton once had and said he liked.

Mock sniffling, Ashton toured the apartment, his arm hooked around Julian's neck, nodding in hearty approval and clutching the Pims and Grey Goose to his chest. "Oh, Auntie Em!" he kept exclaiming. "It's so good to be home!"

They furnished the place together. They painted it all sorts of manly colors, dark blue, dark gray, dark green. As a joke they painted the bathrooms girly pink, "so when the girls come, they'd feel right at home," Ashton said. "Well, by girls, I mean just Riley, of course."

"Of course."

"And by come, I mean visit, not..."

"Of course."

"Though I still have that one condom, Jules. It's waiting for you. Rubber burning a hole in my wallet. You want it?"

"Thanks, man. You hold on to it for me."

"Anything for you, buddy."

They bought real beds and stage lights. Ashton bought a king bed for himself, since he took the large master, but when he saw that Julian was about to buy a twin bed, he rioted.

"I swear on all that is holy," Ashton said, "I will beat the shit out of you right here in the mattress store. You are not a monk, you're not in prison, you're not in college, you are not an asshole."

Julian relented and bought a full-size bed, but in his room he pushed it against the wall. For weeks after, every time Julian showered, Ashton would run into his room and drag the bed out into the middle of the floor.

They bought a big TV and two long leather couches, one for Julian, one for Ashton. They stocked the fridge—with more beer—they hammered framed movie posters into their blue walls, hired a cleaning lady, learned something real about Notting Hill, became dues-paying members of the local Electric Cinema Theatre. They got up every morning and together took the Central Line to work.

"How are you enjoying Notting Hill, bro?" Julian would say after spending an hour each morning strap hanging on the tube.

"Yes, you're right, we both should've moved into your attic room on Hermit Street," Ashton would reply. "Because when you lived there, you always got to work on time."

After Ashton moved to London, Julian's life improved. He didn't want to admit it, but it improved considerably.

Julian was surprised and not surprised by how easily he and Ashton fell into a familiar routine, how good it was to live with his friend again, to work together every day, to debate the top ten Dire Straits songs: "Brothers in Arms," "Love Over Gold"—and the saddest Tom Waits songs, no question "Time" (time, time) with "The Part You Throw Away" a close second; to order takeout, walk to the local pub, grab a pint and some grub, discuss plans for the weekend, to argue which Kanye album was better, *College Dropout* or *808s and Heartbreak*.

How much Julian had missed Ashton and not even know it.

How good it was not to be alone.

Never one to exclude Julian from anything, Ashton invited Julian to go pub crawling with him and Nigel and Sheridan and Roger. Julian tried to remind Ashton that with his father semi-retired, he was now boss at Nextel, and it was no good for the boss to become too chummy with the help. Often, Julian refused to join them. They drank too much. He couldn't keep up, and he didn't like to be hungover. And on top of it, he still couldn't stand Nigel. The man was put on earth as irrefutable proof that not everything in nature had a purpose.

Sometimes on the weekends Anne and Malcolm from editorial joined Julian and Ashton for a drink and a meal, and when Riley visited, she'd make Julian the fifth wheel, and a few times, to make it less awkward, a Camden chick with a nose ring came along, to round out the number to six, almost like a dinner party, though Julian didn't want to think of Callie as his date or anything. Julian met her when he and Ashton had been browsing through the Portobello market one Saturday morning. Callie was selling historical maps of the world for a crazy chunk of change. She told Julian she was a copy editor and looking for work. He asked Ashton to hire her, and to thank Julian, Callie gave him the expensive maps for free.

∞

And then one night, when the moon was new, Julian dreamed of Josephine again.

She strolled toward him waving, twirling her umbrella, a beret on her head, a smile on her lips and love on her face. When he woke up, Julian sat in his bed for a long time, staring ahead, not moving, barely breathing. He was trying to catch the threads of Devi's words and the pattern of the dream and knit them together to make a fragile tapestry to cover himself with, to comfort himself with.

Had he been looking at everything all wrong?

Mary wasn't dead.

She was *alive*!

She was *still* alive.

He didn't save her *that* time, yes, but if Devi was right, and her soul was new, didn't that mean that she was still out there?

Didn't that mean that she was out there...waiting for him?

"What?" Devi said when Julian expressed this in a poorly worded, stilted monologue. "Waiting for you *where*?"

"In the future. I dreamed of her, Devi. Why would I dream of her again?"

"I don't know, but so what?"

"She doesn't have a future. That's what you said. That means I'm dreaming of her in *my* future."

"Or you could just be dreaming."

"Thanks, Dr. Weaver." Awkwardly, Julian tried again to express the inexpressible. He had nine months before the equinox in March. Their lease wasn't up until next April. Julian would do what he could. He'd prepare. Improve, recover, be better.

"Go *where*?" Devi said. The shaman almost laughed before he saw the somber expression on Julian's face. "Oh, you're not joking. Um, *no*. You *can't* go again."

"Why not?"

"Because. You know why not."

"I don't. Tell me why."

"Why is the sky blue. Why is the grass green. That's why."

"Because you think it will change nothing?"

"Yes, Julian." Like Devi was talking to a child. "That's one of the reasons. Because it will change *nothing*. Also, not for nothing, but it nearly killed you."

"It didn't though."

"It took a terrible toll on your body."

"What do I care about my body."

"Oh, you should care," Devi said. "It's the only one you've got. And it's got to last you a long time, the rest of your life, really. You don't look the same, you don't walk the same. The trip has aged you a decade. You survived it once, I don't know how, but you won't survive it again, Humpty Dumpty."

"I'm fine," Julian said. "Good as new. I started boxing again."

"Why?"

"I don't know. To get strong, get in shape. Plus, let's be honest, what took a toll on my body was the involuntary return. I'll just have to make sure *not* to return."

"How do you plan to do that?"

"Um, by not returning."

"Please, *please* tell me you're not serious." Devi looked stunned and troubled.

"Calm down." Julian backed off. A little later he tried again. "But what if I was?"

"Julian...why would you ever want to do it?"

"Because I didn't save her, Devi."

"You didn't go to save her, Julian. Do you remember what I told you when we first met? It wasn't that long ago. I had hoped you were listening."

"You said so many things. I can't be expected to remember them all. You know what you didn't say? Bring a flashlight, a flotation device, a grappling hook."

"You know what I *did* say, though? That your greatest delusion is thinking you have any control over whether another human being lives or dies."

"Yes," Julian said, "you're right. I forgot that part. I was too busy remembering you telling me that my *other* greatest delusion was thinking she was *mortal*."

"It'll behoove you to recall *all* my words right about now."

"I remember your words," Julian said. "You told me you couldn't find her in the spiritual realm because her soul was lost. You told me she ran out of time. That's how I feel, Devi, now more than ever. That she and I ran flat out of time. When she died, the most important work of my life—I mean *her* life—was not yet finished." He took a breath. "I think I could do better if I had another chance with her."

"Oh, dear boy, trust me, if that's what you heard, then you heard all the wrong things."

"You told me I have free will," Julian said. "Was that another lie? Do I or do I not have it?"

Devi took Julian's hands and looked him in the eye. "Listen to me very carefully," Devi said. "What you're calling free will is nothing but your irrevocable pride talking. Be humble, Julian! Bow your head. Think of your *great* accomplishment. Not just for yourself, but for me, too. Truly you have done the impossible. Because of your remarkable effort, your faith has been answered. And you've let me in on that mystery as well, and for that I thank you. This is your gift eternal—to know the truth and to stand witness to it. You had asked for *one* thing. And you've been given two. You've been given proof that you will die. And, much more important," Devi said, "you've been given proof that you will live forever. How can *that* not be enough? It's everything. Now, please—don't tempt the dark forces, I beg you. Don't get into a fight with them. You won't win. Take the bounty you've been given, take your marbles and go."

What dark forces, Julian wanted to say. But he knew. The

forces of treachery and vengeance. The forces of death and disease and despair.

Devi muttered something in a foreign language under his breath. "Don't make me regret helping you," he said. "With faith as your guide, you can start afresh. Your closest friend has moved to London for you. He gave up his life to help you! If that's not a sign of his devotion to you, I don't know what is. Does his friendship mean nothing? You're finally off Klonopin— and have lived to tell about it. You've got a good job, you found a nice apartment. You're young and single. You're moderately handsome, I suppose—more so if you'd ever shave that thing on your face." Devi wrinkled his nose. "The women you meet might be even more complimentary. You've got your whole life ahead of you. You can stay in London, this incomparable city, or you can move back to California. Right now, all you have is options. Right now, all you have is a future. What a place to be. And you're welcome, by the way."

Julian sat on the stool, chewing his lip, appraising Devi, by equal measures courageous and afraid, resolved and uncertain.

Devi let go of Julian's hands and waited with a look on his face that could only be described as desolation. "I asked you about your friend."

"What about him? He has nothing to do with this."

"No?"

"No!"

"You only think the answer is nothing." The two men stared at each other. "What if it's everything?"

"Devi, help me unpack this," Julian said. "You're keeping something from me. Why shouldn't I go again? The truth now. You told me she's lived more than once. That means I have another chance. She could be anywhere this time. Things will only get easier. What can possibly be worse than living within a sewage-filled moat with no electricity and no running water?"

"Famous last words," said Devi. "Pity the fool who thinks he is the reason the bell clinks, and rejoices."

"Who said that?"

"Me. I'm saying it now."

"No matter what, I'll be better prepared," Julian continued confidently. "I will train my body to be strong, now that I know I need to protect her. Maybe she'll even remember me." He smiled.

"Oh, because you've trained to be strong? Or because now you know things?"

"Don't mock me."

"Now you know only in part." Devi looked so unhappy. "And Ashton?"

"I'll be doing him a favor," Julian said. "He likes it here well enough, but his real life is in L.A. There he's got his store, his girl, all his other friends. He'd never be here if it weren't for me."

"That's certainly true," Devi said. "But are you sure you know where Ashton's real life is?"

"Yes, this is just an interlude for him," Julian said, "the London thing. It's not real. Not for him, not for me. We belong somewhere else. Ashton belongs in L.A."

"And you?"

"With her," Julian said. "Somewhere out there, there's a foreign country that's called the past, where she still lives. She lives! I've seen her with my own eyes, Devi, thanks to you, and I can't unsee her."

Devi groaned. "I wish I'd never opened my big mouth. I wish my mother never spoke to you. I gave you the Transit Circle so you could save your life, not destroy it."

"How can I not try again?" Julian exclaimed. "Are you telling me you wouldn't try again if you could?" He was deeply irritated by Devi's stubborn ambivalence. The conflict over the wisdom of Julian's choices played out in a cage match on Devi's impassive face. There was curiosity and excitement, anxiety and fear, there was something for Julian, and something for Devi, too, all in the barely animated face of a Vietnamese man who spent his life hiding his feelings from others.

"So the future I have laid out for you full of hope and promise, it's nothing to you?" Devi said. When Julian didn't reply, the shaman persisted with implacable conviction. "There's great peril in what you're contemplating. There is mortal danger."

Julian began to waver. "You're just trying to scare me."

Devi said nothing.

"Oh, for God's sake!"

"I can't see it," Devi said. "I can only feel it."

"Feel what?"

"A weight, a magnetizing block laid on the compass of my intuition. I feel terrible suffering all around you, at the root and the tree and all its branches. Not just for you. For those close to you."

"That's crazy. So I'm supposed to listen to your *feelings* before I decide what to do?"

Devi kept his thoughts to himself.

"Are you really telling me I must choose between my friend and my girl, because you have some vague *worries*?"

"How hard a choice can it be?" Devi said. "Your girl is gone, and your friend is right here. And you have your life. Seems barely a choice at all."

But she wasn't gone! That was the point. She wasn't gone. She was out *there*. Smugly, Julian took an assured breath, a lawyer about to dismantle the opposition, a boxer who sees a weakness in his opponent and gets ready to pounce. "Devi, you're not making sense," he said. "You just told me I can't control whether somebody lives or dies. And now you're saying my actions—that have nothing to *do* with Ashton—actually control what happens *to* Ashton."

"Oh, you're adorable thinking you can control anything," Devi said. "You can't even control your temper."

"You can't have it both ways, Devi. Pick a side."

"It's not me who's trying to have it both ways, you mule-headed fledgling."

"Okay, fine. But if I can be an instrument of destruction," Julian said, "why can't I also be an instrument of salvation?"

"You can or you cannot," Devi said. "It's a false choice. You can be one without the other. You can be both. You can be neither. That's not what I'm asking. Have you thought of a worst-case scenario outcome in this? What you can and can't live with, what you can and can't bear?"

"Of course not. I'm not a pessimist like you. I'm not a fatalist."

Devi demanded an answer. "For another chance to save her, what are you prepared to lose?"

The smugness left Julian. He didn't dare say *everything*. He said, "Nothing else."

"Yes, because that's how life works," Devi said. "To have what you want, to live how you want, you usually sacrifice nothing. Besides, I said *worst*-case scenario. Not unicorns riding butterflies."

"I don't want to talk to you anymore. Goodbye."

"I'll see you next Wednesday," said Devi.

Julian staggered back to work, a shell on the outside, a whirling storm inside.

∞

A few days later, on a Saturday morning, Ashton caught Julian staring into the toilet. The door was ajar, and they were about to head out to the market, yet there Julian was, in a trance in the pink bathroom.

"Um—Jules?"

"Isn't the toilet remarkable?" Julian said. "Did you know that in half the world they still practice open defecation?"

"Well, you know what they say," Ashton said, "practice makes perfect." He grinned. "Still, I didn't know that, and more important, didn't wish to know that."

"In the old days," Julian went on, "the castles where royals lived had garderobes, which were basically stone seats that emptied down a trough into the moat surrounding the castle. And the gong farmer cleaned out the moat every day. And he never washed his hands, and he'd walk through the house infecting every person he came near. Is it any wonder so many died before they were eighteen." Julian shook his head.

"What the hell? Lots of people lived past eighteen," Ashton the history major said. "The eighth Henry. The first Elizabeth. The second Charles. Queen Victoria."

"Let's go," Julian said, pushing past his friend. "Before the market closes." He could never ask Ashton's advice about this, even in the hypothetical, much less tell him the truth. "You want to eat at the Granger if the line's not too long?" The Granger was the hottest brunch place in West London.

At the Granger over ricotta waffles, Ashton caught Julian staring at him. "Jules, why are you gaping at me the way you were just gaping at that toilet an hour ago?"

Julian blinked and looked away. "What way is that, Ash?"

"Like on the one hand you're pleased I'm so shiny and new, but on the other, ashamed by how you're about to desecrate me." Ashton laughed.

And Julian forced out a laugh also.

Before going out drinking they headed to the Electric Cinema in Notting Hill to catch a documentary about a British explorer named Robert Falcon Scott, and his failed expedition to claim the South Pole for Britain in 1912. Failed in every sense of the word. He and his four men had arrived at the South Pole 34 days too late. Roald Amundsen from Norway got there first ("Those damn Vikings!" Ashton said). Heartbroken, the five men trudged nearly *900 miles* back to their ship through blizzard winds and 50 below temperatures before freezing to death a few miles from the coast. Some of their bodies have never been found. "I knew you'd like that film, Jules," Ashton said as they left the theatre. "It resonates with you, don't it? You *love* taking the scenic route and ending up where you're not supposed to be."

"I wind up on Antrobus Street, not in Antarctica!"

The quote from the film that stayed with Julian was from Charles Bukowski who said that it wasn't whether you succeeded or failed that mattered most. *What mattered most was how you walked through the fire.*

Bullshit, Julian thought. What mattered most was whether you succeeded or failed in the one irreducible imperative of your life.

And Robert Falcon Scott had failed.

∞

What was the irreducible imperative of Julian's life? And what was he prepared to give up in his quest for it?

All the documentaries and late night pubs, all the stars over London and the ceilings in his apartment and the pavements under his feet, all the wrong cafés with metal tables and golden awnings couldn't help Julian wade through a future he did not know and could not know, did not see and could not see.

What should he do?

Julian hated, *hated* to admit it, but he feared Devi was right. It seemed better to leave well enough alone, make peace, move forward, stay put, rebuild what he had.

Certainly, it was easier.

But was it?

Julian didn't feel easy. He felt hard and heavy.

When you didn't know what to do, how did you decide which path to take, with the future unknowable? What was the right choice?

Julian knew how you decided. It was one of his least popular life hacks. *The thing you didn't want to do was nearly always the right choice. That's* how you made your decision in the absence of other compelling evidence. You did the thing you didn't want to do. Did you train first or go drinking. Did you eat first or go running. Did you stay in bed or get up and get on with your day? Did you stay put or run away. Did you do the impossible thing and fly through a black hole in search of the missing or did you stay put and forge a new life? Were you made to last or made to be broken?

But even here, nothing was clear. On the surface, though to stay seemed the easy choice, it was also the hardest.

Because Julian didn't want to stay.

Everything felt so fragile, all his mutually exclusive options dangling above him on silk spider threads.

He remembered the debt to Sweeney, returned to Greenwich, gave the man two hundred pounds for the coat, apologized. Sweeney's reaction puzzled Julian. The guard struggled to remember him. He recalled a man being naked in the middle of the Transit Room, but had forgotten giving Julian his coat. He thought he had misplaced it. "This is what happens when you get to be my age, mate," Sweeney said. "Your memory goes. Don't take it personal." He took Julian's money, because what sucker wouldn't, and he shook Julian's hand, but then without interest stared at Julian who stood by the telescope holding up the quartz crystal to the sky, as indifferent to him as the old guard.

You be sure to come back and see us again, Sweeney said before going on break.

I'm not coming back, Julian wanted to say. You will never see me again. But he couldn't say it. Couldn't say it because he didn't mean it.

Julian kept asking Devi what he would do if he was in Julian's shoes.

For weeks Devi wouldn't reply. The man's black eyes would rest on Julian, bottomless, fake-calm, judging, appraising, beseeching.

"I'm not the center of your newfound life," Devi finally said. "*You* are the center of your life. The question in front of you is a question each of us must answer for ourselves. You, me, Ashton, Josephine. Each one of us is the keeper of our own souls. What are you prepared to give up to live how you want? What are you prepared to lose to try to attain it? And what if you fail? Because that's also what's at stake here. That is also one of your options. That you will sacrifice everything and gain nothing. Can you live with that?"

For a long time Devi waited while Julian gathered his thoughts to speak.

Why would I gain nothing, Julian said, weakened in spirit. That is just one unlikely possibility. One among many.

I'm asking you only about that one, unlikely as it may be, Devi said.

Don't you think there *could* be a fate beyond the fates, said Julian, not answering.

"I showed it to you already," Devi replied. "If there is another fate, I do not know it. Would it help you if I answered your question? All right. I'll tell you. I would never go." Devi looked away. "I would never go *again*."

While Ashton slept away his hangovers, Julian kept coming back to Greenwich on Sunday mornings, standing as if at an altar in front of the black mute motionless telescope pointing up at the infinite meridian. Julian wished Devi understood something. Not just Devi. Ashton, too, and Riley, and Nigel, and Callie. What Devi was talking about, it meant nothing. London, Los Angeles. The comfortable bed Julian slept in, his liquid brunches, the walks through Portobello Market, the coffee he liked and couldn't go without, the great new song, the latest book, the blockbuster movie. None of it meant anything without her. He knew he'd feel better eventually. But after what happened to her, life would never again mean to him what it used to.

Devi responded poorly to this. "The sullen are punished by being drowned in muddy waters until the end of forever," Devi said. "Is that what you want?"

It wasn't what Julian wanted. He wasn't sullen. He wasn't drowning. What he wanted was to take back his life. Not to turn his back on her, not to take a beating, not to be swallowed, hidden, left behind, but to start over. Not to feel so alone. Falling in love with her had changed everything he knew.

Ask yourself the only question worth getting an answer to, Devi said. Are you prepared to risk everything to gain *nothing*?

Julian didn't know if he was prepared to do that. But it was also difficult to state exactly what it was he'd be losing.

"Everything you have, and everything you love, and everything you know," Devi said with dark certainty.

How could Julian take a stand against that? The ground was shifting under his feet.

A small voice tried to make its timid exit out of Julian's throat. But wasn't there another outcome? Couldn't he lose everything—*and gain everything*? Wasn't that also a possibility?

When they first met they were lovers for barely a minute. They didn't talk enough about the future or the past, about the profound or the mundane. They stepped into Eden where the unreal was real and their little L.A. life was nothing but a dream. Who had time to shoot the breeze when they had been so busy living. She acted breathy and carefree, though many things frightened her. The ocean, the fiery Santa Ana winds, traffic, gangs, hard drugs, loud noises, explosives. Don't worry, he told her, a fake cavalier knight, you're safe with me.

Once when the ocean was clear, he carried her in and they bobbed shivering in the slow lapping tide, her arms around his neck. Even now he felt her cold slender body in his hands wrapped around him in the Pacific off Zuma. It's better with you, she said. Everything is better with you. Wasn't that the truth, he thought, but what he said was, it's call time. Dante and Beatrice are waiting for you on stage at the Greek. No, don't make me, she said. I don't want to go back. I just want to stay here with you, in the ocean. Please. I don't want to go back.

But they went back.

Julian remained haunted by her face. She had come to him for a few days—once in L.A. and once in Clerkenwell long ago—and walked off with his life. He had hoped for so much more. He had hoped for love. He did not wish to know only the meaning of despair. Would she feel betrayed to be deserted by him when he was supposed to be at his post? Would she even care? Had she already forgotten him, the one who had mourned her, the one who mourned her still, who loved her still?

Julian's human heart was in conflict with itself, trembling. *Josephine...Mia...Mary...*

His choice wasn't the lady, or the tiger. The lady and the tiger were both behind door number two. Behind door number one was nothing.

He stood for a long time on the meridian even after noon had come and gone, his hand half outstretched, the crystal silent, the sun in hazy retreat. The holy girl asked, will you remember me? Will you ever remember how you once loved me, or will you forget that, too, as you've forgotten the other joys in your life? How could he leave her. In her was the soul of the prophets and the saints and of all those slain upon the earth. In her soul was a heart that was his. It was by her side that he must end his life. Julian knew it. He felt it. He was a soldier, and she was his country.

As the fool thinks, so the bell clinks. There is no return from death, the wise man said.

And the fool replied, but what if there was?

Read on for an exclusive extract from

A Beggar's Kingdom,

book two in the *End of Forever* saga...

Real Artifacts from Imaginary Places

ASHTON STOOD, HIS BLOND HAIR SPIKING OUT OF HIS baseball cap, his arms crossed, his crystal eyes incredulous, watching Josephine cajole Zakiyyah into going on Peter Pan's Flight. Julian, Josephine, Ashton, and Zakiyyah were in Disneyland, the last two under protest.

"Z, what's not to love? You fly over London with Peter Pan aboard a magical pirate ship to Never Land. Come on, let's go, look, the line's getting longer."

"Is it pretend fly?" asked Zakiyyah.

"No," replied Ashton. "It's real fly. And real London. And real magic pirate ship. And definitely real Never Land."

Zakiyyah rolled her eyes. She almost gave him the finger. "Is it fast? Is it spinny? Is it dark? I don't want to be dizzy. I don't want to be scared, and I don't want to be jostled."

"Would you like to be someplace else?" Ashton said.

"No, I just want to have fun."

"And Peter Pan's magical flight over London doesn't qualify?" Ashton said, and sideways to Julian added, "What kind of *fun* are we supposed to have with someone like that? I can't believe Riley agreed to let me come with you three. I'm going to have to take her to Jamaica to make it up to her."

"You have a lot to make up for all around, especially after the crap you pulled at lunch the other week," Julian said. "So shut up and take it."

"Story of my life," Ashton said.

"What kind of fun are we supposed to have with someone like that?" Zakiyyah said to Josephine. "His idea of fun is making fun of me."

"He's not making fun of you, Z. He's teasing you."

"That's not teasing!"

"Shh, yes, it is. You're driving everybody nuts," Josephine said, and then louder to the men, "Z is new to this. She's never been to Disneyland."

"What kind of a human being has never been to Disneyland," Ashton whispered to Julian.

"That's not true!" Zakiyyah said. "I went once with my cousins."

"Sitting on a bench while the kids go on rides by themselves is not going to Disneyland, Z."

Zakiyyah tutted. "Is there maybe a slow train ride somewhere?"

"How about It's a Small World?" Ashton said, addressing Zakiyyah but facing Julian and widening his eyes into saucers. "It's a slow *boat* ride."

"I guess that might be okay. As long as the boat is not in real water. Is it in real water?"

"No," Ashton said. "The boat is in fake water."

"Is that what you mean when you say he's teasing me?" Zakiyyah said to Josephine. "You sure it's not mocking me?"

"Positive, Z. It's a world of laughter, a world of tears. Let's go on It's a Small World."

After it got dark and the toddlers had left and the crowds died down a bit, the three of them convinced Zakiyyah to go on Space Mountain. She half-agreed but balked when she saw the four-man luge they were supposed to board. Josephine would sit in front of Julian, between his legs, and that meant that Zakiyyah would have to sit in front of Ashton, between his. "Can we try a different seating arrangement?"

"Like what?" Ashton said, keeping his voice even.

"Like maybe the girls together and the boys together."

"Jules, honey, what do you think?" Ashton asked, pitching his voice two octaves higher. "Would you like to sit between my legs, pumpkin, or do you want me between yours this time around?"

"Z, come on," Josephine said. "Don't make that face. He's right. It's one ride. You'll love it. Just…"

"Instead of you sitting in front of me," Ashton said to Zakiyyah, as cordial as could be, "would you prefer I sit in front of you?"

"You want to sit between my open legs?" Zakiyyah's disbelieving tone was not close to cordial.

"Just making suggestions, trying to be helpful."

"Aside from other issues, I won't be able to see anything," Z said. "You're too tall. You'll be blocking my view the whole ride."

Ashton knocked into Julian as they were about to get in. "Dude," he whispered (hissed), "you haven't told her Space Mountain is a black hole with nothing to see?"

"We haven't even told her it's a roller coaster," Julian said. "You want her to go on the ride or don't you?"

"Do you *need* me to answer that?"

They climbed in, Ashton and Julian first, then the girls in front of them. Zakiyyah tried to sit forward as much as possible, but the bench was narrow and short. Her hips fitted between Ashton's splayed legs.

"Can you open your legs any wider?" she said.

"The bishop said to the barmaid," Ashton said.

"Josephine! Your friend's friend is making inappropriate remarks to me."

"Yes, they're called jokes," said Ashton.

"They're certainly not jokes because jokes are funny. People laugh at jokes. Did you hear anyone laughing?"

Zakiyyah sat primly, holding her purse in her lap.

Ashton shook his head, sighed. "Um, why don't you put your bag down below, maybe hold on to the grip bars."

"I'm fine just the way I am, thank you very much," she said. "Don't move too close."

"Not to worry."

They were off.

Zakiyyah was thrown backwards—into Ashton's chest. Her hips locked inside Ashton's legs. The purse dropped in the footwell. She seized the handlebars and screamed for two minutes in the dark cavernous dome.

When it was over, Julian helped a shaky Zakiyyah out, Josephine already jumping and clapping on the platform. "Z! How was it? Did you love it, Z?"

"Did I love being terrified?"

They had a ride photo made of the four of them: Zakiyyah's mouth gaping open, her eyes huge, the other three exhilarated and laughing. They gave it to her as a keepsake of her first time on Space Mountain, a real artifact from an imaginary place.

"Maybe next time we can try Peter Pan," Ashton said as they were walking out.

"Who says there's going to be a next time," said Zakiyyah.

"Thank you for making this happen," Josephine whispered to Julian, wrapping herself around his arm in the parking lot. "I know it didn't seem like it, but she had fun. Though you know what didn't help? Your Ashton pretending to be a jester. You don't have to try so hard when you look like a knight, you know. Is he trying to be funny like you?"

"He's both a jester and a knight without any help from me, believe me," said Julian.

Josephine kissed him without breaking stride. "You get bonus points for today," she said. "Wait until we get home."

While she walked through Limbo past the violent heretics and rowed down the River Styx in *Paradise in the Park*, Julian drove around L.A. looking for new places where she might fall in love with him, like Disneyland. New places where his hands could touch her body. They strolled down Beverly and shopped for some costume jewelry, they sat at the Montage and whispered in nostalgia for the old Hotel Bel Age that overlooked the hills. He raised a glass to her in the Viper Room where not too long ago someone young and beautiful died. Someone young and beautiful always died in L.A. And when the wind blew in from Laurel Canyon, she lay in his bed and drowned in his love and wished for coral trees and red gums, while Julian wished for nothing because everything had come.

But that was then.

Author's Note

I have taken a few liberties with mathematics, longitude, geography, various disciplines of science, the calendar, and the English language.

There will also undoubtedly be some unintended tiny errors of fact. For all this, I beg your indulgence.

As for the tale's more fantastical assertions, I stand behind them. First, tiger catching is a real thing. Second, shame toast is crazy delicious. And, when properly applied, love can accomplish remarkable feats.

Paullina Simons is the author of *Tully* and *The Bronze Horseman*, as well as twelve other beloved novels, a memoir, a cookbook, and two children's books. Born in Leningrad, USSR, Paullina immigrated to the United States in the mid-seventies; has lived in Rome, London, and Dallas; and now lives in New York with her husband and half of her children.

COMING SOON:

A Beggar's Kingdom
Inexpressible Island

While you wait read these other fabulous Paullina Simons titles:

The Bronze Horseman

Tatiana and Alexander

The Summer Garden

Children of Liberty

Bellagrand

Lone Star

Road to Paradise

Red Leaves

The Girl in Times Square

Song in the Daylight